THESE GUNS FOR HIRE

EDITED BY
J.A. KONRATH

MJF BOOKS

NEW YORK

*For Mickey Spillane and Ed McBain—you will be
missed, but your work will never be forgotten.*

━━━━━━━━━━━━━━━━ ⊕ ━━━━━━━━━━━━━━━━

mjf

Published by MJF Books
Fine Communications
322 Eighth Avenue
New York, NY 10001

These Guns for Hire
LC Control Number: 2009932341
ISBN-13: 978-1-56731-965-1
ISBN-10: 1-56731-965-3

This edition is published by MJF Books in arrangement with Bleak House Books, an imprint of Big Earth Publishing.

CONTENTS

CONTENTS

Introduction
J.A. Konrath

"Murder didn't mean much to Raven. It was just a new job."

So begins the 1936 novel THIS GUN FOR HIRE by Graham Greene. Raven, a hit man, was one of the first anti-heroes in crime fiction. But he was far from the last.

Since Greene's groundbreaking creation, assassins have been a mainstay in mysteries and thrillers. They're the dark reflection of the cops and private eyes that populate the genre. Mobsters. Snipers. Sociopaths. Bounty hunters. Spec-Ops soldiers who ruthlessly dispatch the enemy. Aging mafia loners troubled by conscience.

Sometimes the villain, sometimes the hero, always compelling.

They're also more popular than ever.

Perhaps this is because conventional genre protagonists have constraints built into their character. Heroes are expected to adhere to a code of ethics. They seek to do good, solve the crime, catch the bad guy, rescue the victim, all while keeping within the boundaries of morality. Through the hero, the reader can witness the day being saved by those who evoke the best traits humanity has to offer: Courage, compassion, and firm sense of right and wrong.

But this also hinders a main character's actions, and restricts a hero's motivation. A genre protagonist must conform to reader expectations, or lose reader sympathy.

Enter the hitman. No morals or ethics. No compassion. Some may have rules, or a code of behavior, but the bottom line is that they murder people for money. Assassins don't suffer from the same constraints as a homicide cop, a private eye, or an amateur sleuth. They can be as bad as the writer wants them to be. Which, for the writer, is very liberating.

It's also a lot of fun.

Amoral characters allow writers to explore the darker side of human nature. To kill for cash is as cold-blooded as a human being can get. What kind of character would do something like that? What would it be like to bounce around in that person's skull for a few dozen pages?

Hitman stories offer writers the rare opportunity to thumb their noses at conventional genre ethics, to write without limits. They appeal to that childhood sense of right and wrong, without risking the actual punishment for wrong-doing. Forbidden fruit is the tastiest, and when children gather in groups to play cops and robbers, the robbers invariably outnumber the cops.

It's like dressing in a monster costume for Halloween. No one would actually like to meet a real monster, but it's good fun to pretend.

This anthology is packed with monsters. Monsters who wear human masks.

THESE GUNS FOR HIRE offers readers a unique opportunity, to vicariously experience some very bad people, courtesy of the best writers in the mystery thriller genre. They're all here. Cold blooded mobsters (Rob Kantner, Victor Gischler,) series characters from novels (David Morrell, Lawrence Block, Max Allan Collins,) humorous killers (Brian Wiprud, Jeff Strand,) hitwomen (Libby Fischer Hellmann, MJ Rose,) and even some forays into the supernatural (Jay Bonansinga, Robert W. Walker.)

So without further ado, let the assassinations begin …

THESE GUNS FOR HIRE

VICTOR GISCHLER

VICTOR Gischler's debut novel GUN MONKEYS was nominated for the Edgar Award. His current novel is SHOTGUN OPERA. Victor's work has been translated into French and Japanese. He lives in Skiatook, Oklahoma with his wife Jackie and his son Emery.

When asked about his affinity for hitmen stories, Victor replied: "I like it when the bad guy is the good guy. Makes a nice change of pace from the squeaky clean hero doing all the usual good guy things. If a reader finds himself/herself cheering for the protagonist to commit an act we'd normally consider wrong, then the author has really accomplished something."

Visit Victor at www.VictorGischler.com.

THEY ALWAYS GET YOU
Victor Gischler

I WATCHED THE fire march up the hill. Just the smoke actually. The flames were still a mile off, maybe two, across the valley. Then the call came.

"You recognize this voice?" asked the guy on the other end of the phone.

It took me a second. Rusty parts of my brain creaked into motion, reached back twenty years. Yeah, I recognized the voice. I told him so. No emotion in my tone. Let's see what this long lost voice wanted before I got too worried.

"You were hard to find," the voice said. "But I know some people."

"I'll bet you do."

"Whispering Lenny is sending some boys. He knows where you are, so I thought you'd want a heads up."

"His personal boys?"

"No," said the voice. "It's an open contract, so you'll be getting a mixed bag. Anyway, I thought you'd want to know. See ya."

"Wait."

He waited.

"Why the phone call?"

"You took a bullet for me. I owe you."

Oh, yeah. Funny how I'd forgotten. I looked down at my right hand, the bird finger and the ring finger gone at the first knuckle. Strange, they'd been gone so long it was almost like I'd never had them. "Okay then. We're square."

"I figured." A long pause. "Good luck, Blake." He hung up.

I sat there a long time, wondering what to do next, if I should do anything at all, and smelled the fire in the valley creep closer.

⊕

ON THE BACK deck, I watched the fire through a pair of good binoculars. I hoped the wind would shift but knew it wouldn't, and through the binoculars I could actually see the flames now, not just the smoke.

Part of my brain considered the fire, assessed risk. It was early in spring, plenty of green. The fire wouldn't catch much. Anyway it wasn't climbing the trees, just sweeping through the underbrush, clearing out the dead limbs and leaves. Hell, the Oklahoma Parks Service often let those kinds of fires burn on purpose. Spring cleaning. The fire would most likely climb the hill, hit my freshly mown lawn and circle around. A hell of a lot of smoke, but I didn't think the house would catch.

Still, I thought I might hook up the hoses, park the sprinklers at the south and east sides of the lawn, wet everything down, encourage the fire to go around. I'd have to watch the sun shed. It was set off in a patch of dry trees, lots of dry, loose stuff around the fire would like to eat up and crap out as ash, and I didn't spend three weeks building the thing just to see it torched.

Even as I made these plans, watched the fire and the smoke and the direction of the wind, the other part of my brain wondered how Whispering Lenny Diamond had found me. Had someone told him? Had an old acquaintance seen me in town? How long had he known?

I glanced at the double-barrel shotgun leaning against the railing next to me. It was a short coachman's gun, a trigger for each barrel. Squeeze both triggers at once and you got a nice spray of buckshot. Hard to miss. I'd practiced long and hard after losing the fingers, waiting for Lenny or one of his goons to come after me. I could fire off both barrels, break the breach, eject the old shells and thumb in new ones in two seconds flat. But Lenny'd never come. Nobody had. And I was out of practice.

The .38 police special on the hall table was good within a dozen feet. Beyond that I might as well be spitting watermelon seeds. I was never worth much with my left hand.

I walked back through the house to the front porch, scanned my property and the driveway. I hadn't thought much about defending the place in recent years. Better think about it. I was fifty-six years old which meant Whispering Lenny must be almost eighty. A long time to hold a grudge.

I'd need to go into town. Pick up a few things.

But first the fire. I estimated the flames would be getting close to the headstone down in the valley. I hadn't been down there in six months. The winter was always bad on my knees; I could get down the hill okay, but coming back up was hell. There'd be a lot of branches and leaves around the grave, and I hated the thought of the headstone all scorched up with soot and black streaks. Nothing to be done about it now.

I stuck the police special in the back of my pants, went outside, and started arranging the hoses and sprinklers. The smoke was already thick coming up the hill, even though the flames were still a long way off. The wind picked up.

"How's it going, Blake?"

I spun quick, drew the pistol. My own speed surprised me. I hadn't drawn on anyone in more than a dozen years. My heart beat fast. I had a steady, left-handed aim at the guy's chest. Took me a split-second to realize it was my neighbor.

"Whoa!" Roy Jenkins held his hands up, palms toward me. A weak smile. "Didn't mean to sneak up on you. You didn't hear my truck?"

"No." I lowered the pistol. "Sorry about that."

Roy smiled bigger now, walked toward me, his hands down. He eyed the revolver. "You gonna shoot the fire?"

"I thought I saw a coyote."

He nodded, pretended to believe me even though nobody had seen a coyote around here in about a hundred years. "Anyway, I thought I'd check on you. You fixed okay for hoses and sprinklers?"

I showed him what I'd done.

"That's about all you can do, I guess. It won't burn anything green. Too early in the season. We'd be bad off if it was along into August."

I told him I'd figured the same thing.

"All the same," Roy said, "you give me a holler if it gets bad. It'll circle around your place first before it gets to me. Gimme a ring you need some help."

I thanked him, and he left.

Roy was my "neighbor," but his house was still far enough away that we had plenty of privacy. He lived across the valley on the other side, atop the next hill. From my yard, I could just stretch my neck and see his house. His hill was higher, and Roy said he could see me grilling or mowing my lawn from his upstairs window. It was good of him to check up on me, but I'd nearly shit myself when he caught me by surprise. I was more nervous than I thought. I checked the sprinklers again and went inside.

My upstairs office happened to have a window facing out back, so I could keep tabs on the fire. I pulled an old strong box out of the closet, sat at my desk, and opened it. Old papers, photographs. The picture of me at Scallywag's Alley on Bourbon Street was a shock. I don't remember ever being so young. It was a candid shot, me looking at old Ronny Doyle, reaching for a beer, and I was laughing. Probably at one of Doyle's dirty jokes. I don't even remember that night or what the occasion might have been, but there I was with black hair and a smooth face, looking like I owned the world. Stuck there in time in the faded color of the photo, eternally cock of the walk with my *compadres*, and nobody looked at us crossways because we were Whispering Lenny's boys. It couldn't have been too long after that when it all went to shit.

⊕

NEW ORLEANS, 1975

"You wanted to see me, boss?"

"Sit down, Blake."

Lenny looked worried, dark circles under his eyes, clothes all out of whack. He probably hadn't slept.

He said, "I need you, Blake. This is a big one. Important." As always, the words came out like a hoarse croak. Back in the day, he'd taken a bullet in the throat and got the nickname Whispering Lenny.

"Tell me who you want killed, boss." I was Lenny Diamond's trigger-man. Feared and hard. I didn't blink or flinch.

"This is more important." He poured a tumbler half full of Cutty Sark, tossed back nearly all of it in one gulp. "You know we're in the middle of a turf war."

I knew.

"The other side is starting to play rough. They're pushing hard."

"You want me to push back?"

Lenny shook his head. "I told you. It's not that kind of job." A long pause. "My daughter's back in town. She just graduated LSU."

I'd forgotten he had a kid. I'd never seen her, never heard Lenny talk about her.

Lenny said, "There have been threats. I want you to watch her. I've got a cabin on the bayou. Keep her there for a few days, just until we get on top of the situation."

I frowned. "I can help you better here, boss. I'm your best gun."

"Dammit, do what I say."

"Okay."

"Her name is Alison."

When Doyle came to the cabin to warn there were killers on the way, it was already too late. They'd followed him. I lost the fingers, but I got Alison out of there safely. We ran north and west and maybe even then we sort of knew we weren't coming back.

⊕

I FOUND THE picture I was looking for, almost at the bottom of the strong box. Alison looked young and fresh and freckled, hair red and blowing, lips parted in that imp smile that made her eyes scrunch up. The picture hit me right in the chest, a pang I hadn't felt in so long. I put the picture on my desk, looked at it for a while.

Out the window, the fire was still doing its slow march.

I needed to think about supplies. I got in the pickup truck and went to town.

In Oklahoma, a pickup is like local camouflage. A red Ford, 1986. It ran okay. All I ever asked it to do was take me to town and back. I hadn't been down to Stillwater or as far as Tulsa in a long time. I parked in the alley behind Jordan's Market. I left the tire iron on the seat and went inside, the police special under my shirt. The shotgun was behind the truck seat. I wouldn't be able to grab it quickly, but it made me feel better being there.

Inside the market, I bought lunchmeat, bread, new flashlight batteries, and another box of 12-gauge buckshot. Halfway through my shopping, I saw a guy, maybe twenty-two years old. He looked way out of place, black slacks, green Polo shirt, rings, gold chains. Way too slick. The local costume was denim and a John Deere cap. I kept an eye on him as the clerk rang up my stuff. I headed back out to the alley. I set the groceries in the bed of the truck, opened the driver's door, didn't turn around. I saw him coming in the mirror. I kept still, went though my pockets slowly for the keys. Everything normal. He went into a pocket, came out with something that glinted in the sun. I thought it might be a small pistol and almost went for the police special under my shirt. But I saw it flick open. A switchblade.

I waited until he was almost on top of me, then turned around fast, swinging the tire iron from the car seat. It hit his jaw with a sickening crunch, and he spit blood and teeth. He staggered, dropped the knife so he could hold his shattered jaw. I kicked him in the knee and he went down.

I stood over him. One of his hands snaked towards his belt. Now he was going for the pistol. I smashed his wrist hard with the tire iron, and heard the bone snap. He let out a sound that was a yelp and a wheeze and a sob all at the same time.

"What's the bounty on me, slick?"

He shook his head.

I lifted the tire iron. "You want another whack?"

"Fifty thousand dollars." I barely understood him. He could hardly move his mouth.

"You working with a partner?"

He shook his head again. "But there's three guys working together, I heard. Pros. I haven't heard of nobody else."

I recognized his accent now. Back East. New York. Some slick wop wannabe-tough-guy with a knife. The warning voice on the phone had told me to expect a mixed bag, and here was this kid trying to make his bones or impress his neighborhood pals, thought he was going to make a quick trip to the sticks and whack an old man.

And this dumb fucking kid in his gold chains just lay there being a problem. I couldn't do anything with him. There was no way to let him go. He might've lied about having a partner, or the cops would find him and ask questions and that would be bad, too. I felt sick and held the tire iron tighter and there just wasn't anything else to do. You don't leave live ones behind.

I lifted the tire iron, brought it down, his eyes so big. He started to scream, swallowed it when the iron hit, skull smashing and blood after the second strike. I hit three more times, just to make sure, but there hadn't been any need. He was dead dead dead and his face looked like so much mush. I quickly went through his pockets to make sure he hadn't written down my name. I wiped the tire iron on his pants and drove away, my hands trembling on the steering wheel.

✛

I SET MOTION detectors along the driveway, connected them to bright, battery-powered lamps. Anybody who drove or walked through would light the place up real good. I had planned to use the detectors four of five years ago when the deer kept eating the leaves off the grape vines. But the vines had died, and I'd never used the detectors.

I checked on the fire. The flames were bright and close. No need for the binoculars. The smoke was thick. It smelled like camping.

Night fell. The flames were only ten yards from the house now, the orange flickering hellish through the smoke. I unhooked one of the sprinklers, took the hose around the house to the shed, wet everything down real good. As predicted, the fire split at the green lawn, started circling the house. If I just kept watch with the hose everything should work out okay. The fire would burn through the underbrush and move on.

I kept looking over my shoulder at the driveway. Nothing tripped the motion detectors.

Way off to my right, at the edge of the lawn, some fire had broken through, started climbing a dry, dead tree. Too far for the hose. I grabbed a shovel, jogged toward the tree. I shoveled dirt at the base, but it was no good. The fire was fast.

I looked back at the house but couldn't see it. The smoke was that thick. If it hadn't been for the fuzzy shimmer of the porch light, I couldn't even be sure I was looking in the right direction. I coughed. The smoke stung my eyes.

I started back for the porch, saw the porch light flicker and froze. Then the porch light went out. I dropped the shovel, pulled the police special out of my pants, stood in the smoke and tried to see. A shape. A body. Somebody on the porch.

I glanced at the driveway. Still dark. Nothing from the motion detectors.

And then my instincts kicked in. They hadn't come from the driveway. They followed the fire up the hill. They'd lit the fire as cover and had followed it up the hill. Pros, the kid had said. Three of them. And if I hadn't been out in the smoke playing fireman, they'd have greased me no problem. I wouldn't have known what hit me.

I circled around, decided to make for the pickup truck. Run for it. One against three wasn't anything I'd tried in a long time. No pride. Time to haul ass. But they'd been to the truck first. All four tires were flat.

Son of a bitch.

I crouched next to the truck, eased open the driver's door and pulled out the shotgun. I empted the box of shells onto the seat, grabbed a handful and shoved them into my pants pocket, stuck the police special back into my belt. I held the shotgun close, thumbed off the safety.

Through the smoke I saw my house, lights blazing in the windows. No curtains—no need, I thought, way out here in the middle of nowhere. I watched, waited. A figure passed by one of the downstairs windows. A moment later another shape in an upstairs window. Maybe the same guy, maybe not.

My eyes felt like hot coals in my skull, snot pouring from my nose. So much smoke. They'd been clever. The smoke provided good cover. But it was good cover for me, too. I circled around back, watched the deck and the sliding glass doors.

I shrank against the trunk of a scrub oak. Against the backdrop of flame, I'd just look like part of the tree. I stayed there as long as I could, lungs burning. I'd almost given up when the guy came out the sliding glass door. He held some sort of big automatic, but it was lowered. He'd searched the house and I wasn't there. Sorry to disappoint him.

For a second I thought he'd spotted me. He looked right in my direction, and I thought that was it. I could see him good now, yellow hair over the ears, lantern jaw, rough pink skin. He turned away, and I knew he hadn't seen me in the smoke and the dark. I stepped away from the tree to get a clear shot, and I had him easy.

I squeezed the triggers and both barrels exploded, peppered him with buckshot. I shattered the glass in the door behind him, a few stray pellets scarring the vinyl siding. He grunted and went down.

I'd already popped out the spent shells, thumbed in new ones. The gun blast would bring his buddies. I went around the side. From there I could see the front door, but they didn't come spilling out in yahoo fashion. The lights went out on the bottom floor, and I backed up against the house. If it had been me in there, I'd have done the same thing, put out the lights and check the windows. They didn't want out, and I wasn't going in.

At least that would've been the smart thing, but I figured they were smart enough to know I wouldn't try anything so dumb. Wrong guess. I climbed the porch steps fast, kicked open the front door, and blazed away with the shotgun without bothering to see if anyone was there. I didn't hit anyone, but I made a hell of a racket, and I saw a body upend the dining room table. I dropped the shotgun and drew the police special, pulled the trigger four times. Wood chips and splinters flew as the slugs went right on through. It was a cheap table.

A pause, then a sound like somebody dropping a bag of oranges. I looked behind the table. I'd only hit him once, but it was right in the face. Same lantern jaw and pale hair as the last guy, but more meat around the middle.

I heard the ceiling creak and knew the third guy was in my office upstairs. I stuck the police special back in my belt, picked up the shotgun and reloaded it. Now the decision. Wait down here for him to get bored or go up after him?

He knew I was downstairs and that his two buddies had probably taken some lead. It might not take him too long to realize he could kick out the bathroom window, drop down to the front porch roof and then jump to the ground. He'd get away if I jerked around too long, and I didn't want him coming at me again in a day or a week.

With the shotgun out front, I started up the stairs. Sweat under my arms and across my forehead. I forced my breathing down to normal. Tried to get the heart to stop pounding. I told myself I'd done well so far, an old man with tired knees, but the reflexes were still there. I could do this. I was steady. Even as I tried to talk myself up, my legs hurt, lungs and eyes burned from smoke, back sore. It was turning into a long night, and I wanted it to be over, wanted so many things to be over.

It happened fast.

He'd gotten impatient, leapt in front of me at the top of the stairs, jerking the trigger, the shots flying high. I'd dropped flat, pulled the triggers on the shotgun and blasted his shins into hamburger. He fell down, dropped his gun and writhed and screamed like a dying animal.

I climbed the stairs, pulled the police special. I noticed he looked like the other two, some kind of family resemblance, but he was a lot younger. I shot him in the head, and he quit screaming. Blood soaked my carpet.

I got halfway back down the stairs when I felt my legs go watery. I sat on a step. My hands shook. I started to hyperventilate. Embarrassing. I closed my eyes, got myself under control. I found it hard to believe that there'd been a time I was proud because I was good at this sort of thing.

I pulled myself together, reloaded my weapons, and checked the house. All clear. I took the jug of water out of the refrigerator and drank half.

The bodies would be a problem. I couldn't call the cops for this, didn't know how I'd explain. I could bury them, but they'd still be there, and I wanted to be rid of them in some way I knew was permanent.

Roy Jenkins had a wood-chipper. It would be messy, but it would work. I picked up the phone to call him. No dial tone. Either the killers had cut the line or maybe it was something to do with the fire.

I stepped onto the front porch. The air had cleared. The fire had moved around my house and was inching toward Roy's place. I craned my neck, saw his place through the trees. His lights were on. Roy was a good guy. He'd lend me his truck and the wood-chipper. I wanted it done before daylight. I moaned with fatigue at the thought of it, the twenty-minute walk to Roy's, hooking the chipper up to Roy's truck, the messy work with the bodies. But I wouldn't be able to sleep until it was finished.

I started walking. I took the guns. There might be others out there. A mixed bag, the voice had warned. I jumped when my motion detectors triggered the flood lights. I forced a laugh, kept walking, held the shotgun tight. I walked the long way around, the orange glow from the valley the only light.

Standing on Roy's front porch, I started to reconsider. The smoke was back, the fire down in the valley between his hill and mine. Roy would think it a peculiar time to come asking for the chipper. I knocked anyway, waited, knocked again. No answer.

I turned the knob and pushed the door open. Sometimes, I thought I was the only one in the county who locked his door. Country living.

Inside, I heard the TV up loud, so I guessed Roy hadn't heard my knock. "Roy?" I walked through the front hall, into the living room where Roy reclined in the big, leather La-Z-Boy. His feet were up. Eyes open and rolled back. A neat hole in the center of his forehead, a trail of dried blood over his nose and lips.

I turned, ran for the front door. Something hit my legs, and I flew, hit the hardwood floor, and slid three feet, the shotgun knocked out of my hands and rattling away. I turned over, still on the floor, the police special digging into my lower back. I reached for the shotgun.

"Hold it!"

I froze.

The black woman who'd tripped me held a small automatic, maybe a .380. It was pointed at my face. She had very dark skin, hair in corn rows, lithe, athletic build. She wore jeans and a Sooners t-shirt and boots. The glint in her eye told me she'd have no trouble pulling the trigger.

She said, "Scoot back up against the wall and sit still."

I scooted, sat still.

She picked up the shotgun, emptied the shells and dropped it behind her.

"I'll double the bounty if you let me go." Maybe she'd even believe I had that kind of money.

She shook her head. "Sorry. I'm not one of the freelance guns. I work for Lenny Diamond."

"You cut the phone line at my house?"

"Nope. Must've been the Schmidt brothers. Clever lighting the fire, huh? But I'm not sure it was necessary. They always did make things more complicated than they needed to be. I guess you took care of them since you're here. Not bad. You must be more dangerous than you look."

I glanced at Roy. "Was that necessary?"

"Only place I could keep tabs on you was from the upstairs window. A good view of your house," she said. "He was in the way."

"Go ahead and shoot then. Finish it." I leaned forward, tensed to make a hopeless play for the police special.

"Not yet." She took a cell phone from her back pocket, dialed. "Mr. Diamond? It's Keesha. Yeah, I got him. Okay. Hold on." She handed the phone to me.

I swallowed hard. "Hello?"

"You know who this is?" he whispered.

"Lenny."

"That's right. I told Keesha if she got you before the others did, that I wanted a last word. Then she's going to kill you, you rat bastard dumb fuck."

I started to say something. The words caught in my throat.

"You were supposed to protect her," Lenny said. "But you took her away. My only daughter and you took her."

"We loved each other." I couldn't imagine it would make any difference to him, but I had to say it.

"Fuck you. Now she'd dead. I heard it through the grapevine. She's dead, and I don't even know how."

"Bone cancer," I told him. "I loved Alison, Lenny. I was with her to the end, and I loved her so much."

"Oh, God." His voice was rough, choked up. "My beautiful daughter."

"She couldn't live in your world," I said. "So I took her away from it. She was happy, Lenny. I promise."

But he wasn't listening. I heard him sniff. "Goodbye, Blake." He hung up.

I looked at Keesha, took the phone away from my ear, hesitated a split second, then said, "He wants to talk to you." I tossed the phone at her. It sailed too high. She reached for it, realizing at the same time it was a trick. I went for the police special.

I never really had a chance, but the diversion forced her to shoot from the hip. The little automatic spat flame, and I took the slug in the gut two inches left of my navel. I grunted, fought down the pain and shot her three times in the chest. She twitched, took three steps back, and fell over flat on her back.

The blood seeped between my fingers where I held my gut, the smell of cordite hanging in the room. I shut my eyes tight, sat a while, summoned Alison's face. Oh, baby, we never planned all this, did we? Still, we had some good years. I wished I'd brought the picture of her from the strong box. I wanted to hold it.

I lurched to my feet, pain lancing through my gut. There was a chunk of lead lodged in something important. I left the guns and cell phone and dead Keesha and stumbled out Roy's back door. The smoke hit me at once, and my whole body wracked with coughing. I almost gave up right then, every part of me screaming to lie down and close my eyes and just forget everything.

The fire lit the valley between my hill and Roy's.

I started down, knowing my knees couldn't bring me back up again. It didn't matter. Down and down, picking up speed, holding my guts and tripping on rocks, straight down into a hellish realm of smoke and ash and flame.

When I got to the fire line, I found a place where the flames were only shin high and ran through. Each step made my gut blaze.

The other side of the fire was a different world. Ash and darkness lit only dimly by orange-glowing embers. I knew where I was, headed along the valley floor toward the head-stone. The air was clean.

In the darkness, I missed the grave and had to circle back, but I finally found it and slumped down against the rough stone. It hadn't been scorched too badly, the name Alison clearly visible. No last name. No dates. I already knew, and nobody else came to visit.

"It's me, baby."

I sat, back against the stone, legs extended in front of me. My fatigue was total. No force on Earth would be able to move me. I took deep gulps of night air. My throat was so dry.

I looked up and saw the stars, remembered when Alison and I had first moved to the country. We'd been in the house only a week. A big thunderstorm and a power outage. We'd gone outside after the rain. The clouds had cleared away, and in the total darkness, the velvet night glittered with a million stars. Never a view like that in the city.

My gut was numb now, but I felt light-headed, like I was floating. I understood my life was leaking out of me. It was okay. I felt calm, and I looked at the sky and the stars went on forever and ever and I was drifting and it felt like my body was lifting up and away and the sky was so big.

And the stars. So many stars.

RAYMOND BENSON

RAYMOND Benson is the author of nine James Bond novels, the suspense novels FACE BLIND and EVIL HOURS, and the non-fiction books THE POCKET ESSENTIALS GUIDE TO JETHRO TULL and THE JAMES BOND BEDSIDE COMPANION. As "David Michaels" he recently wrote the action/adventure novel TOM CLANCY'S SPLINTER CELL and its sequel, OPERATION BARRACUDA. He is married, has one son, and is based in the Chicago area. His latest novel is the noir thriller SWEETIE'S DIAMONDS.

On the subject of hitmen in fiction, Raymond remarks: "I'm a big fan of noir fiction and film noir. Nine times out of ten you're going to find a hitman somewhere in that genre. While often despicable characters, hitmen have to possess a certain coolness and professionalism that is compelling in any story."

Visit Raymond at www.RaymondBenson.com.

ANOTHER ROCK 'N' ROLL HIT
Raymond Benson

THE ASSASSIN ALWAYS slept late.

Like so many of his colleagues, he was a night person. Sometimes he didn't go to bed until the first sign of dawn streaked across the sky. Everything he did usually occurred between the hours of eight PM and six AM He was normally in Dreamsville between six and noon unless he had to catch an early flight, which was something he strove to avoid. Better to take a red-eye than try to show up at an airport when most people were punching in at their mundane nine-to-five jobs.

It was the nature of the business.

Nevertheless, the assassin made it a point to be up and about after the noon hour. For someone who dealt with death on a day-to-day basis, he was a man who enjoyed life. He felt that sleep was a waste of precious time, albeit a necessary one. He had thus trained himself to survive on anywhere from two to six hours of sleep for every twenty-four. The afternoons of his days were reserved for his cover job, personal business, his family, and the preparation for the tasks he was paid to perform. Those hours were precious and he didn't like to miss them. Then, after an early dinner, the assassin was ready for the critical evening hours when his various disciplines came into play.

He opened his eyes when he heard noise in the hallway outside his hotel room. A mother was shouting for her kids to hurry up or they weren't going to the swimming pool.

For Christ's sake, can't they read? There was a "DO NOT DISTURB" sign on his door, but of course, no one paid attention to those things.

He glanced at the digital clock on the nightstand and saw that it was just after noon. Sighing, he stretched beneath the sheets, yawned, and slowly sat upright.

The assassin had a job to do that night.

⊕

"I HEAR THERE'S a contract out on you."

Giovanni blinked and then laughed loudly with his trademark boisterous voice that carried through the restaurant.

"Well, I'll just have to make sure the manager clause is airtight and that I have complete control, including ownership of copyrights and masters," the portly music executive boomed. He raised his wineglass to his companion and said, "Cheers."

Deborah smiled and shook her head. "You never take anything I say seriously, Maxie. What if I'm right?"

Maximillian Giovanni shrugged and said, "My dear, what else is new? If I had a nickel for every contract that was put out on me, I'd be a rich man."

"You already are a rich man."

"True. So I'd be a richer man." He took a bite of his swordfish steak and chewed it with delight.

They were an odd couple but one that was always good fodder for tabloid newspapers—Maximillian "Maxie" Giovanni, the sixty-something record mogul and promoter of some of the world's biggest rock 'n' roll acts, and Deborah Carlucci, his twenty-something girlfriend of three years, former runway model and occasional "celebrity host" on various reality shows featured on MTV and VH1. He was eighty pounds overweight and had a white David Crosby mustache that drooped below the corners of his mouth. His hair—what was left of it—was just as white. She, on the other hand, was about as beautiful as a young woman could be. Six feet tall with long, straight red hair and round green eyes, she possessed a body that *Playboy* magazine had offered a half-million dollars to reveal *au natural*. She had declined.

They sat in the chic Sacred Sea Room, one of the many restaurants located within the ultra-kitsch Luxor Hotel in Las Vegas. Giovanni had asked for a private table but the best the management could do was supply one next to the large plate glass window that overlooked the casino floor. The couple still had to put up with stares and pointing fingers belonging to the common folk at other tables. The seafood was excellent, so Giovanni didn't mind too much. Such was the price of fame and he had been paying it for over thirty years.

"So what makes you think there's a contract out on me?" he asked, taking another bite of swordfish.

Deborah twirled linguini around her fork and stuck the prongs into a shrimp, then placed the medley into her mouth. She savored the flavors, chewed, and swallowed before answering.

"Just something I heard. You know how David mouths off when he's had too much to drink."

"David, eh?" Giovanni frowned. Suddenly his good humor disappeared. David Lee Roth was a thorn in his side. "I thought you two were history."

"We are. I ran into him at Steven Tyler's poker party the other night." She picked up on Giovanni's displeasure and added, "Don't get all hot under the collar. We just said 'hello, how are you,' that sort of thing. He even asked about you."

"Gee, what a nice guy."

"And that's when he said that Spoons wanted your head on a platter."

"*Spoons?*" Giovanni wiped his mouth with a napkin and looked at her. "What the fuck does David know about Jimmy Scarlotti?"

Jimmy "Spoons" Scarlotti was reputed to be one of Las Vegas's old school *mafiosos* that still had a piece of the action in town. He was nearly seventy, a mobster with a colorful history who had always managed to weasel his way out of legal predicaments. Besides operating a substantial drug trade in Vegas, he had a stranglehold on musical acts that appeared in the city. Although it had never been proven, the stagehands' union was reportedly in Scarlotti's pocket and he could command whatever prices he wanted from the managers of bands that wished to perform live in the town.

Deborah took a sip of wine and said, "Come on, you know David. He knows everybody. He had to deal with Spoons when he played Vegas. Or his management did. Whatever."

Giovanni rubbed his chin. "So what did he say?"

Deborah looked at her companion sideways. "Oh, you mean to tell me there's something to it?"

"No, no," Giovanni said, faking a laugh. "I'm just curious to hear what the greasy slimeball is saying about me, that's all."

"Who, David or Spoons?"

"Spoons! David's not a greasy slimeball."

"That's not what you said when you found out we went to Barbados together."

"That was two goddamned years ago, Deborah, so drop it. So what did Spoons say?"

"Apparently the word is out that you've stiffed him for the last time. Do you owe him money, Maxie?"

"Hmpf. So *he* says. Spoons thinks he runs Las Vegas when it comes to rock 'n' roll. That guy tries to squeeze every major act that comes to town—he won't let 'em perform unless a special compensation is made. Otherwise the stagehand union mysteriously goes on strike. Well, fuck that. I'm not putting up with it any longer. I told that asshole a year ago that he wasn't getting any extra money from me. And nothing's happened. I brought the Red Hot Chili Peppers and Metallica to Vegas in the last eight months and there were no union strikes.

Spoons is all hot air. I've called his bluff. He can't do anything to me. I'm Maximillian Giovanni, after all."

"You certainly are," Deborah said. She put down her fork and looked out the window.

"What's the matter? You're not eating."

"This is too heavy a meal for lunch," she said. "This is more like dinner. I'm not that hungry."

"Suit yourself," Giovanni said. He resumed attacking the swordfish and ignored the beautiful woman across from him. Sometimes she could be a real pain. Mostly, though, he didn't want to let on that he was truly frightened by what she had said about Jimmy Scarlotti.

⊕

THE ASSASSIN SHOWERED, shaved, and combed his long hair back so that it flowed evenly over his shoulders. He dressed in simple blue jeans and a Hawaiian shirt, put on expensive Nike running shoes, donned sunglasses, and left his hotel room.

He found the interior of the Luxor Hotel gaudy and ridiculous. There was something very Disneyland about the fake pharaohs and Egyptian statuary that surrounded the casino. The so-called King Tut Museum was beyond kitsch, as if guests were supposed to believe the stuff was real. The mechanical camels were the ultimate in cringe-worthy contrivances.

Nevertheless, the assassin didn't mind staying at the hotel. As far as resort hotels in Vegas went, the Luxor was as good as any. It amused him to compare the various establishments and examine the types of people that were drawn to a particular theme. The really wealthy preferred places like the Bellaggio while the family crowd liked the Excalibur. The Luxor fell somewhere in between. It wouldn't have been his first choice for a hotel but he had little say in the matter. The show was scheduled to go on that night in the 1200-seat Luxor Theater. It was the one night of the week that the Blue Man Group had off.

Most of the hotel guests had already finished lunch. The assassin wanted breakfast but he dared not appear in public. Not yet, anyway.

After a discreet walk-around through the casino, he went back up to his room and ordered from the room service menu. A plate of scrambled eggs, pancakes, and strong coffee would do the trick. Afterwards, he would receive the massage he had scheduled when he had checked in, perhaps take a swim in the outdoor pool, and relax until the evening's festivities. He could take care of some personal business in his room by using his laptop computer and the hotel's modem. Non-sensitive phone calls could be made on his mobile. For other calls he'd have to find a pay phone.

It might have seemed that he had several long hours to kill but the assassin relished this time of day.

He wouldn't be bored at all.

✛

AT SEVEN THIRTY PM, Maximillian Giovanni checked with the theater's house manager from the stage manager's phone backstage. The concert was sold out, of course, but whether or not all the ticket holders would show was another story. That was the thing about putting on a concert in Vegas—some people who had tickets were invariably held up by flights or whatever. Giovanni had left instructions for the box office to resell any seat that wasn't claimed by the eight o'clock showtime.

Giovanni left the stage manager's station and went into the green room, where three of the band members sat with cold beers, ogling Deborah and chatting her up. She appeared to be enjoying herself, laughing at Mickey Johnson's jokes and at Rick Gould's come-ons.

"Where's Dave?" Giovanni asked.

Keyboard player Greg Planer shrugged. "Hell if we know."

"He hasn't shown yet?"

"Nope."

Giovanni grumbled. The War Room's drummer was always pulling this kind of stunt. He was as bad as Keith Moon or John Bonham during their heydays.

Rick Gould spoke up. "Don't worry, Maxie, Dave'll show. He always does, you know that."

Giovanni rolled his eyes and sat beside his girlfriend. She snuggled against him but continued her conversation with the band's bass player, Mickey Johnson, without stopping.

"Do you have your set list handy?" Giovanni asked.

Gould, the band's guitarist *extraordinaire*, dug into a satchel on the floor and removed a sheet of paper. He handed it to the promoter and said, "Here you go, chief."

Giovanni took it and read through the song titles. "You're saving 'Blast Me' for the encore?"

Gould shrugged. "Makes sense to me."

"I think that's a better opener."

Planer answered, "Nah, 'Blast Me' is our biggest hit. We can't open with that. It's got to be the one everyone waits for. It's perfect for the encore."

Giovanni handed the list back to Gould. "Whatever."

The War Room was his biggest act. A heavy metal thrash outfit that had taken the States by storm three years previously, the band consisted of four talented young men who *Rolling Stone* predicted would be the "next Led Zeppelin." That comment raised some eyebrows in the music industry because it was tantamount to saying a new pop band would become the next Beatles—which of course was an impossibility. Still, Giovanni had jumped on the publicity and used the quote to promote The War Room's eponymous first album to *Billboard's* number one position, where it stayed for seven weeks. The new CD, *You Can't Fight In Here*, debuted at number two when it was released three months prior to the Vegas gig. It reached the top slot after two weeks and was still there. The War Room, Giovanni realized, was going to be huge.

"Speak of the devil," Deborah said, looking toward the green room door. Dave Bennett walked in looking like death warmed over. Although he had obviously combed his long blond hair the bags under his eyes looked like Samsonites.

"Jesus, Dave, where the hell you been?" Giovanni asked. He stood and put his hands on his hips.

"Don't ask," Bennett said. He immediately went to the ice chest and removed a beer. "I sure need this."

"You look like you've been drinking all day."

Bennett shrugged. "I have. So what?"

"You go on stage in twenty minutes, you dumb fuck."

Bennett looked at Giovanni and said, "Have I *ever* let you down?" He addressed the rest of the band. "Have I ever let *any* of you down?"

Gould, Planer, and Johnson shook their heads.

Bennett threw his gaze back at Giovanni and said, "So don't worry."

"Fine," Giovanni said. "I'm going to check on the house. Have a good show. I'll see you backstage afterwards."

"Hey, Maxie," Bennett said, stopping the promoter. "I have a question."

"Yes, Dave?"

"Why the hell are we playing here?"

"What do you mean?"

"I mean, this theater is what, a thousand seats or something? Shouldn't we be playing a goddamned football stadium? We've had the number one album for, what, two months now? And you have us in a thousand-seat theater? What the hell for?"

Giovanni turned and addressed them all. "I thought I explained it to you when I first booked the gig. Playing a casino theater like this may not bring in the big bucks but what it does for your prestige is immeasurable. We got away with charging a thousand bucks a seat for this show and it sold out in two minutes. Your audience tonight are the rich and famous. Now we can ask to play the House of Blues or the Event Center or Harrah's or whatever—and command top dollar from the middle class."

The band members said nothing.

"Okay?" Giovanni asked.

"Okay, Maxie," Bennett said.

There was a moment of awkward silence. Finally, Rick Gould stood and said, "I'm gonna go get my axes. See you guys on stage." He moved past Giovanni and went to his dressing room. Like most musicians, he refused to let the road crew handle his beloved instruments and preferred to take the two guitars with him personally.

Giovanni left the green room and was stopped in the hallway by Charlie Nix, the stagemanager.

"You got a letter delivered by Fed Ex, Maxie," he said, handing the envelope to the promoter.

"Really? Who's it from?" Giovanni asked.

"I dunno. Doesn't say." The stagemanager walked away and Giovanni opened it. His heart skipped a beat when he read it.

MAXIMILLIAN GIOVANNI—CALL SPOONS ON PRIVATE NUMBER BEFORE EIGHT PM TO VERIFY COMPLIANCE WITH TERMS.

The note wasn't signed. It didn't say much but Giovanni knew there was an implied threat. The words "or else" were understood. Giovanni crumpled it up and threw it in the trash. *Fuck him*, he thought. It was about time that someone stood up to a guy like Scarlotti. If it had to be Maximillian Giovanni, then so be it.

The promoter tried to ignore the rising apprehension he felt in his chest and went on his way to check on the house.

⊕

AT FIVE MINUTES after eight o'clock, the assassin heard the roar of the small but noisy crowd in the Luxor Theater. From his position backstage, he could see the comings and goings of every person associated with the band from the musicians down to the stagehands. The assassin had especially kept his eye on the target, the fat promoter Giovanni, and made sure the man would be where he was supposed to be during and after the concert.

Had the people around him known his "true" profession, they might have questioned why he needed to do what he did. Wasn't he happy? Didn't he have enough money? Why was he drawn to a vocation that was so dangerous and morally objectionable?

The assassin had no simple answers to these questions. Sometimes he even asked himself the same things. Perhaps it was the power he felt when performing his job. It was an entirely different sort of power than the kind he enjoyed in his "cover" occupation. One of his employers once called him a "god." Maybe that was it. The assassin liked to play god. He had control over life and death.

Putting such thoughts away for the time being, the assassin opened his case and inspected the weapon.

Everything was ready.

A quick phone call to his employer assured the assassin that Giovanni had not called Scarlotti as he had been instructed. The job was to be executed as planned.

The crowd in the theater shouted, "War Room! War Room! War Room!" When the house lights dimmed, a cacophony of cheers enveloped the building. The assassin couldn't hear his own thoughts.

That meant it was showtime.

⊕

THE WAR ROOM hit the stage and the Luxor Theater vibrated with the crashing chords of the opening number from the band's latest album. "Miss Missile" was a heavy rock anthem that got the enthusiastic on their feet and the concert off to a great start.

Giovanni put his arm around Deborah as they stood in the stage left wings. Deborah moved with the pounding rhythm section of Dave Bennett's Tama/Sabian drum kit and Mickey Johnson's thumping Rickenbacker bass. Rick Gould hit power chords on his Fender Stratocaster, evenly complimented by Greg Planer's Roland and Yamaha keyboards. The quartet grooved into the song, rocking the house, and finally Gould stepped up to the mike to sing the first verse.

The band's onstage performance was spectacular, although the Luxor Theater management wouldn't allow the band's pyrotechnics engineer to operate his gear for the evening's show. They would have had to go through the Luxor's special effects guy and The War Room's technical director didn't want to bother. So for once the group had to depend on the lighting effects, their skin-tight stage clothing, their long "hair band" locks, and their good, beefy looks to provide the visual stimulation.

"They sound pretty good!" Giovanni said into Deborah's ear.

"What?" she shouted.

"Never mind!"

Giovanni left his gyrating girlfriend and walked to the stage manager's console, where Charlie Nix was calling lighting cues into his headset.

So far, so good. The band was in top form, the house was a sell-out, and Maximillian Giovanni felt on top of the world. And there had been no union strike.

What could possibly go wrong now?

⊕

THE CONCERT ENDED at ten minutes to midnight. The War Room had played two full hour-and-a-half sets with a thirty-minute intermission in the middle. The encore stretched out to another forty-five minutes. By the time the Meet 'n' Greet backstage was finished, it was nearly one o'clock. The Meet 'n' Greets were obligatory after-show events in which the band met with privileged audience members who copped backstage passes. These people were usually family members, important press personages, or celebrities. The band members stood with Sharpie pens in hands in case they were asked to autograph something. They smiled and nodded at the comments made by their effusive fans, but most of the time the group was anxious to get the hell out of the building and move on to the next city and venue.

Deborah Carlucci hugged Mickey Johnson and Rick Gould as they started for the green room door. "You guys were fantastic tonight!" she gushed.

"Thanks, honey," Gould said. "I gotta get my gear. You riding in the limo or do you and Maxie have a private car?"

"The limo, of course!"

"I'll see you there."

Deborah found herself alone in the green room and wondered where Maxie was. He had been present throughout the Meet 'n' Greet but was now nowhere in sight. She often wondered if she was doing the right thing by sticking with a man old enough to be her grandfather. He certainly provided for her in the monetary department but in the bedroom he left something to be desired. Perhaps it was time for her to move on and find someone younger. As a matter of fact, Deborah thought, Mickey Johnson was a definite possibility. She had had her eye on him for some time. It probably wouldn't sit too well with Maxie, but to hell with him. He had to understand that she had her whole life ahead of her and he was knocking at death's door.

She didn't realize how true that thought really was.

✛

GIOVANNI GRABBED HIS bag and went to the washroom located backstage. He had needed to take a leak since the end of the show but had been caught up by the people he was forced to see during the Meet 'n' Greet. Finally, as he stood at the urinal relieving himself, he could relax.

He had done it. He had beaten Spoons Scarlotti. The guy was all bluff. The concert was a smash success and nothing bad had happened. It was a major victory for concert promoters in Las Vegas.

The washroom door opened behind him and he heard the footsteps on the tile. Giovanni turned his head and saw who had entered.

"Oh, hey," he said.

"Hey," the assassin said, as he raised the suppressed Glock to the back of the promoter's head and fired.

⊕

DEBORAH WAS ALREADY in the limo with Johnson and Planer when Gould brought his two guitar cases out the stage door and loaded them into the open trunk. The driver shut the trunk and Gould got inside, facing the others.

"Where's Maxie?" he asked.

"Didn't you see him?" Deborah asked.

"Nope."

"Where the hell is he?"

"You want me to go look for him?"

"No, just wait a minute," she said. "He knows our schedule."

"Did Dave already take off?" Gould asked.

"Yeah," Planer said. "He goes his own way, as usual. He loves that SUV of his."

They sat there another minute as Johnson pulled a bottle of champagne out of the ice bucket. "We might as well get this started," he said.

That's when Charlie Nix came out of the building and leaned into the limo. His face was pale and he looked as if he'd just witnessed the apocalypse.

"Guys," he whispered.

"Charlie, what's wrong?" Gould asked.

"It's Maxie. He's … he's dead! He's been shot! I found him in the bathroom!"

"What?" was the collective response from the four people in the car.

"Yeah," Nix said. "The cops are on the way."

⊕

IT **TURNED OUT** to be a long night.

The homicide detectives interviewed and took statements from the three present members of The War Room, Deborah Carlucci, and the remaining tour crew. Because Dave Bennett had disappeared from the site prior to the discovery of the body, he was immediately under suspicion. The police in the next venue, Lake Tahoe, were alerted to pick up the drummer as soon as the man's SUV was sighted. At nearly five in the morning, the witnesses were released and the limo finally made its way out of Las Vegas. Deborah, who had shown remarkable restraint during the questioning, ultimately broke down and cried. Mickey Johnson was happy to offer her solace. Greg Planer sat and stared out the window, numb and silent. Rick Gould absent-mindedly rubbed the calluses on his fingers, lost in his thoughts.

Eventually they all fell asleep and didn't wake until the limousine reached the Hyatt Regency in Lake Tahoe. Subdued and exhausted, the four passengers removed their belongings from the trunk of the car, checked into the hotel, and went to their respective rooms.

Rick Gould closed the door behind him and gently placed his two guitar cases on one of the double beds. As he made the phone call to Scarlotti's liaison, Gould thought about that old cliché from the gangster films of the thirties. A mobster could hide a tommygun inside a violin case and get away with it. What irony.

When the liaison answered, Gould said, "All sewn up."

"We heard," a rough voice replied. "The other half of your fee has already been wired to your account."

That was all that needed to be said. Gould hung up and opened the two guitar cases. One contained the Fender Stratocaster that provided The War Room's signature sound. The other held a beloved Dean USA V Custom that he used to alternate with the Fender on stage. Hidden in the secret compartment of that case was Gould's Glock 34 9x19mm handgun.

He sighed, for he would need to sleep a little into the afternoon to make up for the lost morning. Gould didn't like messing with his routine, but that was one of the few pitfalls of touring with a popular heavy metal band.

Another town, another show, another rock 'n' roll hit ...

The assassin sat on the edge of the bed, removed the Dean guitar, and proceeded to polish. He wanted it to look brand spanking new at that evening's gig.

JEREMIAH HEALY

JEREMIAH Healy is a graduate of Rutgers College and Harvard Law School. A past president of the Private Eye Writers of America, he is the current president of the International Association of Crime Writers. He has had published 18 novels and three collections of short stories.

On the subject of literary contract killers, Jerry says: "There is something very fundamental, even primitive, about someone who could take the life of another member of the same species. It is the ultimate crime, and therefore, I think, the ultimate mystery as well."

Visit his website at www.JeremiahHealy.com.

THE CONFESSIONAL

Jeremiah Healy

STANDING ON THE sidewalk at 4:15 PM during a bell-clear, mid-August Saturday, Anna Maria Saracino first stared down at her shoes. Plain, matte-brown, sensible heels. No black patent leather today, no. As her mother had always admonished her, black patent leather reflects up, enabling boys to glimpse the panties you wore under a parochial school's tartan-plaid skirt.

Now Anna Maria willed both eyes and both feet to cross the sidewalk—empty of anyone else on such a beautiful summer's day—and climb the impressive granite steps, topped by the imposing double doors of the old Catholic church. She'd never been inside this one, but she'd seen plenty of others, if none for a long while. And, at age thirty-three, if ever there was something that could make Anna Maria Saracino feel seven years old again, it was going into such a daunting house of worship.

But, she'd made up her mind, and promised the family, so Anna Maria hefted her large tote in her left hand, used her right to pull on the massive bronze ring of the closer door, and entered the church itself. In order to start a new "life chapter" by going to confession for the first time since—what, high school?

⊕

FATHER RICHARD WAS pissed.

No, not drunk, though in a few hours that was a distinct possibility.

Rather, he was pissed at Father Paul.

And for no good reason, Father Richard (or "Dick," as he thought of himself), recalled. After all, Dick was the senior priest in the parish, now that old Monsignor Concannon had died suddenly of a heart attack.

Dick never felt close to the man, despite the near parent-son differential in their ages, though Dick did learn from him. "You're a Catholic before you're a priest, Richard, so be smart about it: Always be posted to a seminary or a large parish, so that you'll have others around to administer the Last Rites and hear your final confession."

Too bad the old monsignor went out like a candle in the wind, unable to take advantage of his own sage advice.

Dick also was appreciative that Concannon allowed the priests under his tutelage a "free rein" as they "tended" to the large congregation.

But now the parish's population was dwindling, the church's contingent down to just Dick and Father Paul, and the former had told the latter to cover the Saturday activities at the diocesan orphanage toward the special High Mass the next morning to celebrate the Feast of the Assumption.

Hell, I should be grateful we still have an orphanage. Or even a parish.

The newspapers—public articles, mind, for all to read— were full of the disaster in Boston, less than two hundred miles distant. The "scandal" of priests "molesting" little brats who wanted it enough—begged for it—only to later cry wolf. The worse scandal of the "cover-up," transferring priests with known prior "tendencies" to unsuspecting new parishes. And the greatest scandal of all, to Father Richard's thinking, the new archbishop in Boston actually selling off the Cardinal's mansion in order to fund the settlements with alleged victims and their families, even auctioning off churches to real-estate developers, who would turn the sacristy into a "duplex condo with garden" and the choir's section of the balcony into an "artist's loft."

Sacrilege, plain and simple. Yield to blackmailers, and we've lost any hope of retaining respect, not to mention peace of mind.

Father Richard wished he could spit, but he was in the center booth of the confessional, covering Father Paul's hours on a golf-glorious Saturday afternoon while the younger priest tended to an even younger flock. Stuck, Dick was, in a stuffy, cloth-lined coffin, wearing the rosary beads his own bishop insisted be visible whenever "on-duty." The scent of fear and anxiety permeated the enclosure, even when nobody occupied either confessional to his sides.

Not that anyone had, mind. Never, on such a day as this.

Here I am in this musty, vertical coffin, while Father Paul frolics in the fresh, open air with just the sort of "little gentleman" I always fancied. After being broken in just right by another seminarian with a more conscious devotion to that particular desire.

Father Richard sighed deeply. Lovely times, those.

The boys' names hardly mattered, as he had his own nicknames for them, occasionally puns on their given ones. "RamRod," for a boy named Rodney, and a game called "Pecking Peter's Pipe," for a boy with that first name. And none of his "little gentlemen" ever turned on Dick—ah, the puns even the boys enjoyed on that one—the way those ingrates in Boston did on their mentors and teachers, best friends and first lovers.

The hypocrisy of it all: Showing the eager boys "the way," then having them claim rape? Absurd.

Not that Father Richard had to worry about that anymore himself. No, his prostate surgery the prior year pretty much wrecked the nerve bundles around the removed gland, and "Dick's dick" could no longer manage an erection. He still could ejaculate, after vigorous, near painful masturbation, but it was rather a brief and, frankly, un-sensual—much less "sexual"—experience.

So, instead, there Father Richard sat, on a day nobody—not even harrowed sinners—wanted to be indoors. And should business suddenly pick up unexpectedly, it would still be the same old, same old: housewives fantasizing about soap-opera heartthrobs whose names Dick didn't recognize. Or the occasional young boy who could be coaxed into cleansing his soul by describing a bit more elaborately his "unclean thoughts and deeds," which almost always were heterosexual and soul-numbingly boring in their redundancy.

Oh, for just a single, solitary "new" sin, one I haven't absolved a thousand—

At which point, Father Richard heard the kneeler on his left side creak through the gauzy screening, and he drew in a breath, one which he was pleased to find smelled mildly exotic, like a perfume expensive enough to be subtle rather than obvious.

Well, if I must listen to somebody's tale of time-worn misbehavior, better it be a rich somebody who might ease the financial burden under which our, and many other parishes, unavoidably stagger.

✜

"BLESS ME, FATHER, for I have sinned," began Anna Maria Saracino, hoping the traditional opening hadn't changed during the interim decades. "It has been … oh, God— years and years since my last confession."

And, to Anna Maria's complete surprise, she began to cry. Hard and genuinely—the full-body variety—for the first time since … Well, she couldn't recall that, either.

"There, there, my child," came the soothing, if oily and patronizing, voice from the other side of the eye-level screen. Anna Maria suspected there was a liturgical word for the thing itself, but after stating the correct words to kick-off her confession, the rest of her memory appeared to have gone south. "Take your time. I'm here for as long as you need me."

Anna Maria got a grip, even felt a twinge of guilt over the sympathy the man tried to extend her. "You're Father Richard, correct?"

A hesitation? "Why, yes. I am. But are you one of our congregation?"

She steeled herself to follow through. "No, I grew up in another parish, far away from here. But I moved nearby recently, and I was given your name by a couple who used to live and go to church where you were pastor ten years ago."

A longer pause before, "St. Cecilia's?"

"Yes, yes," said Anna Maria, grateful to be prompted. "The Dunnes, Rita and Ed?"

"Ah, of course. I remember them well."

"And their son, too, named Damian?"

"Him, also. Dark hair, blue eyes?"

"I've seen only pictures of the boy, but yes, I think so." Anna Maria cleared her throat. "I've been carrying secrets with me for what seems like forever, Father Richard. Horrible, mortal sins that I have to confess."

"Well," a little roundness in the voice now, the reassuring teacher tone. "As you certainly know, my child, that's the purpose of the sacrament we're performing right now."

"Yes, that's why I'm here." Anna Maria had never actually said the words out loud to anybody, to anything besides the mirror in her bedroom, with the windows closed and the door locked. "You see, Father, I kill people. For money."

The pause now so long … "Father Richard?" said Anna Maria Saracino very softly. "Father, are you still there?"

✢

DICK, THIS FALLS under the category of "be careful what you wish for." He had to catch his breath at the young woman's—and she did sound young, early thirties at most—admission. Good Christ, an actual contract … hitter?

In my confessional?

No. No, the poor child must simply be deluded. "Surely you aren't telling me the truth."

"But I am," came back, the voice laced with the kind of desperation Father Richard had heard, and later verified, hundreds of times a year. "It began when I was fifteen. My stepfather—he wasn't a religious man, you see—and he … wanted me. Sexually. He watched me when I'd … take off any piece of clothing. And then, one school afternoon when Mom was at work … he … he cornered me in the basement near his little 'workshop,' and he … made me …"

The tsunami of tears began again. Great choking sobs. Father Richard found himself actually glad the church was probably still empty, as surely the woman's anguish, if not her exact words, were echoing across every pew.

But this was turning out to be good enough to be worth sacrificing a Saturday on the golf course. "The man forced himself on you?"

"And … and in me, Father."

A wail now, the way she must have sounded that afternoon, half her lifetime ago. Not to Dick's taste, but exquisite in its sincerity. This woman was definitely not faking her story of rape.

He said, "Did you become pregnant, my child?"

"No," a concluding sob. "No," the voice stronger now. "Thank God, at least that didn't happen."

"But this sort of man. Well, he didn't leave you alone after the first time, did he?"

"No." Her voice cold as a tombstone. "Once, maybe twice a week until I could get out of the house, find a place of my own."

"I see." That path now seemed dismally barren. "But you also mentioned … 'killing'?"

"Yes, yes." The cold tone now replaced with something like … hope? "A few years later, when my stepfather was dying of cancer, I visited him. In the hospital."

"That was extraordinarily charitable of you, child," said Dick, meaning it.

"Charity had nothing to do with it." The cold voice was back, with a vengeance now. "I watched him lie there, recognize me, even try to smile." A sniffly breath, but the voice remained strong. "Then, after I moved the nurse's call button out of his reach, I took another pillow from his bed and smothered him."

Mary, Mother of God! "You … you murdered your own stepfather?"

"I evened our accounts."

Oh, I wish Father Paul were the sort who would enjoy this lurid, sordid tale as much as I do, so the entire confession could be recounted—without even the need for any embellishment—later over a glass of wine in the rectory.

Father Richard tried to keep an excited tremor from his voice. "Then what, my child?"

"I put the pillow on the other, vacant bed in the room, and walked out. I never signed in as a visitor, so there was no record of me even being in the building. And his doctors assumed a heart attack had taken him. Mercifully, given the cancer and all."

A woman to be taken seriously, indeed, Dick decided. "So, you smothered your stepfather to pay him back for raping you."

"That's right."

"Didn't …" What were this arctic bitch's exact earlier words? "Didn't you say earlier, though, that you'd actually killed … 'people,' plural?"

"That's right, too. And for money, mostly with guns. Here are their names."

Father Richard absently counted them off on his rosary beads, reaching twenty-three victims before she stopped. "But, my child, that's—"

"Could we maybe cut the 'my child' crap and just call me 'Anna Maria.'"

It was phrased as a question, but stated as an order.

"Very well, 'Anna Maria.' You wish me to absolve you of all these sins, then?"

A click, like from the latch on a handbag. "Don't you want to?"

For the first time, a coy tone in the sinner's voice, as though she was flirting with him the way those disgusting baby boom spinsters always did after Sunday Mass. And, to his surprise, Dick realized he didn't want to hear another word this monster on the other side of his venerable wood and cloth had to tell him.

"Very well, you are absolved," in the sternest tone Dick could muster, dispensing with the usual request for sorrow and remorse over having committed the sins themselves. "But, I warn you, you must never—"

"Do you know how the Dunnes came to recommend you, Father?"

"The … Dunnes?"

"You remember. Damian's parents. After they left St. Cecilia's parish, their son had to go into a mental institution over what you'd done to him with your nickname for him, and the perverted … 'games' you made Damian play with you."

Father Richard felt physically ill himself. Dizzy, nauseous. "Get out! Get out of—"

"I promised the family: This one's on the house. The house of God."

Three sounds—like hiccuping coughs—but they rocked him in his chair, splintery holes in the wood before him. Father Richard could feel the impact of the silenced bullets, ripping through his robe and flesh and organs, scalding lava surging inside his chest, shoving him toward eternity.

No, dear God. No!

Trying to rise, Dick slid from his chair, crumpled now between it and the doorway out. To the church, the sanctity of ...

Father Richard felt himself falling, far further than the cold church floor beneath his palms.

Not yet, please. I need a ... priest, like Monsignor Concannon always said ... for Last Rites ... and my final confession before ...

JULIE HYZY

JULIE Hyzy, vice-president of the Midwest Chapter of Mystery Writers of America, is the author of three novels, and many mystery and science-fiction short stories. DEADLY BLESSINGS, the first in Julie's mystery series, introduced readers to Alex St. James, a Chicago-based researcher who uncovers a conspiracy of organized prostitution in the Chicago Catholic Church. DEADLY INTEREST, the second in the series, will be released in October 2006.

On the topic of this anthology, Julie says: "Hitmen (and hitwomen) are bad guys I can root for. After all, they're usually targeting villains much more despicable than themselves. They inhabit a treacherous world. They live on a perilous edge. They're cool. They're professional. Their stories give us a chance to step into their lives—to experience the dangers they face every day. How much more fun can you ask for?"

Visit Julie at www.JulieAHyzy.com.

STRICTLY BUSINESS
Julie Hyzy

DONNY FIRST CAUGHT sight of her over the rim of his shot glass. He drained the scotch and smacked his lips, holding the empty glass eye-height while he watched her saunter toward the bar. It had to be her. Tall and sleek, like a championship racehorse. Gorgeous little filly, he thought, half-expecting her to shake back that mane of sorrel-brown hair as she sashayed in. Yeah, she was a stunner, all right. Perfect.

Tight in low-slung blue jeans, her hips swayed from side to side—in precise time to Sinatra crooning about witchcraft—as she wound her way through the smoke and mood-lit tables that cluttered the main floor. She shifted the weighty backpack on her shoulder, then sidled up to the bar, leaning her back against it, surveying the establishment like she owned the place.

Donny did own the place. And pretty soon, he'd own a whole lot more, too.

He banged the shot glass down on the booth's tabletop with a crack that made Bobby and Mark sit up. "There she is," Donny said.

All three men leaned forward, looking down over the balcony from their perch a half-level up from the rest of the bar. Donny couldn't drag his eyes away.

Bobby gave a low whistle. "You sure?"

Al, the bartender had obviously seen her, too. Dragging the red terry towel from its perch on his shoulder, the old guy gave her a long appreciative look as he lumbered to the far end where she stood. He said something. She responded. They spoke, briefly, until Al nodded, then pointed toward Donny's table with a tilt of his head.

She took her sweet time before directing her gaze upward, but when those blue eyes finally met Donny's, he sucked in a white-hot breath. "Oh, yeah," he said, still staring. Nodding a greeting, his right hand swept sideways in a casual gesture of invitation. She smiled and started for the steps.

"Beat it," he said.

Bobby gave Mark a look that ordered him to follow, before squeezing his big gut out from the far side of the booth. He stood next to the table as Mark scrambled out behind him. Mutt and Jeff. Fred and Barney. What a mismatch. Bobby big and solid, Mark puny and blond. These two didn't talk much between themselves, and Mark almost never addressed Donny personally, but both could be counted on when it mattered. And it had never mattered more than it did now.

"Keep an eye on who comes in," he said as the woman cleared the top of the risers and began to make her way across the wood floor of the long balcony.

"Got it," Bobby said.

She turned sideways to get past the departing men. "Excuse me," she said, in a husky bedroom voice, just loud enough to be heard over the bar's muted conversations and Sinatra's final notes. Donny sat up a little straighter, fighting the jolt that had just zinged its way from his eyes to his crotch; as she neared the table, he stood.

She stopped when she was still about an arm's reach away. Tilting her head, she ran her fingers up through the shining brown tresses, looking like a model who'd just stepped off a magazine cover and into his life. Dark brows lifted expressively over amused blue eyes, and she touched her top lip with her tongue before smiling at him. Those were some fine lips.

"Mr. LaRocco?"

Donny grinned. Shit, if she was half as good as she looked, she'd be worth twice what he was paying her. "Call me Don," he said. He always liked the sound of that. Don LaRocco. Like he was the don already. He grinned again, and waited for her to slide into the booth before taking the seat across from her. "And I take it you're Susan. Susan … what?"

Easing the backpack off her shoulder, she set it next to her, then perched her right foot on the seat, draping an arm over her up-turned knee. She fixed him with a blue-eyed stare. "Just Susan."

Donny sat back, assessing her for a long moment. His cousin Leo in New York had promised she was good, but had warned her that she wouldn't take the job if she didn't like the employer. "She's the best," he'd warned. "But don't push her."

Smiling, he leaned forward. The booth, tucked into the far corner of this upper level, was lit by a sole high-beam lamp that hung over the table's center. He noticed she kept her back against the booth, her face away from the circle of light. "Something to drink?" he asked.

She nodded.

With a hand motion, Donny summoned his waitress. "Ladies first," he said with a gallant smile Susan's direction.

"Bottled water," she said.

Donny raised his eyebrows her direction before ordering another shot with a beer chaser. "You ought to take it easy on the hard stuff."

She didn't respond to his attempt at humor, leaning on the table now, but still keeping her face in the low light until the waitress left. "Tell me more about this job."

Man, this broad really cut to the chase.

Dragging his eyes from the very impressive tanned cleavage staring up at him from beneath her lacy white top, Donny adjusted himself in his seat. "So is that from the sun or do you use one of those tanning beds?" he asked, imagining that bronzed body sprawled out on silky satin sheets.

She licked her lips in an impatient gesture. "Mr. LaRocco …" she began. "Let's get one thing straight. You're not paying me to sit here and chat with you." Her face took on a look that Donny might almost describe as amused. "This is strictly business."

They were interrupted by the waitress, back with their drinks. Susan pushed aside the glass and took a moment to inspect the seal on her bottle before opening it. She wasn't obvious about it, but Donny noticed the measure of caution just the same. This chick didn't trust anybody. Good.

Susan took a long drink from the blue-labeled bottle. Holding it in both hands, she sat like a prim school girl till Donny downed his shot. "The job?" she asked.

With a sudden burst of giddy power, he shoved the beer toward the wall with the back of his hand. Time to set it all in motion. He'd gone over the plan in his head for months, and he'd just waited for the right vehicle to implement it.

And what a vehicle she was. Donny wondered what a spin round the block would cost him once the business end of the deal was done. Didn't matter. He'd have the money. He'd have the power. When she finished the assignment, he'd have the girl, too.

Donny chewed the inside of his cheek, wondering for a moment how he looked to her. Though in his late thirties, he took pride in the fact that he could still best the twenty-somethings on the racquetball court. Women always told him he was handsome. Tall, dark, and handsome. He considered taking off his sport coat to give her a glimpse of his black t-shirt, tight over his muscular chest, but thought better of it. He'd wait. Later, maybe. For now, he ran a hand through his hair, thanking Jesus, Mary, and Joseph that he'd taken after his mother's side and still had it all, nice and full. "You recognize my family name?" he asked, finally.

An abbreviated nod. "I've heard it around," she said.

"My uncle," he said. "Is Frederico LaRocco."

She nodded, giving a husky rumble that Donny couldn't interpret.

"What?" he asked.

"Your Uncle Fred," she said. "I've met him."

As though the vengeful old bastard had suddenly appeared at the table, fixing those murderous eyes on him, Donny sat back with a start. He shook his head to clear the image. "Shit," he said, looking down over the balcony's railing. He sat back and formed both hands into fists. He pounded them on the table. Leo should have done a better job of checking. "Shit," he said again. Plans were beginning to unravel.

"Take it easy," she said. "I said I met him. I didn't say he'd remember me."

Donny dragged his attention back to her. "He hired you for something?"

She shook her head.

"How did you meet him? Does he know what you do for a living?"

She licked those lips again, unscrewed the bottle and took a long drink before taking her time meeting his eyes.

He wanted her to answer now. Right now. Maybe there was still a chance things could work. Damn it, why didn't she tell him? He hit the table again. "Will he recognize you?"

With an elbow still positioned on her knee, she curled a finger in front of her lips, her other hand holding the water. She rolled her eyes. "Way back then I was bleached blonde, scrawny, and flat-chested." Donny saw the angry set of her lips around the water bottle's top as she tilted it back for another drink. "The good old days," she said with a stiff smile.

Donny knew his uncle had a good memory for faces, but the geezer's eyesight wasn't so hot anymore. Glaucoma. If this Susan really changed as much as she said she had …

He wiped sweaty hands on the sides of his pant legs before bringing them up to the table again. Shit. This was it. This was the moment. Leaning forward, he ran a blunt fingernail over a small crack in the table's center. "Listen," he said, "my uncle is ... going senile," he said. His eyes flicked up a quick glance at Susan before he stared at the crack again. "He's been making bad decisions for the family."

"And you want him taken out? Is that it?" she asked.

Over the smoky ambiance her words were smooth, like the warm path of whiskey down his throat. It sent another shiver up his spine.

He nodded the affirmative. "But I can't take any chances. If he finds out ... if he somehow knows you ... I'm dead." She didn't flinch at that. She didn't so much as blink. "And you're dead, too," he said.

The woman's icy demeanor under such circumstances made Donny want to slap her. Wake her up. This was a big-time hit. Didn't she get that?

"I didn't say he'd know me," she said, leaning low enough that the light topped her forehead, sending her features into shadowed relief. "Nobody knows me if I don't want them to." Susan's eyes held Donny's for a piercing moment. "I can do this job," she said, then looked away, nodding, as though remembering some long-ago hurt. Her face set in a mask of anger.

"I have to have a guarantee ..." he started to say.

"Guarantee?" she asked, leaning back in her seat again, this time dropping her foot to the floor. "How long you been in this business, bud? There are no guarantees."

"What I mean is ..." Donny hated the way she intimidated him. "Are you positive he won't recognize you?"

She pursed her lips. "I met him about four years ago," she said. "Out in Vegas. Late. I'd seen him on TV and knew who he was."

Vegas. Uncle Fred spent every vacation out in Vegas. He would've run into a million girls out there. Had his pick. But this chick sounded like she had some ax to grind. Donny prompted, "I get the impression you're not too fond of him."

Susan shrugged. Took another drink.

"How come?" he asked.

She fixed him with another one of those stares of hers. This one carried the unmistakable message of "back off." After a long moment, Susan slid her gaze far off to the right, then lowered her eyes momentarily, before she turned back to face Donny. Staring at him now, her eyes hardened. Blue steel, he thought, as she continued. "I have a score to settle, okay? This hit can help me accomplish that." She smiled now, with frightening calm. "I want this job."

Donny slid his butt farther forward on the seat, till his body touched the table. Time to take control again. He lowered his face and spoke softly, but clearly. "Have it your way," he said. "I don't care what your beef is with the old man, but I want this thing done my way, and I want you to listen to how it's going to go down."

Her face impassive, she nodded.

"Okay," Donny said, encouraged. "Saturday next week, there's going to be this big seventieth birthday bash at the house. Everybody's going to be there, but I know my uncle and he's going to think that this party shit is boring. He's going to be looking for some reason to escape all the little half-pints screaming and running around." Donny rolled his eyes heavenward. Too many kids at these things lately. When he took over, he'd start enforcing some of the old rules, like no women and no kids. Well, he amended, looking at Susan, he might make an occasional exception.

"At nine o' clock, you're going to show up, and I'm going to sneak you into his room. I'll let him know he's got a surprise waiting for him ..." Donny smiled at his choice of words, before continuing, " ...   and then I'll introduce you to him as his very special birthday present from me."

Susan held the water bottle. She gave a short nod.

"You're going to give him a glass of sherry. The idiot drinks sherry, of all things. Like he's some damn Brit or something. Anyways, you're going to have this sherry that he keeps next to his bed and you're going to put a little of this into the glass before he drinks it."

Donny pulled a small vial out from his jacket pocket. He held it in his palm, shielding it from view of anyone who might be looking their direction.

"What is it?"

"Concentrated dose of rohypnol."

"Roofie." Susan lifted one eyebrow, as though impressed. "Go on," she said.

"This'll take effect pretty quick. Maybe ten minutes or so. That's why you can't give it to him right away. It'll be too suspicious if he keels over right after you get there. You're going to have to … you know … keep him happy for a while. Once he's out, you slip a plastic bag over his head, he suffocates, and it'll look like he died from a heart attack."

She didn't say a word.

"You get me, right?"

She ignored the question. "And you don't think they're going to look for drugs in his system when they do the autopsy?"

Donny had thought of that. "This stuff's pretty undetectable. Anyway, he's under doctor's care for some heart troubles—no way anyone's going to ask for an autopsy."

Licking his lips, Donny finished, "You just slip him the mickey and you keep him quiet till it's done. Then you come out and find me and I'll take it from there."

She appeared to be waiting for him to say more.

Donny spread out his hands, eager—frustrated. "You understand the instructions, right?"

"And how do I get out of there?"

"The kid, Mark, is going to sneak you out the back stairway and to a car around the front. My guy Bobby will drive you anywhere you want to go."

"Your uncle doesn't have any bodyguards? Anyone who watches his back?"

The look she shot him said, "amateur," and that got Donny's back up. "Uncle Fred's goon squad will be there, but they always hang outside. He doesn't like them mingling with the family," he said. "And inside, Fred has me to cover his back." He barked a laugh.

She didn't respond. "And the money?"

"In the car, in a duffel bag. Just like in the movies."

Susan let her gaze drift upward—pursed her lips. "I want half up front."

"Yeah, I thought you might." He watched out over the balcony for a minute, his eyes taking in all the happy drinkers, carousing like they were perfectly hilarious. Raucous conversations and the clanking of glassware accompanied the movement of the waitresses through the smoky room. The background music had switched from Sinatra and was now playing an upbeat Dean Martin tune. Donny let his eyes skim the area several times before they rested on Bobby, who acknowledged Donny's gaze with a lift of his chin.

A minute later, Mark was at the table, carrying a shopping bag from Victoria's Secret. Donny checked Susan's expression as she caught sight of the distinctive pink-striped package. "Half is in there," Donny said, "along with the address, the stuff you'll need," he placed the rohypnol in a small padded envelope and reached over, adding it to the bag, "and a little something I thought you might want to wear when you work on the old man."

Taking the bag from Mark with a nod, she set it on the seat next to her.

"Don't you want to look?" Donny heard the disappointment in his voice and he hated knowing she could probably hear it too. He'd taken care to pick the lingerie item out himself and he thought it was a sweet little piece. It should make even this cold fish's eyes light up. She didn't seem to care one way or another. "I mean, don't you want to see if you like it? Count the money?"

She arched an eyebrow. "I'll look at it later." She paused, as if waiting for him to argue, before continuing. "This is a job and I'll wear what I want. And," she said, leaning her face near the table, "if the money isn't right, I'm out of here." She smiled. "So I figure you're not about to mess with me."

With that, she stood, slinging her backpack over her shoulder and grabbing the pink bag. "I'll see you Saturday."

Donny watched her go, left with the lingering wonder whether that hollow feeling in the pit of his stomach was annoyance or relief.

⊕

SATURDAY NIGHT, DONNY had his arm around his wife's waist. She was talking to his cousin Benny and Benny's wife, telling them the story of the past week home with two kids having summer colds and being miserable in front of the TV. He'd been hearing her tell it all night, and his arm tightened around her so as to keep himself grounded while his mind drifted away from the conversation. He looked around for Bobby.

Uncle Fred's house had the feel of comfortable money, Donny thought, as he spied Bobby and Mark near the front door. And soon all of it would be his. He caught Bobby's eye and shrugged as the big guy made a pantomime of checking his watch. Just closing in on nine. He would have expected this Susan to be on time.

Uncle Fred, the target of tonight's plans, wandered through the celebratory collection of family, a fresh Manhattan in one hand, a half-smoked stogie in the other. Hard drinking, hard living, his being alive and active at seventy refuted all the conventional wisdom about exercise and eating right. Fred moved through the small clusters of cousins, friends, and business associates with the presence of a monarch, reigning supreme over his little fiefdom.

The guy never lifted a finger except to issue orders, yet there he was, mingling, his fat cheeks wobbling and red—his head full with silver-glinted white hair. Smiling that warm, encompassing grin at the guests who all wanted a moment with the man. Smiling like he was really the grandfather type and not the cold-blooded killer of Donny's drug supplier.

Right now that bright white hair was catching the light from the recessed bulbs overhead, and Uncle Fred leaned in to listen to something his young great-niece Rebecca had to say. As the little girl reached up on tiptoe to whisper, Fred's face fixed in a somber look, as though what she had to say was of the utmost importance. In a moment, he threw his head back and laughed, pulling the blonde-curled baby close into the crook of his cigar arm.

Sure, everybody thought Fred was God around here. Just wait. They all depended on the old guy for their meager handouts. Just wait. Everyone would forget the tightfisted geezer in a heartbeat once Donny took control.

Mark tapped Donny's shoulder. He didn't say anything, simply twisted his head toward the back end of the home. Donny broke away from his wife, who'd now lapsed into a discussion of children's bowel movements with Benny's wife. Benny flung Donny an exasperated look of boredom and the two men went separate directions.

Donny checked his watch as he made his way to the back. "In here," Bobby said, in front of the rear study's oak double doors.

Nine o'clock on the nose. Donny grinned as he walked in. His time had come.

He suppressed a low whistle when he caught sight of Susan. While she'd been beautiful the other night, she'd been so in an almost wholesome way. Her face had been clear of heavy makeup and her whole demeanor that of a free spirit, girl-next-door. Tonight, however, she'd gone all out to fit the role she needed to play. She was wearing a low-cut yellow teddy-top—lacy and sheer with the skimpiest of spaghetti straps holding it up—over an ultra-short black leather skirt. A tiny purse swung near her hips. She'd arranged the rich brown hair into curly waves that rested on nearly bare shoulders. Her three-inch black stiletto heels showcased shapely legs, and she approached him, licking her lips.

"I'm ready," she said, breathing the words into Donny's right ear. "Are you?"

Reflexively, yet not, Donny's arm reached around, trapping her tiny waist. He then slid his hand down over the supple leather to grab her ass and pull her close.

She arched away from him in a move of coy refusal that made him start to get hard.

"Not now, big boy," she said, pressing her hands against his chest and easing herself out from his hold. "Your time comes later."

Donny blew out a high-octane breath of frustration. Delayed gratification. He could deal with that. Waiting always made it more fun anyway. With a nod of acquiescence, he led Susan to Uncle Fred's room upstairs.

Though he was prepared for its sumptuousness, having been in Uncle Fred's private sanctuary many times before, Donny still reacted to the high-ceilinged space with awe. As large as the ballroom two floors below, this was more an apartment than a bedroom. Surrounding the custom-made four-pillar canopy bed were individually lighted paintings and handcrafted furniture pieces, each commissioned work by a real artist. Everything that inhabited this room was one-of-a-kind and irreplaceable.

Except for Uncle Fred, of course.

Donny smiled at his private joke.

He waited in the doorway, and let her pass. "You like?" he asked, sweeping out his hand expansively.

Susan's eyebrows raised as she stepped slowly into the room, her eyes scanning the gold brocade-papered walls, the fireplace with two easy chairs set before it, and the thick maroon Oriental rug at her feet. Keeping an unhurried pace, she wandered across the room, to the closed door near the corner. Grasping the gold handle, she opened it. Through the dark opening, Donny could see the flickers of candlelight reflecting on the marble bathroom's walls. Good, he thought. The maid had set the mood, just like he'd ordered.

Susan closed the door again, stopping briefly at Fred's nightstand where she ran a finger over the decanter of sherry standing there and sent Donny a pointed look. "Very nice," she said, reacting in her understated way. Donny grimaced. Just wait till he had her alone, later. He'd find ways to make her react, all right.

He'd been about to go over the plan with her one more time, when Bobby interrupted. "Boss?" he said.

Donny turned to see Uncle Fred clearing the uppermost landing with a huff of effort, his hand gripping the banister. His bigger-than-life voice boomed his presence, like it always did. "What's the big secret, Donny-boy?" Fred's smile was wide and as he passed beneath the overhead lamps toward his bedroom doors, Donny was struck again by the halo-like effect of the light on the man's silver hair.

"Got a ..." Donny stopped, cleared his throat, started again. "I got a birthday present for you, Uncle Fred. A special surprise, from me to you."

"Oh?" the older man's tone spoke of pleasured curiosity as he drew closer. "Should I close my eyes?"

"Not now," Donny said, with a wink. "But you might want to, later." He answered the older man's grin with one of his own and stood in the open doorway, holding a hand out Susan's direction, as though making introductions.

"Hello," Susan said in that husky voice as Uncle Fred cleared the threshold. She crossed the room in three leisurely strides, then lifted her index finger to caress Fred's five o'clock shadow. "I've been waiting for you."

Donny searched the old man's eyes for some look of recognition, some measure of wariness, but all he saw there was instant enthusiasm. "Oh," Fred said, dragging the exclamation out in a slow release of breath. His arm encircled her waist and she molded herself against him. "Hello."

Donny tamped down the rush of excitement that shot hot prickly tingles through his brain. Keep calm, he told himself. Not much longer now. "Well then," he said, striving to maintain a composed outward appearance. "I'll leave you two to get acquainted."

⊕

AT TEN FORTY-FIVE, carrying on an insipid conversation about golf games with fat cousin Craig, Donny thought his lips would crack from the stupid smile he'd pasted on. The bitch hadn't come down yet. How goddamned long was she going to take up there? Maybe she lost her nerve.

Craig leaned close. "Don? You listening?"

"Yeah, sorry," Donny said, lifting his scotch and soda to his lips. "Long day."

"I bet," Craig said, his plump lips twisting into a sausagey smile against pale freckled skin. "You're Fred's right-hand man. You gotta have a lot on your mind every minute, eh?"

"You don't know the half of it," Donny said with a snort.

Godammit. He thought she'd be perfect. A sultry, sexy hitwoman. Nobody'd suspect she was anything more than a high-priced hooker. She'd do her thing, Uncle Fred would be dead—apparently from sexual exertion—and Donny, suitably grief-stricken, would move in to take over, just as soon as the body was cold. But it all depended on this Susan coming through for him. And she was taking her goddamn sweet time about it.

"So can you?" Craig asked, in a conspiratorial whisper. He'd been blathering incessantly for the past minute and Donny had tuned him out again. Craig sidled closer, his eyes roving the room. Donny didn't have to have heard the earlier part of the conversation to know that Craig was pushing for another drug buy. He had a hundred Craigs out there all waiting for him to come through. And he wouldn't be able to keep any of them happy until Uncle Fred was out of the picture.

"Next week."

"Next week?" Craig's voice was plaintive, too loud.

"Keep it down, asshole," Donny said. "I'll get you what you need, but you have to wait till next week. I lost my contact."

"Lost, how?"

Donny ignored him, letting his gaze wander toward the doors again. He wanted to know, right now, what was going on upstairs. He took another look at the Rolex on his left arm. "Damn it."

"What's wrong?" Craig asked, putting a brotherly hand on Don's shoulder.

Donny shook it away. "Nothing," he said in a voice too sharp. "I'm expecting … a phone call, okay?" He twisted away from his cloying cousin, and stormed out of the room, letting the music, conversation, and birthday party sounds fade behind him as he made his way to the quiet back staircase of the home, where Bobby stood.

"What the hell is taking so goddamn long?" he asked in a tight whisper.

Bobby's big face paled as his eyes widened. "Beats me. I been sending Mark up there every so often just to see if he can hear anything going on in there."

"And?"

"He says he can't hear nothing."

As if summoned, Mark appeared next to Bobby. Silent, he shook his head, underscoring Bobby's words.

Bobby shrugged. "Should we go up there and check?"

Donny wanted to slap the big man's stupid face. "What are you, an idiot?" He gazed off down the long corridor that led back to the busy family festivities. "We'll give it another—" He stopped himself short when he heard fast footfalls approaching from above. A half-second later Susan appeared at the top of the stairs, staring down at the threesome with wide blue eyes. Barefoot, she wore only a man's shirt, open, the tails skimming the tops of her tanned thighs. She gestured frantically.

"Hurry," she said. "Please."

Donny froze, looked all directions at once. Maintain control, he told himself. Don't panic. "What happened?" he asked, taking the stairs two at a time.

She didn't answer. Instead, she turned and fled up the remaining flight and scurried into the master bedroom before Donny could get another word out.

"Damn it," Donny said, breathless as the three of them came through the door. "What? What is it? Is he here? Did he recognize you?"

She shook her tousled head and bit her lip. "Shut the door," she whispered. "We've got a problem."

Donny ordered Bobby and Mark to stand outside. "Don't let anyone in," he told them.

As soon as they were alone she grabbed Donny's sleeve, tugging him deeper into the room. "Listen," she shot a terrified look at the slightly ajar bathroom door. "He wanted his sherry in there. I tried to keep him distracted, I tried to put it off, but he said he needed it to relax."

Donny made a move toward the bathroom. He'd had enough waiting; he needed to know what the hell had happened. Susan grabbed him again, this time with a strength that surprised him, holding him back. "Is he dead?" Donny asked, forgetting to keep his voice low.

"It didn't go down the way you wanted. He wanted us to get into the Jacuzzi together," she said. One hand rose to her forehead, and she stroked an eyebrow, her face tightening as she spoke. "But that roofie took effect too fast. He slid under the water," she said, finally. "I think he drowned. This is going to screw up your plans isn't it?"

Donny broke away from her long-fingered grasp. "Goddamn right it is." He shook his head, grabbing both her shoulders, shaking her. "Goddamn now they're going to do an investigation and they're going to point the finger at me." He stopped shaking, then worked to settle his mind—to gather his wits, pacing. "We need damage control here. I have to figure this out." Donny clenched and flexed his fists as he reasoned it all out. "I'll have to make it look like I came up to check on the old man and found him in the tub."

Donny glared at Susan again. "And you, bitch," he said, nearly spitting, "don't expect another penny from me. You screwed this one up royally."

"Hey," she said, starting to put her clothes back on, "You wanted your Uncle Fred killed, right? You owe me the rest of it."

"I don't owe you anything," Donny said, poking her chest.

"The hell you don't."

"Look," Donny said between clenched teeth. "I paid you to make it look like a heart attack. I told you I wanted this done my way. You got sloppy. You ought to give me back the cash I already gave you, you dumb bitch."

Susan finished pulling her skirt on. "Not so fast," she said.

The panicked terror she'd displayed moments ago had been replaced by cool confidence once again. Nice try, Donny thought, but I'm not falling for that "I'm in control" shit. If she thought she was going to weasel the rest of the cash from him, she had a big surprise in store for her.

Donny addressed her in a guttural voice. "Get the hell out of here before I tell Bobby to take care of you, too." He turned toward the bathroom, and slammed open the six-panel door with the palm of his hand, but it met with an obstruction, and stopped short.

Uncle Fred emerged from the shadows behind the blocked door. "I believe the lady said, 'not so fast,'" he said calmly. The old man's eyes were bright over a pouchy, malevolent grin and he spoke in cool, measured tones. But it was the sleek, silenced Walther PPK pointed directly at his chest that caught Donny's attention. His brain stutter-stepped.

"Uncle Fred," he said, with forced joviality. "She ... she said you were dead. Thank God you're okay." Too late, Donny noticed his uncle was perfectly dry and fully clothed. He shot an accusatory look at Susan. "You bitch. You lied to me."

She blew him a kiss. Smiled.

Donny thought about calling for help from Bobby and Mark, just outside. His quick glance toward the door must have telegraphed his thoughts because Uncle Fred shook his head. "Don't even think about it, Donny. My guys are taking care of your two clowns right now." As though by pre-arranged signal, a half-second later, one of the goon squad came through the door. He nodded to Fred, then stood behind Donny, pressing something metal and hard against Donny's back.

"You," Donny said, glaring at Susan. "You did this." He looked back to his uncle, but saw nothing there but cold hatred. "She did this. She's setting me up."

Uncle Fred shook his silver head. "I heard everything, boy. And it goddamn nearly broke my heart." He shrugged. "Not that I didn't expect something like this from you. God, Donny, you had such a future. But then you tried to pull this shit."

Susan sat cross-legged on the big bed, watching them. Donny couldn't make himself comprehend what was going down. "You said you hated him," he said.

She smiled again. "Nope. You said that."

"But," Donny sputtered, not understanding. "You said ..." he knew he sounded like a whining toddler, but he couldn't go out like this—not knowing. He'd done everything right. He was supposed to be the head of the family now. What had he done wrong? "You said ..."

"I said I had a score to settle," Susan finished for him as she stood and moved close to Fred. "Your uncle got me out of a very bad situation and away from some very nasty people a long time ago. He helped me when I needed it, and he didn't ask for anything in return." She smiled up at the corpulent septuagenarian like he was some sort of God. "I'm just glad I got this chance to pay him back."

Donny's stomach lurched. The big guy behind him yanked at his arms, pulling them back and twisting some sort of scratchy restraint around his wrists.

"Good-bye, Donny," Uncle Fred said. "I'll be sure your family's taken care of."

The bile rose in Donny's throat. He wanted to spit at them both. Instead he fixed Susan with a stare of disgust. "I paid her well, Fred. You might as well get my money's worth with her before you kick her out."

Susan canted her head. Snapped her fingers. "You're right." She reached into her little purse and pulled out the suffocation bag.

Her blue eyes glittering, she advanced on Donny, whipping open the plastic bag with a hollow thwack. "I always repay my debts, Mr. LaRocco." she said. "And I still owe you a hit, don't I?"

JAY BONANSINGA

JAY Bonansinga grew up in Peoria, Illinois. After getting a B.A. in English from Michigan State University, and a Masters in Film from Columbia College in Chicago, he apprenticed as a corporate writer for over five years, drafting everything from commercial scripts to executive speeches. His first novel, THE BLACK MARIAH, was published in 1994 to rave reviews and a lucrative Hollywood deal. Since then he has had eight more novels published, and has worked in Hollywood as a busy screenwriter on various projects. He has been a finalist for the Bram Stoker Award, and has won the prestigious silver plaque at the Chicago International Film Festival. He lives in Evanston, Illinois, with his wife and two sons. His latest novel is TWISTED.

On the topic of this antho, Jay says: "For me, the appeal of the hitman in literature has always been the appeal of being a Jack of One Trade. A true professional. A master of the craft. That's the metaphor, I think, that works in a lot of these stories. And it's a perfect catharsis for frustrated white-collar middle managers in a messy, compromised world. And that's what drives me as a writer. My favorite hitman was Trevanian's Jonathan Hemlock, and he was a true pro. Well groomed. Laconic. Smartly dressed. Good taste. Nothing wasted, no nonsense. But always deadly as ... well ... hemlock."

Visit Jay at www.JayBonansinga.com.

THERE'S SOMEBODY HERE WANTS TO TALK TO YOU
Jay Bonansinga

I**T'S GETTING LATE,** and the shadows are stretching across the bayou, making the little derelict marina look like a graveyard of torn sails and leaning masts swaying in the fishy breeze. The light's different down there below Lake Pontchartrain. That's something I noticed that first night. We got down there about supper time, the kid and I, and the cicadas or the crickets or the frogs—or whatever they got down there in that hot box in the dead of summer—they're like the roar of jet engines in my skull. And the heat's pressing down on us, and our shirts are sticking to our backs from driving all day in that beat-up Jimmy, and I notice everything looks fuzzy and green. Like the sun's drooped behind a pane of insulator glass on the horizon.

"So we don't need a license or anything to go out in this crate?" I ask the old cracker who runs the boat rental place.

His rotten smile widens, his green teeth gleaming in the dusky Louisiana light. "Naw … not unless y'all run into the coast guard."

Then he laughs his phlegmy laugh like a raccoon snorting coke, gesturing down at the cockpit of that rusty bucket of bolts tied to the dock. It's an old Sea Ray diesel pocked with salt sores and a ragged canvas bonnet stretched like a sagging skin across its cabin—a veteran of drug runs and countless illegals rafting out of Mariel, Cuba. I don't know squat about boats. Or the sea. I'm from Chicago, for Christ's sake. Water's for chasing Bushmills and flushing turds. But the thing looks simple enough. A few gauges, a steering wheel, and a couple pairs of stick-shift levers.

"Two bills gets y'all twenty-four hours," he says, "no questions asked."

I look over at Billy. A skinny bundle of bones and zits, draped in an oversized denim shirt with the sleeves fringed off, he's looking down at the GPS receiver with a nervous expression on his ferrety little face. It's gripped in his sweaty palm like a transistor radio, and I can tell when the kid looks up at me that the Freak's moving. We're running out of time. "Uncle Dan, um, we need to, like, make a decision," he says.

I tell him to take it easy. I tell him I got it under control.

He's my cousin Matt's boy—maybe the closest thing to family I ever had. I use him now and again in my skip-trace business, usually as a spotter, or a driver, or whatever. I guess he thinks it's pretty jake having a bounty hunter as an uncle. But this trip is different. We're down here to kill somebody—a first for me—and I still don't like the fact that I brought him along. It's bad enough I expose the boy to the scum-bag bail-bond jumpers I gotta track down.

But now this.

"So uh … fellas … what's the deal?" Mr. Green Teeth pipes up suddenly, and I let out a sigh and offer him a hundred and fifty for the night. He snatches the wad of bills out of my hand with a grumble, then hobbles away toward his tar paper shack at the end of the dock.

We throw the duffel bag in the rear of the cabin, then climb on board the bucket of bolts. The boat pitches like a carnival ride as I thumb the motor on. A gurgling noise, and a fart of exhaust, and then we're launching out of there, the Spanish moss clawing at us like an endless, broken-down car wash as we churn through the soup toward the mouth of the bay. The air smells of rotten eggs.

It takes us maybe fifteen minutes to reach the gulf, and by that time the kid is crawling out of his skin with nervous tension. I tell him to relax. I assure him that the little green dot on that GPS receiver is accurate—I had the kid's mom hide the little pellet of a transmitter inside the Freak's cell phone a week ago—and now all we have to do is close the distance. We won't even have to board the Freak's boat. Just get close enough to get his attention.

Get a clean shot, and we're outta there.

By that point it's already as dark as a stew pot out there, and as we emerge into the open sea, the air changes. I goose the motor a little, and the slimy, sulphurous breeze envelopes us. The sky over the Gulf is frigging huge. I'm not used to seeing all those stars. Where I come from the sky's usually so low and grey you can reach up and scrape your fingertips across it. But this is insane. It's like we just slid out over the edge of the universe.

"The fuck's he doing out there?" Billy hollers over the bellow of the engine, gripping the side of the rocking boat with his free hand, his eyes glittering in the darkness. According to the two little glowing dots on the GPS we're now less than a mile from the Freak's boat, but we still can't see anything out there other than a sheet of black glass stippled with yellow moonlight. I start to wonder if the directions the boy's mother gave me are messed up. Maybe we got the wrong coastline.

"Don't get your piles in an uproar, kid. I told you I got it under—"

The words stick in my throat suddenly.

The first glimpse of the Freak's boat materializes like the tip of a cigarette on the horizon. He's not moving. I yank back on the throttle, and the nose of the Sea Ray sinks, the wake goosing us from behind as we slow down. The kid doesn't say a word when I take the GPS from him and toss it to the deck. "Get the duffel bag."

He goes down below, gets the bag, brings it back up, and I fish around for the Smith & Wesson. It's a chrome .357 I bought off a skel on the street, filed clean, with a red laser sighting device. This is going to be easy, I'm thinking. Right now, I'm thinking this is going to be a piece of cake.

Of course, at that point I had no idea what was about to happen.

⊕

LET ME TAKE A minute to tell you about the Freak, and why I agreed to resort to murder in order to rid the world of this prick. His real name is Calvin Pryce, and with a name like Calvin it's no wonder he turned out to be such a monster.

Anyway: Here's how he got his claws into the kid's family. My cousin Ginny—the kid's mom—she had a tough time after the divorce. She couldn't find work, and half of Matt's income as a pipe fitter didn't help much, so she started flirting with what she insisted on calling 'the exotic dancing field.' Brothers and sisters, let me tell you: I like a good table dance as much as the next guy, but working as a dancer in a strip club is about as safe and secure as being a goddamned mind sweeper. All manner of scum passes through those places, and when Calvin Pryce showed up one night, he set his sites on Ginny.

At first, I guess, she was swept off her feet: this tall, blonde dude with the fake British accent, and this mysterious business that he's got that takes him to far flung places like Indonesia, the Middle East, and South America. But after a few months of dating the guy, he starts playing rough. Worse than that, Ginny starts stumbling on little clues that he's into some freaky shit. Satanic cult type stuff. A desecrated cross in a drawer, a little vial of blood in the guy's coat pocket—stuff like that. And their sex is getting weird: he wants to tie her up, choke her, drink blood with her, and finally he takes her to this sex club where they're sacrificing a goat or some shit like that.

Ginny decides she's had enough, and she bails. And that's when things really get scary. Calvin comes over one night and

beats the shit out of her, and then he ties her up and starts vid-
eotaping himself torturing her. He probably would have killed
her if the kid hadn't come home. Billy tries to intervene and
The Freak does a number on the kid. Beats the tar out of him
and then rapes him in front of his mother.

Next day, Ginny goes to the cops, and the Freak shows up
with a high-powered lawyer, and the whole thing becomes a
he-said/she-said circle jerk.

Now by this point, the kid wants to kill him, and Ginny
just wants to move away. In fact, she did put her place on the
market. But before she could sell the house, she ran across a
stash of videos that the Freak had left there. I never saw the
tapes. Ginny burned them. But she swears to this day they
were the real thing. Honest-to-goodness snuff films. Devil
worship stuff. Horrible shit.

That's when she called me. I guess she figured if I didn't
kill the guy, her son probably would. And she knew I ran in
some petty unsavory circles. Which is kind of funny. Because
even though I've dwelled in the asshole of the world for most
of my working life, I have this thing about sin. I was raised
Catholic for a while—before my drunkard of a daddy skipped
town—and I guess the old catechism just clung to me like a
bad knee or an allergy you can't shake. Killing is a mortal sin.
Thou shalt not do it. Under *any* circumstances. I've had op-
portunities. It would be easy for a guy like me. So goddamn
easy. But then I'd be lost. Lost.

Maybe that's why I start sweating bullets that night as we
float through the darkness toward that idling speedboat.

I'm checking the Smith & Wesson's chamber, snapping it
shut with greasy fingers.

The Sea Ray's rocking, and my hands are shaking, and I
can now see the Freak's boat out there maybe a couple hundred
yards away. It sits there like a black, gleaming coffin, its running
light like the smoldering tip of a cigar, twinkling in the sultry salt

air. I'm not sure about the distance. Your eyes play tricks on you when it's that dark, and the adrenaline's pumping.

"C'mon, let's do it, c'mon, c'mon," the kid's murmuring behind me.

"Go down below."

"C'mon, c'mon, c'mon, c'mon, c'mon." Billy's backing into the shadows of the cabin like a character in some silent horror movie, and the low, strangled, flaky sound of his voice gives me the jeebies. I glance over my shoulder and all I can see is the half moon glow of the kid's pale face hovering in the darkness underneath that parchment bonnet. "C'mon, c'mon, do it … do it, do it, do it, do it!"

By now we're less than a hundred yards away from the Freak's boat, and in the moonlight I can make out the long, pointed prow like the snout of an animal bobbing in the currents. The moonlight gleams off the windshield. Something glows orange within the hold of the boat. The Freak must have dropped anchor because the craft is staying in one place but the optical illusion of white caps pushing across its keel make it look like it's inching backwards across the black void. Like a dream. Or a *nightmare*, I guess.

I thumb the hammer back.

" … do it, do it, do it …"

As we bob and pitch closer and closer in the darkness, maybe twenty yards away now, our engine burbling like an old man choking on his own saliva, I see the weirdest frigging thing I've ever seen—and let me tell you, I've seen my share of weird shit. I realize there's a dark figure, pretty much in silhouette, standing up on the boat, standing near the rear outboard powerplant. I realize it's *him*. He's standing there like he's waiting for us. Dressed in the rags of a bloody shirt, his stringy, greying blond hair tossing on the sea breeze, he's staring at us.

I raise the .357 at him.

" … do it, do it! …"

Now we're close enough to see the blood. It's spattered all around the bulwark of the speed boat. It looks like he tried to fingerpaint words or symbols all over the seats and the deck, and I realize the glowing light from within is coming from about a thousand candles, and there's a moldering carcass of an animal near the stern, a dog or a sheep, dangling, flaccid and gutted, over the rail.

I aim at the Freak's face. The red dot of laser light touches his forehead.

" ... DO IT!! ..."

The son of a bitch smiles at me. The boats are close enough to spit on each other now. Behind me the GPS is beeping. My scalp is tingling.

The flickering light is shining off the Freak's face, and I'm close enough to see he's smiling at me. He's *smiling* and I can't fire.

I can't do it. I can't squeeze off a single shot. The trigger is impermeable like a tree trunk planted deep in the earth's core.

"KILL HIM!!"

I hear the kid's shriek ring out behind me, and then there's this black flash of movement. And before I know what's going on the kid is leaping over the bow of the Sea Ray and vaulting across the ten foot gap between the two boats. I scream at him at the top of my lungs: "BILLY!"

He lands awkwardly on the keel of the speedboat, his feet splashing, the air knocked out of his lungs. The impact makes the speedboat lurch, and sends the Freak staggering backward until he falls on his ass.

It all happens so quickly I don't even get a chance to make any moves before the Freak is crawling toward the kid. I slam down on the throttle, and the Sea Ray booms, and then it bucks in the water. The gun is still glued to my hand as the Sea Ray rams into the speedboat ... tossing both vessels like dominoes ... sending me sprawling across the bow ... tangling the boats like train couplers locking ... but it's too late now.

The Freak already has Billy in his clutches, and is pulling the kid up into the speedboat. Into the candlelight and sheep's blood.

The kid screams, and the Freak wraps his gnarled hands around the boy's neck, and the kid starts kicking and choking and making these weird mewling noises. And I know this is hard to believe but the Freak is smiling through all this. I'm back on my feet by this point and I've got the .357 in both hands now, and I'm standing on that rocking deck, gasping for breath, drawing a bead on that prick—

—and I still can't get one off, I just can't fire, I can't do it, my finger's like the Rock of Gilbralter on that trigger … right up until the moment I hear him speak. And then everything changes.

"What are you waiting for, friend?!" he calls out to me, and he's staring at me with that sick fish-belly smile, his unblinking eyes locked onto me while the kid's dying in his hands. And in that one crazy instant in the darkness, as the passage of time seems to hang in front of me like a veil, I see something in the Freak's eyes that I hadn't noticed before. I wouldn't exactly call it suffering or pain … I guess the best word for it is *torment* … as he sneers his words at me: *"Are you gonna do it or do I have to gut this dirty little mongrel open like a suckling pig?"*

I empty the gun into him.

I don't really know what I'm doing at that point, I just squeeze and squeeze, the wet blasts popping open the humid air, the sparks like a photographer's strobe documenting my little moment of truth. The Freak's head turns to red mist. It's amazing. His hands still clutch the boy's neck beneath him long after his face is gone.

Then the clicking noise, and the gun is empty. The Freak sags backward and falls to the deck with a wet splat. My ears are ringing.

The silence seems to close down over us like a great black canopy.

⊕

I WISH I COULD tell you the kid made it. I didn't blubber or anything. To be honest I wasn't really feeling much of anything at that point. I'm pretty much in shock by that point. But I hated boarding that slimy black casket of a boat. It's like hopping into a dead shark.

I work in the flickering candle light, my hands shaking, my brain like a frozen stone. I drag the kid's body over to the rail and pause for a second. His eyes are still open. Like a doll's eyes. What a goddamn waste. I want to hug him. I want to say something but all I can do is toss him into the drink.

The kid barely makes a splash.

The rest of it goes fairly quickly. I toss in the Freak, toss my gun, kick the carcass over the side, and find a plastic gas jug in the aft storage compartment. I douse the bulwark, then hurl the tank into the Gulf. I pull my Zippo out and I'm about to torch the boat when I notice a little silver object lying up on the console by the steering column.

It's the Freak's cell phone, the one Ginny rigged with the transmitter bug.

I don't know why I didn't just leave it on the boat to burn with the rest of the shit but for some reason I feel compelled to fling the little silver gadget as far as I can out into the open sea. The thing arcs out into the night air, the moonlight flashing on it for a nano-second, and then … plop! The thing lands and sinks.

The guy at the boat yard told us one of the deepest parts of the Gulf is just a mile or so off shore. Said the Tarpin fisherman have to use military depth finders to locate it. I stand there for a moment, breathing hard and fast, soaked with sweat, imagining that cell phone plummeting down and down through that endless black murk.

I imagine it hitting the bottom.

Then I spark the rest of the boat and I'm out of there.

⊕

FOR A WHILE I don't even realize I'm lost. A wall of humid fog has unexpectedly rolled in but I keep expecting the lights of the coast to materialize like a diamond necklace in the distance. But it never does. My only reference point is the orange spot of that burning speed boat on the horizon behind me but soon that's gone as well. I guess the thing has finally sunk or maybe just passed out of sight.

I inch along in the pea soup, blind and desperate, the Sea Ray gurgling and sputtering, for another hour or so—like I said, I'm not sure about lengths of time—until finally I realize that the green-toothed, hillbilly asshole put us out with half a tank of gas.

Now I'm running on fumes, and all I can do is sit there with my hands glued to that greasy steering wheel, staring at the blanket of darkness in front me. Then the engine gives up the ghost. Now I'm just drifting, the boat pitching and yawing at the whim of the endless black Gulf of Mexico. The air is so thick and humid it feels like gauze on my face.

I think they call it 'dead calm,' something like that. Real funny. I'm drifting and drifting, lost in the night, and I'm *dead calm*. Ha ha, real ironic. But all I can think about in that lapping silence is the fact that the kid is dead, and I finally stepped over that imaginary line, finally committed the act.

The only other thing I can think about, for some reason, is that little bugged Nokia cell phone, plunging and fluttering down, down, down, down … into the darkest, emptiest, coldest place on earth.

And that's when the little telltale chirping noise pierces my skull.

Look: the truth is I had no reason to believe there was anything weird going on when I heard my cell phone ringing. I'm a freelancer. I get calls in the strangest places, the most inopportune times. I figured it was some sleaze-bag bail bondsman calling about another skip. But when I finally fish through my pockets, find my cell, dig it out, and look at the caller-ID glowing in the darkness, I jerk backward and drop the phone like it's a hot coal burning my hand.

"No way," I utter in the silence, my voice sounding hollow and distant in my ears.

The cell phone continues trilling and vibrating on the deck, creeping across the varnished surface like a beetle, the display sending a tiny beam of sickly light through the fog. I can see the caller-ID number. I can see it. There's no mistake. I needed to memorize that very same number in order to set up the GPS device last week.

The Freak's number glows on the little LED screen shivering at my feet.

I turn away from it in a fever of chills. I convince myself I'm just seeing things. My guilty brain has scrambled a few digits. That's it. That's got to be it. The cell phone keeps chirping behind me as I gaze out at the wall of dirty grey cotton encapsulating me. If I ignore it maybe it'll go away. If I just keep staring out at that soupy fog, the thing will stop ringing or my voice mail will pick it up. I'm drenched in sweat and my heart's pulsing in my neck as I stand there, gripping the rail, waiting for it to stop.

And it does.

The silence that slams down on me is almost worse than the ringing noise.

The faint patter of seawater lapping against the hull is barely audible now above the sound of my ragged breathing. I've got that coppery-sour taste in my mouth from all the adrenaline, and I can smell the rank, dead-rot odor of the stagnant tide. The boat is gently pitching, and I've got that woozy, twilight feeling you get when you've just awakened from a dream—that sense of primal relief with the return of mundane reality.

I turn away from the railing and stagger over to the place I dropped the phone. I kneel down and pick it up. It's blinking—a little mail box cartoon in the display window. Someone has left me a message. I start to retrieve it but I stop, my thumb poised above the message button.

I don't want to hear it. Whatever it is. I don't want to know.

The phone rings again and I jerk like I've got a poisonous snake in my hand.

I hurl the little device across the cabin, and it strikes the windscreen, then bounces to the floor in the shadows under the bonnet. I slam my hands over my ears, and bark at the empty night sky—I'M NOT HEARING THIS SHIT!!—and I lose my balance as the boat lists suddenly. I fall on my ass. I see stars and I can still hear that thing ringing in the cabin.

"Aw fuck it," I say and climb back to my feet and then edge my way under the canvas roof. I find the cell phone, pick it up, and thumb the answer button on the fifth ring. "WHO THE HELL IS IT? THIS BETTER BE GOOD!"

My first impression is that the sound is coming from a great distance. A burst of static sizzling in my ear. But under that, a faint voice saying something I can't quite make out yet. The closest analogy would be maybe an overseas operator speaking some language unlike any language I've ever heard. Or maybe an ancient wax-disk recording so full of pops and scratches and crackling noises that you can't make out the words but that's not exactly it either.

"Crrrrrhhhhhhhhh—*ssuh*—crrrrhhhhhhhh!"

"What!? HELLO?!"

Now maybe I'm in shock or something. I don't know. Maybe it's the trauma of being lost at sea after losing the boy, adrift with my own thoughts after having just committed the unthinkable. In my mind I keep going back to *Exodus 20:13— And God spoke these words, 'You shall not kill!'* And I keep seeing the Freak's little Nokia wireless, no bigger than a silver bar of soap, skimming the surface of that obsidian sea where I pitched it, then sinking, then fluttering down and down through the black void, and maybe even coming to rest in the silt at the very bottom of the deepest part of the ocean.

And now maybe all this overactive imagining has basically snapped my wig, popped the fuse of my sanity like a light bulb flaring out.

But I swear to God I can hear a familiar voice between those bursts of static.

C R R R R R R H H H H H H H — *s o m e b o d y* — CRRRRRHHHHHH!

"What?! Who *is* this goddamnit?!"

CRRRHHHH—*therrrre's sssomebody*—CRRHHHHHH!

"Somebody? Somebody-what! Somebody-WHO?!"

CRRRHHH—*there's somebody here*—CRRRRH!

"Okay, whatever, there's somebody there, but where's *there*, okay, and while you're at it why don't you tell me just who the fuck this—AAHHHHH!"

All of a sudden there's this terrible, watery shrieking noise coming over the line, but it's not exactly a scream, it's more like a howl, like something other than human is roaring on the other end of the line, and I just let out a yelp and hurl the phone into the sea.

The little thing skips a couple of times across the glassy surface of the water, then vanishes, and I'm assuming it's sunk, you know, I'm thinking the thing is long gone. And I'm catching my breath, leaning back against the bulwark, pretty frantic by that point. I'm thinking about getting out of there with any means necessary, maybe using a piece of the boat as a paddle, or finding something to use as a signal, when all at once I see the little silver device floating alongside the boat in the gentle lapping water.

That telltale chirping sound has started up again, and I don't even have to look to know what number is flickering on that caller-ID display.

"Heh heh heh heh heh, go to hell, go to hell, nobody *home!*" I'm raving now in a sing-songy rant, my voice sounding mechanical and garbled in my ears. "Nobody home, nobody nobody, just reading my bible, thou shalt not kill … nobody hommmmmmmmme!"

The thing keeps ringing.

I can't resist. I wish I could tell you I could. I wish I could say I resisted leaning out over the keel and fishing that thing out of the water. But then I'd be a liar and I'm only good for one mortal sin at a time, if you know what I mean. So, anyway, what I do is, I reach down and pluck that thing from the black lapping waters, and it slips out of my trembling wet hand, *plop*, and I reach down again and finally I get a good grip on it and put the dripping thing to my ear and scream: "WHO THE HELL IS THIS?!!"

And what I hear coming out of that phone, and what I hear in the distance, in the darkness … well, let's put it this way: that's when things go from bad to worse.

⊕

I NEED TO TAKE another drink before I tell you this next part, the last part, the part about the water. And the voice. And what happened then.

Okay, here goes: I'm standing there hanging over the water with my heart slamming in my chest and my ear pressed to that dripping cell phone and I hear that wet, hoarse voice piercing the static on the other end of the line: "CRRHHH—*there's somebody down here wants to*—CRRRRRHHHHHHHHH!"

I'm about to scream another series of obscenities when I realize I've been hearing another sound off in that empty, black distance for quite a while now and haven't even realized it. But something out of the corner of my eye catches my attention then, a blinking light off to my right, on the floor of the boat, a faint beeping sound.

I don't put the two things together at first, but when I suddenly realize what I'm hearing out in that fog, and what I'm seeing on the floor of the boat, my heart jumps in my mouth and all my sweat turns to ice.

The GPS receiver.

"Don't, don't, don't don't do this to me," I mutter with whatever breath I have left, and I go over and snatch it up with my fee hand. Now I'm standing there on that rocking bucket of rust with my knees wobbling and heart thumping and that GPS in my shaking hand and the cell phone glued to my ear.

"CRRRRRRHHHHH—*there's somebody down here wants to talk to you*—CRRRH!"

I can see the tiny glowing dots on the GPS again. I see one of the dots moving.

Which brings me to the noise I've been hearing. Very faint at first. Like I'm feeling it more than hearing it. But there's something massive out there, gathering energy, moving toward me. Like a fold in the fabric of the ocean rolling toward my boat.

And I look down at the GPS again, and I see that little glowing spot moving across the little spider web of a grid toward the other one, the stationary one. Impossible. Right? I'm just saying. Totally impossible. But here it comes, the little dot moving *toward* me. And I'm dumb with terror right then, backing away from the rail with the cell phone still pressed to my ear.

CRRRH—*there's somebody down here wants to talk to you!—CRRRHHHHHHHHHHHHHHHHHH!!*

Okay, this isn't easy, describing it, reliving it, but I'll give it a shot, I have to, I owe it to all of you. You've seen submarines when they rise to the surface? Or you've seen films of submarines?

First you just see that vague disturbance in the ocean coming toward you, just a nauseating kind of folding in of the water that seems to gather as the gigantic sub starts to materialize from the deep. Then the water begins to implode into itself as the sub emerges with a great torrent of sound and backwash.

This kind of thing had been building out there in the fog for what seemed like hours, a kind of low, vast rumble, and that shadowy undercurrent that I'd been sensing, and now it was

approaching, coming up from the depths, and it was *huge*—
Huge!—like a mountain rising out of the Gulf.

"No Jesus no fuck," I'm backing away on trembling legs
and I finally fall down the steps into the shadows of the cabin,
dropping the gadgets, seeing stars.

Now maybe this is how those poor sons of bitches felt in
Moby Dick when that monster came out of that black void, a
vast monolith under the surface, displacing a black glacier of
sea water as it rises toward you. But I start shrieking like a
baby on the floor of that dark cabin, curled into a fetal position,
my brain a mess of tangled panic, sparking like an overloading
switch board.

Whatever it is coming out of the sea, it reaches my pathetic little boat on a great WWWWWWWWWWWWWW
WWWWWWWWWHHHHHOMPP! of air pressure collapsing
and the seams of the universe ripping apart, and I can't describe
that last sensation before I blacked out. I've tried to put it into
words. I can't do it. Best I can manage is that the ocean itself
opened its mouth, a great chasm of festering black bile, a raging aperture of rotting fangs and teeth and poison, and it swallowed me, and that was all.

Except for one thing.

One thing.

✛

SCREW IT. THAT'S the best I can do. Why bother?
Nobody's going to believe it. And what do I care anyway?
Obviously I didn't die out there. Obviously I made it back to
the shore that night. Somehow. Don't ask me how.

So here I am in my little flop house trying to tell the story.
Jesus. Who am I kidding? What am I going to do, write my
memoirs?

I got the windows painted black, aluminum foil on some the panes. Nobody can see inside. Which is good since I need to prepare for my work in private.

I tend to rotate my tools to keep the cops off the scent so I usually have a lot of stuff laid out on work tables. Knives for one, poison for another. Various and sundry handguns. I'm good at what I do. I can clear 50k on a single mob hit.

Maybe more if some captain of industry wants his loud-mouth wife out of the picture.

Oh yeah. I almost forgot. That last sensation before I blacked out on the boat that night? There was one realization that struck me before I lost consciousness. I realized the Freak's cell phone had fallen right through a hole in the bottom of the earth.

And I realized who it was wanted to talk to me.

SEAN DOOLITTLE

SEAN Doolittle is the author of the novel DIRT and BURN (Gold medal winner, Mystery category, *ForeWord Magazine* 2003 Book of the Year Award). His latest novel is THE CLEANUP. Doolittle's short fiction has appeared in THE YEAR'S BEST HORROR STORIES, THE BEST AMERICAN MYSTERY STORIES, and various magazines. He lives in Omaha, Nebraska.

Sean says: "I like stories about hitmen for the same reason I'd probably like an anthology of short stories about alligator wranglers. I can't help being intrigued by people who occupy such niche professions—people who make their living doing work which requires a high degree of specialized skill, can be unforgiving to moments of weakness or lost focus, and exists solely in society's margins. Throw in a little debatable morality, maybe a job satisfaction issue or two, you've got me hooked ..."

Visit Sean at www.SeanDoolittle.com.

THE PROFESSIONAL
Sean Doolittle

AROUND ONE IN the morning, two guys walk into the GitGo wearing hoodies and wraparound shades.

My friend John has the register open even before they open their mouths. They go through the tough-guy stuff anyway, lifting their sweatshirts, pulling pistols.

"Put the money in a sack," the tall one says. He sticks his gun in John's face. "Hurry up."

The short one comes over to where I'm standing and points his gun at my eye. It's a little .38 revolver with tape on the handle. "Just be cool there, dad."

I show him my palms. "Sound advice."

"Are you fuckin' with me?"

"I'm not fucking with you."

He thumbs back the hammer, sour breath in my face. "Motherfucker, I will flat-out shoot your ass." His hand isn't shaking. "You want to get shot?"

"I don't." It's the truth.

"Then shut the fuck up."

I look beyond his shoulder. Behind the counter, John transfers grubby stacks of bills from the register drawer into a green plastic sack. He moves reflexively: maximum cooperation, zero resistance, absolutely no eye contact.

Watching him, you might get the idea he's done this before. It makes sense. He works nights at the GitGo; he's had practice being robbed.

But I know more.

I know, for example, that my friend John was hacked in the face by a machete when he was fifteen years old. His skin is dark black, the scar even darker, a worm of thick tissue from eyebrow to chin. I know that he's been shot before. More than once. I know that his name isn't John.

The tall one snatches the sack of money. It can't be more than a couple hundred bucks.

"What, are you kidding me?" He checks the door, the empty parking lot, the security monitors. "Open the safe."

The short one seems to tense up. This isn't the usual script.

John lifts his hands higher, dips his head lower. "I do not know the combination."

"You don't know the combination?" The guy mimics John's speech: de comb bee naysun? "Bullshit. Grab some sacks, Moomba."

"He's telling the truth," I say.

The short one jams his gun barrel into my cheek. "Man, what the fuck did I tell you?"

I point to the sign taped up on the wall: BE ADVISED THAT OUR EMPLOYEES CANNOT ACCESS THE SAFE.

The tall one checks the parking lot again. He knows I'm right, but it doesn't make him happier with the take. He waggles the gun and says, "Gimme yours."

John doesn't look up. "I do not understand."

"Ooga booga," the tall guy says. "Fuckin' spearchucker. Your wallet. Hand it over now."

John doesn't have a wallet, but he reaches into the front pocket of his pants. He pulls out a roll of cash. The roll is big around as his wrist, tied with a frayed piece of twine.

The guy looks at the roll, looks at John. He snorts and shakes his head. "Jesus, look at this pimp. Drop it in the sack."

No hesitation, no quick movements. John simply does as he's told.

The guy pistol-whips him anyway. There's a fleshy smack; John grunts and sags to his knees.

By now the tall one is halfway out the door. The bell jingles. Over his shoulder, he says, "Get his. We're gone."

The short one smirks, still holding his gun to my face. He holds out his other hand and wiggles his fingers. Give it here.

I give him my wallet.

He gives me a push in the face with the gun.

Then he hustles after his buddy, shoving the ramshackle pistol back into the waistband of his jeans.

The bell jingles. Outside, car doors slam. An engine growls; tires bark. After they're gone, I go behind the counter and help John to his feet.

"Are you okay?"

"Yes," he says.

"Let me see."

He takes his hand away from a small cut on his cheek. It isn't bad. A jot of pink tissue, a little blood.

There's a first aid kit in back, but it's poorly stocked; I get some Band-Aids and a tube of ointment from the shelves. I fill a cup full of ice from the soda machine.

While I fix him up, I ask the obvious question. "John, why were you carrying all that money around?"

He shrugs. "The building where I stay is not safe."

I smile. "Bad part of town, huh?"

My friend John just gave two stickup guys his entire savings account. But he smiles back at me. It could be worse. His teeth are white, and his eyes hide nothing. The scar tugs at his features like a badly sewn seam.

⊕

I FIND THEM where they live: a shabby apartment in a rundown building near the meatpacking district on the south side of town.

The light in the outer hallway is broken. I pick the lock in the dark. Inside, the flickering television throws blue shadows on the walls.

The tall one is sitting on the edge of the couch. He's shirtless, hunched over the coffee table, sucking the business end of a ceramic water bong.

I close the front door behind me.

His head snaps up. "What the fu …"

I shoot him once in the chest. Once more in the head.

The muzzle suppressor gulps down the noise. Two quiet hiccups, and that's all. He sits up straight, then falls back. He sinks into the cushions, and then he's still.

The apartment smells like gunpowder, body odor, and cheap weed. In the light of the television, I can see tendrils of smoke trailing from the end of the suppressor. Smoke trails from the mouth of the bong.

A toilet flushes; the short one shambles back into the room. He's also shirtless, baggy jeans low on his hips.

I place a red dot in the center of his chest. He stops in his tracks.

"Keep walking," I tell him. "Come over and sit down."

He sees his dead friend on the couch.

He sees the fan of wet blood on the wall.

But he's stoned. I give him a moment to process the situation; I want us to be able to start on the same page.

You can almost track his progress. I'm the old dude from the GitGo; forty minutes ago, he was pointing a gun at my face. Now I'm here. Pointing a gun at him.

"Professional advice." I reach over and turn down the television. "Before your next robbery, rub mud on your license plates."

He looks at me, eyes wide. "Man, what the fuck?"

I nod him toward the couch.

"Holy shit."

"Try to calm down."

"Jesus." He edges around the coffee table. He sits as far from his friend as he can. He tries not to look, but he can't help it. "You whacked Darryl."

"Was that his name?"

"Jesus Christ."

"What about you? What's your name?"

"What do you want, man?"

I bend down and take what I want: John's roll of cash. It's sitting there on the coffee table, along with the sack of money from the register, the bong, a baggie of grass, two pistols, and my wallet.

"You know the guy with the scar on his face?" I hold up the roll of bills. "The guy who gave you this?"

"Jesus, take it. No prob."

"Last year, his father organized the bloodiest coup attempt in his nation's history." I nod. "It's true. Small country, I doubt you've heard of it. It wasn't even in the news. But it happened."

"Man, I don't ..."

"His father and brothers were killed. His mother and sisters were jailed." I lower my weapon. The red dot slides down his stomach, over his leg, across the floor, back to my side. "Raped, tortured ... look, trust me, you wouldn't even want to know."

"Then why are you telling me? Jesus, who are you, man?"

"They eventually escaped." I hold up the roll of cash again. "Thanks to money John sends home for bribes. One of his sisters made it to a refugee camp in a bordering province."

The whole time I'm talking, I can see his hand creeping toward a gap between the sofa cushions. I decide I'll call him Mike.

"His mother and his other sister were captured," I tell him. "They were dragged behind Jeeps all the way back to the jail. A little over forty kilometers. Do you know how much forty kilometers is, Mike?"

Of course he doesn't.

"About twenty-five miles," I say. "Can you imagine what was left of them, after twenty-five miles?"

I look at his hand. He stops moving it.

"Don't be an animal," I tell him. "That's the lesson I want you to take from this. Do you understand?"

"Jesus." He nods his head. "Yeah, man. Fuckin'-A."

Of course he doesn't.

The moment I turn, he goes for the gun stashed in the sofa cushions. When he looks up, he sees his mistake. Even if he can't see the red dot between his eyes.

I leave my wallet on the table. It contains fifty dollars in cash, a falsified driver's license, two major credit cards issued under the name on the license, and pictures of kids I don't have.

I have five more like it.

⊕

THE TRUTH IS THIS:

My friend John and I aren't really friends. We've known each other for about two days. Everything I know about John, I knew when I got here.

Everything he knows about me, he knew the moment I walked into the store.

Yet here we stand at the GitGo, John on his side of the counter, me on mine. The police are long gone, and the store is still open. Dawn is just around the corner. The world outside is beginning to stir.

"Stop sending the money." I press the roll of cash into his hand. "Your friends earn more by telling where you are."

He doesn't ask me how I know this. He doesn't ask how I found his money, or what I did to get it back. He doesn't ask why I'm doing what I'm doing.

I wouldn't know what to tell him if he did. John is my job; I'm a professional. What's happening hasn't happened before.

Very soon now, I'll be asked to provide a status report to the people who paid me to execute this young man.

For the third night in a row, I tell him:

"Don't be here when I come back tomorrow. Do you understand?"

For the third night in a row, he says, "I understand."

We're not animals.

MAX ALLAN COLLINS

MAX Allan Collins has earned an unprecedented fourteen Private Eye Writers of America Shamus nominations for his historical thrillers, winning twice (for the Nathan Heller novels TRUE DETECTIVE and STOLEN AWAY). He is one of publishing industry's leading authors of tie-in novels, including the USA TODAY bestselling CSI series, and penned the New York Times bestselling graphic novel ROAD TO PERDITION and its prose sequels, ROAD TO PURGATORY and ROAD TO PARADISE. He is a leading indie filmmaker in his native Midwest, with a current boxed DVD set—BLACK BOX—collecting four of his five features and two of his documentaries. He lives in Muscatine, Iowa, with his wife, writer Barbara Collins; their son Nathan is pursuing post-grad studies in Japan.

Collins's hitman Quarry, created by Collins at the University of Iowa Writers Workshop in 1972, was the first series character of his kind, an innovation worth noting here. THE LAST QUARRY, the killer's first full-length adventure in nearly two decades, was recently published by HardCase Crime.

On inventing the hitman sub-genre, Al says: "In the late '60s and early '70s, antiheroes took hold, in response to the Vietnam/LBJ/Nixon era. Audiences for films and books had no trouble identifying with thieves like Westlake's Parker, whose collective lead I followed into my Nolan-and-Jon pro-thief series. At the same time, Vietnam was playing out on the nightly news and we were eating off TV trays, watching body bags—seemed to me we were getting dulled by it all. I wanted to take the antihero the next logical step and see if (a) I could get the reader to identify as easily with a killer as with a thief, and (b) confront the reader toward the end of each tale with just-who-the-hell-am-I-identifying-with-here. Key to both was removing the safety of the distance of the Westlake/W.R. Burnett third-person and putting the reader directly into the first-person head of the killer."

Visit Quarry and Al at www.MaxAllanCollins.com

GUEST SERVICES
Max Allan Collins

AN AMERICAN FLAG flapped lazily on its silver pole against a sky so washed-out blue the handful of clouds were barely discernible. The red, white, and blue of it were garishly out of place against the brilliant greens and muted blues of the Minnesota landscape, pines shimmering vividly in late morning sunlight, the surface of gray-blue Sylvan Lake glistening with sun, rippling with gentle waves. The rails of the grayish brown deck beyond my quarters were like half-hearted prison bars that I peeked through, as I did my morning sit-ups on the other side of the triple glass doors of my well-appointed guest suite.

I was not a guest of Sylvan Lodge, however: I ran the place. Once upon a time I had owned a resort in Wisconsin not unlike this—not near the acreage, of course, and not near the occupancy; but I had *owned* the place, whereas here I was just the manager.

Not that I had anything to complain about. I was lucky to have the job. When I ran into Gary Petersen in Milwaukee, where he was attending a convention and I was making a one-night stop-over to remove some emergency funds from several bank deposit boxes, I was at the loosest of loose ends. The name I'd lived under for over a decade was unusable; my past had caught up with me, back at the other place, and I'd lost everything in a near instant: my business yanked from under me, my wife (who'd had not a clue of my prior existence) murdered in her sleep.

Gary, however, had recognized me in the hotel bar and used a name I hadn't used since the early '70s: my real name.

"Jack!" he said, only that wasn't the name he used. For the purposes of this narrative, however, we'll say my real name is Jack Keller.

"Gary," I said, surprised by the warmth creeping into my voice. "You son of a bitch ... you're still alive."

Gary was a huge man—six six, weighing in at somewhere between three hundred pounds and a ton; his face was masked in a bristly brown beard, his skull exposed by hair loss, his dark eyes bright, his smile friendly, in a goofy, almost childlike way.

"Thanks to you, asshole," he said.

We'd been in Vietnam together.

"What the hell have you been doing all these years, Jack?"

"Mostly killing people."

He boomed a laugh. "Yeah, right!"

"Don't believe me, then." I was, incidentally, pretty drunk. I don't drink often, but I'd been through the mill lately.

"Are you crying, Jack?"

"Fuck no," I said. But I was.

Gary slipped his arm around my shoulder; it was like getting cuddled by God. "Bro—what's the deal? What shit have you been through?"

"They killed my wife," I said, and cried drunkenly into his shoulder.

"Jesus, Jack—who ...?"

"Fucking assholes ... fucking assholes ..."

We went to his suite. He was supposed to play poker with some buddies but he called it off.

I was very drunk and very morose and Gary was, at one time anyway, my closest friend, and during the most desperate of days.

I told him everything. I told him how after I got back from Nam, I found my wife—my first wife—shacked up with some guy, some fucking auto mechanic, who was working under a car when I found him and kicked the jack out. The jury let me off, but I was finished in my hometown, and I drifted until the Broker found me. The Broker, who gave me the name Quarry, was the conduit through whom the murder for hire contracts came, and, what? Ten years later the Broker was dead, by my hand, and I was out of the killing business and took my savings and went to Paradise Lake in Wisconsin, where eventually I met a pleasant, attractive, not terribly bright woman and she and I were in the lodge business until the past came looking for me, and suddenly she was dead, and I was without a life or even identity. I had managed to kill the fuckers responsible for my wife's killing, but otherwise I had nothing. Nothing left but some money stashed away, that I was now retrieving.

I told Gary all this, through the night, in considerably more detail though probably even less coherently, although coherently enough that when I woke up the next morning, where Gary had laid me out on the extra bed, I knew I'd told him too much.

He was asleep, too. Like me, he was in the same clothes we'd worn to that bar; like me, he smelled of booze, only he also reeked of cigarette smoke. I did a little, too, but it was Gary's smoke: I never picked up the habit. Bad for you.

He looked like a big dead animal, except for his barrel-like chest heaving with breath. I looked at this man—like me, he was somewhere between forty and fifty now, not the kids we'd been before the war made us worse than just men.

I still had liquor in me, but I was sober now. Too deadly fucking sober. I studied my best-friend-of-long-ago and wondered if I had to kill him.

I was standing over him, staring down at him, mulling that over, when his eyes opened suddenly, like a timer turning on the lights in a house to fend off burglars.

He smiled a little, then it faded, then his eyes narrowed, and he said, "Morning, Jack."

"Morning, Gary."

"You've got that look."

"What look is that?"

"The cold one. The one I first saw a long time ago."

I swallowed and looked away from him. Sat on the edge of the bed across from him and rubbed my eyes with the heels of my hands.

He sat across from me with his big hands on his big knees and said, "How the hell d'you manage it?"

"What?"

"Hauling my fat ass into that Medivac."

I grunted a laugh. "The same way a little mother lifts a Buick off her baby."

"In my case, you lifted the Buick onto the baby. Let me buy you breakfast."

"Okay."

In the hotel coffee shop, he said, "Funny … what you told me last night … about the business you used to be in?"

I sipped my coffee; I didn't look at him—didn't show him my eyes. "Yeah?"

"I'm in the same game."

Now I looked at him; I winced with disbelief. "What … ?"

He corrected my initial thought. "The tourist game, I mean. I run a lodge near Brainerd."

"No kidding."

"That's what this convention is. Northern Resort Owners Association."

"I heard of it," I said, nodding. "Never bothered to join, myself."

"I'm a past president. Anyway, I run a place called Sylvan Lodge. My third and current, and, I swear to God, ever-lasting wife, Ruth Ann, inherited it from her late parents, rest their hardworking souls."

None of this came as a surprise to me. Grizzly bear Gary had always drawn women like a great big magnet—usually good-looking little women who wanted a father figure, Papa Bear variety. Even in Bangkok on R & R, Gary never had to pay for pussy, as we used to delicately phrase it.

"I'm happy for you. I always figured you'd manage to marry for money."

"My ass! I really love Ruth Ann. You should see the knockers on the child."

"A touching testimonial if ever I heard one. Listen ... about that bullshit I was spouting last night ..."

His dark eyes became slits, the smile in his brushy face disappeared. "We'll never speak of that again. Understood? Never."

He reached out and squeezed my forearm.

I sighed in relief and smiled tightly and nodded, relieved. Killing Gary would have been no fun at all.

He continued, though. "My sorry fat ass wouldn't even be on this planet, if it wasn't for you. I owe you big-time."

"Bullshit," I said, but not very convincingly.

"I've had a good life, at least the last ten years or so, since I met Ruthie. You've been swimming in Shit River long enough. Let me help you."

"Gary, I ..."

"Actually, I want you to help me."

"Help *you*?"

Gary's business was such a thriving one that he had recently invested in a second lodge, one across the way from his Gull Lake resort. He couldn't run both places himself, at least not "without running my fat ass off." He offered me the job of managing Sylvan.

"We'll start you at 50k, with free housing. You can make a tidy buck with no overhead to speak of, and you can tap into at least one of your marketable skills, and at the same time be out of the way. Keep as low a profile as you like. You don't even have to deal with the tourists, to speak of—we have a social director for that. You just keep the boat afloat. Okay?"

"Okay," I said, and we shook hands. Goddamn I was glad I hadn't killed him ...

Now, a little more than six months into the job, and a month into the first summer season, I was settled in and damn near happy. My quarters, despite the rustic trappings of the cabin-like exterior, were modern—pine paneling skirting the room with pale yellow pastel walls rising to a high pointed ceiling. It was just one room with bath and kitchenette, but it was a big room, facing the lake which was a mere hundred yards from the deck that was my back porch. Couch, cable TV, plenty of closet space, a comfortable wall bed. I didn't need anything more.

During off-season, I could move into more spacious digs if I liked, but I didn't figure I'd bother. Just a short jog across the way was an indoor swimming pool with hot tub and sauna, plus a tennis court; a golf course, shared with Gary's other lodge, was nearby. My duties were constant, but mostly consisted of delegating authority, and the gay chef of our gourmet restaurant made sure I ate well and free, and I'd been banging Nikki, the college girl who had the social director position for the summer, so my staff relations were solid.

I took a shower after my push-ups and got into the usual gray Sylvan lodge t-shirt, black shorts, and gray-and-black Reeboks, to take a stroll around the grounds, and check up on the staff. I was sitting on the couch tying my tennies, with a good view of the patch of green and slice of sand below my deck, when I heard an unpleasant, gravelly male voice tearing somebody a new asshole.

"Why the fuck *didn't* you rent the boat in advance, Mindy?"

"I'm sorry, Dick."

"Jesus fucking Christ, woman, you think I want to come to a goddamn lake without a goddamn boat?"

His voice carried into my living room with utter clarity, borne by the wind coming across the lake.

I looked up. He was big—not as big as my friend Gary, but big enough. He wore green-and-red plaid shorts and a lime-green golf shirt and a straw porkpie hat with a wide leather band; he was as white as the underbelly of a crocodile, except for his face, which was a bloodshot red. Even at this distance I could see the white tufts of eyebrows over narrow-set eyes and a bulbous nose.

He was probably fifty, or maybe more; his wife was an attractive blonde, much younger, possibly thirty-five. She wore a denim shorts outfit that revealed an almost plump but considerably shapely figure, nicely top-heavy. Her hair was too platinum for her age, and too big for her face, a huge hair-sprayed construction with a childishly incongruous pink bow in it.

Her pretty face, even from where I sat on my couch, was tired-looking, puffy. But she'd been beautiful, once. An actress or a dancer or something. And even now, even with the too big, too platinum hair, she made a man's head turn. Except maybe for my chef.

"But I thought you'd use your brother's boat …"

"He's in fucking Europe, woman!"

"I know … but you said we were going to use Jim's boat …"

"Well, that fell through! He loaned his place *and* his boat to some fucker from Duluth he wanted to impress! Putting business before his own goddamn brother …"

"But I didn't know that …"

He grabbed her arm; hard. "You should've made it your business *to* know! *You* were supposed to make the vacation arrangements; God knows you have little enough to do otherwise. I have a fucking living to make for us. You should've got off your fat ass and …"

"Let's talk to Guest Services," his wife said, desperately. "Maybe they can help us rent a boat somewhere in the area."

"Excuse me!" I called from the deck.

Still holding onto the woman's arm, the aptly named Dick scowled my way.

"What do you want? Who the hell are you?"

I was leaning over the rail. "I'm the manager here. Jack Keller. Can I be of any help?"

He let go of her arm and the plump, pretty blonde moved toward me, looking up at me with a look that strained to be pleasant. "I called both numbers your brochure lists, and wasn't able to rent a boat …"

"It's a busy time," I said. "Let me look into it for you."

"We're only going to be here a week," Dick said. "I hate to waste a goddamn day!"

She touched his arm, gently. "We wanted to golf while we're here … we did bring the clubs … we could do that today …"

He brushed her hand away like it was a bug. "Probably have to call ahead for that, too."

"I'll call over for you," I said. "You are … ?"

"The Waltons," he said.

"Excuse me?"

"We're the fucking Waltons! Dick and Mindy."

The Waltons. Okay …

"Dick, I'll make the call. After lunch, around one-thirty a suitable tee time?"

"Good," Dick said, pacified. "Thanks for your help."

"That's what I'm here for," I said.

"Thank you," Mindy said, and smiled at me, and looped her arm in his, and he allowed her to, as he walked her over to the restaurant.

I called over to the golf course and got the Waltons a tee time, and called Gary over at Gull Lake Lodge to see about a boat.

"They should've called ahead," Gary said. "Why do you want to help these people? Friends of yours?"

"Hardly. The husband's an obnoxious cocksucker who'll browbeat his wife into a nervous breakdown, if I don't bail her out."

"Oh. The Waltons."

"Addams Family is more like it. So you know them?"

"They were at Sylvan the last two seasons. Dick Walton is a real pain in the ass, and an ugly drunk."

"Maybe we don't want his business."

"Trouble is, he's as rich as he is obnoxious. He's from Minneapolis—runs used car lots all over the Cities. Big fuck-ing ego—does his own commercials. 'Big Deals with Big Dick' is his motto …"

"Catchy."

"It's been popular with Twin Cities school kids for a couple decades. He's worth several mil. And he brings his sales staff up for conferences in the off-season."

"So we cater to him."

"Yeah. Within reason. If he starts busting up the bar or something, cut him off and toss his ass out. When he starts spoiling things for our other guests, then fuck him."

"I like your attitude, Gary. But what about a boat?"

"He can use mine for the week. It's down at dock nine."

"That's generous."

"Generous my ass. Charge him double the going rate."

⊕

THE RESTAURANT AT Sylvan's is four-star, and it's a real asset for the business, but it's the only thing Gary and I ever really disagreed about. Dinner was by reservation only, and those reservations filled up quick; and the prices were more New York than midwest.

"The goddamn restaurant's a real calling card for us," Gary would say. "Brings in people staying at other lodges and gives 'em a look at ours."

"But we're not serving our own guests," I'd say. "We're a hotel at heart, Gary, and our clientele shouldn't have to mortgage the farm to buy supper, and they shouldn't get turned away 'cause they don't have reservations."

"I appreciate your dedication to the guests, Jack. But that restaurant brings in about a third of our income, so fuckin' forget it, okay?"

But of course I didn't. We had this same argument at least twice a month.

That particular evening I was having the house specialty—pan-fried walleye—and enjoying the way the moon looked reflected on the silvery lake when I heard the gravel-edged sound of Dick Walton's voice, singing a familiar tune.

"You're a stupid cunt!" he was telling her.

They had a table in the corner, but the long, rather narrow dining room, with its windows on the lake, didn't allow anyone much privacy. Even approaching nine thirty, the restaurant was full—older couples, families, a honeymooning couple, all turned their eyes to the asshole in the lime sportcoat and green-and-white plaid pants who was verbally abusing the blonde woman in the green-and-white floral sundress.

She was crying. Digging a Kleenex into eyes where the mascara was already smeared. When she got up from the table to rush out, she looked like an embarrassed, haunted raccoon.

He shouted something unintelligible at her, and sneered, and returned to his big fat rare steak.

The restaurant manager, a guy in his late twenties who probably figured his business degree would get him a better gig than this, came over to my table and leaned in. He was thin, sandy-haired, pockmarked; he wore a pale yellow sweater over a shirt and tie.

"Mr. Keller," he said, "what should I do about Mr. Walton?"

"Leave him alone, Rick. Without his wife to yell at, I doubt he'll make much more fuss."

"Should I cut him off with the bar?"

"No."

He gave me a doubtful expression, one eyebrow arching. "Personally, I …"

"Just leave it alone. If he passes out, he won't bother his wife or anybody, and that would probably be ideal."

Rick sighed—he didn't like me much, knowing that I was lobbying to have his four-star restaurant turned into a cafeteria—but he nodded in acceptance of my ruling, and padded off.

I finished my walleye, touched a napkin to my lips, and headed over to Walton's table.

"You got my message about the boat?" I asked.

His grin was tobacco-stained; the tufts of white eyebrow raised so high they might have been trying to crawl off his face. "Yeah! That was white of you, Jack! You're okay. Sit down, I'll buy you one."

I sat, where his wife had been (her own walleye practically untouched on the plate before me), but said, "I had enough for tonight. I know my limit."

"So do I, buddy boy ..." He pointed a steak knife at me and winked. " ... it's when the fuckin' *lights* go out."

I laughed. "Say, what was the little woman riding you about? If you don't mind my asking."

His face balled up like a fist. "Bitch. Lousy little cunt. She fucked up royal this afternoon."

"Oh?"

"Yeah, fuck her. We're playing with another couple—the Goldsteins, from Des Moines. He's a dentist. Those docs are loaded, you know. Particularly the Hebrew ones."

"Up the wazoo," I affirmed.

"Anyway, Mindy is a decent little golfer ... usually. Shoots a 19 handicap on the country club course back home ... but this afternoon she didn't shoot for shit. I lost a hundred bucks because of her!"

"Well, hell, Dick—everybody has a bad afternoon once in a while."

His aftershave wafted across the table to tickle my nose—a grotesque parody of the pine scent that nature routinely provided us here.

"I think she did it just to spite me. I'd swear she muffed some of those shots just to get my fuckin' goat."

His speech was pretty slurred.

"That sounds like a woman," I said.

He looked at me with as steady a gaze as he could muster. "Jack—I like you."

"I like you, Dick. You're a real man's man."

I offered him my water glass for him to clink his tumbler of scotch on the rocks against.

"I'll have to sneak away from the little woman," he said, winking again, "so we can spend some *quality* time together."

"Let's do that," I said. "You going fishing tomorrow?"

He was lighting up an unfiltered cigarette; it took a lot of effort. "Yeah—me and that kike dentist. Wanna come along?"

"Got to work, Dick. Check in with me later, though. Maybe we can take in one of the casinos."

"One of the ones those injuns run?"

Gambling having been ruled legal on reservation land, casinos run by Native Americans were a big tourist draw in our neck of the woods.

"That's right, Dick. A whole tribe of Tontos looking to fleece the Lone Ranger."

"Hah! How 'bout tomorrow night?"

"We'll see. If you're getting up early tomorrow morning, Dick, to fish, maybe you ought to hit the sack."

He guzzled at his drink. "I ought to hit that fuckin' cunt I'm married to, is what I oughta hit."

"Take it easy. It's a hell of a thing, but a man can get in trouble for hitting a woman, these days."

"Hell of a thing, ain't it, Jack? Hell of a thing."

I walked out with him; he shambled along, slipping an arm around me, cigarette trailing ash.

"You're a hell of a guy," he told me, almost crying. "Hell of a guy."

"So are you, Dick," I said.

Outside the real pines were almost enough to cancel the room-freshener cologne he was wearing.

Almost.

⊕

I WAS SITTING in the dark, in my underwear, sipping a Coke in the glow of the portable television, watching a Randolph Scott western from the 1950s. I kept the sound low, because I had the doors to the deck pushed open, to enjoy the lake breeze, and I didn't want my movie-watching to disturb any of the guests who might be strolling along the beach, enjoying the night.

Something about the acoustics of the lake made her crying seem to echo, as if carried on the wind from a great distance, though she was at my feet, really—stumbling across the grass beneath my deck.

Underwear or not, I went out to check on her—because the crying sounded like more than just emotions: there was physical pain in it, too.

"Mrs. Walton," I called, recognizing her. She still wore the flowered sundress, the scoop top of it displaying the swell of her swell bosom. "Are you all right?"

She nodded, stumbling. "Just need a drink ... need a drink ..."

"The bar's closed. Why don't you step up here, and I'll get you a beer or something."

"No ... no ..." She shook her head and then I saw it: the puffiness of the left side of her face, eye swollen shut, the flesh already blackening.

I ran down the little wooden stairs; if somebody complained to the manager about the man running around in his underwear, well fuck 'em: I was the manager. I took her by the arm and walked her up onto the deck and inside, where I deposited her on the couch in front of the TV, where Randolph Scott was shooting Lee Van Cleef.

"Just let me get dressed," I said, and I returned with pants on and a beer in hand, which I held out to her. "It's all I have, I'm afraid," I said.

She took it and held it in her hands like something precious; sipped it like a child taking first communion.

I got her a washcloth with some ice in it.

"He's hit you before, hasn't he?" I said, sitting beside her.

She nodded; tears trickled from the good eye. Her pink-bowed platinum blonde hair wasn't mussed: too heavily sprayed for that.

"How often?" I asked.

"All ... all the time."

"Why don't you leave the son of a bitch?"

"He says ... he says he'll kill me."

"Probably just talk. Turn him in for beating you. They go hard on guys who do that, nowadays, and then it'll be harder for him to do it again."

"No ... he would kill me. Or have somebody do it. He has ... the kind of connections where you can get somebody killed, if you want. And it'll just be written off as an accident. I bet you find that hard to believe, don't you?"

"Yeah." I sipped my Coke. "Sounds utterly fantastic."

"Well, it's true."

"Are you sure you're not staying 'cause of the prenup?"

She sighed, nodded slowly, the hand with the ice in the washcloth moving with her head. "There is a prenuptial agreement. I wouldn't get a thing. Well, ten thousand, I think."

"But you're not staying 'cause of the money."

"No! I don't care about the money ... exactly. I got family I take care of. A younger sister who's going to college, mom's got heart trouble and no insurance."

"So it is about money."

The good eye winced. "No! No ... it *was* about money. That's why I married Dick. I was ... I was trash. A waitress. Topless dancer, for a while. Anything to make a buck ... but never hooking. Never!"

"Where did you meet Dick?"

"In a titty bar a friend of his used to run. I wasn't dancing, then ... I was a waitress. Tips in a topless place are always incredible."

"So I hear."

"This was, I don't know … over ten years ago."

"You been taking this shit all that time?"

"No. He was sweet, at first. But he didn't drink as much in those days. The more he drank, the worse it got. He calls me stupid. He can't have kids … his sperm count is lower than he is. But he calls *me* 'barren' and hits me … says I'm fat. Do you think I'm fat?"

I'd been looking down the front of her sundress at the time, and swallowed, and said, "Uh, no. I don't like these skinny girls they're pushing on us, these days."

"Fake tits and boy's butts, all of them." Her lips were trembling; her voice sounded bitter. "He has a girlfriend … she works in a titty bar, too. A different joint—this is one that he's got money in. She's like that: skinny little thing and a plastic chest and a flat little ass."

"You should leave him. Forget his threats. Forget the money."

"I can't. I … I wish he was dead. Just fucking dead."

"Don't talk that way."

Her whole body was trembling; she hugged herself with one arm, as if very, very cold. "I need a miracle. I need a goddamn miracle."

"Well, here's a suggestion."

"Yes?"

"Say your prayers tonight. Maybe God'll straighten it all out."

"With a miracle?"

"Or something," I said.

⊕

"HOP IN," HE SAID.

He was behind the wheel of a red-bodied, white-topped Cadillac; his bloodshot face was split in a shit-eating grin as he leaned over to open the door on the rider's side. He was wearing a green-

and-orange plaid sportcoat—it was like a Scotsman had puked on him—and orange trousers and lots of clunky gold jewelry.

I slipped inside the spacious car. "Didn't have any trouble getting away?"

"Naw! That little bitch doesn't dare give me any lip. I'd just knock some *more* sense in her! Anybody see you go?"

"No. I think we're all right."

I'd had him pick me up at the edge of the road, half a mile from the resort, in darkness; I said I was on call tonight and wasn't supposed to be away.

"You tell your wife where you were going, and who with?"

"Hell no! None of her goddamn business! I tell you, Jack, I should never have married that lowlife cunt. She's got a family like something out of *Deliverance*. Poor white trash, pure and simple. No fuckin' class at all."

"Why don't you dump her, then?"

"I just might! You know what a prenuptial agreement is, don't you, Jack?"

"Got a vague idea."

"Well, my lawyer assures me I don't have to give her jack shit. She's out in the cold on her flabby ass, soon as I give the say so."

"Why don't you, then?"

"I might. I might ... but it could be bad for business. I use her in some of my commercials, and she's kinda popular. Or anyway, her big ol' titties are, pardon my French."

"She helps you put up a good front."

"Hah! Yeah, that's a good one, Jack ... that's a good one ..."

The drive to the casino was about an hour, winding through tall pines and little bump-in-the-road towns; the night was clear, the moon full again, the world bathed in an unreal, and lovely, silver. I studied the idyllic landscape, pretending to listen to Walton blather on about his accomplishments in the used car game, cracking the window to let some fresh air cancel out his Pine-sol aftershave and cigarette smoke.

It was midweek, but the casino looked busy—just a sprawling one-story prefabricated building, looking about as exotic as a mobile home, but for the huge LAKEVIEW CASINO neon; the term "Lakeview" was cosmetic, as the nearest lake was a mile away. Some construction, some expansion, was going on, and the front parking lot was a mess.

He pulled around back, as I instructed; a couple of uniformed security guards with guns—Indians, like most of the employees here—were stationed in front. None were in back. A man and a woman, both weaving with drink, were wandering out to their car as Walton found a place to park.

"No limit here, right?" he asked.

"Right. You bring a pretty good roll?"

"Couple grand. I got unlimited cash access on my gold card, too."

The car with the couple in it pulled out, and drove unsurely around the building. Once their carlights were gone, it was as dark as the inside of a cow, back here. I got out of the Cad.

"If you need a couple bucks, Jack, just ask."

He had his back to me, as we walked toward the casino. When my arm slipped around him, it startled him, but he didn't have much time to react; the knife had pierced his windpipe by then.

When I withdrew the hunting knife, a scarlet geyser sprayed the night, but away from me. He fell like a pine tree, flopping forward, but the sound was just a little slap against the pavement. The knife made more noise as it clattered against the pavement; I kicked it under a nearby pick-up. He gurgled a while but that stopped soon.

Yanking him by the ankles, I dragged him between his Caddy and the dumpster he'd parked next to; a slime trail of blood glistened in the moonlight, but otherwise he was out of sight. So was I. I bent over him, using the same flesh-colored, rubber-gloved hand that had held the knife, and stripped him of his gaudy gold jewelry and lifted his fat wallet from his hip pocket, the sucker pocket the dips call it. I removed the wad of hundreds and tossed the wallet in the dumpster.

The jewelry was a bit of a problem: if somebody stopped me to talk to me about the dead man in the parking lot, I could be found with it on me. But a thief wouldn't leave it behind, so I had to take it, stuffing it in my jacket pockets. Tomorrow I would toss it in Sylvan Lake. Right now, with my couple of thousand bucks, I walked around the front of the casino, said, "Nice night, fellas," to the Indian security guards, who grunted polite responses to the paleface.

Inside, the pinball-machine-like sound of gambling fought with piped-in country western—the redskins seemed to favor cowboy music. I found Nikki where I knew she'd be: at the nickel poker machines. The slender girl had a bright-eyed, pixie face and a cap of brown curls.

"Jack! I'm doing *fantastic* ... I'm up four dollars!"

"Sounds like you're making a killing."

"How about you?"

"Same."

I had told Nikki I'd meet her here—we usually took separate cars when we went out, since the manager and his social director weren't supposed to fraternize.

She moved up to the quarter poker machines, at my urging, and ended up winning about thirty bucks. Before long, I was up two hundred bucks on blackjack. If somebody found the body while I was there, things could get interesting; I'd have to dump that jewelry somewhere.

But I didn't think anybody would be using that dumpster tonight, and I knew nobody would use the Caddy. Leaving too soon would be suspicious. So I stayed a couple hours.

"Jeez," I said, as we were heading out finally, her arm in mine, my hand on my head. "I think I drank a little too much."

"That's not like you, Jack."

"I know. But you better drive me home."

"What about your car?"

My car was back at the resort, of course, parked where Nikki wouldn't see it when she went to her own cabin.

"I'll have Gary drive me up for it tomorrow."

"Okay," she said, and she steadied me as we walked back around to the parking lot in the rear.

It was still dark back there, and quiet. Very quiet. I could barely make out a dried dark streak on the pavement, over by the Caddy, but nothing glistened in the moonlight, now.

First thing the next morning, the police came around to see me; Gary was with them, a pair of uniformed state patrolmen. It seemed, around sun-up, that one of our guests had been found dead in the parking lot at the Lakeview Casino. His wallet, emptied of money, had been found nearby.

"Mr. Walton wore a lot of jewelry," I said. "The gold kind?"

"Asking for trouble," said one of the cops, a kid in his mid-twenties.

Gary, wearing a gray jogging suit, wasn't saying anything; he was standing behind them like a mute grizzly, his eyes a little glazed.

"That casino's probably gonna get sued," the other, slightly older cop said. "Bad lighting in the parking lot back behind there. Just asking for it."

"Both Walton *and* that casino," the young one said.

I agreed with them, said sympathetic things, and pointed them to the cabin where they could find—and inform—the new widow.

Gary stayed behind.

"You know," he said quietly, scratching his beard, "I'm glad that bastard didn't get killed on our grounds. We might be the ones getting sued."

"Right. But that's not going to happen around here."

"Oh?"

"Don't worry, Gary." I put a hand on his shoulder; had to reach up to do it. "We have adequate lighting."

He looked at me kind of funny, with narrowed eyes. He seemed about to ask me something, but thought better of it, waved limply, and wandered off.

⊕

I WAS DOING my morning sit-ups when she walked up on my deck, looking dazed, her perfect, bullet-proof platinum hair wearing the girlish pink bow, her voluptuous body tied into a dark pink dressing gown. She stood looking through the cross-hatch of screen door, asking if she could come in.

"Of course," I said, sliding the door open, and took her to the couch where she'd sat two nights before.

"You heard about Dick?" she said, in small voice. She seemed numb.

"Yes. I'm sorry."

"You ... you won't say anything, will you?"

"About what?"

"Those ... terrible things I said about him." Her eyes got very wide; she seemed frightened, suddenly, but not of me. Exactly. "You don't think ... you don't think I ..."

"No. I don't think you did it, Mrs. Walton."

"Or ... or hired somebody ... I mean, I was saying some crazy things the other night."

"Forget it."

"And if the police knew about Dick hitting me ..."

"Your face looks pretty good today. I don't think they'll pursue that angle."

She swallowed; stared into nothing. "I don't know what to do."

"Why don't you just lean back and wait to inherit Dick's estate? You can do those TV commercials solo, now."

She turned to look at me and the faintest suspicion seemed etched around her eyes. "You've been ... very kind, Mr. Keller."

"Make it Jack."

"Is there anything I can do to … repay your kindnesses?"

"Well … you can keep coming to Sylvan Lodge, despite the bad memories. We could sure use your business, for those sales conferences and all."

She touched my hand. "I can promise you that. Maybe we could … get to know each other better. Under better circumstances."

"That would be nice."

"Could I just … sit here for a while? I don't really want to go back to the cabin. It still … still smells of Dick. That awful cologne of his."

Here all you could smell was the lake and the pines, real pines; the soothing touch of a breeze rolled over us.

"Stay as long as you like," I said. "Here at Sylvan Lodge, we strive to make our guests' stay as pleasant as possible."

P.J. PARRISH

P.J. Parrish is actually two sisters, Kelly Nichols and Kris Montee, who write the Edgar- and Shamus-nominated Louis Kincaid series. Their books have appeared on the *New York Times* and *USA Today* bestseller lists. Their latest is AN UNQUIET GRAVE.

Hitmen have always had a special place in their hearts. Kelly created her first one in the fifth grade for a story she wrote called "The Kill" in which The Beatles manager Brian Epstein was bumping off his Fab Four. Kris "hired" her first hitman in one of her romances in the 1980s to knock off the fictional version of her slimeball ex city editor. They believe it is always nice to have a hitman around the house.

Visit them at www.PJParrish.com.

GUTTER SNIPES
P.J. Parrish

THE NEON WAS A slash of red in the oily puddles of the asphalt, and every time a car went by it sent the red quivering.

It looked just like Helen's mouth, he thought.

Moon Renfro tossed his butt out the window and leaned back in the seat. He didn't need to be thinking about Helen. There was too much other stuff he needed to be using his brain for right now and there was just no extra space for trying to figure out what the hell he had done this time to set those lips of hers flapping again.

The neon sign was making this annoying buzzing sound. He looked up at it.

PAUL STROFFMAN'S LUCKY STRIKE

A couple of the letters were flickering, getting ready to die. He stared at the sign in admiration. It was original, put up there in the '60s when Paulie "Sour Kraut" Stroffman bought the place. It was big and flashy and when it was working right, a neon ball would roll across the top of the letters, knock down the pins at the end, and the red letters STRIKE would turn to yellow. The sign never worked right since back in '79, but then the city passed some dumb-ass ordinance so Paulie couldn't replace it even if he could afford to. So it kept breaking and Paulie just kept trying to fix it.

It was a fucking work of art after all. They didn't make 'em like that anymore.

Just like the Lucky Strike. He had to admit the place wasn't much to look at on the outside. Just a brick slab in a dying strip mall. But inside …

Paulie kept the insides up real good, kept the lanes oiled with the best stuff, and stripped them down twice instead of once a year. Had the best computerized scoring program that not only marked your score, but flashed these cartoons of grinning turkeys and pins being sucked to dust. Things that really made you feel good about what you had just done.

Moon had been bowling at the Lucky Strike every Tuesday and Thursday night for ten years, and he loved it. Loved the sharp smell of acetone, beer, and smoke. Loved the constant clattering of the wood. Loved the feel of that old bowling shirt on his back and the idea that only four other guys in the whole world had one just like it.

It was his life, and for ten years it had been a good life, one that provided him with friends, beer, and even sex from the alley kittens who worked the snack bar. But best of all, he was somebody here. He carried the second highest average in the house, a 239. Only Bulldog Baker had a higher one at 240.

Moon sucked on his cigarette.

One goddamn pin.

It started to drizzle so he cranked the window up halfway. He exhaled and watched the smoke swirl in the clammy air of the truck. His eyes were locked on the front door of the bowling alley and his insides were churning as he considered what he was about to do.

He had gone over every detail in his head, thought about every angle, asked himself every question. Well, every question but one: Did he have the balls to really go through with this?

A sudden noise made him jump. The neon sign was spitting and flickering. He leaned forward and looked up at the sign.

PAUL STROFFMAN'S LUCKYSTRIKE

Then, suddenly, with a loud *pop!* some of the letters were gone. Moon stared through the wet windshield at the sign, frowning. He switched on the wipers.

U MU STRIKE

His mouth fell open and he had to grab at his crotch to slap away the cigarette. He found the butt on the floor mat and then swung back up to look at the sign again. Damn. The letters were still there, big as life against the black sky. U Must Strike? Shit … it was a sign. It had to be.

The clatter of falling pins drew his eyes back to the entrance of the bowling alley. A guy had come out and was slinking across the lot.

Moon stuck a hand out the window. "Shaky!"

Shaky Cruthers slumped toward Moon's car. He opened the passenger door and climbed inside, flipping his stringy black hair like a wet dog.

"Whatcha doing here, Moon?" Shaky asked. "You didn't bowl tonight, did you?"

"No," Moon said. "I came to talk to you."

Shaky pulled a crumpled pack of Camels from his shirt pocket and started patting at himself, looking for a match. Moon tossed him a book from the bowling alley. Shaky lit his cigarette and settled into the seat, drawing one knee up.

"So, what did you want to talk about?" he asked.

"I want to win the championship for the Triple J Doubles," Moon said. "I want that thousand dollars prize money and that trophy."

Shaky laughed. He had a weird laugh, like one of those little dolls with the talking strings in their necks. "You better run that by Bulldog first," he said.

Moon almost reached out and choked Shaky for his bad joke, but he didn't want to piss him off right now. But he did throw him a sneer and Shaky mumbled an apology.

"Hell, we're in good shape," Shaky said. "We're tied for first."

"But we've been sucking hind tit most of the year," Moon said. "We got only next week. I want you to do something for me."

"Anything, Moon."

"I want you to make sure we win."

Shaky almost laughed again, but he caught Moon's eyebrow slant and he sucked it back in. "What do you want me to do? Stand back there and blow the pins down?"

"I want you to fuck with Bulldog Baker."

Shaky choked on his cigarette smoke. His hacking filled the car and Moon looked away, out to the darkness to tune him out.

"You done coughing?" Moon finally asked.

"Yeah," Shaky gagged. "Yeah. But man … I thought you was serious there for a minute."

"I am serious."

"Bulldog is big as a damn semi, Moon," Shaky said. "How am I suppose to fuck him up?"

"Not him, asshole," Moon said. "His equipment."

Shaky stared at him, and suddenly Moon could see the reflection of the sign in his big brown eyes.

"Listen," Moon said. "Bulldog bought a pair of Kangaroo Ultras at the beginning of the season. Second week he wore those shoes, he bowled a 300. He calls them his magic slippers."

"So?"

"I want you to steal them just before we start. It'll mess up his head."

"What? How?"

"It'll be easy," Moon said. "Before practice, Bulldog always goes in the bar to get his beer and play that stupid poker machine. That's when you steal his shoes."

"I dunno, Moon," Shaky said, tossing his cigarette butt out the window. "Why don't you do it?"

"Because it'd be bad karma for me to do it," Moon said. "You know how important karma is in bowling. I'll be plagued with ten pins the rest of my life."

Shaky fell quiet, picking at his fingers, trying to peel off the little pieces of rubber left from his thumb tape.

Moon looked down at his cigarette, trying to decide if he could get one more puff out of it. It was important to get all the puffs you could, just like it was important to always get one of the pins of the 7-10 split because that's what a lot of games came down to. And a lot averages, too. One goddamn pin.

Moon slid a glance to Shaky. "I'll give you my old Red Inferno ball," he said.

"That ball has so many potholes it rolls down the alley like a moon rock," Shaky said.

"Okay, what then?"

"Man …"

"Okay, the Inferno and my Brunswick three-baller bag. But you'll have to fix the right wheel. It keeps falling off."

Shaky pulled a long string of thumb tape from his hand and started rolling it between his fingers. When he had it into a tiny ball, he tossed it out the window.

"What about your Atomic Revolution?" he asked. "Can I have that?"

"No fucking way," Moon said. "I worked three weeks OT to get that damn ball. It's a friggin' two-hundred-dollar piece of art. No way. No way."

"Buy a new one with the prize money," Shaky said.

Moon shook his head again, trying to find his cigarettes. His hands were trembling so badly, he couldn't pull one out and when he did, he broke it.

"I got other bills to pay," Moon said, ripping open the pack to get the last smoke. "I'm two months behind on the mortgage and one month on this friggin' truck. And Helen's bitching at me to get her a new washing machine. I can't give you no money."

Shaky was still staring at his fingers and Moon finally tossed the cigarette pack to the dash and grabbed Shaky's collar, jerking him toward the windshield.

"See that up there?" Moon asked.

"What?"

"The sign," Moon said, pointing up. "See the sign? Don't you get it? It's telling us something. It's telling us to strike."

Shaky blinked up at the sky. "Yoo … moo..stttt … kee?" he said slowly.

Moon tapped the windshield. "No, stupid, can't you fucking read? You … Must … Strike. It's talking about Bulldog."

Shaky's eyes widened. "Wow," he whispered.

They both stared at the sign for a few moments, then Shaky slumped back against the door. His eyes stayed glued on the flickering neon.

"Just steal the shoes, huh?" he asked. "That's all I have to do?"

"That's all you have to do."

⊕

IT RAINED ON position night, like it did most nights in May in Memphis. For some teams, the downpour would mean a forfeit since half the streets would be flooded and most bowlers—those that didn't have a true heart—would stay home. After all, the league was ending and if you weren't one of the top few teams, you were already a loser anyway, so why risk your life driving through a lake just to win games no one cared about?

Moon was sitting at one of the tall back tables, a beer in his hand, his eyes scanning the emptiness. Moon couldn't imagine not showing up every week, rain or sleet. It was what being a purist was all about.

He hadn't known that until a few years ago, when in a drunken bar conversation, the pro shop guy, Al "The Hawk" Hawkins, had first called Moon a purist. Moon had gotten mad until he looked up "purist" in the dictionary and realized The Hawk had paid him a helluva compliment.

Shaky had a good heart, but he wasn't a purist. Like his average. For as long as Moon had known him, Shaky had never gotten above a 199, and he seemed content to let that one pin stay beyond his reach, like there was absolutely no difference between a 199 and 200 average.

Now Bulldog Baker. Not even close to a purist.

Yeah, he wore the silver Dyno-Thane Kangaroo Tour Ultras, and a glove called the Power Paw, and had made a name for himself a few years back by throwing a ball called The Thing. One day The Thing cracked in half on its way to the seven pin, only because Bulldog hadn't respected it enough to take it out of his car trunk all summer. Bulldog tried to get another Thing but it was out of stock, so he bought The Thing's new version, a purple and orange monstrosity called The Thing Lives.

Jesus. Having a ball with that stupid name was bad enough. But Bulldog also liked to act the fool out there, sometimes wearing a dog mask, or bowling with his eyes closed, or clipping a rubber chicken to his teammate's ass and then laughing like hell as it swung and bounced during the guy's approach.

You didn't do stuff like that in a league.

Moon took a drink and spun his chair to look around. On the wall above the alleys was another version of PAUL STROFFMAN'S LUCKY STRIKE sign. Moon stared at it for a moment, waiting for a message, but he knew none would come. This sign was newer, and not the classic symbol the one outside was.

A few dripping bowlers were straggling in. Tony Valleni, who had memorized every page of the ABC rule book, and Bald Leo, whose thumb was sliced off a few years back but who had worked real hard to learn to throw a helluva curve using just his two fingers in the holes. True hearts at their best.

At five thirty-seven, Bulldog came through the front door, lugging his rain-speckled bag. Bulldog always carried two balls—The Thing Lives and a second ball he used only for spares. After he was done hugging the girls, shaking hands with the guys, and talking about last night's scores, he made his way toward alleys eleven and twelve. He had small, penny-colored eyes pressed into a catcher's mitt face and they glinted with something Moon read as victory, even though not a ball had been thrown yet.

"You're here early," Bulldog said. "What are you doing, soaking up the atmosphere for inspiration?"

Moon drew hard on his cigarette and just stared.

Bulldog gave him a smile, then set his bag against the rack that held the ugly pink and green house balls. He glanced up at the computerized scoreboards. The teams and names were already up there. THE STEEL BALLS VS. BULLDOG'S BEST.

"I didn't know we were playing you," Bulldog said.

"It's friggin' roll-off night," Moon said dryly.

"Good Lord," Bulldog said, giving Moon a wink. "Is the season almost over already?"

Moon stubbed out his cigarette, crunching his teeth to avoid saying anything that would get him punched. Besides, he needed to stay focused.

Bulldog unzipped his bag and pulled out The Thing Lives and started toward the ball return to place it on the rack. Moon gaped. Bulldog was going to walk on the polished approach with wet shoes.

"Hey!" Moon called. "Watch it, your feet are wet."

Bulldog looked down at his black work shoes, then came back to his bag. He set The Thing Lives back inside then bent to untie his shoes.

"My apologies, Moon," he said. "Last thing I'd want is someone sticking on the approach and getting hurt on my account."

Bulldog took off his street shoes. Then to Moon's surprise, he pulled out his Dyno-Thane Kangaroo Tour Ultras and started to put them on.

He was putting the shoes on now ... before he went to the bar. Shit! Shit!

"You going to walk around this whole place in your bowling shoes?" Moon asked. "They'll be soaked."

Bulldog unzipped a pocket on the bag and held up a limp pair of red leather slip-on shoe covers. "Have no fear, my friend," he said. "I always use protection."

Then he laughed, that horrid hoarse chuckle that always sounded like he had a rag caught in his throat. He was still laughing as he pulled the covers over the Kangaroos and sauntered off into the bar to play his poker machine.

Moon couldn't stand it, couldn't sit still, and he pushed away from the counter so fast he almost tipped his beer. Winding his way between bowlers, he shoved the front doors open and stepped outside.

Shit! Fuck! Motherfucker! Tits!

How could he have been so stupid? Why didn't he just keep his mouth shut? Why couldn't he just let some stuff go instead of worrying about a few drops of water getting on the approach?

Because you can't, he thought. It's who you are. You're a purist.

The red neon of the sign cracked and buzzed, drawing his gaze up to the gray sky. Moon stepped out from under the overhang and looked up. Different letters were struggling to stay aglow in the rain. Suddenly, the sign steadied itself, and a handful of letters grew bright and solid.

T OFF   LUC

Moon squinted up into the rain. A new message.

Toff luc? Tough luck?

He stared harder, waiting for something else, waiting for the sign to show him the rest, tell him what to do now. But the letters just stood there, tall and fuzzy and red in the mist.

Tough luck. Tough luck. Tough luck.

Moon spat on the ground. This was bullshit. The sign wasn't some mystical crystal ball that was going to help him beat Bulldog and light the way for a re-purification of the greatest game ever invented. It was just a rusty old relic of a vanishing era.

He reached for the door. The boom of a blown electrical transformer snapped his head back toward the sign. With a groan and a crackle, three new letters came to life. **TRI**

T OFF   LUC TRI

The last three—TRI—were blinking on and off.

TRI? Try? Try ... that was it. Try. Try. Try!

Moon looked up to the clouds, his heart swelling with wonder and gratitude. His eyes filled with tears.

"You okay, Moon?"

Moon jumped, then looked at the man who had spoken. It was Al 'The Hawk' Hawkins, the pro shop guy. Moon's eyes slid back to the sign, but he knew The Hawk couldn't read it.

"I'm cool," Moon said.

The Hawk motioned to his van. "I had to close the shop early. My old lady's in labor again. Good luck tonight. Seven years in a row finishing second, that's gotta hurt after a while."

Moon couldn't even fake a smile. The Hawk hurried off across the parking lot. After a few seconds, a yellow Camaro with confederate flag window decals swung in. Shaky was here.

Moon waited under the overhang until Shaky was almost to the doors then he stopped him with a palm to his chest. Shaky stared at him, his black hair looking like leeches stuck to his forehead.

"What?" Shaky asked. "What's wrong?"

"He's already wearing the shoes," Moon hissed. "You got to do something else."

"Like what?"

"Go to my truck. Inside is a full tube of epoxy. Bring it to me and don't let anyone see you with it."

"Huh?"

"Just go. I'll explain inside."

Moon pushed him out from under the overhang. Shaky planted his feet, blinking like he was figuring something out. "I do something with that epoxy then you gotta give me something better than your old Red Inferno."

"What?" Moon demanded. "What the fuck else I got you want?"

"What about a roll with Helen?"

"What? She would never sleep with you."

"Get her drunk enough, she might."

Moon came off the concrete, fist clenched and Shaky quickly back-pedaled. "I was just kidding, man."

Moon stopped himself, and for a few seconds, both of them stood in the rain, silent. Moon sighed. Man, he had to give Shaky something better than the pitted Red Inferno. Shaky didn't have much else. Hell, maybe the thrill of winning this was enough. Maybe Helen's new washer could wait.

"All right," Moon said. "I'll give you my Atomic Revolution."

In the gray mist, Shaky's face lit up like a headlight. He loped off toward Moon's truck. A few seconds later, he was back.

"You get it?" Moon asked.

Shaky patted his dripping shirt, his voice low. "I'm packin' man."

✣

IT WAS CROWDED by the time they got back to alley eleven. Beefy men hunched over black bowling bags. Shoes scattered everywhere. The counters covered with the fine white powder from tiny bags of Easy-Slide. Paulie had music playing from the speakers, the kind Moon knew would give him a headache if he listened to it too long.

They had both dried off in the john, changed into their yellow and black shirts, and Shaky had opened the epoxy inside the stall, making sure it would be warm and ready when he needed it. He was only going to get one good squeeze per hole.

Back at alley eleven, Moon provided the cover for Shaky. He heard Shaky unzipping Bulldog's bag.

"Good luck tonight, Moon!" someone called.

Moon gave the man a tight nod, keeping his eyes on the alleys. The smell of epoxy was everywhere.

"Hurry up," Moon hissed.

"Do you want I should do the spare ball, too?"

"Yeah."

Moon heard the draw of a zipper and suddenly Shaky appeared in front of him, a tight smile on his face. "Mission accomplished."

Moon watched as Shaky wandered off and dropped the epoxy into a full trash can, then he looked toward the bar. Bulldog was coming out the door.

It was time to get ready.

As Moon put on his shoes, he snuck a look at Bulldog. He hadn't touched his bag yet. Still busy jawing about his recent 300 game and wondering when his award ring would come from ABC.

Moon's eyes slipped quickly to the only ring on his hand, his wedding ring, but he didn't like thinking about that. He set his Atomic Revolution on the rack and looked down at the pins. They stood like polished teeth at the end of the gleaming wood tongue. Pearly and ripe.

"Who's been fucking with my ball?"

Bulldog had pulled The Thing Lives from his bag and was jabbing at the thumb hole with his finger.

"It's ... filled up with something."

Moon resisted the urge to walk over. Bulldog poked at the clogged hole a few more times, then the copper eyes came up. Right at Moon.

"You," Bulldog whispered.

Moon gave him a dry smile. "Things happen to balls when you leave them in hot car trunks," he said. "Maybe it melted."

Bulldog stared at him, The Thing Lives cradled in his hands like a dead pet.

People started to gather around, taking turns sticking fingers inside Bulldog's thumb hole and mumbling about how the new kind of resin used to make balls nowadays just didn't hold up very well in the southern heat.

"Maybe Al the Hawk can drill it out for you real quick," someone said.

Moon let Bulldog take a few steps toward the pro shop before he called out."Hey Bulldog," Moon said. "I saw Al leaving about thirty minutes ago."

Bulldog turned slowly back to Moon. The mumbling all around them grew louder. Everyone knew what this meant.

"You want to borrow one of my balls, Bulldog?" someone asked.

"You know I can't," Bulldog said. "I got fat fingers."

"Maybe you can use a one of those pink house balls," Moon offered.

Bulldog glared at Moon, so hard he didn't even notice that Bald Leo had walked up. "Man, that's tough luck," Leo said. "Want me to show you how to throw it without sticking your thumb in?"

Bulldog's head jerked to Bald Leo. "Yeah," he said quickly. "Show me."

✛

THEY WERE ALLOWED fifteen minutes of practice. With only two on a team, that gave everyone a chance to throw at least twenty shots. Normally Moon took every one he could, but not tonight. He was watching Bulldog.

At first, Bulldog threw a couple of gutters, then Bald Leo worked on his grip, showing him how to cup to ball to get it stay on his hand. Eight practice balls later, The Thing Lives, with the clogged holes, was rolling down the alley and getting strikes.

Moon was pissed. No one could learn to bowl with two fingers instead of three that quick. In fact, unless you were thumbless, there ought to be a rule against it. They put three holes on a ball for a reason.

"This sucks," Shaky said, coming up next to him. "What now?"

Moon's gut was so hard, he couldn't speak. He shoved Shaky aside and ripped into his bag for his shoe covers. He was still struggling to get them on as he hobbled away from the alleys.

Moon shoved open the front doors. He stepped out from under the overhang and into the hard rain. Every damn letter was off.

"Okay!" Moon shouted at the sign. "Okay! Now what? What do I do now?"

The sign stood dark and silent.

"Dammit!" he screamed. " I did everything you wanted me to! Talk to me. C'mon, one more time!"

Nothing.

"You fucking piece of shit!" Moon shouted, fist raised. "You lousy, stinking piece of cheap neon! Talk to me!"

It started with a buzz, then a crackle and a few letters began to glow. First a K, then a second K.

"C'mon," Moon said. "I'm running out of time here!"

More letters. Then the sign stopping buzzing, leaving only a handful of letters lit.

M A K   SIK.

What did that mean?

Ma..k … Make? S..i..K … Sick.

Make sick.

Yes! That was it. He would make Bulldog sick.

Moon rushed back inside, dripping all the way back to alley twelve. The whole place was alive now with clatter, but to Moon, it seemed strangely muted, like it did sometimes at the end of a one-pin game when he had to tune everything else out in order to throw the perfect ball.

Bulldog was humping strikes every time now and his teammate stood in awe, watching him. Everyone was watching him.

Moon grabbed Shaky's sleeve and pulled him over to the counter.

"Get your acetone," he whispered.

Shaky reached down into his bag and pulled out a small plastic squeeze bottle. Moon glanced at the crowd around Bulldog, then tipped his head toward Bulldog's Rum and Coke.

"Pour some in there," he said.

"You want me to poison him?" Shaky asked.

"He won't die," Moon said. "He'll just get sick."

"I dunno, Moon. This is bad stuff."

"Just do it!" Moon hissed.

Shaky hesitated, then took the cap off the bottle. "I want a bigger pay-off," he said.

"You already got my Revolution. I ain't got nothing else!" Moon said.

"But I could go to jail for this."

Moon looked up, his throat tight. Behind him, he heard the smash of a sure strike, followed by laughter. Man, could he really do this? Yes. He could. He would make it up to her somehow.

"Okay," he said, looking back at Shaky. "If you want Helen—and I mean for one quickie—I'll get her to do it."

Shaky's eyes widened, then he slurped the acetone into the drink and quickly put the bottle away. The scoreboards suddenly turned a bright blue, indicating practice was over. Everyone started back to their own lanes. Moon turned to look at Bulldog.

He was standing by the approach, holding The Thing Lives in his arm. He made a sweeping gesture toward the lanes.

"You're up, Moon."

⊕

BULLDOG THREW UP in the wastebasket in frame nine of the first game, and no one was sure if he was going to be able to continue, but right after, he got back up and threw another strike—a Moses ball—the kind that hits the head pin and divides the pins right down the middle.

It was the kind of thing that always happened to unpure bowlers when they found themselves up against real talent. Moon called them ugly strikes, the ones that never should have been and although everyone took them—you had to take them—Moon thought there was an element of shame in having too many. Bulldog didn't seem to think so.

Moon glanced up at the scoreboard. Dammit.

They were going to lose this game. Shaky wasn't concentrating. His shots were laden with guilt, and he was having a hard time keeping his eyes off Bulldog's drink.

Shaky apologized five times for losing the game, even though he had bowled a 218, nineteen pins above his average. Moon had bowled a 266. Any other night, it would have been more than enough. But not tonight.

Bulldog spent most of the second game in the bathroom. Moon wanted to call Tony Valleni and his rule book down to see if there was a set number of minutes someone could delay a game before they forfeited. But half the damn league was in the john, worried about Bulldog, and Moon didn't want to come off as a jerk, so he stayed quiet, just sitting at the table, staring at the scoreboard, which by the end of the second game, read: THE STEEL BALLS 521, BULLDOG'S BEST 499.

It was even up. All they needed to do was to win the third game, and the league, the thousand dollars and that big-ass gold trophy would be his.

Moon rubbed his face, wishing the knot in his belly would go away. He looked out at the lanes. Most of the bowlers had stopped their own games to gather behind eleven and twelve to watch the championship. The alleys were so quiet, Moon could hear his own heart.

Someone called his name and he looked to see Bulldog and his entourage heading back to the alleys. Bulldog's fat face was sweaty and white as the pins, and he was walking unsteady, but he managed to find his way to the approach and grab The Thing Lives.

⊕

SHAKY STARTED OFF the third game with a Moses ball strike. Moon followed with a perfect pocket hit, but so did Bulldog and his partner. By the middle of the game, amidst rolls of thunder and flickering lights, the game was tied, with X's in every box on the scoreboard. The crowd behind was thickening.

The score stayed almost tied through the ninth, even though Bulldog was staggering, with sweat running down his face and only the cheers of the faithful behind him to give him strength.

Moon looked up at the scoreboard. They were a few pins behind, but it was not out of reach. He was calculating up how many pins he would need if Bulldog struck out when he heard a groan from the spectators and he looked at the alley.

Bulldog had done the unthinkable. The Thing Lives was rolling down the gutter.

Moon watched the ball until it disappeared into the black abyss behind the pins, then his eyes flicked up to the scoreboard. His brain worked like lightening. All Moon had to do was get a spare. Two balls to get all ten pins. It was theirs. Goddammit. The whole thing was theirs!

Bulldog lofted his final ball, a weak hook that toppled the pins in slow motion. He stumbled back to his chair, holding his stomach, falling into the arms of a dozen other bowlers.

It was time to end this.

Moon picked up his Atomic Revolution and took his place on the approach. Lowering his head and concentrating on every step, he threw his first ball. It was perfect—absolutely fucking perfect—and he felt a surge of greatness as the Revolution exploded into the pins and scattered them.

Wait … there was one left. One damn pin. The ten pin.

Dammit. Dammit to hell.

Moon grabbed the Atomic Revolution off the return and cradled it, staring at the ten pin. If he missed this, it was over. Everything was over.

He set himself, his heart starting to pound, beads of sweat forming on his palms. Just as he started his first step, thunder rolled overhead. Moon stopped, waiting for it to pass before he set himself again.

He wiggled his fingers into the ball, then slipped in his thumb and stared down at the pin. It stood gleaming and silent, waiting for him.

As he took a step, another explosion from outside vibrated through the building, sending the lights flickering and the pin trembling. He stopped again.

The sign outside must be flickering, too, trying to talk to him, and he wished he could go look at it to see what the message was, but he couldn't leave now.

But then, suddenly, imaginary letters started flashing in his head. They made no sense, like one of those scrambled word puzzles in the newspaper that he couldn't do.

He set himself again, trying not to think about the letters. But now words were starting to form in his head and with every step he took, another letter would drop into place.

S ... T ... A

Third step and the swing of his arm.

Y ... P ...

It amazed him that he could see his messages now in his mind, and that realization, more than the letters themselves, filled him with a sense of magical power as his arm started forward.

U ... R ...

The ball was cupped in his hand like a perfect size C boob, and as he started to lay it down, the last letter dropped into place in his head.

E.

In an instant, he saw it, all the letters blinking as sure and strong in his head as he knew they were blinking outside.

STAY PURE

What? That wasn't the right message. It couldn't be the right message. He was already pure.

Wasn't he?

The Atomic Revolution was just coming off the tips of his fingers when something pulled at him, something powerful and creepy and irresistible, and he did something he never thought he would do. He flipped the ball just a half-inch to the left. The moment it hit the wood, he knew it would miss the pin.

And it did.

The ball disappeared into the dark bowels of the alley, and Moon stood and stared at the ten pin.

It stared back, silent and defiant.

Somewhere in his brain, he could hear cheering and then the rattle of the Revolution coming up the ball return. But everything he expected to feel—rage and disappointment—were not there. All that was there was a scary kind of peace.

He turned slowly and packed up his stuff. Shaky was talking about next year and Bulldog was shaking hands and someone was on the loudspeaker announcing that BULLDOG'S BEST were league champs. In the corner of his eye, Moon caught sight of the huge, gold trophy coming through the crowd.

He headed outside, Shaky hustling along behind him, still yakking about next year and summer leagues and tournaments, but Moon wasn't hearing him. He wanted to see the sign and he wanted to make sure the message he had seen in his head was the right one because if it wasn't, then everything that had happened to him in those last few seconds had been fake.

He stopped under the overhang and told Shaky to shut up. They both stood there, staring at the sign, watching and waiting.

With a crack of thunder, all the letters went out. A few seconds later, they flickered back on.

U L
U   L O
U   L O S R

Moon stared, and blinked, and kept staring. Then he started slowly off across the parking lot. Shaky trailed behind.

"Do I still get your Atomic Revolution, Moon?"

"No."

"What about Helen?"

"No."

"Well, then do I get the old red Inferno?"

"No."

"Well, then, what do I get out of all this?"

Moon stopped and faced him. "Purity, my friend. We get purity."

ED GORMAN

ED Gorman has published more than thirty novels in twenty-five years as a full-time writer. *Booklist* noted, "In Gorman's novels good and evil clash with the same heartbreaking results as they do in the more urban crime novels of Block and Leonard." Gorman has also published six collections of short stories.

On the subject of this anthology, Ed says, "I suspect that hitman stories are voyeuristic exercises for both reader and writer. How simple life would be if we could just bump off those who displease us."

Visit Ed at:

www.geocities.com/Athens/Acropolis/3192/ejgorman.html

BEAUTY
Ed Gorman

MOST OF US USE code words. I suppose that sounds a bit melodramatic, but how else are you going to separate the wheat from the chaff? Or, more specifically, the real client from the undercover FBI agent who wants to bust your ass and send you away for a long, long time.

The lady called me while I was on the Stairmaster in my hotel room. She'd guaranteed a nice sum to fly to her city. I was nice and winded from my workout while she went through this nervous little introduction without once giving me that one word that could put us in business.

"Oh, damn," she said. "The—what do you call it?—the code word. You want that, don't you?"

"Be nice to hear it."

"Associates."

"There you go."

"So how do we proceed from here? I suppose you can tell I'm sort of nervous."

"Where are you?"

She told me. I mentioned a nice little Chinese place two blocks from her hotel.

⊕

DURING MY BRIEF tenure in the loving arms of the fine folk who run Joliet state pen —bank robbery gone wrong;

nothing to do with my present occupation—I spent a lot of time reading psychology books. I figured that psychology would be useful no matter what kind of work I took up when they gave me back my cheap suit and the free bus ticket.

I had a friend in high school that had spent every possible minute tending to this cherry 1957 red Ford Thunderbird his wealthy father had bought him at the start of our senior year. Ken had once been a fun guy. No more. After he got the T-Bird, he lost interest in girls, smoking dope, cruising our hangouts, and even the XXX videos that had just become available to the general public.

The woman who slid into the booth across from me also had an obsession. Her obsession wasn't with a thing. It was with herself.

I don't keep up on all the things women can do to keep themselves beautiful if they have the money. I know about plastic surgery, of course, and facials and bikini waxes and things like that. But I'm sure there are at least a dozen devious little tricks most men know nothing about. With her, it was probably two dozen devious little tricks.

She was stunning more than beautiful. A lot of her appeal was in the important way she carried herself. She was fighting forty and winning.

The smile disarmed you. One of those ridiculously outsize Hollywood smiles that mere mortals can't muster. And what the smile couldn't accomplish, the blue blue eyes did. Now you were not only disarmed, but raising your arms in surrender. The elegant suit looked to be Armani, the enormous tooled earrings looked to be real gold, and the long, calculatedly tousled golden hair finished you off.

But she irritated me immediately. "What if I change my mind?"

"I'm told that's a woman's prerogative."

"Do you have a kill fee?" The smile was genuine. "Oh, God, I used to work at a magazine and that's what we called it when we canceled an article but wanted to give the writer something for his work. A kill fee. In this case, I guess it's a bad choice of words."

I smiled. "Nothing to worry about. And a kill fee is already taken care of."

"It is?"

I nodded. "Remember what I said on the phone. First half is payable right here, right now. If I don't have the second half in cash by the end of the day, I keep the first half whether I do the job or not."

"What if I called the police?"

"Again, your prerogative. But you'd be implicated in hiring me to kill someone. Conspiracy to commit murder probably wouldn't go over too well with your friends at the country club."

"How do you know I belong to a country club?"

"Please."

She frowned. "What you're saying is that I'm a cliché."

Never accuse a narcissist of anything. Their egos move in for the kill.

"You have a manila envelope. Let's get to it, shall we?"

"I resent your remark."

I started to slide out of the booth.

She held up her perfectly manicured hand. "Oh, forget it. I am very country club and I may as well admit it. It's just that common people are so snobby about country clubs. They don't know about all the fine people you meet at them."

Like ladies who hire hitmen, I thought. Not to mention robber barons that cheat their employees out of their pensions, and then go home to sleep on thousand-dollar silk sheets in their ten-bedroom mansions.

She opened the 8-by-10 manila envelope and slid out a small package wrapped in brown paper, accompanied by a newspaper story that included a full-color photo with the caption: Beauty of Beauties. The rest of the text listed the names of the three runners-up and the beauty pageant winner. The runners-up tried desperately to look happy. The queen didn't have that problem, flashing a Hollywood smile that made you reach for your sunglasses.

"You won this beauty contest."

"State winner. I went on to Miss USA. I was eighteen, just a sophomore in college." When she mentioned her age, melancholy hushed her voice to a whisper. I wondered if she'd cry. She wasn't putting me on. She was lamenting her lost youth. I suppose we all do that, though given all the time I'd spent in county jail, my youth wasn't much to lament. "I didn't win Miss USA. I was the second runner-up." She mentioned the name of a prominent male singer popular at that time in the mid-80s. "He was one of the judges. He knew I should have won and he wanted to help me get through it. He took me dancing and other things."

I knew better than to inquire about those "other things."

"Now my daughter is in a beauty contest and I don't want the same thing to happen to her."

"What 'same thing?'"

"To be cheated out of it. The word I'm getting is that the advertising agency man who runs this particular pageant is actually the father of one of the contestants. He got a girl pregnant when he was already married and now the daughter is in his show. I think the mother is blackmailing him. He won't have any choice but to figure out some way for his daughter to win. This could be a very important stepping stone for my daughter. I don't want some dirty old man to ruin it for her."

"When's the pageant?"

"Tomorrow night." She named a convention hall. "Eight o'clock. My daughter's all ready to go. She's not only the most beautiful, she's also the most talented."

"If you do say so yourself."

Another genuine smile. "If I do say so myself. I'm sorry if I sound egotistical. It's just that I want my daughter to win this."

"So I address my skills to the advertising man?"

"Oh, no. The man might be dead, but his illegitimate daughter would still be alive and ready to compete again. I hate to admit this, but she's a very good looking girl. And not bad in the talent department."

"So I direct my attention to her."

She leaned forward. "Yes, but not the full thing."

"The full thing?"

She nodded. "Right." Her voice dropped even lower. "I don't want her killed. I just want her disfigured. Permanently."

⊕

I SPENT THE REST of the day deploying all the things I'd need for a perfect strike. Access would be the first problem. While the girl would be in her hotel room at various times, her floor would be shared by other contestants. A whole lot of problems there. She would be at a banquet tonight. I could get the security uniform I'd need, but again, the contestants would be everywhere. A clean getaway was dicey. My client had given me an itinerary that the girl followed every day. Up early for a quick jog around the hotel pool and then fifteen minutes of swimming before showering, eating a light breakfast, and then her singing and ballet lessons. A star in the making. The only problem was that this star seemed to always be accompanied by another woman, an older one, perhaps her mother or aunt or someone. It didn't matter to me; she was an inconvenience, nothing more.

I disguised myself for a quick tour of all the hotel sites that were possibilities for the attack. Late in the day, I went downstairs to where the maids and the bellboys check in and check out. They each had their own small locker room. I always carry a few elementary burglary tools with me. In one locker I found a bellhop uniform still in its dry-cleaning plastic. It wouldn't fit perfectly, but it would fit well enough.

Tonight, coming back from the banquet, the girl and her escort would probably walk back to her room via a wandering garden-like area that led directly to her entrance. My client said that this was the route they had followed the last three nights. She also said that the two never joined the other contestants in staying out a little longer. They went right back to their room. They would be virtually alone on the garden walk. Neither one would be startled by seeing a bellhop.

✛

I DON'T PRETEND to be Superman. I don't even pretend to be Jimmy Olson. Over the years, I've found that my job-related anxiety is at its worst two or three hours before the gig itself. I've tried antidepressants, a few shots of whiskey, even a joint or two of pot. But they all left me logy. Maybe the worst danger of all to a man in my profession.

Then I discovered the Stairmaster. I now insist on hotel rooms with Stairmasters. Pricey, yes, but invaluable. An hour of hard exercise and then a cold shower leaves me not only wide awake but focused entirely on the task ahead.

I'd just stepped out of the shower when the call came that I'd been expecting.

"I guess I'm backing out."

"Figures."

"You don't have to be sarcastic."

"I'm ready to go. Guess I'll have to find some other amusement for tonight."

"I was just thinking to myself I'm not this kind of woman. I'm a Junior Leaguer, for God's sake."

"All right. I've got the money and I'm hanging up now."

"I feel foolish. You must think I'm an airhead."

"A Junior League airhead? A contradiction in terms."

"There's that f-ing sarcasm again."

"Good night, Madam."

I was just adjusting the clip-on necktie that fitted the white shirt I wore under the uniform jacket when the second call came.

"I've changed my mind."

"Who is this?"

"You know damn well who this is. Now quit playing around."

"Oh, yes, the Junior League lady."

"I ought to hang up on you, you bastard."

"Go ahead. It's your turn."

"I want you to do it."

"I've already made other plans."

"You prick. You've got my money and I want satisfaction. And don't get cute with that last word."

I checked my Rolex. If I was going to do it, I had to move fast.

"One thing," I said.

"What?"

"I never want to hear your voice again."

I hung up, grabbed my stun gun, and drove over to the hotel.

⊕

THE BANQUET RAN LATE. A minor celebrity sang some songs and an even more minor celebrity gave a speech about why beauty pageants were the best expression ever of true American values. If there'd been a vomitorium nearby, I would have gladly bought my ticket.

Someday when I tell this story again to a few friends of mine, I'll fill it with a lot of intrigue and suspense. The whole stalking sequence you see in all those noir films. Close cuts of me hiding in the front of the garden area. The beautiful contestant coming out the door that leads to the garden, her mother holding her hand. Her innocently looking around. My hand tightening around my weapon of choice for this evening. Her walking briskly toward her entrance door. And then me coming up behind her, devilishly disguised, and saying in a safe, sensible voice, "Excuse me."

And her turning around and—

⊕

I'D JUST POURED myself a drink when the phone rang in my hotel room. I picked up and said, "I thought I told you I never wanted to hear your voice again." Nobody else it could be. Nobody else knew where I was.

"I just wanted to thank you."

"I did my job."

"You did a fine job. Of course, I feel terrible about it. It's not the sort of thing I'd normally do but my daughter—" Then, "But this Tiny Tiara contest is real important to her." I could feel rather than hear her smile on the other end of the phone. "Call me the ultimate stage mother, I guess."

"I'm hanging up now."

"Well, that's nice. All I wanted to do was thank you. I mean it must've been weird for you throwing acid in the face of a little five-year-old girl. I'm just glad you could get through it."

I hung up.

The local news was all over it of course. A beauty contest for five- to seven-year-old girls. A barbaric act unheard of in the history of these pageants. Police searching for a dark-haired man dressed as a bellhop. So stealing the uniform and spending the time to get just the right wig had been worth the trouble.

Sleep didn't come easy but when it finally arrived I had an unwanted dream about screwing the woman who'd hired me. She was a lot better than I would've thought.

MICHAEL A. BLACK

For the past twenty-eight years Michael A. Black has been a police officer in the south suburbs of Chicago. His short stories have appeared in various anthologies and magazines, including *Ellery Queen*, *Alfred Hitchcock's Mystery Magazine*, and *Detective Mystery Stories*. He's the author of the Ron Shade novels, and the stand-alones THE HEIST and FREEZE ME, TENDER. Michael has worked in various capacities in police work including patrol supervisor, tactical squad, investigations, raid team member, and SWAT team leader. He is currently a sergeant on the Matteson, Illinois Police Department.

On the subject of literary hitmen, Michael comments: "The role of the hitman in crime literature is fully entwined with that of the private detective. Both are steeped in a romantic mysticism that transcends reality and builds a mystique all its own. 'Down these mean streets, a man must go … ' Raymond Chandler once said. What he didn't say was that Marlowe was worried there was a hitman waiting somewhere in the shadows and the fog. But since hitmen and gangsters aren't unique to the United States, I tried to give my story an international feel."

Visit him at www.MichaelABlack.com.

THE BLACK ROSE

Michael A. Black

BRAX WATCHED AS THE muscular men danced around the picturesque courtyard, chopping at one another with those three-foot bamboo swords, their arms, chests, and backs covered with colorful tattoos, their bodies glistening with sweat.

"They do that with real blades, too?" he asked. The wood of the raised porch-like balcony that overlooked the courtyard below was hard and his legs were beginning to ache from sitting there.

"Of course." Kiroshi cast an amused looking smile his way. His English was good, but heavily accented. "Those are called *shinai*. Used for practice. But there are times when a *yakuza* must use a real *katana*."

"A what?"

Kiroshi smiled again and stood up. "A *katana*." He touched the handle of the long sword sticking out from his belt. "For us, it is part of our culture. A sacred part." With a quick movement, Kiroshi pulled the long sword from its holder and held it out in front of Brax. The shiny metal gleamed in the fading sunlight like sterling silver. "They were used to guard the Emperor and his lords. A true warrior used his *katana* as an instrument of honor. They were fashioned by … artists with metal. It would take them many months. They would fashion the blade over and over, never allowing any weakness or impurity." He turned it, catching the light. "During this time, they would not eat meat, bathed only in cold water, and would not have sexual relations. Not until their task was complete. Not until the blade was perfect." He swiftly raised his arm and with a quick motion sheathed the sword.

Brax shook his head. This whole country was nothing but fanatics. In the distance, symmetrical rows of trees and circular patterns of crops gave way to a once scenic mountain, now obscured by a cloud of brown fog. Like everything else here, crowded, polluted, and inscrutable. The sooner he could get himself and crazy Stevie out of this damn country, the better.

"We're used to guns in the States," he said.

"Guns are illegal in Japan," Kiroshi said, grinning as he pulled back his jacket to display the grip of the pistol, "but they are not unobtainable."

Kiroshi murdered the pronunciation of the last word, but Brax figured he'd better not say anything. After all, these were the guys who were protecting them. He looked around again at the remote house where they'd been hiding out, waiting on that flight back to the States in twelve more hours. It seemed pretty secure. They were a good distance from the city, in a maze of gardens or farms or something. The long house was set back from the yard, and the whole place was surrounded by a five-foot brick wall. Embedded fragments of broken glass adorned the topping cement. Plus there must have been at least fifteen *yakuzas* here. It should be safe enough. He glanced at his watch again, wondering what time it was in LA right now, and thought about the reason he was sitting here, sweating it out.

"You're sure that Tanaka dude ain't gonna find us?" he asked.

Several of the men in the courtyard yelled in unison, brandishing their bamboo swords and charging their opponents.

"Tanaka Mishima knows where we are," Kiroshi said. "But he will not come."

Brax thought about that and decided if two foreigners had whacked his daughter, he'd be sure to try and ice them before they took off for parts unknown. He hurled another silent curse at Stevie for getting him into this mess. Taking the boss's son along on a business trip like this had been a mistake from the get-go. He'd known it, and Stevie's excesses when it came to hookers was what did them in. Instead of completing the simple transaction agreement like he wanted, and getting the hell back to the States, idiot Stevie had to get laid.

And how was I supposed to know he liked things rough, Brax thought. Real rough. And then the dead hooker turned out to be this ex-hitman's daughter …

"So just how good is this Tanaka guy?" Brax asked.

Kiroshi's eyes narrowed and he held up his thumb. "I trained him to be the best-best."

One of the female servants, dressed in a flowing kimono, stepped on to the porch and bowed, saying something in Japanese. Kiroshi grunted a response and motioned for her to set the tray down.

"He was a cast-off of your army's occupation," he said picking up one of the small cups and sipping from it. "His father was a GI, his mother Japanese. When I found him, he was an *einoko* running the streets. I took him in, raised him as my *shatei*, taught him the way of the *katana*." Kiroshi paused and Brax thought he saw something akin to pride in the older man's expression. "In the years that followed, after the occupation, he became legend among the *yakuza*, able to master every technique, every weapon, and completely without fear. And yet he also had honor. He would leave a black rose with each of his … assassinations." He murdered the pronunciation again, but Brax got the idea. It sent a cold shiver up his spine. "It would be," Kiroshi continued, "the last thing seen before his *katana* struck."

One by one, the combatants in the courtyard were being eliminated in their swordfighting contest. Only two of the tattooed men remained now. Brax watched as they circled each other warily. The larger of the two made a deft movement, sweeping the other man's *shinai* out of his hands. The big guy followed up with a quick slashing motion, smacking the other man's gut and leaving a bright red welt below a feathery tattoo pattern.

Kiroshi called out in Japanese. Brax could tell that it was an order because the men quickly turned and bowed toward him. Then they picked up their gear and dispersed.

"That big guy looks pretty good with that thing," Brax said.

"Kiro was taught by Tanaka," Kiroshi said. "He is very skilled with *tanto*, *katana*, and guns." He turned and pointed to the tray. "Have some tea, Brax-san."

"So the guy who's stalking me is the guy who taught your crew all they know?" Brax said, ignoring the cups. "How do I know this guy ain't crazy enough to follow me once we get outta here?"

Kiroshi chuckled. "He could never find you in your country. He does not speak the language. And if he tries here, tonight, he knows it means defying me, which will necessitate his death. I am his *saiko-koman*." His expression turned stern again. "Believe me, Brax-san, once we get you and your friend on that plane in the morning, you will be safe." He leaned forward. "Just do not let your superiors forget about our agreement. And the special reward you promised me."

One of the flunkies from the courtyard approached them and bowed, then went into a crouch, holding out his open palm like he wanted to shake hands. Brax noticed that the little finger was missing on the guy's left hand. Kiroshi regarded him for several seconds, and then said something in Japanese. The man responded, bowed again, and backed cautiously away.

"He told me your friend has refused food," Kiroshi said. "He is very strange."

You got that right, Brax thought. The dumb son of a bitch.

"He's also the big man's son," he said. "My boss, Sal Payne."

Kiroshi nodded and brought the small cup to his lips, sipped, then barked out an order and two men, each with small machine guns, began walking around the courtyard.

"Looks like they're ready for action," Brax said, feeling slightly better that they were packing heat and not some kind of samurai sword bullshit. "You said that guy Tanaka is no longer with the organization?"

Kiroshi set the small cup down and nodded. Almost noise-lessly, the servant girl appeared and took the tray away.

"So what did he do?" Brax asked. "Screw the boss's daughter?"

If Kiroshi got the joke, he didn't show it. He simply shook his head.

"I told you Tanaka was an *einoko* … Mixed blood. As it stands, it is our custom that he never marry a full blood Japanese. But he did.

"He came to me almost twenty years ago, and asked to be released from the …" he paused, as if searching for the right word, "organization. He offered me *yubitsume*." Kiroshi held up his own left hand, which was missing the tip of the little finger.

The corners of Brax's mouth turned downward. "That other guy was missing one, too. Some kind of sword-play accident?"

Kiroshi shook his head. "*Yubitsume* … An atonement. If a *yakuza* has offended his *oyabun*, he may offer his finger as an apology."

"You cut off your own finger?"

"*Hai*. I was his *kumicho*, but I forbade him to do it."

The image of some dude fanatical enough to go chopping off the tip of his finger flashed through Brax's mind. "Why was that?"

"Tanaka was the greatest kendo master I had ever seen. A throwback to the days of the samurai. And I owed him a debt of honor. I once saw him kill ten men at one time."

"Sweet Jesus," Brax said. "You mean with one of them swords?"

Kiroshi nodded. "Yes, with a *katana*." He stared off into space. "Tanaka saved my life that day, so I went to the *oyabun* and offered myself in his place. My *yubitsume* was accepted. I went back to Tanaka and told him our debt was paid. He left on the condition that I never see him again."

"Or what?"

"Or," Kiroshi looked toward Brax with an obvious expression of disdain. "I would kill him."

Brax wrinkled his nose. "You guys got some funny rules over here, I'll say that. But I gotta tell you, I don't get a lot of what you're telling me."

The older man smiled. His teeth were gold outlines reinforcing crumbling enamel. "I did not imagine you would. You are a westerner ... an American." His word had a measured, contempt-filled tone. "I speak of *bushido* ... The warrior's code. It is very important here in Japan, even today."

"I'm sure it is," Brax said, rising. "I gotta use the bathroom."

He went inside the structure and saw the shadows of a group of men moving behind the long paper wall of the main room. They were obviously playing one of their damn Jap card games. Christ, it seemed like that's all they did. He went to the third room, slid open the door, and checked to see if Stevie was still sleeping it off. The fat slob was lying on his back clad in his dirty underwear, snoring and stinking of booze.

Brax would have liked nothing better than to boogie on out of there, take a taxi back to the city, and wait by himself in the airport for the next flight out. But bringing the boss's kid home safe was part of the deal. Sal Payne's boys were almost, but not quite, as serious as these *yakuza* fuckers. He didn't have to worry about cutting off any fingers. They'd probably cut something else off, though, before they put a bullet in his brain.

Two of the gangster dudes ran down the narrow hallway talking Japanese into a portable radio. They looked agitated and alarmed. He could see it in their eyes. He slid the door closed and followed them, noticing for the first time that it had suddenly gotten very dark. Lighted Japanese lanterns ringed the hallway and the perimeter of the courtyard.

Kiroshi stood by the doorway, his hands on his hips, surveying the yard as the other guys rushed out.

"What's up?" Brax asked.

Kiroshi frowned. "Just checking on the guards. They did not answer their radios."

Oh shit, Brax thought. That don't sound too good. "What does that mean?"

Kiroshi glared at him momentarily, then his radio squawked with some kind of gibberish, and he smiled and held the radio up. "See, it is as I told you. All is good."

Brax looked dubious.

"Do not worry, Brax-san. As I told you, Tanaka is a man of honor. He cannot defy me, without it meaning his own death." Kiroshi turned and gestured down the hallway. "Do you want me to teach you how to play our game of cards?"

Brax glanced at the gesticulating images against the opaque wall again. "You guys do that a lot, don't you?"

"It is our tradition. We take our name from it. The word *yakuza* means twenty-three."

"Is that lucky or something?"

Kiroshi shook his head and smiled. "No. It means to lose."

Great, Brax thought. Just what I wanted to hear.

"Another time," he said. "I'm pretty beat."

"Go to your room, then. Rest for your long journey home."

"Ah, I'd feel better if I had a piece," Brax said. "At least until we leave in the morning."

Kiroshi shook his head. "A gun would do no good against Tanaka, and you might accidentally shoot me."

Brax swallowed hard and eyed the butt of the automatic in the other man's belt. He didn't dare to reach out and try to grab it.

"All right," he said. "But keep me posted on what's going on, okay?"

Kiroshi bowed his head slightly.

Brax went back to his room and pulled out the small mattress they'd given him.

Christ, it isn't bad enough that I have to spend my last night in Japan cooped up in some little shithole, but I have to sleep on the goddamn floor, too. He stretched out and tried to sleep, but it proved elusive. Stevie's sonorous breathing carried through the thin wall with the precision of a buzzsaw. Brax lay on his back listening to it, strangely reassured that if he could hear it, he knew the other man was still alive.

Still alive, he thought. Something he wouldn't be if he failed to bring the idiot back unharmed to his old man.

The buzzsaw stopped and Brax wondered if he should get up and check. Then the snoring resumed and Brax felt relief wash over him as he fell into a light slumber.

⊕

HE AWOKE FROM a bad dream, and lay there in the dark trying to figure out if the loud noise was what he thought it was. It had sounded like a gunshot. Or had he imagined it? Blinking, he couldn't be sure. Could he have dreamed it? Then he heard it again. A gunshot. Another one, followed by a scream. No, this sure as hell ain't no dream, Brax thought.

A shadow flickered across the translucent door panel. Someone was outside. Before Brax could even get to his feet, the door slid open. Kiroshi poked his head in, his face drawn and tight in the moonlight that filtered in after him.

"Tanaka is here," he said. "You no move." He slid the door closed.

Brax was on his feet, thinking the hell with that. I ain't gonna be no sitting duck. It took him several seconds to slip on his pants and shirt.

Better go check on Stevie, he thought.

He heard footsteps on the other side of the far wall and saw a shadowy figure running toward the front.

Must be a hallway on both sides, Brax thought. Great. Those paper walls would offer about as much protection as a silk nightgown.

He eased open the sliding door and peered out. Several *yakuzas* ran down the hallway. Glancing both ways, Brax looked for Kiroshi, but saw only a lone guy standing at the end of the hallway where it opened up into the courtyard. A pistol dangled from the man's hand.

Being as stealthy as he could, Brax moved into the hall, and crept down the ten feet to the room Stevie was in. He pushed on the sliding door and slipped inside, closing it after him.

The big slob lay on his side, still snoring, his swollen gut looking like a distended bladder. Brax grabbed the other man's shoulder and shook him.

Cursing and muttering, Stevie shoved Brax's hand away.

"Whatcha doing?" he asked, his tone loud and full of anger. "I was sleeping, for Christ's sake."

Brax couldn't afford to waste time. He slapped the fat cheeks twice and put his face closer.

"Listen to me," he said, keeping his voice low. "We're in the middle of a real bad situation here, see? Now I'm going to go outside and get us a gun, then I'm coming back for you and I'll get you outta here." He stared into the pale brown eyes, hoping to see a glimmer of understanding. "But I can't waste time looking for you, so I need you to stay right here, got it?"

Stevie's hot, fetid breath stung Brax's nostrils.

"Got it?" he repeated, slapping the other man again.

"Yeah," Stevie said.

Brax knew for sure, as he got up and moved to the door that he was going to have to answer to Sal for roughing the punk up, but, hell, what other choice did he have? He thought momentarily about cutting and running, but then if Stevie did survive, how would Brax's exit be explained? It'd be answered with a bullet, that was for sure.

The hallway was deserted as Brax moved toward the guard at the end.

Easy does it, he thought. All I need is for this dude to turn around and think I'm Tanaka. Staccato sounds ripped through the night again, and Brax figured the sound would cover any noise he made.

There were three more rooms separating Brax from the other man and all were standing open. That meant three more recesses. Once he got up next to the guy, he'd call out, and get him to give up a gun or something. If worst came to worst, he could try knocking the dude out and taking what he needed. From there he'd collect Stevie and make a run for the front gates while all the confusion was still going on. Who could blame him? It sounded like a war zone out there punctuated by gunshots and screams. Brax moved down to the second open door. A running silhouette shot past on the opposite wall. It startled him, but he kept moving. Just as he reached the final door, Kiroshi appeared and began shouting orders at the guy who'd been standing guard.

The guy said, "*Hai*," bowed quickly, and moved off to the left. Kiroshi's head bobbled as he looked down the hallway and obviously saw Brax.

"I told you, stay in room," he said, his English slipping into less comprehensible pronunciations. "Now, go!"

Kiroshi raised his arms and Brax saw the man was holding a gun. A chrome, snubnosed revolver. Kiroshi opened his mouth, as if to shout another order for Brax to leave, when his lips twisted downward in a lugubrious scowl. Slowly, Kiroshi's head lowered, as if he was testing to see if he could put his chin on his chest. But out of the front of his shirt something long and pointed protruded. An arrow. Kiroshi reached up and touched it with his left fingers as a crimson stain blossomed around the point. He looked slowly up at Brax, took two steps toward him, and twisted down in a tangled heap. After a quick glance around, Brax knelt beside him and peeled the fingers off the butt of the gun. A large, blood-tinctured bubble spread over Kiroshi's lips, and stayed there without bursting.

Brax pressed the cylinder release button and checked the ammo. Six shots, all good primers. This was his ticket out. He moved to the door and looked around. At least seven guys lay in the middle of the courtyard, some with long arrows sticking out of them, others with their bellies sliced open. He estimated about thirty yards to the gate.

To his left Brax saw the *yakuza* who'd been guarding the hallway moments ago. The man stood glancing around, his eyes so large and scared-looking that Brax was afraid the guy would shoot the first thing that moved.

"Hey," Brax called, pointing down the hallway. "Kiroshi wants you."

"Kiroshisan?" the guard said, and took a step forward just as a shadow moved behind him. The guy lurched forward, crying in pain, then as he whirled around, trying to raise his pistol, Brax saw a flash of light as a blade whistled up and back. The *yakuza* twisted, stumbling down the walk-way, his expression stupidly benign. He gripped his abdomen, which had an immense slash across it, the dark intestines rhythmically winding out from between his fingers with each step. The gun he'd been holding clattered to the floor and fell over the edge into the darkness. When the guard fell after it, Brax saw a figure in a black pajama-looking outfit standing there holding a long, bloody sword.

Tanaka!

Raising the gun, Brax started to squeeze the trigger, but the figure dashed to his right, into the adjacent hallway.

Brax ran back into his hallway and threw open the first paper door. Nothing. He ran to the second room where the door was already open. The shadow in the pajamas was silhouetted against the white rice paper wall. Brax brought his gun up and fired once, twice, three times. The shadow on the other side fell out of sight.

Never take a sword to a gunfight, Brax thought, and moved down to Stevie's room. It was still time to get the hell out of there, and he had three shots left as a buffer.

He threw open the door and yelled.

But Stevie stood there dumbly looking back at him, his fat cheeks covered with sweat. He was standing at the far wall, in the corner.

"Let's go, dammit," Brax said.

"Is it ..." Stevie finally muttered, "is it safe?"

"As safe as it's gonna be," Brax said. But before he could add anything else, Stevie stiffened and rose up on his toes, the point of a *katana* protruding from his chest. The blade rotated, and Stevie did a little dance step before crumbling to the floor. Brax fired at the shadow behind the wall, aiming for the open slit as the blade withdrew.

He couldn't tell if he'd hit the guy, or not.

His mind raced: But, Christ, I thought I hit him before.

An eerie silence crept over everything, punctuated only by the racking coughs of Stevie's death throes. Nothing to do but get out myself, Brax thought, looking at what was now the corpulent corpse of his boss's son.

Turning, Brax moved down the hallway, the gun extended in front of him, ready to fire at whatever moved. Nothing's gonna stop me from getting to that gate, he thought.

He came to the edge of the hallway exit. Moving to one side, he surveyed the flat platform that led to the stairway down to the courtyard. Once he got down there, he could cover the distance in a few seconds. Zigzagging to make himself a harder target for the arrows. Unless Tanaka had picked up a gun along the way ... That would be a problem. But Kiroshi had said the guy didn't operate that way. Old school, he'd called him. Traditional. A samurai.

Putting all that *bushido* crap out of his mind, Brax moved to the other wall and checked that direction also. It was clear, as far as he could see. Stepping onto the wooden platform, he did another fast survey and went to the steps. It was perhaps eighteen feet down to the court yard. How many rounds did he have left? He'd used three at the first shadow, one at the slit. That meant two left. Plenty of cushion. Something creaked under the porch as Brax stepped forward, but a quick look indicated nothing. He could feel the sweat starting to wind down his face, collecting on his neck, and running onto his back.

"Like I said," Brax muttered, "Never take a sword to a gunfight."

The best thing would be to just make a run for the front gate. Go out and try to find some way back to Tokyo. Maybe a cab or something. Hell, he'd even pay one of these farmers for a ride.

Brax turned and worked his way cautiously down the stairs, wheeling quickly from side to side.

He thought about calling out to Tanaka, telling him he had no quarrel with him. That he only wanted to leave. Maybe it would buy him passage, or trick the Jap into showing himself so he could get a clear shot. But yelling would only give away his position.

No, he thought. Got to keep moving. If the guy showed himself, he'd shoot first and say he was sorry later.

Two more steps and he'd be at the bottom. He surveyed the yard again. Nothing, except for a whole lot of bodies. Brax felt his feet on solid ground and was moving forward, toward the gate when a noise over to his left made him whirl. Nothing. He started to turn back, his gun arm still outstretched, when a shadow moved from under the wooden porch's support pillars, and something flashed in front of him.

He turned, trying to pull the trigger but his hand wouldn't work. Instead, he felt a strange numbness, and looked downward. The gun lay there, in front of his feet, his fingers still curled around it, the bloody cut that severed it from his wrist looking smooth and even. Like a chopped-off piece of meat. Something flittered in front of him and landed next to the gun on the ground. He squinted to see what it was in the poor light, and then, suddenly, he understood.

It was a black rose.

LIBBY FISCHER HELLMANN

LIBBY Hellmann writes the Chicago-based series featuring video producer and single mom Ellie Foreman. AN EYE FOR MURDER debuted in 2002 and was nominated for an Anthony Award. A PICTURE OF GUILT was released in 2003 and was nominated for a Benjamin Franklin. They were followed by AN IMAGE OF DEATH and A SHOT TO DIE FOR. All four were simultaneously published by Poisoned Pen Press (in hard cover) and Berkley Prime Crime (mass market). In addition, her short stories have appeared in American and British magazines. When not writing fiction, Libby produces industrial videos and trains individuals to be better speakers. She lives in the Chicago suburbs with her family and a beagle, shamelessly named Shiloh.

When asked about the appeal of assassin stories, Libby remarked: "This is the first hitperson story I've written; in fact, it's probably the first really hard-boiled story I've written. In a word, it was exhilarating! The freedom to venture out of my safe corner has been liberating—even cathartic. To create a character who has few boundaries, values the rest of us would abhor, and yet is true to her own—but skewed—moral code is exciting, sexy, and challenging. It unlocked something in me I never knew was there … I think I'm going to have to do more of this …"

Visit Libby at www.Hellmann.com

DETOUR
Libby Fischer Hellmann

I WASN'T EXPECTING a hit that hot August morning. I was barreling east on a stretch of 94 between Indiana and Michigan that just begs you to floor it. Newly paved, with two wide lanes, it's practically uninhabited at six in the morning. Compared to 96, or even 69, you feel like you're about to take off, like the frigging crows on the power lines at the side of the road. At least the ones that haven't been dropped by West Nile.

I'd headed out from the Michigan shores before dawn. I hadn't slept much—Christ—I hadn't even changed my clothes. I was still trying to figure out what the old lady was up to. I hadn't seen her—or the place—in ten years. Why did she invite me back? I'd been living in the Motor City, trying to keep a low profile, when all of a sudden the phone rings, and there she is with that high-class way of talking. You know, the kind that reminds you of your fourth-grade teacher. Asking could I please do her the honor of visiting?

The honor?

It'd been too long, she said, with just a trace of regret. We needed to catch up. I could stay overnight. She'd put me up in the guest cottage, she said, and we could bond. What was I, Elmer's Glue?

So I met her yesterday afternoon for tea. Tea, for Christ's sake. So bitter that even with sugar and cream it sucks out the insides of your cheeks. She had those stupid little sandwiches and biscuits. Scones, she called them—all arranged on a silver tray you only see at weddings. She also had this thick white stuff in a bowl. Clotted cream, she smiled. "You'll like it. It's sweet."

As she poured, she made small talk. How was I, Teresa dear? What was I doing? Such a shame about my father. Hey—no one calls me Teresa. It's Terry. Tare, sometimes, or TJ. But never Teresa. Who did she think she was, the Queen of England?

Afterwards I meant to grab a burger and a couple of boilermakers in town to rinse the taste of the tea out of my mouth, but I took a walk along the lake instead. The old lady's place went on forever now. Much farther than it used to. She'd bought up even more of her neighbors' land. I couldn't understand why. She didn't have any kids. What was she gonna do with it when she croaked? What is it they say, the rich get richer, and we get screwed?

It was after midnight when I got back to my room. I lay down on the bed, and the next thing I knew some bird was chirping outside the window, and it was four in the frigging morning. I took a quick shower and left. I wasn't looking forward to the drive home.

Once I was on 94 , I pulled into a truck stop for breakfast. Not only was I wiped, but I was starving. That's probably where he picked me up. I was wolfing down three eggs over easy with toast and bacon. A bunch of farmers in plaid shirts, jeans, scuffed boots were there. Plus one creep in a yellow slicker, even though the sun was blistering hot. There was a map of the state on the wall with one of those "you are here" pins stuck to it. Christ. I knew where I was. And where I was going. But I didn't think it meant trouble.

Thirty minutes later I was back on I-94, the oldies station blasting. My head was bobbing to Del Shannon's "Runaway" like one of those sappy little dogs you see in the back of cars when I caught him. At first I thought it was just some jerk riding my tail. A kid coming down from a wild night. Or a trucker in a car instead of an eighteen-wheeler. I switched lanes and slowed down, thinking the asshole would blow by me. But he didn't. He switched lanes, too, and slowed down.

He was in a blue Buick. Who drives a Buick anymore? I was in a gray Camry I'd ripped off last week. Had to be nearly six years old, but it still drove like a champ. I checked the rearview mirror. A man. Older, from what I could tell. Maybe fifty. Shades covering his eyes. Looked like he was wearing a sports coat. I frowned. It was close to ninety degrees already.

I floored it. The Camry hesitated for a second, like the transmission was about to AWOL. But then it gathered itself together and surged ahead. The lane dividers flashed past so fast the stripes ran together into one straight line. Kind of like the blades on a prop plane. Speaking of flying, I realized I was clocking almost a hundred. I checked the rear view. The creep was still on my ass.

I gripped the wheel. Who knew I was here? I thought about the last job I'd pulled. It'd been riskier than usual. I'd taken all the normal precautions. Stole some plates. Wore a disguise. Made sure to use a throw down. But I didn't figure the mark would have his kid with him. I don't do kids. I had to wait until he dropped the kid off. Which meant tailing him all afternoon. First to some fancy toy store in the mall whose name I couldn't even pronounce. Then to a bookstore. And then the Dairy Queen.

Too much time is a danger in my line of work. Things change. People take notice. Someone could have picked me up. He did have two bodyguards, but for all I knew, there could have been another—a guy who was supposed to watch the watchers.

I slowed and checked the rear view again. Still there. I fished out my cell phone and punched in a number. "Hey."

"Hey, babe. What's happening?" His voice was as smooth and mellow as always.

"You get the package for the last job?"

"Just came today. And very sweet it is. You do fine work."

"Yeah, well, you hear about anything strange going down?"

"What do you mean?" A trace of caution crept into his voice.

"Some guy's riding my ass." I explained what was going on.

"There's nothing on the street. In fact, I got another job for you. It's all lined up. You know, the jerk's probably just a redneck having some grins. You see that a lot in the country."

"I don't think so, Johnny."

There was a beat of silence. "Well, if makes you feel better, why don't you take the long way home?" That was code to hole up for a few days. "I'll be waiting for you whenever you show up. We need to spend time together."

I smiled as I disconnected. Johnny D was my boss. And my man. It didn't matter he was twenty years older than me. Or that he'd been one of Pop's buddies. His partner, as a matter of fact. Johnny D taught me a lot about my job. And after Pop died, he taught me other things. A shiver of pleasure ran up my spine.

I took another look in the rear view. The Buick was still there, but it was holding steady fifty yards back. Maybe Johnny D was right. Maybe this was just some joker getting his rocks off by scaring me. Like I said, I didn't get much sleep last night. I could be a little paranoid. I decided to hang tight for a few more minutes.

I thought back to my visit with the old lady. There was a lot of history between us. Pop used to do jobs for her. When he wasn't using a gun he was using a hammer, and for a long time he was the caretaker at her place. A huge estate overlooking Lake Michigan, it was in the kind of neighborhood no one pays much attention to. Mostly because the rich families who live there make sure of it. Private roads. Private beaches. Private clubs. There's a shitload of Detroit money up there, Pop used to say. And the old lady's place is sitting pretty, right in the middle of it.

Once I asked my father how he met her. He said he knew her husband first, and had promised Grayson—what kind of a name is Grayson?—that he'd look after the old lady if anything happened. And, wouldn't you know it, Grayson up and died one night. Helped along by the .38 slug that blew his brains over the desk and against the wall. But that was a long time ago, when I was still a little girl. After that we started to visit the old lady a couple of weeks in the summer. To make sure she was okay, Pop said.

At first my mother came too, and we stayed in the guest cottage. My mom, my dad, and me. Mom tried to pretend I was one of *those* girls. She even bought me this fancy white dress with lace all over it. Except I got a big fat blueberry stain on the front the first time I wore it. I never put it on again.

I always wondered if that's why she took off. It was only a few days later. Pop and I had been fixing a pipe in the old lady's kitchen, and we went back to clean up for supper. Mom wasn't there, but there was a note on the table. Pop read the note, then crumpled up the paper and pitched it into the trash. He didn't read it to me, and I was too scared to ask. I thought she left because the stain wouldn't come out of the dress. When I was older, though, I figured she just couldn't hack it. Pop once told me she liked living on the old lady's estate. Said it made her feel respectable. But I guess when you can't have what you want all the time, you want it even more. And when there's no chance in hell of getting it, you just give up.

Which is why I try not to want anything.

I checked the rear view again. The asshole was still there, but now he was closing. Christ. I didn't think a Buick had that much in it. Who was this creep? Who sent him? Johnny D said everything was quiet back in Detroit. Unless one of the mark's bodyguards had one of those bugs you stick to a car to track someone. I'd been thinking of getting something like that myself. Make my job a whole lot easier. Damn. I should have looked under the Camry at the truck stop.

But what if it wasn't the guy or his men? The only other person besides Johnny D who knew where I'd been was the old lady.

Think, Tare. What happened yesterday?

After the preliminaries, she started to talk about my father. She had this strange way of describing his work, using plain words but weird inflections, kind of like a drama queen, to get her point across. Either she didn't want to admit what he did, or she wasn't sure if I knew. Which made me realize she didn't know what I did, either. Then again, how could she? I hadn't seen her since I was fifteen, well before I started following in Pop's footsteps.

I decided two could play her game, and when she asked what I was up to, I kept it vague. "A little of this, a little of that," I said, shrugging my shoulders.

"Do you have any thoughts of going back to school, Teresa dear?"

"It's a little late for that."

"You're only thirty. It's never too late for an education," she smiled.

I shrugged again. "I never was much good in school."

"I see." She stirred her tea with this tiny little spoon, then set it down on her saucer.

We were circling each other like two wary cats. I guess she realized it too, because, all of a sudden, she came out with it. Did I know the kind of work Pop did?

"I think so." I answered cagily. "He worked for you."

She pressed her lips together. Did I ever hear from my mother?

"Nope." I shook my head.

Now, I looked in the rear view mirror. The tail was only thirty yards back. Much too close. I hunched my shoulders and squinted through the windshield. I was cruising over eighty, and there weren't any other cars on the road. No rest stops, either. But Pop taught me not to panic. "All you need is a plan, TJ. You got a plan, nine times out of ten, you can get out of a tight spot."

I tried to focus. Trees and billboards zipped by. A green sign said I was forty miles from Kalamazoo. It could have been forty million for all the good it'd do me. But then, on the side of the road, an orange sign flashed. Detour Ahead. A smaller sign underneath said that Route 131 was closed for repairs.

I was still in the left lane; I twisted around. Nothing on either side except the Buick. The detour was only half a mile ahead. I kept my foot on the gas. Pop used to say never advertise your plans. I tightened my seat belt. A quarter mile. I sucked in a breath. A few hundred yards. I veered sharply to the right and tore up the exit ramp. I threw myself off balance, but I managed to hold onto the Camry. I glanced at the speedometer. I was clocking in at 82.

As I charged up to the stop sign, I heard the screech of brakes. He'd overshot the exit! The plan had worked—I'd bought myself some time. I looked both ways down the road. On the left was a gas station and quick mart, then the entrance back to 94. On the right, nothing but farmland.

I turned right and nudged the Camry up to sixty. I sped by fields of corn and hayfields with bales of the stuff curled up like pinwheels. A farmhouse with a barn on the side. In between the fields were woods with lots of trees. Ahead of me on the left was a farmer riding a tractor. He stared at me as I passed. For him, it was just another day with nothing but work to do.

I opened the glove compartment and slid out my Sig. The nine has always been my favorite. Hardly any recoil. I slammed in the clip, then set the gun on the passenger seat.

I felt a chill on the back of my neck. When I looked in the rear view, I tensed. He was only a speck in the distance, but he'd be closing fast. I passed a few dirt paths that bisected the fields. They probably led back to homes or barns or storage sheds. Plenty of cover back there. Getting to it was the problem. Everything was out in the open. Too risky.

I kept driving. The Buick was gaining. My hands grew slick with sweat. Ahead of me were more woods. They ended at the side of a cornfield, but continued around the back. At the far edge of the field was a dirt road. As I got closer, I could see it led back into the woods.

I slowed and swerved onto the dirt path. Trails of dust blew up behind me. Damn! I might as well send up smoke signals. But I had no choice. I kept going. The path was studded with rocks, and the Camry lurched unevenly. I heard a squeal from the chassis. I couldn't think about it now. The woods were just ahead. A few more seconds. I let myself glance back at the road. The Buick was making the turn.

When I pulled into the woods, the Camry was swallowed up by trees and underbrush. No way was I going any farther. I braked and switched off the ignition. I opened the car door, grabbed the Sig, and launched myself into the brush. I thrashed through bushes, ignoring the branches and brambles that scratched my skin. The thicket was so dense I couldn't see much in any direction. I squatted on the ground and pointed the Sig back toward the road.

A minute later the Buick drove up. I heard the engine idling. I pulled back the slide on the Sig. He knew I was hiding. He wouldn't get out of the car without reason. Still, the longer he waited, the edgier he'd get. Another lesson from Pop. Be patient and let him come to me.

I was ready. It was silent. Even the bees stopped buzzing. My calves started to cramp. All that crap about women crouching in the fields to give birth and then getting up to work was bullshit. No way could you stay in this position for long. I swatted away the gnats and tried to work out why the old lady sent him. I thought back to her questions. She'd been fishing—she wanted to know how much I knew.

What she didn't know is that I was fishing too. See, when Pop died last year, he left me a letter. Written in a scrawl with all those spelling mistakes, it said he wanted to clear the record. Seems as if after her husband died, one of her neighbors put some heat on her to sell her land. She asked my father for help, and two months later, the neighbor dropped dead of a heart attack. Instead of the neighbor buying her out, she was the one who bought. A few years after that, when the neighbor on the other side tried the same thing, he died in a car accident. The old lady ended up with a compound that stretched over a mile of lakefront property.

But I knew all that before I went to see her. In fact, that's why I went. Pop's death had been real sudden. One night he was fine, and the next morning, he keeled over. The doctors said it was a heart attack. He was almost seventy, he liked booze and cigars, and he ate all the wrong things. But there are chemicals that can simulate heart attacks, and any professional knows how to use them. So when Pop said he had visited the old lady before he died, well, let's just say coincidence isn't a word in my vocabulary.

But now I realized she must have figured out I knew. Don't know how. I thought I'd been careful not to spill anything. Unless Pop told her I knew before he died. Which meant the guy following me was hers. She had the connections—hell, Pop probably gave 'em to her. "Use him for back-up," I could hear him saying, "if I'm not around to help you out."

A car door squeaked. I tore myself back to the present. With one hand I grasped the end of a branch and carefully pulled it back. I caught a glimpse of the Buick. The driver's door was open, but there was no sign of the goon. I kept perfectly still. Just one opening. That's all I needed.

Suddenly he stepped in front of the car door, his gun drawn. He started toward the bushes. Christ. Had he spotted me? My heart went ballistic, and it was tough to breathe. Then he stopped, uncertain, maybe, which way to go. It was only a brief moment, but it was enough. I raised the Sig, aimed, and squeezed the trigger.

I waited until I knew he wasn't going anywhere, then scrambled to my feet. I rolled him and found a few hundred in his billfold. I stuffed them in my jeans. I didn't expect to find any ID, and I didn't. The road looked deserted, but I dragged his body back into the woods. When I got back to the Camry, I stripped the plates and wiped all the surfaces. Then, just for the hell of it, I checked under the car. No bug. I got all my stuff out of the back then inched the car as far into the brush as I could. With luck they wouldn't find it for a few weeks. Hell, maybe the whole season.

The door to the Buick was still open, and the keys were in ignition. I slid into the front with the Sig beside me. I backed out onto the road, running through the checklist Pop taught me. Everything was accounted for. Even the farmer I passed on the way had left.

✛

IT WASN'T HARD to take care of the old lady. She was still in her bathrobe, her clothes laid out on the bed. She didn't scream or struggle when I broke in—it was almost like she was expecting me. I didn't say anything, and I was quiet when I used the pillow. I didn't want one of the maids barging in. I wore gloves, and made sure there were no marks. With luck they'd think she had a heart attack. But even if they didn't, the only thing the cops would have was a description of a blue Buick, not a Camry. Afterwards, I slipped out the door and for second time that day, headed back to 94. I ditched the Buick just outside Detroit and hitched the rest of the way.

I lay low for a few days in case there was any heat. I didn't even call Johnny D. I saw something in the paper about the old lady's death—they said it was a heart attack—but there was nothing about a Camry or a body in the woods near a cornfield. After four days I was running out of clothes and money, so I decided to go home. I staked out the place until two in morning before I went in. Nothing suspicious.

I didn't check my messages till the next morning. There were three: two from Johnny D and the third a thin nasally voice I didn't recognize. Said he was Kenneth McCarthy, the old lady's lawyer. I grabbed some clothes, stuffed them in a gym bag, then pried up the floorboard next to the bathroom. I threw my entire stash into the bag, grabbed the keys to my Honda, and bolted.

It took an hour of driving around to realize I probably panicked for nothing. If someone out there had made me, the call would have been from the cops, not a lawyer. And theirs would have been in person. This had to be something else. I drove to a diner for some food. Behind the register were these crummy little paperweights with tiny dogs and cats and butterflies suspended inside a glass ball. The butterfly had some silver stuff on its wings, and it sparkled in the light. I could hardly take my eyes off it.

After I ate, I called the man from a pay phone.

"Teresa Nichols?" The nasally voice asked after I'd waited about a year on hold.

"You got her."

"Yes, well …" McCarthy cleared his throat but when he spoke again, his voice was still nasally. Almost whiny. "It seems as if you've been named the sole beneficiary of my client's will."

"What?"

"My client has left everything to you. The estate. The bank accounts. The investments. Even her jewelry. Over ten million dollars in assets."

"Are you fuck—I mean are you out of your mind?"

He cleared his throat again. "There's a letter for you from her. It's marked confidential. If you'd like to come down to our offices, I can give it to you personally."

Yeah, right. I wasn't born yesterday. "Why don't you read it to me?"

"As I said, it's marked confidential."

"You got my permission."

"You won't mind putting that in writing?"

"What the—sure—whatever."

"In that case, well …" I heard the rip of an envelope, the crackle of paper. His tone was so emotionless he could have been reading a grocery list.

"Dearest Teresa,
After Grayson died, your father was my confidante and clos-
est friend. But you were the most precious thing in his life.
He always wanted to give you a better life, and he never
stopped trying. He talked about you so much I felt like I knew
you. And though I wasn't your birth mother, I loved you, too.
Now that I'm gone, I'm in a position to help your father ex-
press his love for you. Just consider it my way of repaying
all the favors."

The lawyer was quiet. I stared out at the street but to this day, I don't remember what I saw.

"Miss Nichols, are you there?"

"Yeah." I grunted after a pause.

He started spewing details about what I was supposed to do and when, but I wasn't paying attention. He said he'd send me a registered letter and checked my address. I hung up the phone and started to walk back to the car. My head was spinning. The old lady didn't order the hit. I took out the wrong target. And now I was rich. I massaged my temples.

But if she didn't do it, who did? I stopped. There was only one other person who knew where I was going. Johnny D. He knew everything about my father. He'd been there when Pop died. He was the only man I trusted. We'd even had our wills done together. He'd promised Pop, he said. It was the best way to protect me from the occupational hazards of our jobs.

I walked around some more, then headed back to the car. I had one more job to do. It would probably be my last. But I'd do it, and I'd do it well. Pop would have wanted me to. The old lady, too. But first maybe I'd go back to that diner and buy the frigging butterfly.

DAVID MORRELL

DAVID Morrell is the award-winning author of FIRST BLOOD, the novel in which Rambo first appeared. He holds a PhD in American literature from the Pennsylvania State University and taught at the University of Iowa until he gave up his tenure to devote himself to a full-time writing career. "The mild-mannered professor with the bloody-minded visions," as one reviewer called him, Morrell has written numerous best-selling thrillers that include THE BROTHERHOOD OF THE ROSE (the basis for a highly rated NBC miniseries), THE PROTECTOR (which features Cavanaugh, the hero of this story), and CREEPERS, his latest. Eighteen million copies of his books are in print. His fiction has been translated into twenty-six languages.

On the topic of this anthology, Morrell comments: "Stories about hitmen take us to the edge of our civilization and perhaps also to the core of it. Dispassionate violence. Indifferent brutality. Somehow, during recent decades, these became familiar rather than exceptions. *In Cold Blood* now seems almost quaint. Perhaps stories about hitmen can help us understand where we are and how our society needs to change."

Visit his website at www.DavidMorrell.net.

THE ATTITUDE ADJUSTER
David Morrell

A ROAD-RENOVATION crew. Trucks, grinders, roll-
ers. Only one lane of traffic is open. As you drive toward the
dust and noise, a man holds a pole with a sign at the top. The
pole's bottom rests on the dirt so all he needs to do is turn the
shaft to show you one side of the sign or the other. SLOW, you
are directed, or else STOP.

The man is tall and scarecrow lanky, exuding the impression
of sinewy strength. He wears battered work boots, faded jeans,
and an old blue work shirt with the sleeves rolled up, revealing
a rose tattoo above the hand with which he holds the pole. His
shirt has sweat blotches. His face is narrow, sun-browned, and
weather-creased. He wears a yellow vest and hard hat.

According to the radio's weather forecaster, the temperature on this Illinois August day is ninety degrees Fahrenheit,
with eighty-seven percent humidity. But the sun radiates off
the road, increasing the temperature to one hundred. Because
the project is behind schedule, the man is required to work
overtime. He has held his sign twelve hours a day for the past
three months. You've seen countless versions of him. Passing
him, you never wonder what he thinks.

*Stupid son of a bitch. Sits in his damned air-conditioned
SUV, stares at my sign, speeds past, almost hits me, throws dust
in my face. Can't you read, you moron? The sign says SLOW!
One of these days, I'll whack this pole against a fender, hell,
through a back window. Teach these bastards to show respect.*

Everybody's got a snotty attitude. Here comes another guy barreling toward me. King of the road. Hey, see this sign I'm pointing at, dummy! SLOW! It says SLOW!

The man's name is Barry Pollard. He is thirty-nine, but years of working outdoors have made him look much older. His previous jobs involved strenuous physical labor, lifting, carrying, digging, hammering, which he never minded because he felt satisfied when he had something to fill the time, to weary him and shut off his thoughts. But months of nothing to do except stand in the middle of the road, hold the sign, and watch motorists ignore it have given him plenty of opportunity to draw conclusions about the passing world.

Dodo, how'd you ever get a driver's license if you can't read? The sign says SLOW. For God's sake, you came so close, you almost knocked it out of my hand! You think you can do whatever you want? That's what's wrong these days. Nobody pays attention to the rules. When I was a kid, if I even thought about doing something my old man didn't like, he set down his beer can and punched me to the floor. Certainly taught me right from wrong. 'You've got a bad attitude,' he used to tell me. 'We gotta correct it.' From what I've seen the past three months, there's a lot of bad attitudes that need correcting.

A voice squawked from a walkie-talkie hooked to Barry's belt. "Okay, that's enough cars going north for a while. Stop 'em at your end while the cars on *my* side get a chance to go through."

"Roger," Barry said into the walkie-talkie, feeling a little like he was in the military. He swung his sign so the message now read STOP.

A guy in a van tried to go past.

"Hey!" Barry shouted and jerked his sign down in front of the windshield.

The guy barely stopped before the pole would have cracked the glass.

"Back up and get off the road!" Barry shouted. "There's a bunch of cars coming this way!"

Red-faced, the guy charged from the van. "You almost broke my windshield!"

"I could have, but I didn't!" Barry said. "Maybe next time!"

"You jerk, I ought to—"

Barry pointed the pole at the guy. "Oughta what? I told you to back up your van and get off the road. You're interfering with the project."

"You could have waited to stop traffic until I went past!"

"When the boss tells me to stop vehicles, I do it. You think you're more important than the guy in the car behind you. I should stop *him* but not *you?*"

"I've got a job I need to get to!"

"And *he* doesn't have some place to go? You think you're a big shot? A VIP? That stands for Very Important Prick. An attitude like yours, it's no wonder the country's going to hell. Here comes the other traffic, bozo! *Move your vehicle.*"

The guy spit on Barry's work boots, then stormed back to his van.

Barry stared down at the spit.

A sign on the van read MIDWEST CABLE AND HIGH-SPEED INTERNET INSTALLATION. A phone number was under it, along with a Rockford, Illinois address. As the guy got into the truck and backed from approaching traffic, Barry took his cell phone from his belt and pressed numbers.

"Midwest Cable," a female voice said.

"One of your installers was at my place today. He did such a good job, I thought I'd phone and tell you how impressed I am."

"What's his name?"

"Just a second. I've got his … Of all the … Dumb me, I lost the card he gave me. He's about forty-five. Kind of on the heavy side. Real short red hair."

"Yeah, that's Fred Harriman."

"He did a great job."

At seven, after the job shut down for the day, Barry drove into nearby Rockford, stopped at a convenience store, found Fred Harriman's name in the phone book, and made a note of his address. He waited a month, wanting to be certain that no one at the cable company would remember his phone call. At last, he drove to Fred's neighborhood, passed a white ranch house with two big flower beds, saw a pickup truck in the driveway, and stopped at a park down the street. With lots of other cars near him, no one paid attention as Barry watched the truck. Soon, the sun set, and the people in the park went home, but Barry continued watching. The house's lights were on. Curtains were drawn.

At nine thirty, as Barry began to worry that a police car would cruise the area and wonder why he was sitting alone in a car in the dark, the front door opened. Fred came out, got in the truck, and drove away.

Barry followed him to a bar called the Seventh Inning Stretch, where Fred joined a couple of buddies at a table, drank a pitcher of beer, and watched the end of a baseball game. They cursed when the Cubs didn't win. Fred was such a putz, he didn't notice Barry watching among drinkers in the background. But Barry was gone when they paid for their beers.

In the shadowy parking lot, they made a couple of jokes. One of them burped. They went to their separate vehicles. Fred got to his about the same time the others got to theirs. He climbed into the truck, started to drive away, then felt something was wrong, and got out. The shadows were so dense that he had to crouch to see the flat tire on the front passenger side. He cursed more seriously than when the Cubs lost. His pals were gone. As he straightened and turned toward the locked tool kit in back of his truck, he groaned from a two-by-four to the side of his jaw, although he never knew what hit him or saw who did it. Barry felt the satisfying crunch of flesh and crack of bone. To make it look like a mugging, Barry took all the cash from Fred's wallet.

Two weeks later, the road work was finished. With time on his hands, Barry unhappily discovered that everywhere he went, people had attitude problems. A guy in a sports car cut him off at an intersection and gave him the finger when Barry blared his horn. A woman pushed in front of him at Starbucks. A clerk at a convenience store made him wait while the clerk used the store's phone to gab with his girlfriend. A waiter at a diner brought him a bacon and tomato sandwich that had mayonnaise, even though Barry had distinctly told him he didn't want any mayo. When Barry complained, the waiter took the sandwich away and brought a replacement, but when Barry opened it, he saw traces of white. All the waiter had done was scrape some off.

"I wouldn't go into that warehouse," a woman said.

"The cop should radio for backup," the man next to her said.

"He didn't radio for backup when he searched the abandoned house, either."

"Well, if he did, the stupid writers wouldn't have a plot."

"Please, be quiet," Barry said.

"And look at this. The lights don't work, and he doesn't have a flashlight, but he's going inside anyhow."

"Please, don't talk during the movie," Barry said.

"Yep, here's the vampire sneaking up on—"

"SHUT THE HELL UP!"

The man turned and glared. "Have you got a problem, buddy?"

"This isn't your living room! I'm trying to—"

"You want me to shut up?"

"That's what I've been trying to—"

"Make me."

Barry left the theater, waited outside, followed the couple home, and taught them to shut up by knocking their teeth out. Then he smashed all their TV sets and set fire to their car. Another job well done.

"There, your computer system's updated," the Midwest Cable installer said.

"High-speed Internet." Barry marveled. "I saw one of your company's trucks the other day and figured it was time I joined the twenty-first century."

FOLLOW ANYBODY ANYWHERE, the pop-up ad announced:

JUST HIDE THIS TINY RADIO TRANSMITTER ON THEIR CLOTHES OR IN THEIR BRIEFCASE OR THEIR PURSE. IT GIVES OFF A SILENT BEEP THAT ONLY YOU CAN HEAR THROUGH YOUR MATCHING RADIO RECEIVER.

But when Barry got the transmitter, it was the size of a walkie-talkie and the even-larger radio receiver needed to be no more than thirty feet from the transmitter or else Barry couldn't hear the beep.

He sent an email, asking for his money back, but never got an answer. He repeatedly phoned the number on the company's website, but all he ever heard was a recorded message, telling him that "every available technician is talking with another customer."

Barry drove four hours to St. Louis, where the company had its post-office box. From his car in the parking lot outside the post office, he stared through windows toward the company's PO box. After a rumpled guy took envelopes from the box, Barry followed him to an office above an escort service. When Barry finished teaching the guy the error of his ways, he had his money back, plus the guy's FOLLOW ANYWHERE business card, which allowed Barry to cash all the money orders in the envelopes (no checks accepted, the ad had warned).

Compensation for my time, Barry thought. It's only fair. Back home after the long drive, he counted his money, eight hundred dollars, and opened another beer. Sure beats standing on the road, holding that damned sign. He chased a shot of bourbon with a gulp of beer and told himself that he was actually performing a public service. Protecting people from jerks. You bet. Teaching bozos to mend their ways.

He slumped on his sofa, chuckling at the thought that some guys with attitude problems might even be thankful if Barry set them straight. *For all I know, they're ashamed of being dorks. Like my father said, everybody knows they need direction.*

Amused, Barry staggered to his computer. Alcohol made his fingers clumsy. He thanked God for the computer's spell-check program. After all, he needed to make the proper impression.

E-BOD
THE ADULT ALTERNATIVE TO EBAY
LOWER COMMISSION—LESS
INTERFERENCE—MORE FUN
SELLERS ASSUME ALL RESPONSIBILITIES
FOR LISTING ITEMS

I WILL ADJUST YOUR WAYS
ITEM 44735ABQE

High bidder receives an attitude adjustment. I am strong and tough from years of outdoor work. If you win this auction, I will teach you to walk the straight and narrow. I promise not to cripple or kill you. No weapons, just my boots and fists. Maybe a club, depending on how much your attitude needs adjusting.

(Barry chuckled.)

I will perform this service only if you promise not to resist and not to have me arrested afterward.

(Clever, Barry thought.)

You will provide travel expenses and directions to your home and work. You will also provide motel expenses, but these should be low because I plan to do the job swiftly so that I can proceed to other adjustments. I will pick a time that you least expect. Perhaps while you're asleep or in the bathroom or going to work. During your adjustment, I may be forced to break windows or furniture. Those are your responsibility. If you have a family or whatever, warn them to stay out of my way unless you want their attitudes adjusted also.

(Barry laughed.)

No checks or PAYPAL. I only accept money orders made out to CASH. Good luck in the auction.

The next morning, Barry foggily remembered what he had done and cursed himself for wasting time when he could have continued drinking. E-bod was part of a porn site, for God's sake. The only reason he'd used it was that eBay wouldn't have allowed him to post his auction. For all he knew, nobody visited that portion of the site, and anyway, who's going to bid on getting beat up? he asked himself. To prove his point, all week he didn't get a response.

Then, on Sunday, with a half hour to go in the auction, he received the following:

QUESTION TO SELLER

I thought about your auction quite a while. All week, every day and night. I have done something bad that makes me feel awful. I can't stop thinking about it. I need to be punished. How could I have done such a terrible thing? Are you serious that you won't kill me? I'm a devout Roman Catholic, and if you kill me, God might see it as suicide. Then I'd

*go to Hell. I need to know that you won't endanger
my soul, which is in danger enough already.*

✛

DAN **Y**ATES STUCK the OPEN HOUSE sign into the
lush lawn and walked past rose bushes toward the two-story
Spanish Colonial Revival. Another sign was prominently displayed: YATES REALTY, under which was a phone number and
a website address. He wore a navy sport coat, white shirt, and
conservative tie. He paused on the porch, surveyed the handsome yard and pleasant neighborhood, and nodded with confidence that someone would make an offer by the end of the
afternoon. He left the front door open, then proceeded to the
kitchen, where he brewed coffee and arranged cookies next to
bowls of peanuts and potato chips. He set out bottled water and
canned sodas. He stacked brochures with eye-catching photographs of the house and information about it. $949,000. Two
months ago, the price had been $899,000, but low mortgage
rates were creating a real-estate frenzy. The smart tactic now
was to encourage potential buyers to bid against each other and
raise the price to the $999,000 that the owners wanted.

His preparations completed, Dan gave his best smile to
his first visitors, a man and a woman, who were obviously impressed by the marble-floored kitchen but tried not to show it.
Thirty seconds later, another couple arrived, then another soon
after, and the show was on.

"The house is three years old. This subdivision used to
be the Huntington Beach airport. As you can see, there's no
house behind you, only this low attractive wall beyond which
is a Mormon church. Very quiet. Plenty of sky. You attend
that church? The Latter Day Saints? My, this house would
certainly be convenient for you. On Sundays, you could practically crawl over the wall and go to services. The subdivision has
its own swimming pool and park. There's a golf course down

the street as well as a shopping center three blocks away and a school three blocks in the other direction. You've heard the old saying about what makes property valuable? Location, location, location. Five minutes to the beach. Honestly, this has it all."

And so it went, forty visitors, three promises to make offers and one firm offer for cash. Not a bad afternoon's work, Dan thought. "The owners are vacationing in Hawaii," he told the prospective buyers. "I'll fax the material to them. They have until noon tomorrow to respond. I'll let you know what they say as soon as possible." He escorted the couple to the door, checked his watch, saw that the hours for the open house were over, and allowed himself to relax. When the last visitors drove away, he went to the street and put the OPEN HOUSE sign in his SUV. He returned to the kitchen, where he cleaned the coffee maker and cups. He put all the empty cans and bottles into a garbage bag along with the coffee grounds and the remnants of the cookies, the peanuts, and the potato chips.

The Baxters are coming for dinner, he thought. Sarah's expecting me to bring home the steaks. I'd better hurry. Giving the kitchen a final inspection, he saw movement to the right and turned toward a lanky man standing in the doorway to the living room. The guy had a creased, rugged face. He wore sneakers, jeans, and a pullover. His hair was scraggly.

"I'm sorry," Dan said. "The open house is over. I was just about to leave and lock up."

"I warned you I'd show up when you least expected," the man said.

"Excuse me?" Dan asked.

"You've been bad."

"What the hell are you talking about?"

"Your attitude adjustment."

"Adjustment?"

"The one you paid for. You're Dan Yates, correct?"

"That's my name, but—"

"Two-one-five Sunnyvale Lane?"

"How do you know my—"

"No sense in putting it off." The guy shoved up his long sleeves, as if getting ready for physical labor. He had a rose tattoo on his right forearm.

"Look, I don't get the joke. Now if you'll come with me, we'll step outside and—"

"No joke. You bid on the attitude adjustment. You won the auction. Now you get what you deserve. I don't know what you did that was so terrible, but I swear I'll ease your conscience. You'll be sore, but you'll feel a whole lot better after I finish with you."

Dan reached for his cell phone. The man threw it against the wall, punched him in the stomach, kneed him in the face, whacked his cheek, struck his nose, then started beating him in earnest.

At five, when Dan didn't return home with the steaks for the dinner with the Baxters, his wife Sarah called his cell phone. An electronic voice announced, "That number is out of service." Out of service? Sarah wondered. She called several more times, with the same response. The Baxters arrived at six. At seven, when Dan still had not arrived, Sarah phoned the police, but no one named Dan Yates had been reported in a traffic accident. The Baxters agreed to watch the Yates's ten-year-old daughter while Sarah went to where Dan had the open house. The front door was unlocked. She found him unconscious on the kitchen's marble floor, lying in a pool of blood.

"Fractured arm, ribs, and clavicle," an emergency-ward doctor told her after an ambulance hurried Dan to the nearest hospital.

"Auction. Rose tattoo," Dan murmured as he drifted in and out of consciousness.

"Must be the pain killers. The poor guy's delirious," a police detective said.

Barry, who had never been to California, used the generous travel fee he'd demanded to stay a few extra days. He watched the surfers near Huntington Beach's famous pier. He planned to drive north to Los Angeles and cruise Hollywood

Boulevard, then head up to Malibu. With luck, he'd cross paths with movie stars.

Those plans ended when he read the next morning's edition of *The Orange County Register*. With increasing anger, he learned that Dan Yates had attempted to identify him. *Auction. Rose tattoo.* That wasn't the damned deal! Barry thought as joggers passed him at the beach. You weren't supposed to resist, and you weren't supposed to try to have me arrested afterward! Doesn't anybody keep his word? Didn't I adjust your attitude hard enough?

"Dan Yates's room."

"Are you a member of his family?" the hospital receptionist asked.

"Brother."

"Eight forty-two."

One of many things Barry learned while holding the sign for the road crew was that people got so absorbed in their affairs, they didn't pay attention to what was around them. They'd drive over you before they noticed you. Walking along the hospital corridor, a newspaper in one hand, a bunch of flowers in the other, just one of many visitors, he might as well have been invisible. The door to room eight forty-two was open. He passed it, glancing in at banged-up Dan lying in a bed, the only patient in the room. Dan's face looked like a raw beefsteak. Various monitors were attached to him. An IV tube led into his arm.

I'd almost feel sorry for you if you hadn't broken our agreement, Barry thought.

A not-bad-looking woman sat next to Dan. Roughly Dan's age, she was pale with worry. The wife, Barry decided.

That was all he saw as he continued down the corridor. He went into a men's room, lingered, then came out, and returned along the corridor. Visiting hours were almost over. People emerged from various rooms and headed toward the elevators. The woman left Dan's room and did the same.

Barry went into Dan's room, used a knee to close the door, set down the flowers, and pulled his shirt sleeve over his hand so he wouldn't leave fingerprints. He turned off the monitors, grabbed a hospital gown from a table, shielded himself, pulled a section of garden hose from the newspaper, and whacked Dan several times across the face. Blood flew. He set the crimson-soaked section of hose on Dan's chest, dropped the spattered gown, opened the door, and went down the corridor with the other departing visitors.

Twenty seconds, Barry thought. Damned good.

A nurse went into Dan's room and screamed. After ringing for an emergency team, she hurried to turn on the monitors, which immediately began wailing, the waves and numbers showing that at least Dan was still alive.

Keep our agreement, jerk, or you'll get an even worse adjustment, a typed note with the flowers said.

"Mrs. Yates, do you know anything about the agreement the note refers to?" a detective asked.

"I haven't the faintest idea." Sarah trembled.

"Any idea what the reference to 'worse adjustment' means?"

"No." Sarah wept.

From:Sarah Yates <earthlink.net>
To: <jamietravers@gps.com>
Subject: trouble, postpone visit
Jamie, I hate to do this at the last minute, but I've been so worried and tired that I haven't had the time or energy to send an email. I've got so much trouble. I need to withdraw my invitation for you and your husband to stay with us for a few days while you're in LA on business. Dan was nearly beaten to death on Sunday afternoon at an open house he was giving. Then he was beaten again in his hospital room. We have no idea who on earth did it or why. I spend

so much time with him at the hospital that I won't be able to see you. Plus, I'm so sick with worry that I won't be very good company. Sorry. I was looking forward to meeting your husband and reminiscing about our sorority days. Life can sure change quickly. Sarah.

From:Jamie Travers <gps.com>
To: sarahyates@earthlink.net
Subject: coming regardless
Sarah, Since we're in the area, we've decided to visit you anyhow. But you won't have to babysit us. This won't exactly be a social occasion. My husband's in a line of work that might be helpful to you. I'm pretty good at it myself. Apologies for sounding mysterious. It's too complicated to explain in an email. Kind of a secret life I have. All will be revealed tomorrow. What's the name and address of the hospital? Can we meet you there at noon? We'll see if we can sort this out. Don't despair. Love, Jamie.

Although Sarah hadn't seen Jamie in five years, her former college roommate looked as radiant as ever. Five feet ten, with a jogger's slim build. A model's narrow chin and high cheek bones. Long brunette hair. Bright green eyes. She wore brown linen slacks, and a loose-fitting jacket over a beige blouse. But Sarah processed these details only later, so distracted by her emotions that all she wanted to do was hug Jamie as she came into the room.

Sarah wept again. She'd been doing a lot of it. "I'm so glad to see you."

"You couldn't have kept me away," Jamie said.

Sarah's tear-blurred gaze drifted toward the man next to her.

"This is my husband," Jamie said proudly. "His name's Cavanaugh. And this is my good friend Sarah," she told her husband. "She and I raised a lot of hell at Wellesley."

"Pleased to meet you," the man said. Again, Sarah paid attention to his appearance only later. He was around six feet tall, solid looking, especially at his chest and shoulders. Handsome, with a strong chin and forehead that somehow didn't intimidate. Hair that wasn't quite brown and not quite sandy, not long but not short. Alert eyes that were hazel and yet seemed to reflect the blue of his loose sports coat. He had an odd-looking black metal clip on the outside of a pants pocket. But all that mattered was his handshake, which was firm yet gentle and seemed to communicate a reassurance that as long as you were with him, you were secure.

"Cavanaugh?" she asked. "What's your first name?"

"Actually"—he grinned—"I've gotten in the habit of just being called 'Cavanaugh'."

Sarah looked at Jamie. "You call him by his last name?"

"It's sort of complicated," Jamie said.

"But it sounds kind of cold."

"Well, when I want to be friendly, I call him something else."

"What's that?"

"'Lover.'"

"Perhaps I should leave the room," Cavanaugh said.

"No, stick around," Jamie said. "We're finished talking about you. You're not the center of attention anymore."

Cavanaugh nodded. "*He* is."

They turned toward Dan, who lay unconscious in the hospital bed, all sorts of equipment and tubes linked to him. His face was purple with bruises.

"Sarah, the initials gps on my website address stand for Global Protective Services," Jamie said. "My husband watches over people in trouble. He takes care of them. He's a protector."

Sarah frowned, puzzled.

"Sometimes I help," Jamie said. "That's why we're here. To find out what happened."

"And make sure it doesn't happen again," Cavanaugh said.

"But I *don't know* what happened, only that Dan was attacked. *Twice*." Sarah's voice shook.

"Tell us what you can," Jamie said. "Tell us about Sunday."

Ten minutes later, wiping more tears from her cheeks, Sarah finished explaining.

"'Agreement'?" Cavanaugh asked. "'Worse adjustment'?"

"That's what the note mentioned. I don't understand *any* of it." Sarah raised her hands in a gesture of helplessness.

"Has Dan been able to say anything?" Jamie asked.

"Nothing that makes sense."

Unconscious, Dan fidgeted and groaned.

Cavanaugh studied the room and frowned. "Why isn't someone watching the door?"

"The police said they don't have the budget to keep an officer here."

"Jamie said you had a daughter."

"Yes. Meredith. She's ten years old."

"And where is she now?"

"At school. I need to pick her up at two forty-five. She's worried sick about her father."

Cavanaugh pulled out his cell phone and pressed numbers. "Vince," he said when someone answered, "can you stand it if you don't do any sightseeing in LA? I need you to come down to Huntington Beach." Cavanaugh mentioned the name of the hospital. "A patient needs watching. Dan Yates. Jamie went to college with his wife. That's right—this one's for friendship. I'll fill you in when you get here. If Gwen's available, bring her with you. A little girl needs watching. Great. Thanks."

Cavanaugh put away his phone and told Sarah, "They're a brother and sister team. We brought them with us on the Gulfstream for a job that starts two days from now."

"Gulfstream?" Sarah looked more bewildered.

"Global Protective Services has a lot of resources," Jamie said. "That's why I married him."

It was a joke. Jamie, who sold a promising dot-com company during the Internet stock frenzy of the 1990s, owned plenty of resources of her own.

"Sarah, we need to ask the obvious question," Jamie said. "Does Dan have any enemies?"

"Enemies?" Sarah made the word sound meaningless.

"Surely, the police asked you the same question."

"Yes, but ... Enemies? Dan's the nicest man in the world. Everybody likes him."

"From everything Jamie told me, he's kind and decent," Cavanaugh agreed.

"That's right."

"A loving husband. An attentive father."

Sarah wiped her eyes. "Absolutely."

"Good-natured. Generous."

Sarah frowned. "Where are you going with this?"

"In my experience, a certain type of person hates those virtues," Cavanaugh said. "Despises anyone who exhibits them. Takes for granted that someone who's kind and good-natured is weak. Assumes he or she is a mark to be exploited."

Sarah looked at Jamie in confusion and then again at Cavanaugh. "That's awfully cynical, don't you think?"

"I work in a cynical profession," Cavanaugh said. "You'd be surprised how many kind, good-natured, generous people have enemies."

Sarah, who'd been thinking a lot about the times she and Jamie shared at Wellesley, recalled an American fiction course they'd taken. "*Billy Budd?*" She referred to a work by Herman Melville, in which a ship's officer hates a kind-hearted sailor simply because he's kind-hearted.

"Something like that," Cavanaugh said. "Some people—sociopaths—get their kicks taking advantage of what they consider weakness."

"Then *anybody* could be Dan's enemy."

"It's just something to think about," Jamie said. "The point is, often the enemy isn't obvious."

"Often, it's someone who appears to be a close friend," Cavanaugh said. "You mentioned *Billy Budd*. Think about Iago in *Othello*."

Again Sarah looked at Jamie. She might have been trying to change the subject. "I doubt many bodyguards know Shakespeare."

"Not a bodyguard," Jamie said. "A protector. As you'll see, there's a difference. We need to consider something else, Sarah. Please, don't take this wrong. Don't be offended. Are you absolutely certain Dan's faithful to you?"

"What?" Sarah's cheeks reddened.

"Stalkers tend to be motivated by sexual anger," Cavanaugh said. "If Dan were having an affair, if the woman were married, the husband might have been furious enough to attack Dan. Or if Dan tried to call off the affair, the woman might have hired someone to put him in the hospital. 'Keep our agreement, jerk, or you'll get an even worse adjustment.' The note can be interpreted to fit that scenario."

"I don't want to talk about this anymore."

"I understand," Cavanaugh said. "I'm a stranger, and suddenly I'm asking rude questions. I apologize. But I did need to ask, and now it's important for you to look at your world in a way you never imagined. Suppose someone thought Dan was making sexual overtures even when he was perfectly innocent. Did you ever have a fleeting suspicion that someone was needlessly jealous? If we're going to find who did this to your husband and stop it from happening again, we might need to suspect what seemingly couldn't be suspected."

Sarah eased into a chair. "I don't feel well."

"I'm surprised you're holding up as strongly as you are," Cavanaugh said. "Why don't you let Jamie take you home? There's nothing you can do for Dan at the moment. Get some rest."

Sarah looked at Dan unconscious in the bed. "But …"

"I'll stay with him. Nothing's going to happen to him here. I promise."

Sarah studied Cavanaugh for several long seconds. "Yes," she finally said. "I could use some rest."

Jamie helped her to stand. As they walked toward the door, Sarah turned and studied him again. "What's that metal clip on the outside of your pants pocket?"

"This." Cavanaugh pulled on the clip and drew a black folding knife that he opened by torquing his thumb against a button on the back of the blade. He touched his loose-fitting jacket. "I also carry a firearm that I have a permit for."

"So do I," Jamie said.

Bewildered but more certain of the reassurance they communicated, Sarah let Jamie guide her from the room.

⊕

CAVANAUGH IDENTIFIED HIMSELF to a nurse and doctor who came in. They frowned and yet seemed relieved by his presence. Sitting next to the door, out of sight from the hallway, he performed the hardest, tensest activity in his profession: waiting. Bodyguards might pass the time by reading, but protectors didn't distract themselves—they watched.

In a while, he sensed a change in Dan and glanced toward the bed, keeping most of his attention on the doorway.

Dan's bloodshot eyes were open, squinting. "Who …"

"I'm a friend."

Dan's eyes closed.

In a further while, a man walked into the room. Like Cavanaugh, he had strong-looking shoulders and wore a loose sport coat. He looked immediately toward Cavanaugh's sheltered position next to the door, as if that were the proper place for Cavanaugh to be.

"Vince, thanks for coming," Cavanaugh said.

"Well, you said the magic word 'friendship.'"

"Where's Gwen?" Cavanaugh asked.

"Jamie phoned and gave me directions to this guy's house. They're picking up the little girl from school."

"That finally covers the bases," Cavanaugh said.

Again, Dan's eyes struggled open. "Who ..." He squinted at Vince.

"Another friend," Cavanaugh said. "Isn't it nice to be popular?"

Dan's eyes drooped.

"Somebody sure worked him over," Vince said.

"Had a tattoo," Dan said a day later. His words were hard to understand—he spoke through mangled lips. "A rose. Here." Dan pointed toward his right forearm.

"Yes, you said that when you were unconscious. Ever see him before?" a police detective asked.

"No." Dan breathed and rested. "But he knew my address."

Cavanaugh leaned close.

"He claimed I paid him. For what he called an attitude adjustment," Dan said, wincing when he moved.

"What does *that* mean?" the detective asked.

"He said I won an auction."

"Yeah, you mentioned that, too. He must have been crazy. A crackhead who wandered into the house you were showing," the detective said.

"But then why would he go to the hospital and attack Dan a second time?" Jamie wondered.

"That's the thing about crackheads. They don't make sense."

"He said I'd done something terrible." Dan forced out the words. "He was easing my conscience."

"By beating you? Crazy for sure," the detective said. "We'll check our files for crackheads who are religious fanatics."

A physician entered the room, examined Dan, and announced that there wasn't any reason for him to remain in the hospital. "I'll prescribe some pain medication. You'll probably get a quieter rest at home."

There, once Dan was settled in the master bedroom, Cavanaugh asked, "Do you feel alert enough to answer more questions?"

"Anything to catch him." Dan took a painful breath. "To stop him."

"Do you have any enemies?"

Dan looked puzzled.

"Sweetheart, he asked me the same thing," Sarah said. "I told him I couldn't imagine anybody hating you."

"How big is your real-estate firm?" Jamie asked.

"Twenty brokers."

"One big happy family?"

"They're all a great team."

"No exceptions?" Cavanaugh asked.

"No." Dan's pain-ridden eyes clouded. "Except …"

"There's always an 'except'," Jamie said.

"Now that I think about it …"

"Exactly. Now that you think about it … It's a great team because the ones that didn't fit got sent away."

"Six months ago. I had to tell a broker to leave the firm," Dan said.

"Why?"

"Sexual harassment. Sam Logan. He kept bothering a secretary."

"I remember now," Sarah said. "But that's so long ago …"

"Wouldn't he have tried to get even with me earlier?"

"Not if he made himself wait until he hoped you'd forgotten him," Jamie said.

"This wasn't him," Dan said.

"So he hired somebody," Jamie said.

"Auctioned you," Cavanaugh said. "That's the expression he used. He placed a winning bid at an auction."

"But *what* auction?" Dan winced from the pain of talking.

"Set that aside for the moment. Tell me more about your business," Cavanaugh said. "Is anything unusual or dramatic happening?"

"Just that this year was fabulous for us. Enough that Ed Malone made an offer."

"Ed Malone? Offer?"

"He's the best broker I have. He wants to buy a share of the firm and open a branch office close to the beach."

"You seriously considered his proposal?" Jamie wanted to know.

"Not much. I told him I liked things the way they are."

"Do you suppose he wanted a share strongly enough that he decided to put you on your back for a while?" Cavanaugh asked. "If business suffered, maybe he could buy a share of the firm for a lower amount."

"Ed?" Dan's face was a mass of bruises, his look of astonishment giving him obvious pain. "Never in a million years. We get along perfectly."

"Tell us about the Baxters. Sarah told Jamie you were supposed to have dinner with them the day you were beaten."

"Yes," Sarah agreed. "They watched our daughter while I went to try to find Dan. They're close friends. They'd never do anything to hurt us."

"Because of the dinner invitation, they'd be the last people you'd suspect," Cavanaugh said.

"You know," Dan said with effort, "I don't like the way you think."

"I don't blame you," Cavanaugh said. "You're tired and sore, and we're badgering you with questions. We'll talk about this later. Meanwhile, arrangements need to be made. Jamie and I have an assignment in Los Angeles tomorrow. Vince and Gwen go with us. But you need at least two protectors. Also, you need to tell your daughter's school to take precautions while she's there."

"Two protectors?" Sarah frowned.

"Three would be better," Jamie said.

"We'd hire them?"

"Jamie and I were happy to do this for free," Cavanaugh said. "Vince and Gwen did it as a favor to us. But protectors who don't know you would certainly expect to be paid."

"How much?"

"A reasonable rate would be three hundred dollars a day."

"Times *three*? Per *day*?" Sarah looked surprised.

"Good God, for how long?" Dan asked.

"Until you're recovered. Meanwhile, they'd teach you how to secure the house and to change your patterns and behavior when you're outside. There's an attitude we call Condition Orange, a basic alertness that helps you anticipate trouble. You should read Gavin de Becker's *The Gift of Fear*. It teaches you to pay attention to your instincts when they warn you something's wrong."

"*The Gift of Fear*?" Dan said. "Condition Orange? This is insane. You make it sound like we're living in a war zone."

"Not far from the truth. The world's a dangerous neighborhood," Jamie said.

Sarah studied her. "You've certainly changed."

"In any case, think about it while you rest," Cavanaugh told Dan.

"I don't have time to rest." Dan shifted in the bed, grimacing. "Not when I'm losing business. Sarah, get me my laptop. I need to see the new listings and—"

"Do you really think that's a good idea?"

"The alternative is to let Ed try to replace me. That's how your friends have got me thinking."

"Sorry," Cavanaugh said.

Sarah brought Dan his laptop and helped him sit up. Groaning, he opened it and used the hand on his unbroken arm to turn on the computer and try to type commands.

"We'll let you do your work." Cavanaugh and Jamie left the room with Sarah.

"Please, close the door," Dan said.

Halfway down the stairs, Sarah halted. She thought about something, then glanced up toward the bedroom. "Excuse me for a minute." She climbed the stairs and, without knocking, opened the door. After a motionless moment, she stepped inside and closed the door. The back of her neck was red.

At the bottom of the stairs, Cavanaugh and Jamie looked at one another.

"Something's not what it seems," Cavanaugh said. "Sarah seemed more appalled about the expense of hiring protectors than Dan was. Do they have money problems?"

"Not if somebody's trying to buy into Dan's business and he keeps refusing."

"Something else bothers me. The police detective said Dan talked about an auction and a rose tattoo when he was unconscious, but Sarah never mentioned a word about that when we met her," Cavanaugh said.

"Auction." Jamie thought about it. "What does that mean to you?"

Cavanaugh shrugged. "Christie's. Sotheby's. Paintings. Statues."

"Sure. But ... Maybe it's because I used to be in the dot-com business. Christie's and Sotheby's aren't what I immediately think of. They're small compared to the most popular auction in the world," Jamie told him.

"I don't understand."

"I'll give you a hint. The auction's on the Internet."

"eBay?"

"Congratulations. You win a cigar."

"Couldn't you make it chewing tobacco?"

"As long as you don't expect me to kiss you." Jamie went into a study next to the living room and stared at a desktop computer. "You're right. There's more to this than we're being told. Just out of the hospital, Dan was far too impatient to get on the Internet." Jamie turned on the computer, tapped a few keys, and pointed toward a list that appeared on the left side of the screen. "These are the ten sites that this computer accesses the most."

"No eBay," Cavanaugh said. "That hunch didn't work out."

"But what's this bod.com and e-bod? Let's see if this computer and the one upstairs are networked. Yep." Jamie tapped more keys. "Dan already signed off. Strange. He couldn't wait to get on, and now he couldn't wait to get off." Jamie typed www.bod.com. A prompt asked for a password. When she clicked on the empty box, a program automatically supplied the password. "Whoever uses this site wants to save time."

The image that popped up made Jamie tilt her head, trying to look at it upside down. "Gosh."

"Double gosh," Cavanaugh said.

"I didn't know that position was physically possible," Jamie said.

"Just goes to show, we never stop learning," Cavanaugh said. "But I suspect they needed a chiropractor after doing it that way."

"A porn site," Jamie said.

"Chiropractor or not, would you mind if we tried that position?" Cavanaugh asked.

"I have no idea where we'd find the harness."

"Can't wait to see what e-bod is." Cavanaugh pointed toward a directory at the top of the screen, where e-bod was one of the options.

After Jamie clicked on it, the new page made them motionless.

"An auction site," Cavanaugh finally said.

"Well, now we know where to get the harness. Also weird-shaped dildos, erotic creams, exotic vibrators, and inflatable dolls."

"Anatomically correct," Cavanaugh said. "Hey, the bid for that one is only up to twenty dollars. At that price, it's a steal. Maybe I should put in a bid and—"

"Stick with the chewing tobacco."

A directory at the top of the screen included the word "services."

"I wonder where *that* leads," Jamie said.

When Jamie clicked on it and they read about the things that people were willing to be paid to do to one another, Cavanaugh said, "The road of lost souls."

"Seen enough?"

"To last a lifetime."

As they returned to the living room, Sarah descended the stairs.

"Hey, Sarah," Cavanaugh said, "remember, at the hospital, I told you we might need to suspect what seemingly couldn't be suspected?"

Sarah frowned. "What's wrong?"

"How long has Dan been addicted to computer porn?" Jamie asked.

"What kind of question …"

"Is that what he was looking at when you went back to the bedroom just now?" Cavanaugh asked. "Were you checking up on him? Even fresh out of the hospital after taking a beating, he couldn't resist taking a peak. Is he that far gone?"

"I have no idea what you're talking about."

"Bod-dot-com and e-bod."

Sarah's skin paled.

"We all agreed Dan was kind and decent. A loving husband. An attentive father. Good-natured. Generous," Cavanaugh said. "None of that's incompatible with a porn addiction. He's not hurting anybody, right? If he enjoys watching, what's the big deal?"

The room became silent.

"Unless he gets more turned on by fantasy than reality," Jamie said. "Then the expression 'loving husband' has limited application."

"Jamie, you're supposed to be my friend."

"Why were you so concerned about the cost of the protectors? If you were worried about Dan, the price would've been cheap," Jamie said. "Unless you knew who'd attacked him and why. Unless you were fairly confident the guy who did it wouldn't return after the second attack."

"I think you hired the attacker," Cavanaugh said. "You used the auction directory of the porn site Dan's most addicted to. Poetic justice."

Jamie stepped forward. "Did he stop having sex with you? Did he get all his satisfaction from the porn site?"

"Jamie, really, I'm begging you as a friend. Leave this alone."

"Did you resent the way he ignored you? Did you plead with him to stop going to the site? Did you promise he could indulge all his fantasies on you, but even *that* didn't tempt him to pay attention to you?"

Arms trembling, Sarah hugged herself.

"I'm sorry," Jamie told her.

"Damn him," Sarah said, "he wouldn't stop. I wanted to punish him. I wanted to put him in a position where he needed me, where he'd appreciate that I took care of him."

"The second attack?" Cavanaugh asked.

"A mistake," Sarah said. "I contacted the man and made sure he knows not to come back."

"That's why the cost of the protectors bothered you. Because you knew they wouldn't be needed."

Sarah's knees bent. She eased onto a chair. "I don't think I can bear going to prison. Being away from Meredith will kill me."

"We're the only ones who know," Cavanaugh said.

Jamie looked at him in surprise.

"Except for Dan," Cavanaugh said. "*Dan* has to know."

"You mean you're not going to tell the police about this?"

"It seems to me there's been enough suffering."

Sarah looked hopeless. "But you insist I tell Dan."

Cavanaugh nodded.

"When he finds out, he'll leave me."

"Possibly. But the way things were going, one of you would have left soon anyhow. So you're not exactly losing anything."

"Do you still love him?" Jamie asked.

"Yes, Lord help me."

"And maybe, despite everything, he still loves you."

"Do you seriously expect me to believe Dan will forgive me? That's not going to happen."

"Perhaps if you can forgive *him*. There's no denying this is a mess," Jamie said. "But you won't know if this marriage can be saved until the two of you face the truth."

"I feel nauseous."

"I know." Jamie went over, crouched next to her, and held her hands.

No one moved for several minutes. Finally, Sarah took a deep breath, freed her hands, and stood. "There's no sense waiting to tell him. It only hurts worse."

Gripping the banister, Sarah slowly climbed the stairs.

"The attacker," Cavanaugh said.

"He called himself an 'attitude adjuster'."

"What's the email address you used to get in touch with him?"

Sarah paused at the top of the stairs. Her face was even paler.

"Don't worry. We won't tell the police," Cavanaugh said. "If we did, he'd implicate you. He wouldn't be the only one going to prison."

"But he needs to feel responsible for his actions," Jamie said. "*He* should do some soul searching the same as you and Dan are."

E-BOD
I WILL ADJUST YOUR WAYS

*High bidder receives an attitude adjustment.
I am strong and tough from years of outdoor
work. If you win this auction ...*

QUESTION TO SELLER
*I have been bad. Frightfully horribly bad. I
have never felt so ashamed. I can't eat or
sleep because I feel so god-awful guilty. I
need to be punished as soon as possible.
Please. I'm begging you to adjust my ...*

⊕

BARRY PUT ON his leather gloves. A refinement
he was proud of, they protected his knuckles. At the same
time, they guaranteed he wouldn't leave fingerprints. I
don't why I didn't get the idea earlier, he told himself. The
gloves were shiny black. Their thin leather fit snugly on his
hands. He loved their smell.

Time to earn my pay, he thought.

He was in San Francisco, another interesting city he
had not visited until his auctions led him in new directions.
Cable cars. Fisherman's Wharf. The Golden Gate bridge.
The cemetery where James Stewart followed Kim Novak in
that spooky Hitchcock movie. There was certainly plenty
to see, and the food was wonderful, especially at that fancy
Italian restaurant *Fleur d'Italia*, the oldest Italian restaurant in the United States, it claimed, where the waiters wore
tuxedos and the wood-paneled walls were dark with age. A
little pricey, but adjusting attitudes was bringing in cash,
especially when people pissed him off and he took their
money after beating them senseless, making it look like a
mugging. The world was purer by the day.

Almost midnight. A thick fog came in off the bay. A ship's horn blared. Barry was outside a warehouse. At a corner of the building, a light glowed faintly in an office. He peered past moisture condensing on the window. A man sat at a desk. His head down, the man sorted through documents. Crutches leaned against the wall behind him. Barry nodded. The man had sent him an email about a car accident in which his drunken driving had caused his Mercedes to veer toward a van full of high-school kids on their way to a party after their prom. Swerving to avoid him, the kids hit a concrete wall, the impact killing three of them. The man who caused it managed to drive home. Nobody witnessed the incident. Thus he avoided punishment, except for breaking his leg when he got out of his vehicle, drunkenly missed his step, and fell. *That's not enough punishment. I don't want to go to prison, but I can't bear feeling this guilty*, his email said.

You've come to the right person, Barry had replied. *I will make you feel better.*

Now Barry tried the door. As promised, it wasn't locked. He pulled it open, stepped into a dark corridor, and walked toward light seeping under a farther door. As promised, it wasn't locked, either. Barry swung it open, revealing the grief-stricken man hunched over his desk.

"You've been bad," Barry said.

"You have no idea," the man murmured, his face down.

"I'm here to adjust your attitude. You'll be sore afterward, but I swear I'll ease your conscience."

"Actually," the man said, "I planned on doing some adjustments of my own."

"What?"

The man looked up. His intense hazel eyes reflected some of the brown from the desk. His strong chin and forehead radiated the wrath of hell.

"I think I'm in the wrong place." Turning, Barry faltered at the sight of a gorgeous woman with searing green eyes and a pit bull on a leash.

"No, you're definitely in the right place," the woman said.

A noise made Barry pivot toward the man. The noise came from the chair scraping as the man stood and grabbed one of the crutches from the wall.

"Wait," Barry said.

"Why?" The man held the crutch as if it were a baseball bat.

"There's a mistake," Barry said.

"What'll it take to convince you the only attitude in need of adjustment is yours?" the man asked.

"Uh," was all Barry managed to say.

"We'll keep track of you," the man said. "Believe me, we know how. If you ever harm anyone again, we'll come back."

The man swung the crutch with all his might. It slammed across the desk. With an ear-torturing crack, it split apart, one end flying across the roof, crashing against a cabinet.

"Uh," Barry said. Feeling something wet on his legs, he realized that his bladder had let go.

Growling, the dog bared its teeth as the woman urged it forward. Barry stumbled back and tripped over a chair, crashing into a corner. The man whacked the broken crutch against the wall above Barry's head. The impact sent plaster flying. It was so loud it made Barry's ears ring. The dog growled nearer.

⊕

A ROAD-REPAIR CREW. A man holds a pole with a sign at the top. SLOW, it says on one side. STOP, it says on the other. The man holds it listlessly. Tall and scarecrow lanky, he looks even more weary than his dawn-to-dusk workday would explain. His cheeks are sunken. His shoulders sag. A chill November wind blows dust across his face. His coat and yellow vest hang on him. Cars speed past, ignoring the SLOW sign, almost hitting him.

You've seen countless versions of him without ever paying attention. As snow starts to fall, he looks so pathetic that you actually give him a sorrowful look. What kind of dismal life does he have? What on earth is he thinking?

Is that them in that van? The light was so dim, I never got a good look at their faces. The pit bull. Jesus, all I really noticed was that pit bull. Growling. Foam spraying over my face. "We'll come back, Barry." That's what the guy said. "We'll keep a close watch. We'll make sure you've learned the error of your ways. If we find out you've been doing more adjusting, we'll put the fear of God into you." The fear of God? They're the ones I'm afraid of. I was never so shit-scared in my life. That van's gotta be doing sixty. Slow down! You almost hit me! But I don't dare shout at them. I can't risk threatening to break their windshield with my sign. If that's them, they'll wait for me after work. They'll—

"Barry! What the hell's wrong with you?" a voice shouted.

"Huh?" As the snowflakes got larger, Barry turned toward his big-chested foreman stomping toward him. The man had angry red cheeks.

"Don't you listen to your walkie-talkie!" the foreman yelled. "I've been giving you orders for the last five minutes!"

"Orders?"

"To stop traffic from coming through! Turn the frigging sign! Make everybody stop!" As roaring traffic almost hit them, the foreman raised his beefy hands. "This has been going on too damned long. How many times do I have to tell you to do something?"

"I'm sorry. I—"

"Look, I hate to do this. You're just not fit for the job anymore. Don't show up tomorrow."

"But—"

"Can't risk it. Somebody'll get hurt. Get your head straight, man. You need to find a better attitude."

BRIAN M. WIPRUD

BRIAN Wiprud, author of the exceptionally funny PIPSQUEAK, STUFFED and CROOKED lives in New York City with forty pet lemurs and a three-legged badger.

When pestered about his affection for hitman stories, Brian replied: "I have none, but I like stories about lemurs." The following tale contains both hitmen and lemurs.

Visit Brian at www.Wiprud.com.

WHEN YOU'RE RIGHT, YOU'RE RIGHT
Brian M. Wiprud

FBI WIRE TRANSCRIPT 2849-A

Date: November 10, 1997
Time: 8:01PM
Location: Turkey's Nest Bar & Grill, Brooklyn
Participants: Jackie "Jackie Muscles" Napol, Anthony "Louie" DePorta

A:That's fucked up, Jackie.

J:Fucked up is right.

A:(unintelligible …) a lemur?

J:I dunno, it's like a monkey kinda thing, except it looks all cute, like a plush toy.

A:Where they from? Friggin' Africa?

J:Hey, Suze, can I get some of them steamed muscles? What?

A:A lemur. Does it live in Africa?

J:Nah. Some place called Magalaska.

A:So did you do that thing? The lemur, I mean.

J:Hey, they tell me to do that thing to a friggin' whale, I gotta do it, you know what I'm saying?

A:That's the life.

J:The life.

A:Salud … (unitelligible) … his girlfriend?

J:Like I said, the lemur belongs to this guy's comare.

A:Yeah?

J:Yeah, like she sits around all day, watching the boob tube. She loves nature shows, watches the Discography Channel er whatever all day.

A:All day … that's a lotta animals.

J:So this guy goes to visit his comare regular, you know, the way you do.

A:Didn't that guy in Donnie Brasco, what's his name, watch a lotta animal shows?

J:The movie? Yeah, I think. There's a lion in that movie.

A:That's right, and they surprise what's his name with a Lion. This lemur: it big?

J:Big? Nah. Like this. It would sit on his girlfriend's shoulder. Like I was sayin', this guy visits her one day and she's got this lemur thing.

A:Where's she get the friggin' thing? From Magalaska?

J:I dunno.

A:What the fuck? Why does he want you should do a piece of work on this animal?

J:His wife. When he gets home, he's got lemur fuzz on him, and the thing has a smell. She's like, where the fuck do you go at night? Can't have that.

A:(unintelligible) … lint brush.

J:Most guys, they don't want their goombatta to have even a cat just 'causa the fuzz. A bird, yeah, maybe a little dog. Nothin' with a lotta fuzz. But I think this guy really didn't like how much time his girlfriend was spending with the lemur. She loved it like it's her own son. So he decides it's gotta go.

A:You mean the lemur?

J:Yeah. I gotta do a thing on Frankie.

A:Frankie?

J:That's the name of the lemur. I get an apartment number over in Canarsie, and this guy is out with his comare so he knows she won't be there.

A:Where'd they go?

J:Embers.

A:They were closer to Lugers in Canarsie.

J:Yeah, well, I think that was the point. He wanted to give me a good door of opportunity to take care of Frankie. And I needed it, believe me.

A:What's she gonna think when she gets home? I don't get it.

J:Hey. Not like that, Louie. What, I'm gonna … [unintelligible] … my piece on this problem? Nah. He just wants the problem should go away. I open a window, make it look like he run off or something.

A:So you hafta grab this monkey, take it out somewhere and …

J:Lemur. Yeah, like that.

A:I dunno, Jackie. That's kinda sick. It's just an animal, for Christ sake.

J:Hey, you gotta do what you gotta do. That's the life, am I right or am I right?

A:Yeah … yo, Suze, could we get another round? Like a friggin' beer desert over here. Got cactuses growing in my mouth.

J:So I got a key to her place, anna duffle bag to put the thing in. Figure I take it out to the end of Flatlands, bang bang, and throw the bag inna swamp.

A:How'd you get the lemur inna bag?

J:I figure I put a cracker in there, he climbs in t'eat it, I zip him up.

A:A cracker? Parrots eat crackers, you know, Polly wanna a cracker.

J:Fuck, I dunno, what animal doesn't like a cracker?

A:A deer. A deer won't eat no cracker.

J:But this is a lemur. A monkey'll eat a cracker.

A:I woulda brought bananas. Thanks, Suze … this for you, sweetheart.

J:So I get into the apartment, and this thing is sitting inna cage across the room, lookin' at me, y'know?

A:Lookin' at you?

J:Yeah. It's got these big eyes that look at you. Not like, what, a mouse or something. Like a little old lady's eyes, or a baby's, I dunno. He's black an' white. His face is black with white eyebrows. So Frankie is lookin' at me, comes over to the cage door like he expects me to let him out. I offer him a cracker, he takes it, so I figure all I gotta do is put the bag in front of the cage with another cracker an' I'm golden.

A:Yeah, golden. White eyebrows?

J:Uh huh. Except I made the mistake of opening the window first, y'know, to make it look like he escaped.

A:Fuck. So he vamoosed?

J:Right over the bag an' out the friggin' window. Like a shot.

A:Musta shit your pants.

J:So I'm at the window, an' Frankie is out on the ledge eatin' the cracker.

A:The cracker from the bag or the first cracker?

J:He grabbed it from the bag as he went. A lemur is fast, I'm tellin' yah.

A:You grab him?

J:If only I had a net. Lookit, see that?

A:Yeah …

J:Son of a bitch bit me, is what he did.

A:When you tried to grab him?

J:Yeah. So I get some paper towels, y'know, wrapped around my hand like a bandage. I come back an' try to get Frankie to come back in, wavin' a cracker in the air like this …

A:[laughter]

J:Hey, it's not funny, it'd been you.

A:Sorry.

J:That don't work, so I get another idea. I figure I'll get a broom and knock him off the ledge, let him fall to his death. But all I can find is a, y'know, toilet brush.

A:Yeah, that way it'll look like an accident. Like he escaped, went out the window, tripped an' fell. How many floors?

J:Ten, plenty. So I'm holding the toilet brush, y'know, pokin' at him, an' he grabs it an' hits me over the head, throws the toilet brush away. You laughin' again?

A:No ... no. Jesus Christ. Which end did he hit you with? The fuzzy end with the shit on it?

J:Nah, I was pokin' him with the poopy end, so that's what he grabbed.

A:You finally just pop him?

J:Too much noise, Louie. This was supposed to be done very quiet like.

A:I woulda shot the prick, picked his sorry ass uppa the sidewalk and gone to Flatlands to throw him in the weeds. Still seems a shame, just an animal ...

J:[unintelligible] ... all over the sidewalk? How's that gonna look? An' I mess this up, imagine the ribbing I'm gonna take. Nah, I figure a better idea. This comare, she's got like one of them desks with all her makeup on it ...

A:A vanity.

J:Yeah. An' there's a mirror there. One of them hand-held jobs. So I hold the mirror up to Frankie ... I was channel surfing once, and there was this monkey with a mirror, staring at himself. So maybe, I'm thinkin', this'll do the job on a lemur.

A:He didn't hit you with the mirror?

J:Get outta here! Nah, I hold it out so he can't reach it, he looks, y'know, with them lemur eyes I was tellin' yah about, an' sure as shit he starts to come closer. I back up, he comes forward, bam, I close the window.

A:Yo, y'got him.

J:Eh, not 'xactly. I know if I grab him, the fucker'll bite me again, or he'll freak out an' run away. The thing is fast, I'm tellin' yah, and you wouldn't believe how the thing can jump. You could make a basketball team outta these things. Nah. I sit there with him by the window, lettin' him look at himself, y'know, an' very careful like I reach over and touch his arm. Pettin' him, y'know. Well, next thing you know, that thing is sittin' on my shoulder with the mirror. I'm tellin' yah, he was like transfixuated or something by his own image. So I stand up real slow ... like this.

A:He's still on your shoulder?

J:Yeah, an' I got my hand up pettin' him. So I got one problem covered. I could leave with him on my shoulder an' try to get him to the car like that. But I gotta put the mirror back, 'cause the girlfriend will notice it missin' ...

A:Unless she thinks Frankie took the mirror with him.

J:Nah. Couldn't chance it. But how am I gonna go out the building without everybody starin' at me with this animal on my shoulder, a bloody paper towel around my hand? An' I still gotta get the toilet brush, which is ten floors down inna bushes and put that back.

A:People notice stuff like that, yeah. You need a strategy. Couldn't you, like, ease him into the bag?

J:I tried, I tried. But that thing had the mirror in one hand, and the other on my ear. Wouldn't let go, me or the mirror. So I go over to the varsity ...

A:The vanity ...

J:The vanity, right, and get him to look at the mirror there. Big ass mirror. Sure as shit, he gets off and sits on that, staring into the big mirror. I leave him there, go downstairs, get the toilet brush, put it back, an' what do I find but that Frankie had put the mirror down.

A:So now you put the bag over him, right?

J:Not exactly. See, I figure that'll be tough. He's strong, an' got arms an' legs stickin' out while I try to zip it up. And the tail is like a friggin' snake ... like this long. Nah. Again, if he started to freak, I'd never get him. So I move all the makeup an' stuff to the sides, clear things away from him, you know? Real easy.

A:Yeah.

J:Thanks, Suze ... could I have some Tabasco for these here muscles? ... Anyway, I take a plastic trash can, empty it out, and slam it over him. He's bouncin' around in there like a friggin' jumpin' bean, and it's all I can to hold him in there, but I lift him off the varsity …

A:Whoa. Howdja do that?

J:Whaddaya mean?

A:The trash can, how'd you keep Frankie in there?

J:There was like this mat or whatever on the varsity, cardboard kinda thing …

A:Like a blotter?

J:Yeah, like that, but fancy. I go over to the oven, open it with my foot, jam this thing in there, an' before he can scramble out I close the door, lean a chair against the handle so he, y'know, can't get out. He's bangin' around in there, and so I turn the oven on.

A:Sonofabitch. You cooked him alive? That's a sin, Jackie. Just an animal. Musta smelled like friggin' hell!

J:Nah. Before I turned the oven on, I blew out the pilot. I gassed him.

A:[unintelligible] … not so bad.

J:After about ten minutes, he stops movin' around in there, I turn off the gas, and there he is, out like a friggin' light. I pick him up by the tail, put him in the bag, zip it closed, put the trash can an' blotter thing back on the varsity, make things all nice. I open the window wide, air the place out of gas, then close it a little bit so it'd look, y'know, like he just eased it open an' slipped out. Left the cage door open. Either the comare will think she didn't close it OK or that the little bastard managed to open it himself.

A:[laughter] So you got him, took him to Flatlands, and did the thing. Shit, that's one fucked-up story. What's this? You're shaking your head …

J:Not over yet. Thanks, Suze. So I take the bag, right? I lock up, everything is perfect. I put him in the back seat, start driving to Flatlands.

A:I don't get it. What the fuck happened?

J:I'm drivin' down Coney Island Avenue, when suddenly I feel somethin' grab my ear.

A:Jesus Christ! He wasn't dead!

J:Not only that, he got outta the bag, an' he's crawling on toppa my head. Scared the shit outta me, an' I'm swervin' all over the road, almost had an accident. That's when I see the lights.

A:Lights?

J:Yeah, a friggin' cop is pulling me over an' I got a lemur on toppa my my head like fuckin' Davy Crockett.

A:[laughter] Jackie, please, you're killin' me. I don't care what you say, this is one fucked-up story. What'd the cop do?

J:He's on this side, standin' back the way they do so you can't pop them, the other one comes up the other side and starts shinin' a flashlight in the car. Pricks. I can't roll my window all the way down 'cause I don't want that Frankie should, y'know, make a break for it. So the cop asks me, like, to roll the window all the way down an' I say I can't do that causa this lemur on my head, that he might jump outta the window. I tell the guy that, y'know, he escaped an' scared me an' that's why I was all over the road. Now they're laughin', but they wanna see my license and registration. I hand 'em over, they go back to the cruiser. In the meantime, Frankie is still a little groggy, and I manage to like pry him from my head and get him on the seat next to me. I snap the rearview mirror off the windshield an' hand it to him. He starts lookin' into it with those eyes, y'know?

A:Quick thinkin', Jackie. About the mirror. I like the way you do that.

J:Do what?

A:You know, that look you do for Frankie checkin' himself out in the mirror.

J:Yeah, so the cops come back an' say they need me to step out of the friggin' car. They have to do a sobriety check, standard procedure they have to follow whenever they call in an erratic driver, they say. So I quick like slip out, and do the test. Stone cold, I pass, they let me go with a warning, tell me to keep my animal under control. So they drive off.

A:Golden?

J:Heh. I turn to the car an' I can't get in. Frankie dropped the mirror, an' is standin' on the door, his feet on the arm rest, his nose stuck out the little crack I left in the window to talk to the cops. This little bastard put his foot on the door lock, all the doors are now locked, the keys inside.

A:Can we jump to the end?

J:What?

A:I'm dyin' here. The suspense is too much.

J:Take it easy, Louie, we're getting' there. So I call a guy I know, and have my car towed to the airport.

A:The airport?

J:La Guardia. You know the cargo hangar, the one where …

A:Yeah, I remember, that thing. Cargo hangar is a good place to do a thing. So no more Flatlands?

J:Hey, I figure the best thing is to have the car towed out there, I pop the bastard inside my car through the crack in the window and then clean it up right then an' there. I mean, how much blood could there be in a lemur? Couldn't be so bad, just try not to shoot out a window. So I get this guy to tow the car there, he lends me a Slim Jim so I can get back in the car when we're done. We're all alone, Frankie is back sittin' on the passenger seat with the mirror again. I figure the slug'll pass through him an' the seat an' into the quarter panel, no real harm done. Now I'm like this, you know, pointing it at him, about to put the granite hat on him when he looks up at me.

A:So?

J:This isn't like a mouse. He's got these eyes … I dunno. Can I borrow your lighter, there?

A:Sure. So, like I said, it was a sin, you couldn't do it. It's just an animal, for Christ sake. He didn't do nothin'.

J:Believe me, there have been times, Louie. People begging, an' I couldn't give a rat's ass, an' do what needs to be done. But this was like whackin' a friggin' muppet. I'm tellin' yah.

A:What, like Miss Piggy?

J:Miss Piggy? Nah! I could pop Miss Piggy. This was more like Fozzie.

A:Fozzie Bear? Yeah, that'd be tough puttin' the bead on Fozzie. So whadja do?

J:I shipped him home.

A:Back to Canarsie?

J:Back to Magalaska. They got live animal crates there at the cargo terminal. Frankie was still kinda groggy, and he took my rearview mirror with him back to Magalaska. Put him on the next flight, addressed to the zoo or some shit.

A:Marrone! So he went back in a box holding your rearview mirror. Jackie, that was the right thing to do. Where exactly is Magalaska?

J:Shit, I didn't know for sure, but I figured it out by lookin' at the airline names which plane to get him on.

A:There's a Magalaska Airline?

J:Nah, but like I told you, I figured it out. Magalaska. Think about it.

A:[unintelligible]

J:Alaska Airlines.

A:Is that where Magalaska is? Friggin' Alaska?

J:Hey, Jersey City, it's in New Jersey. New York, it's in New York. Kansas City, it's in Kansas.

A:When you're right, you're right, Jackie.

ROB KANTNER

ROB Kantner is the author of nine novels and numerous short stories in the Ben Perkins PI series, which have won him four Shamus Awards. These days Rob knocks out the occasional short story, tinkers with historical fiction and crime novels, and generally contents himself in peaceful obscurity. Rob lives on a farm near Blanchard, Michigan (pop. 200), with his wife, two kids, a dog, two horses, two cats, and others. His latest is TROUBLE IS WHAT I DO.

On the topic of hitmen, Rob says: "I think most of us of the hard-boiled persuasion are drawn to hitmen because as a class they are about as amoral as it's possible to be. Though some play around with justification, for most it's just a job. There's also a feeling of power at having at your command someone who is quite blithely willing to cross boundaries that most of the rest of us would not. And then there's the kind of dark thrill of getting away with things that many don't."

Visit Rob at www.RobKantner.com.

DEAD LAST
Rob Kantner

FROM UTTER INSENSIBLE blackness grew aware-ness: Heartbeat. Breathing. Distant ticking of an admiral clock. Remaining absolutely still, allowing himself to ease awake, eyes tight shut, Bobby wondered: *How sick am I?*

Mentally he took inventory of his sensations: head, chest, abdomen. All quiet.

Another day, then?

So far, so good.

Opening his eyes, Bobby slid back the silk sheet, swung his thin legs off the bed, stood, padded stiffly into the bright pastel bathroom. How different this getting-up ritual was, he re-flected, from earlier days. A nice good-morning hump with the girl of the moment, a quiet first cigarette (the best of the day), a mug of rich black coffee, TV news, a quick phone call with Mister S, and then on into the day, to do his boss's bidding.

Today, he thought as he brushed his teeth, there was no girl. No smoke. No joe. No boss, and no job. And, as evidenced by his reflection in the mirror, no hair. All of that, like the penthouse overlooking the East River, the rambling cottage on Block Island, long behind him.

Now, his day started with the first piss (today blessedly strong and free of discomfort), shower, shave, dress, and on to the kitchen to breakfast on some bland lumpy gruel, to scan indifferently the sports pages, and to plot the day's moves. Will it be *Live with Regis and Kelly*, a nap, and then *Oprah*? Or a walk around the development, *Oprah*, then a nap?

Bobby shaved, unflinchingly navigating the straight razor across the deep indentation in his lower jaw. His scarred scalp showed silver stubble; he needed to see Maricela at the strip mall again—she had the most delicate touch with the razor, and he knew she knew he enjoyed the warmth of her young round hip against his shoulder. It was a quiet reminder of better days, and of his losses, which, like most men his age, Bobby cataloged almost daily. The babes, the booze, the big fast cars. The way strong men's heads snapped his way as he entered rooms. Most especially, the action, the <click> moment. He'd traded all that for golden years in the Nevada sun, which he, like most retirees, felt had been promised to him—only to be betrayed by his body.

But even that, Bobby thought, pulling on khaki shorts, had had its benefits. Many formerly unacceptable situations had become irrelevant. Goals he'd striven for and never achieved seemed not to matter now. Possessions—and people—he'd lost, turned out to be unimportant. And unsettled scores that formerly burned inside him like a bleeding ulcer now lay inert. Bobby's world, once boundless, had gotten very small. And all that was okay.

Interesting thing, a close brush with death. Gets your attention. Not to be underestimated.

In its wake, in these quiet, golden, one-at-a-time days, Bobby felt, for the first time in his life, peace.

And he was grateful.

✛

"TONI PASSED," GRACE said, peering into the screen of her laptop computer. Bobby looked up from his bran-and-skim. *Good Morning America* prattled from the TV on the counter. Filtered desert sun gleamed through the white blinds of the big round-topped breakfast nook window. Grace sat at the computer desk, in half-profile to him. She was short and full-bodied in her snug blue housedress, her rich dark hair coifed to perfection and rigorously lacking in gray.

"Toni?" he echoed. Then, in realization: "Schiavone?"

"Rosario," she corrected, sounding annoyed.

"Still with him?"

"That's what Trixie says."

Antonia Schiavone Rosario, Bobby thought. Gone. This meant something, but exactly what it meant hung back behind a veil of mental gray just now. "The last of them, gone," he murmured.

"Well, there's still Alexa, maybe, who knows," Grace said casually.

Just like the baby of the brood, always throwing darts. Bobby let it pass.

"How'd Toni go?"

"Stroked out," Grace said, with the matter-of-fact casualness of the indestructible. "She was a year behind me at St. Anselm's."

"Ahead of you."

"*Behind.*"

Bobby let it go. "Sweet girl," he murmured.

"Such a joy. And what a *saint*," Grace exclaimed, "staying with Sixto all these years."

"He's still with us, then."

"Threw himself on her coffin, says Trixie," Grace said, tapping the laptop screen with a long red fingernail.

Always the ham-actor, Bobby thought darkly. "She went to the funeral?" he asked.

"No, no. Her Teddy went, to represent the family. Who could go all the way down there. *Florida*," Grace scoffed.

"It's a long way from Beechhurst," Bobby said vaguely.

"Thank God for the email," Grace prattled. "Where are you going?"

Bobby realized he had stood. "Give me a cigarette."

She blinked, round face owlish, and in that instant she looked exactly like their mother. Sounding stung, she said, "I don't have any."

"Come on, you lying sack of shit," Bobby said affectionately, "I know you're sneaking them. Give me one."

Scowling, Grace padded on her pink flip-flops to a drawer by the Bosch dishwasher, took out a cigarette and Bic lighter, slapped them on the table between Bobby's pill box and juice glass. "Not in here. My new drapes." She turned her back on him huffily and resumed her seat at the computer. Out on the grilling patio, Bobby lighted the cigarette—one of those skinny brown menthol jobs. His first toke in six long years went down smooth.

Still in shape.

It was already hot from the burning sun. The blue sky was faintly overlaid by a yellowish brown smutch of smog. Bobby wasn't supposed to be outside without a hat and sunblock, and he was not supposed to smoke. But there he stood, in the full direct sun, smoking, not so much for enjoyment but for the satisfaction. And, he realized, nothing made him feel so alive as breaking rules.

In the distance he could hear the endless roars of dozers and earthmovers and heavy trucks. But Bobby's senses were overwhelmed by the power of memory—of the social club. The one in Bayside, that's right. Where it always seemed to be raining. Where the sidewalk ever teemed darkly with guys practicing their pitches and waiting for an audience.

And where—for the first and only time in three decades of association—he had seen Peter Schiavone cry.

She won't leave him, Mister S moaned, after the long recitation of sins and offenses. *For better or for worse, Antonia keeps saying—keeps to her vows even if he won't.*

So, Bobby had flared, much more of a hothead in those days, let's fix him, Mister S. Let's put Sixto down.

And break my sister's heart? No way can I do that. May God strike me dead.

They had sat there, at the round wood table, alone in Mister S's back room, glasses of Amaretto dell'Orso untouched, silent, as the boss recovered from the storm that had swept through him. It was then that Mister S fixed Bobby with the fierce hooded-eye stare, his dockworker fists—not arthritic yet—clenched on the table: *But after ... AFTER ...* He raised his index finger and jabbed it toward Bobby, just once.

And Bobby had nodded.

That was, when again? Around the time those four hippie protesters were shot dead in Ohio. Somewhere in there, Bobby couldn't remember for sure.

But he had nodded. That Bobby remembered clearly.

Inside he resumed his seat, picked at his suety cereal, let a few moments pass. Grace squinted at the computer screen, pecked at her keyboard, clicks labored and intermittent in deference to her long nails. Tone off-hand, Bobby asked: "That contraption, you can buy airplane tickets on there, can't you?"

She pointedly typed a few more click-click-clicks. "I guess."

"That Captain Kirk on TV, he says so."

She swung around. "Where do you think you're going?" she asked darkly.

"Fort Jackson," he said, continuing to eat.

"No way."

"Pay my respects."

She waved a beringed hand. "She's dead, in the ground, it's done, forget about it."

"Not for her. For Sixto."

"Send a card." She tapped the screen. "This 'contraption,' it'll do that too."

"Not the same."

Her face wrinkled with scorn. "You never liked him."

"That's right."

"He's an asshole. If he hadn't been married to—" She froze, and her dark eyes averted, and in the sudden uplift of

eyebrows, purse of red lips, drop of jaw, Bobby saw her con-
nect the dots. "No," she said.

"Oh yes," he said, and resumed eating.

"Let it go."

"He never did. Ever."

"He's dead. Been dead since—"

"But I'm not."

Grace was flushing, eyes reddening. "You men," she
cried, "you men and your rules!"

He nodded, and flicked his bowl back harder than intended. "Look at me, Grazia," he said, and swept his thin hands
about, taking in their surroundings. "What do I have? What
else is left?"

The tears were rolling, and she made no effort to stop
them. "Don't give me that shit. You just *want* to."

"And I *have* to. And," he could not resist adding, "I still *can*."

"You've been so sick. Haven't I taken good care of you?
Don't go."

"What's the nearest airport to Fort Jackson?"

✛

"ORLANDO," THE TICKET agent said, and clapped
the boarding pass in Bobby's hand. "Seat 2A. We'll be boarding in ... two hours. Have a nice flight."

Bobby had not been in McCarren International in years. He
was alarmed at how vast it had become. The concourses were
jammed, of course, as well as the slot machine areas. The security checkpoint was a mob scene, too. Bobby obediently shuffled
through the metal detector, triggering no alarm, and the TSA officer laughed as he passed: "Another hardened criminal!"

Haha.

It was a long walk to his gate, and Bobby took his time.
He was surprised at the large number of retail shops—the place
was like a strip mall now—and the percentage of people, kids

even, using cell phones. Bobby had never owned one. Who needed to be that reachable, take calls on the shitter? There were, after all, still pay phones, and he found a bank of them across from his gate. Just eleven PM over there, he thought as he dialed, squinting at his phone card.

"Speak to me," came the answer.

"Jimmy."

"Bobby! How the hell are ya. What's it been."

"Too long. Get you up?"

"Who sleeps at our age? Plenty of time for that later. Besides, Bill Maher is on, he cracks me up, the nasty little shit, fuckin' foul mouth on him."

"Yeah. Listen, I need a package."

Silence. "They said you were done."

"Special run."

"Okay. The, uh—the usual?"

"No, a fuckin' rocket propelled grenade. Yes, the usual."

"Okay. Deliver where?"

"I land in Orlando at—" Bobby checked the printout Grace had given him—"six fifty-five your time, tomorrow."

"Night?"

"Morning."

"Red-eye, huh?"

"Best fare that way. Senior citizen on a fixed income, you know."

✛

HE'D NAPPED AT HOME, before leaving for the airport. But as the 737 climbed out, Bobby dropped off. And in his dreams he was twenty-eight again, in that upstairs room in Long Island City, very early morning, the only time he and Alexa could sneak away. They'd just finished making love on the foam mattress on the floor, the room's sole furnishing. Alexa dressed while Bobby, still naked, smoked a cigarette and watched her.

This was his favorite part—well, make that the second favorite. He loved to lie there and admire her long, lush form as she reassembled her blue-suit, English teacher look. Loved to see her go all respectable and solid-citizen in an amazing transformation from the hot, damp, urgent vixen she'd been just moments before.

And then, as she brushed her auburn hair, she told him, with stubborn sad directness, that she needed a "moratorium." That was exactly the word she used. She could no longer stand the suspense, the *fear*, of Peter finding out. He was so strict about these things. He had rules, unbreakable rules. Alexa and Bobby were both married to others—both had kids—if Peter caught them—

Stricken to his heart, Bobby had argued with Alexa, pleaded with her, but she was immovable. Peter would never harm either of his sisters, she said; for Alexa, the punishment would be disgrace and a period of shunning—bad enough. But for Bobby, the retribution would be far more dire, and, Alexa said, she could not bear the thought of that …

When Bobby wrenched awake, the pre-landing announcement was sounding over the intercom. The long-gone ghosts of Alexa fluttered away. He realized he was crying, his left eye leaking tears.

And he had a headache.

⊕

BONOMO, READ THE hand-printed sign in the hands of Jimmy, who stood among a pack of others just past the security checkpoint. Bobby strode toward the shorter man with the crew cut and bull shoulders, hand up in a wave, smiling. "What's with the sign?" he asked. "Think I'd forget what you look like?"

"Hell, man," came the reply, "You haven't seen me since I was about seven." As they shook hands, Bobby realized this had to be Jimmy's son. Jimmy junior, but they called him Jay. He looked amazingly like his dad had, thirty, forty years before. Square head and squint-eyes and that deep, burnt-in Florida tan.

"Suitcase?" Jay asked as they walked companionably up the concourse toward the exit.

"No."

"My compadre's looping the car around," the kid said. "You can't just park at the curb anymore."

"Unless you're a right-wing nut in a Ryder truck."

"Yeah, for them, valet parking."

"Where's Jimmy?" Bobby asked as they stepped out the glass doors into the stifling Florida humidity.

"He don't get out much. Here's my man." The white Escalade sighed up to the curb and Bobby stepped up stiffly and slid onto the cool leather of the front passenger seat. "This is Bobby Bonomo," Jay said, climbing in the capacious back seat. "My man Cliffie."

The driver was squatty and dark-haired, dressed like his boss in a black tee and khaki shorts. He shook hands with Bobby, damn near breaking his bones. "An honor, sir. An honor."

"Better roll," Jay said calmly, "place is crawling with laws."

"National Car Rental," Bobby said, "if you would."

"An honor," Cliffie repeated, easing the blocky Escalade into the flow of traffic. "I gotta ask you," he burbled, guiding the SUV with practiced gestures, "I gotta ask you—weren't you the one who done Archangeli?"

Bobby felt a private glow: *amazing—somebody remembers. Well, when you do good work ...* "I have some familiarity with that," he answered.

"Damn," Cliffie said, "that was so sweet. Shotgun in a rolled-up carpet, walk right past the security guys, and *ba-bing!*"

From the back seat, Jay tapped Bobby's shoulder and handed him a notebook-sized soft brown leather case, squarish and zipped-shut and heavy.

"One dead rat," Cliffie churned on, "and you're through the kitchen and out the back before he even hits the floor."

Bobby reached a thick letter-sized envelope from his jacket pocket and handed it over the seat to Jay. He nodded thanks and said, "Planned it down to the second, dincha?"

"Planning is half the formula," Bobby said. "The other half is brazenness."

"Awesome." Cliffie glanced from over the wheel at Bobby. "What happened to your face, man?"

"Hit a door."

"No, really, your jaw there, look at that."

From the back Jay said easily, "Don't matter, Cliffie, okay?"

"Just wondering," Cliffie grumbled.

They pulled up to the National drop-off. "Wait here," Bobby said.

"What do you need?" Jay asked.

"Gonna trade with you." Jay and Cliffie squinted at him. "You take the rental to the dog track, have a nice day for yourselves," Bobby said. "The extra grand in the envelope, that's what that's for. Meet me back here at six."

"I get it," Cliffie breathed.

"Yeah," Jay said, smiling, "little confusion, little pixie dust, huh?"

"Something like that," Bobby replied.

"I don't give a shit," Cliffie said. "Do you give a shit, Jay?"

"I don't give a shit. Car's going in the container next week anyways."

"Yeah," Cliffie laughed. "Let 'em try to find it in Belarus."

⊕

RELIEVED TO BE freed from the rental car his cheapskate sister had reserved for him, Bobby enjoyed watching it roll away, with the uncomplaining Jay and Cliffie on board. And he enjoyed driving their boxy Caddy monster truck the forty-five miles to Fort Jackson, the thick heavy leather note-book lying on the seat beside him.

The headache lurked like a smoldering ember deep at the base of his skull. An aspirin trio was keeping it at bay. For now.

The Zephyr Estates and Country Club was west of town, along one of the state highways that branched off the freeway. Bobby had committed all the details to memory—this kind of stuff you did not write down—and he drove by the wooded entrance twice, checking it out. There was a white brick wall, row of dense green trees, some low red-tiled buildings beyond, and a security gate. Everything was so lush, so green. Bobby realized how sick he had become of relentless desert tan. But this place here, the humidity would kill him; he had the a/c on full and he was still feeling it.

Wheeling the Escalade into the entrance, Bobby rolled past the wall and some visitor parking to the white guard booth. The security man was on the phone. Bobby powered down his window and waited, glancing past the flimsy wood gate at the pool house, shuffleboard court, and sprawling, low-slung homes packed neatly and closely together along the winding asphalt street. What people he saw were either scooting about in golf carts or power-walking. Most looked to be his age or older: pink, well-scrubbed, well-fed Republican types, enjoy-ing their waning days in their privileged cocoon.

"Help you?" the guard asked. He probably had a decade on Bobby, and a round jovial face, a picture-perfect greeter type whose real function, Bobby judged, was more p/r than security.

Bobby deliberately leaned out the open window, to give the impression of being hard of hearing—which he was not—and to make sure the guard got a good look at Bobby's head and face. "Hi, we're moving down here from New York? And some friends told me about this place?"

"Sure. It's wonderful here," the guard beamed.

"Like to talk to somebody about buying in?"

"That'd be fine. Office is just to your right, by the library. Mary'll be glad to help you."

"Can I," Bobby asked penitently, "can I drive around a little first? Just to get a feel for it?"

"Okay. Speed limit's 15, y'know. Be careful."

"Thanks."

The toothpick gate-arm wobbled up and Bobby rolled the Escalade through, over a speed bump, and then slowly, primly, along the narrow asphalt drive. He could see already that the whole development—which seemed enormous—was built around a sprawling golf course, a network of narrow canals, and clusters of palm trees and thicker, brushier vegetation. The streets, winding about in a confusing tangled maze, were all named after birds. The one Bobby wanted was Chickadee. After making multiple turns and doubling back on his route twice, he found it, and followed it along in search of Number 33.

The homes were single-story with angular roofs and quite large, dominating their patches of grass and nestling under tall palms. Some were rigorously plain. Others were obviously the loving focus of hobbyists overburdened with time and cash, who cluttered each square foot with trinkets, do-dads, knick-knacks, flub-dubs, and dressed geese. Street traffic was, Bobby was glad to see, minimal, and consisted mostly of golf carts. Most were driven by singles and, like the homes, ranged from plain-Jane to custom-painted, flag-bedecked ads for their well-heeled owners.

Bobby slowed as he reached 33. It was a pink frame low-roofed house with no ID outside but the number, and shades drawn over the windows. Inside the open car port sat a white Toyota Camry. Beyond that Bobby got a glimpse of another street and the golf course beyond that still.

Interesting.

Bobby continued to roll at a deliberate 12 mph, waving back at passersby when obliged. Circling left, he caught the street that paralleled Chickadee, and passed by Number 33's back yard. No sign of life from back there, either. But there were people playing the golf course, some on foot, some cruising in their carts. Down the way was a brown tile building with rest room signs on it. Scattered in its vicinity were parked, empty golf carts.

Now this had possibilities.

Bobby passed the rest room building, found a turn-off by a canal, and parked the Escalade under a clump of dense trees. Glancing around for observers, he unzipped the leather case and peeked inside. The Colt Woodsman looked to be the third model, blued with few wear marks, and seemed to be in good shape. Floating loose in the bag was the cylindrical silencer, and a clip. Bobby reached in for the eject button and verified there was a full clip on board. Thoughtful of Jimmy to send the extra ammo, but Bobby had never needed more than one, for straight jobs—or three, when the assignment included delivery of a message.

Zipping up the bag, Bobby stepped out of the Escalade and looked toward the rest room building. The men's and women's doors were on opposite sides. A couple of golf carts parked at angles on the rough grass a few steps away. Presently a man came out of the men's, boarded his cart, and whirred away. Another cart approached, with a couple on board, plus, seated between them, some sort of black-and-white spaniel. No good. Bobby stood and waited. Carts came and went. After a bit another one neared. Just one man this time, and the cart was as plain as could be.

Just right.

As the golf cart drew up, Bobby started walking toward the rest room building. He wore white shorts and sandals and one of the nicer polo shirts, which, aside from being too large for him—as were all his clothes, these days—made him look no different from any other Zephyr resident. The cart parked by the rest room building and its driver, a squat man in a porkpie hat, disembarked and walked with rather awkward haste into the men's. Maalox moment, eh? Bobby thought, grinning. His timing, excellent as ever, had him ten feet from the cart as the man clicked out of sight behind the gray steel door. Without hesitation or furtiveness of any kind Bobby boarded the cart, set the leather case on the seat beside him, and wheeled the machine on its fat rubber tires back toward the street.

Around him, birds soared and chirped and a warm breeze rustled the palm fronds. But there were no cries of protest and no pursuit. There was in fact no reaction at all as Bobby serenely piloted the cart toward the back yard of Number 33 Chickadee.

⊕

ALL WAS BLANK along the pink expanse of the back wall of the house. Here too shades were drawn at every window. A single door offered itself toward the left. Toward it Bobby walked across the coarse grass, hands inside the leather notebook, threading the silencer into the snout of the Woodsman. He worked the action once, enjoying the oiled precision of the double snick. But he left the weapon in the case. For now.

The doormat on the concrete by the back door said GO HOME. With no hesitation Bobby opened the screen door, pulled it back, and turned the knob of the inner door. Promptly it opened. Inside was some sort of sitting room, all done in blue. There was a sewing machine, open and threaded, and some plastic laundry baskets stacked full of folded clothes. As Bobby stepped inside, a man came through the opposite door, stopped and stared. He was in shadow, and this was years later, but Bobby recognized him.

Sixto asked, "What the hell do you want?"

"Pardon me, sir," Bobby said. "Can I have a glass of water?"

"Get lost. This is private property."

Despite his years, Sixto was still beefy, still had the squarish meaty face and jet black hair, glistening and combed just so, still had that looking-down-his-nose air. He wore a white terry cloth robe with wide sleeves flopping at his elbows, and red piping at the hems matched the embroidered initials on the breast.

"Go on," he said sharply, "get out of here!"

"I'm lost," Bobby said plaintively. "I was at my daughter's—I went for a walk—"

Sixto glowered. "Jesus Christ," he breathed. "What a cluster-fuck. All right, all right," he added impatiently, "Wait here. I'll call security."

Bobby followed him up some steps, through a door, past a bathroom, and into the kitchen, wading through Sixto's almost nauseating cologne cloud. The kitchen was a riot of pastels and chrome, and its big windows were securely blinded. *What are you afraid of, Sixto?* Bobby thought, smiling inwardly. Hearing him follow, Sixto turned. "I told you to wait, dickhead."

"Could I have some water?" Bobby asked.

"All right," Sixto said brusquely, and went to the sink. "What's your daughter's name?" he asked as he grabbed a plastic tumbler out of the cupboard.

"Rosario," Bobby said, opening the leather case. "Antonia Schiavone Rosario." Sixto hesitated, glanced over his shoulder. "You're shittin me. That's—"

Bobby let the leather case fall to the floor, having extracted the Woodsman.

"Your late wife's name," he completed. "May she at last rest in peace."

Sixto flinched, dropped the tumbler into the sink, seized the counter edge with one beefy hand, rigidly half-facing Bobby.

"Good God," he breathed, staring. "Oh fuck no."

At which point Bobby used words he thought he'd never again utter: "Greetings from the big guy."

"Bobby! No! Please—"

The first shot, a flat abrupt *cough*, drilled Sixto through the right elbow. As he screamed and grabbed himself, Bobby said, "That's for not letting Antonia visit her mother." He fired again—*cough*—and exploded the opposite knee. Sixto staggered and tottered and clattered to the floor, on the way down whacking his head on the counter's edge. "That's for calling Antonia a cunt that time at the regatta, in front of everyone."

Sixto, bleeding from three places and making that broken-record toneless cry, thrashed himself around on the floor to look up at Bobby through stricken, dark brown eyes.

"Please," he gasped, "*please*, Bobby."

"And this," Bobby said, calmly, instructively, "is for making Antonia cry." And he shot Sixto between the eyes.

The <click> moment. Lights out. Nothing like it.

And then, in the instant stillness of the kitchen, from behind, a soft voice:

"Bobby?"

⊕

AS IF CUED, Bobby's headache rose in his head in a wave of pain. He almost cried out from the force of it. He turned to see Alexa standing at the kitchen entrance: of course much older, a bit stooped, long hair bunned back, its rich auburn given gracefully way to slate gray. She wore white culottes and a sleeveless blue shirt—still the all-eyes English teacher type. But even after all these years, and despite what she had done to him, she could still put Bobby's heart in his throat.

Neither spoke at first. She stepped closer, peered around the counter corner at the forever-still Sixto. "You know," she said, low voice melodious but a little husky, "I never dreamt this would happen. But now ... it makes total sense."

"What are you doing here?" Bobby managed.

"I was taking care of Toni. Couldn't expect *him* to do it. Him and his whores."

"Condolences," Bobby said, "on your sister."

"Thank you." She studied him, mouth a tight line trying to smile. "You haven't been well, I see," she said gently.

With his free hand Bobby touched the depression in his jaw. "Had a mole here, turned out to be melanoma. They took out a chunk of the jaw. Year later, it showed up in the brain. So a slice of that they took. Then radiation." His eyes were leaking tears; Bobby shifted the Woodsman to his left hand and brushed his face with his hand. "For six months I've been better," he added, and the tears came forth fully now, "but I think it's come back again."

"Oh, Bobby. How sad." She reached out a comforting hand, but Bobby flinched back.

"This crying, it's from the tumor," he said brusquely. "That's all it is." Her expression clouded over and she inched back from him. "What is it?" he asked.

She took a deep unsteady breath, swallowed, pursed her lips. "Well," she said, tone effortful, "I can't help thinking … here you are, and there *he* is. And I remember the rule." Bobby said nothing. "No witnesses," she added.

Bobby stared. "Not you. Never." *And not with you looking*, he thought.

The tightness around her eyes eased, and she managed to smile. "That's good. Because there's so much of life ahead yet. For both of us."

Bobby's headache let up a bit. He felt something inside, something that had been locked down for forty years, unclench. "Okay," he breathed. "All right."

"But we should get out of here," Alexa said, and turned. "Could you take me to the airport?" she asked, in that tone Bobby remembered: Peter Schiavone's pampered sister. "I'll call my husband," she added, walking toward the kitchen door, "let him know I'm coming back early."

Silently, Bobby swiveled, leveled, fired. The slug caught Alexa in the back of her skull and knocked her forward, face down flat to the floor—click—lights out.

Going to the sink, Bobby ripped off a paper towel, wiped the Woodsman down, and laid it on the floor. Then he walked toward Alexa, stepped over her still splayed legs, bent slightly to look into her open lifeless eyes.

"No one walks out on me twice," he said, and left.

J.A. KONRATH

J.A. Konrath's first novel, WHISKEY SOUR, introduces series heroine Lt. Jacqueline Daniels of the Chicago Police Department. It also features problem solver Phineas Troutt, the protagonist of this tale. Joe has sold stories to *Ellery Queen's Mystery Magazine*, *Alfred Hitchcock's Mystery Magazine*, and many other magazines and collections. He has one wife, three kids (that he knows of), a few dogs, and a house in the suburbs of Chicago.

Joe says: "I've been a fan of anti-heros in fiction since reading Richard Stark's *The Score* as a teenager. Rooting for the bad guy is good, clean, antisocial fun. THESE GUNS FOR HIRE arose out of my love of this genre. Though the characters in these stories are scary and often horrible, the authors have been a joy to work with, and are some of the nicest folks on the planet. Really."

Visit him at www.JAKonrath.com.

BEREAVED
J.A. Konrath

"**WHY SHOULD YOU CARE?** Guys like you got no scruples."

If I had any scruples, I would have fed this asshole his teeth. Or at least walked away.

But he was right.

"Half up front," I said. "Half at the scene."

He looked at me like flowers had suddenly sprouted out of my bald head, Elmer Fudd-style.

"At the scene?"

I'd been through this before, with others. Everyone seemed to want their spouse dead these days. Contract murder was the new black.

I leaned back, pushing away the red plastic basket with the half-eaten hot dog. We were the only customers in *Jimmy's Red Hots*, the food being the obvious reason we dined alone. The shit on a bun they served was a felony. If my stomach wasn't clenched tight with codeine withdrawal spasms, I might have complained.

"You want her dead," I said, fighting to keep my voice steady. "The cops always go after the husband."

He didn't seem to mind the local cuisine, and jammed the remainder of his dog into his mouth, hoarding it in his right cheek as he spoke.

"I was thinking she's home alone, someone breaks in to rob the place, gets surprised, and kills her."

"And why weren't you home?"

"I was out with friends."

He was a big guy. Over six feet, neck as thick as his head so he looked like a redwood with a face carved into it. Calloused knuckles and a deep tan spoke of a blue-collar trade, maybe construction. Probably considered killing the little lady himself, many times. A hands-on type. He seemed disappointed having to hire out.

Found me through the usual channels. Knew someone who knew someone. Fact was, the sicker I got, the less I cared about covering my tracks. Blind drops and background checks and private referrals were things of the past. So many people knew what I did I might as well be walking around Chicago wearing a sandwich board that said, *PHINEAS TROUTT—HE KILLS PEOPLE FOR MONEY.*

"Cops will know you hired someone," I told him. "They'll look at your sheet."

He squinted, mean dropping over him like a veil.

"How do you know about that?"

The hot dog smell was still getting to me, so I picked up my basket and set it on the garbage behind our table.

"Let me guess," I said. "Battery."

He shrugged. "Domestic bullshit. Little bitch gets lippy sometimes."

"Don't they all."

I felt the hot dog coming back up, forced it to stay put. A sickening, flu-like heat washed over me.

"You okay, buddy?"

Sweat stung my eyes, and I noticed my hands were shaking. Another cramp hit, making me flinch.

"What are you, some kinda addict?"

"Cancer," I said.

He didn't appear moved by my response.

"Can you still do this shit?"

"Yeah."

"How long you got?"

Months? Weeks? The cancer had metastasized from my pancreas, questing for more of me to conquer. At this stage, treatment was bullshit. Only thing that helped was cocaine, tequila, and codeine. Being broke meant a lot of pain, plus withdrawal, which was almost as bad.

I had to get some money. Fast.

"Long enough," I told him.

"You look like a little girl could kick your ass."

I gave him my best tough-guy glare, then reached for the half-empty glass bottle of ketchup. Maintaining eye contact, I squeezed the bottle hard in my trembling hands. In one quick motion, I jerked my wrist to the side, breaking the top three inches of the bottle cleanly off.

"Jesus," he said.

I dropped the piece on the table and he stared at it, mouth hanging open like a fish. I shoved my other hand into my pocket, because I cut my palm pretty deep. Happens sometimes. Glass isn't exactly predictable.

"You leave the door open," I told him. "I come in around two AM I break your wife's neck. Then I break your nose."

He went from awed to pissed. "Fuck you, buddy."

"Cops won't suspect you if you're hurt. I'll also leave some of my blood on the scene."

I watched it bounce around behind his Neanderthal brow ridge. Waited for him to fill in all the blanks. Make the connections. Take it to the next level.

His thoughts were so obvious I could practically see them form pictures over his head.

"Yeah." He nodded, slowly at first, then faster. "That DNA shit. Prove someone else was there. And you don't care if you leave any, cause you're a dead man anyway."

I shrugged like it was no big deal. Like I'd fully accepted my fate.

"When do we do this?"

"When can you have the money ready?"

"Anytime."

"How about tonight?"

The dull film over his eyes evaporated, revealing a much younger man. One who had dreams and hopes and unlimited possibilities.

"Tonight is great. Tonight is perfect. I can't believe I'm finally gonna be rid of the bitch."

"Till death do you part. Which brings me to the original question. Why don't you just divorce her?"

He grinned, showing years of bad oral hygiene.

"Bitch ain't keeping half my paycheck for life."

Ain't marriage grand?

He gave me his address, we agreed upon a time, and then I followed him outside, put on a baseball cap and some sunglasses, escorted him down a busy Chinatown sidewalk to the bank, and rammed a knife in his back the second after he punched his PIN into the enclosed ATM.

I managed to puncture his lung before piercing his heart, and he couldn't draw a breath, couldn't scream. I put my bleeding hand under his armpit so he didn't fall over, and again he gave me that look, the one of utter disbelief.

"Don't be surprised," I told him, pressing his CHECKING ACCOUNT button. "You were planning on killing me tonight, after I did your wife. You didn't want to pay me the other half."

I pressed WITHDRAW CASH and punched in a number a few times higher than our agreed upon figure.

He tried to say something, but bloody spit came out.

"Plus, a large ATM withdrawal a few hours before your wife gets killed? How stupid do you think the cops are?"

His knees gave out, and I couldn't hold him much longer. My injured palm was bleeding freely, soaking into his shirt. But leaving DNA was the least of my problems. This was a busy bank, and someone would be walking by any second.

I yanked out the knife, having to put my knee against his back to do so because of the suction; gravity knives don't have blood grooves. Then I wiped the blade on his shirt, and jammed it and the cash into my jacket pocket.

He collapsed onto the machine, and somehow managed to croak, "Please."

"No sympathy here," I told him, pushing open the security door. "Guys like me got no scruples."

M.J. ROSE

M.J. Rose is the author of seven novels and two non-fiction books. Her fiction and non-fiction have appeared in many magazines and reviews including *Pages*, *The Vestal Review*, *Poets & Writers* and *Oprah Magazine*. She graduated from Syracuse University, spent the '80s in advertising, has a commercial in the Museum of Modern Art in NYC. Her latest is THE VENUS FIX.

When asked what is the appeal of hitman stories, she answered: "I'm fascinated with people who take other people's lives into their own hands."

Visit M.J. at www.MJRose.com.

NOT SHY, NOT RETIRING
M.J. Rose

WITHOUT LOOKING BACK, she left him sitting on the frozen ground with a hypodermic needle stuck in his left arm. The woods were heavy here and dark; a singularly hidden area of a very public park and she was still well camouflaged as she took her first few steps away from the site. Creeping forward, she switched the Whole Foods shopping bag she'd been carrying for a Bloomingdales shopping bag. The one now inside the other as opposed to the way she'd carried them when she'd left her apartment two hours before.

After a job, the heat set in. Her desire ratcheted up to the next level. Someone else's blood wasn't flowing anymore and hers was. And it was flowing hotter and with more urgency, demanding she find a release.

By the time she'd walked another twenty steps she'd thrown on the Calvin Klein trench coat she'd been carrying in the Bloomingdales bag. Her black wool three-quarter-length coat, now totally covered over. Her jeans were the same, her boots were the same but after another five steps her red wig was in the bag along with the silver-rimmed glasses she'd been wearing.

By the time she'd have left the shelter of the shadows just beyond the Belvedere Castle, no one would have recognized her as the woman who'd been hanging on the arm of the bastard who was now dead.

By the time she'd exited Central Park on Fifth Avenue and 80th Street, no one who saw the windblown woman—no longer young, but still very attractive—would have guessed that the secret smile on her face or the flush to her cheeks had anything to do with a drug addicted, sex offender who had gotten off on a technicality and had just ostensibly shot himself into oblivion with an overdose of H.

But if anyone had known that's what she'd just spent the last three quarters of an hour arranging, they certainly wouldn't have guessed how jazzed up and sexually crazed she was. Except she couldn't just go straight home. There were procedures to follow.

Even though she'd entered the park on 55th and Central Park South, and exited it from uptown on the east side, she still had to be careful, had to go out of her way in one direction and then another, using well established protocols to ascertain no one had trailed her out or was following her home.

Actually she didn't even mind. She loved the long wait after a job while the pressure built and the want spilled over and the cravings obsessed her.

In twenty-five jobs spread over ten years she'd never even come close to being tracked. But then again, she was religiously careful, they all were even though they knew it was unlikely anyone cared enough about the rapists and pedophiles and murderers to safeguard them. There was little love lost in society for the psychotic scum who escaped prison sentences on the back of lucky breaks, bad evidence, or stupid police work.

She crossed Fifth Avenue and felt the cool breeze wrap itself around her body, trying to wick away her heat but not managing to lower her temperature by even a degree.

Nothing aroused her like a job. Nothing felt as good as being an avenger who went to work after the system failed. She didn't know how many of her there were, or who they were. She did know most of her legion—this secret society—was made up of other law enforcement officers. There had been rumors that a female judge was at their helm, then that it was the father of one of the victims of a guy who got off scot-free, then that it was an attorney who'd lost a case due to a technicality and had the perp repeat the crime a week later.

Last year, when she'd been made Dean of the forensic psychology department of the John Jay School of Criminal Justice, she'd given up these freelance gigs. Just couldn't take the chance anymore. The job mattered to her too much and she'd worked towards it for too damn long to risk being discovered.

She just hadn't expected the changes.

Walking towards Madison Avenue she passed a couple dressed to the nines and smiled. A month ago she would have expected she'd be going out to some ritzy-ditzy dinner tonight. He'd been surprised when she said she had to work the night of her birthday. Smart guy that he was though, he'd smiled and said they could celebrate another night. She was pretty sure he believed her when she said turning fifty wasn't an occasion she wanted to commemorate. That she just wanted to treat it like any other night.

She meant it too. She didn't lie to him. Well. She did. But only about freelance jobs she took on. He questioned her just enough about the unaccounted hours to make it clear he was concerned but not to crowd her. He knew that about her. He knew almost everything about her.

She shivered. Not cold. Hot. Thinking about him, at home, waiting for her. They'd been together a long time and it felt good that she could still feel like this for him. Shit, the truth was she would have felt like this if no one were home waiting for her.

At the next corner she headed downtown walking past one store after another, watching in the plate glass windows for any reflections that made her uncomfortable.

At 77th and Madison she walked into St. Ambrose, an upscale restaurant with an espresso bar and bakery in the front. There were three men at the bar and she stood among them, the shopping bag on the floor next to her feet, and ordered a cappuccino.

As if they could feel her heat, two of the men shifted toward her, moving their bodies just enough so that she knew they had and they knew she knew. It was a subtle dance. The one on her right, with a slight lift of his head, managed to look her over and the one on her left opened his lips just enough to suggest something more.

She didn't acknowledge either of them as she sipped the steaming foamy concoction of air-blown milk and rich fragrant espresso. Closing her eyes she felt the hot liquid coursing down her throat and the body heat of the two men on either side of her and her own heat building up inside of her, slowly, slowly, like she'd been on slow burn for a long time and was finally, really cooking.

Damn. It had been a long time since she'd felt this good.

With this birthday approaching, and the little lines on either side of her eyes getting deeper, and the gray in her hair showing up more often, she'd been sort of lagging. She'd blamed her low sex drive on her age. Had even started to forget about this feeling, this high, this soaring lightheaded incandescent feeling of being so much more, so much more alive, of being so aware of every inch of skin, every nerve ending and all the potential for mind numbing revolutions into the purple black nothing space where she turned into fireworks of blood rushes and breathlessness.

When her contact had called, asking her to come back for just one more gig, she'd refused flat out. He'd insisted that no one could handle this one the way she could. That he was authorized to double her fee. She'd said no a second time and had hung up. It had taken three days of her almost picking up the phone a dozen times, till she gave in and made the call and said yes, softly, whispering, as if she were agreeing to meet an illicit lover.

She wanted to get home now, to get into bed, to get him into bed. She'd called and talked to him before she'd gone into the park. Made all the small suggestive comments that were the shorthand that lovers of ten years used without having to explain.

He'd responded instantly, offering to bring home dinner if she had to work late, telling her he'd be waiting, really waiting, he'd said with a smile that she could hear over the line, she knew him that well.

And he knew her that well, too. Except for this secret slice of her life.

She'd gotten involved with the organization about a month before she'd met him at a political dinner in the city. He'd noticed her across the room and smiled at her before they'd actually met, and when they had he said he'd been a fan of hers for a while. His compliment made her quiet.

"I'm surprised at your reaction. You never stuck me as the shy type," he said.

"I'm not being shy," she smiled. "Just coy."

He laughed, told her he made a habit of taking note of special law enforcement officials. There was so much suggestion and so much promise in the way he said it she lost her equilibrium for a heartbeat. And that was that. She started seeing the judge that night.

Now ten years later, he was still with her and he was still a fan. She knew that because he hadn't complained once in the last eleven months that their sex life had gone to hell. It was as if her libido had dried up and moved to the Florida Keys and left her behind. She fretted over it. Read up on it. It was her change of life. She was turning fucking fifty years old—but still—why did that mean her volume had to be turned down so low she couldn't even hear it anymore?

She knew though, just didn't want to admit it, that wasn't the problem. Age wasn't the issue at all. The truth was really so horrendous she hardly even allowed herself to think it. Too disturbing. Not something she wanted to know about herself. But now, staring down at the dregs of the cappuccino, she couldn't pretend.

It wasn't turning fifty. It wasn't stinking menopause. It was the jobs. It was retiring from the "revenge squad," as she called it in her own mind. She wasn't stupid. Long ago she'd connected her sexual overdrive with the work she did every few months for the organization.

She just kept denying it.

She put down the coffee cup.

Weeks before a job, as soon as she'd get the call from her contact to meet him for lunch at the Japanese restaurant on University Place, her juices would start to flow and the whole planning stage would keep her in a state of perpetual want. The closer she'd get to the actual implementation the more she'd find herself aroused at all times of the day and night even when it seemed inappropriate. It made her smile in the middle of a meeting to feel prickles of excitement settle on her like a sudden rain. She'd actually be aware of the space between her legs, even ache—in the middle of a meeting—to have it filled. Sometimes she could smell her own scent rising up, wonder if anyone else could too, and then not care.

She could smell it now, hanging right under the heavy coffee aroma in the restaurant.

"Do you want another?" the waiter asked in his musical Italian accent.

She shook her head, "Just the check, thanks."

"The gentleman," he indicated with a nod of his head to her left, "has taken care of that."

Her body was humming. Heat rising up from her skin. She knew this feeling.

Looking to her left, she gave the gentleman a soft smile and a sorry nod, wished him a good night, and left.

It had to be safe out there by now. She'd taken long enough. And at the same time taken pleasure from forcing herself to hold back. Extended the agony of wanting release long past she'd thought she'd be able to. Now. She needed to go home now.

Outside she welcomed the blast of cold air, anything that would keep her tamed until she got home. She wasn't abnormal, she reminded herself as she sat in the back of the cab trying not to let the bumpy ride push her over the edge. She wasn't that wild, she could wait to get home, wait for a man's hands or lips or cock, not use the ruts in the road to send her flying.

No, it wasn't abnormal. Military men often described this desperate need for sexual release after a brutal killing. Replace the specter of death with the explosion of sensation that only the living could experience. Snuffing out one life often made you urgently feel the need to prove your own. Vets she talked to, ostensibly for research she told them she was doing, said that the sex they had after a kill surpassed anything they'd ever experienced at other times.

She would take notes when they talked, not offer any reaction, remain impassive, but she wanted to nod along, to tell them yes, she knew, she felt it too. She too had to have sex after a job, and it was amazing sex. It had nothing to do with love or closeness or meaning: she turned animal, shocked and surprised herself, not understanding where the hungry demanding feral creature came from, not caring.

And yet she'd thought she could give it up. Had been sure she could. Still was. Knew this night was just a slip, an addict going back to cigarettes but only for today. She had a job she loved at the college to protect. A man she cared about. She couldn't do this again.

He was waiting for her. And so was dinner. But they didn't eat it then. He could tell from the minute she walked in the door and helped her off with her coat that she was all charged up and so he kissed her behind her ear where her skin was still cold from the night air and stood up against her back and moved his hands around to her waist and pulled her toward him and when she arched against him and felt his erection on the back of her thigh, she just exploded. It wasn't a big one. Not the one she'd make herself wait for. Not the one she'd prolong until she thought she was going to rub herself raw and lose her mind, but it was a burst that sent a shock up through her system. How long had it been since the last time she'd spontaneously combusted just from the touch of his lips and his hands and his hardness.

She didn't have to guess. She knew. Since she'd done the last job.

By the time they made it into the bedroom, she was only wearing her cashmere sweater and he was only wearing his shorts and as she moved, fast towards the bed, she saw the vase full of big fat blooming red roses on the nightstand.

Her mother had sent them that morning. Right. And she'd put them there knowing they'd scent the whole room. She'd forgotten for a while what day this was, she thought, as she wrapped her legs around his back and shut her eyes, preparing for the ungodly gorgeous feeling of him sliding into her.

He gave her a few minutes of what she wanted and then stopped, raised himself up on his hands, and still connected where it mattered, where she could feel it, looked down at her and smiled.

"So, did you enjoy yourself tonight?" he asked.

"I'm still enjoying myself."

"I mean before."

He moved inside of her. Once. Twice. He still had that smile on his face.

But he didn't know about that, she thought. What she'd done before was her secret. What did he mean?

"Did you like your present?"

"But you didn't get me a present."

He moved inside of her. She thrust back. It was difficult to figure out exactly what he was talking about or else it was very simple. All the sensations were making it damn hard to think straight.

"You are much too young to retire. Happy Birthday, sweetest, and welcome back."

JEFF ABBOTT

JEFF Abbott is a three-time Edgar nominee. His best-selling suspense novels including CUT AND RUN, BLACK JACK POINT, and A KISS GONE BAD. His latest is FEAR.

According to Jeff: "Hitmen are the ultimate anti-heroes in fiction; we should not root for them, but we do, not because we applaud their actions—we can't—but because we so want to understand their unique psychology that, at least in fiction, mixes revenge, business, and honor."

Visit his website at www.JeffAbbott.com.

SEIZE YOUR FUTURE
Jeff Abbott

DERRY HEARD THE murderers talking because he couldn't stand another upbeat commercial for the trade schools, urging him to be his destiny and make tomorrow happen. As if he had a future; he had no money to learn how to fix computer networks or make crème brûlée or repair foreign car transmissions. He had nothing: no money, no wife, no day after tomorrow. He clicked off the TV and wondered how the hell he was going to pay rent and buy food next week when he heard the low voices through the thin wall.

"We're gonna kill him." A man's voice, low.

"I'm scared." A woman's voice, frightened, in answer.

"I'm not gonna let the old bastard walk off with that money."

The woman murmured.

"Tomorrow. Or the day after. We see what he does, and …" and a door closed and the voices went silent.

Derry lay in the darkness. *We're gonna kill him.*

He grabbed an empty beer glass from the side table, pressed it against the wall, feeling silly; listening with glasses was a game for kids. But he heard nothing else, only the distant burr of a snore.

Derry took the glass down from the wall. Picked up the phone to call the police then set it back down into its cradle. He didn't know the neighbors but he had seen them, a melon-bellied guy with thick arms, a thin woman who reminded Derry of a substitute teacher facing a class of delinquents. She was pretty but nervous. The man strutted like he was descended from kings. Lots of jewelry on both of them, more on the man, though, and they drove a new Cadillac, a way-too-nice car for the apartment complex.

Derry lay on the bed and the sweat from his back left a damp oval on the sheets. He wondered who the couple wanted to kill and how much money they would steal from the dead man. He turned the television back on, thumbed the volume low on the remote. Another ad suggested if you wanted a bright new life, seize your future and enroll at the Coastal Bend Advanced Institute of Careers. He didn't write down the phone number. He had a whole new idea on how to seize his future.

⊕

THE NEXT MORNING Derry sat by the window and watched the couple go down the stairs to their Cadillac. Most of the other residents of the Sea Shell had departed for their jobs: shrimping in Port Leo, working retail at the tourist traps in Rockport or Port Aransas, or cleaning the hotels in Corpus Christi. Derry didn't have a job as of two weeks ago and his landlord, retired military, considered rent extensions a symptom of poor discipline. He had a week to come up with the rent money. Lisa—probably in California by now, thanks to hocking the wedding ring—had cleaned him out as neatly as a redfish, gutted from tail to jaw. The classifieds lay folded in front of him, unread. He watched the Cadillac and its bejeweled occupants pull out of the lot.

Even if he got a job today, he wouldn't get paid for two weeks. No rent money in time.

Some people would pay for silence.

He felt his conscience begin to drift away from him, almost like a mist he could see, fading in the morning heat. Maybe just going for a little while, he thought. Just enough to get by.

Derry got in his car and followed them at a discreet distance, easy enough to do in Port Leo. The Cadillac pulled into a diner, the Sailor's Spoon, and Derry followed. They took a

back booth and Derry sat at the counter. He bought a dough-
nut, crusted with glaze, and a cup of black coffee; it was all
he could afford. He watched the couple order a pot of decaf,
orange juice, a fat omelet studded with pink ham for her, steak
and eggs for him, biscuits as thick as a child's fist. The woman
called the man Jack. Then Jack laughed loud, ordering mimo-
sas, trying to be funny with the waitress, knowing she'd have
to laugh at his joke to keep her tip.

Derry wondered what he would say to them after the fact
of the killing: *I know what you did. I can stay quiet. I just need
some money.* And he wondered who they would kill, who was
the old bastard. He would follow them, try to identify their target, wait and see what happened. Then ask for the money once
the deed was done. Enough to run away from this crappy life.
The simplicity of the plan pleased him, like a shelf well made,
wood cut at neat angles.

Cadillac Jack and Mousy (the names he'd coined for them)
walked past him. Derry stared at the coffee smear at the bottom
of his cup. He glanced over to see Cadillac Jack snapping out
two twenties to cover breakfast, from a wad of bills that would
have fed Derry for six months. Making a show of his good fortune,
trying to impress the teenage girl at the register. Mousy ignored
Cadillac Jack as he cracked a joke older than fossils. She stared
at Derry, three stools down from the register, and he saw unex-
pected heat light her eyes, a sudden awareness of him. Her tongue
touched the edge of her front lip. She turned away and walked out
into the morning brightness, glancing back at him once.

When they drove off, Derry followed them. But they went
back to the apartment complex. He thought they might go case
the victim's house, go buy a gun, run the necessary errands of
murderers. He hurried back into his own room and put the beer
glass to the wall, listening for their voices. Muffled. Then he heard
the small, hard shot of a slap. Mumbles, more sobs. Her crying
she was sorry. Then the booming voice of the announcer telling

Cecilia to come on down, you're the next contestant on The Price is Right. No voices talking.

Derry sat near his window, waiting for them to go kill someone.

✛

THE AFTERNOON WAS a cookie-sheet-hot haze. Derry dozed on the couch, fitful, waking with a start at a knock on his door. He looked through the window. The Caddy was gone from its parking slot. Oh, damn. The knock sounded again. He opened the door.

Mousy stood on his doorstep. She'd pulled her brown hair back into a ponytail, changed into a pink T-shirt and khaki shorts. She wasn't wearing the morning jewelry. Again her little tongue dabbed along the lips. Her cheek was still a shade red from the slap.

He stared at her in surprise; he thought she was off committing a felony.

"Excuse me, I'm your next door neighbor?" Her voice rose at the end, like she wasn't sure. "My name's Gina. I saw you this morning at the Sailor's Spoon."

"Uh, yeah."

"Would it be okay if I came inside and we talked?"

"Sure." He stepped back, his heart pounding. She came in, glancing at the sparse furnishings, keeping her smile fixed in place.

"Your place is nice."

"It's a dump, but you're nice to lie," Derry said. "You want a Coke?" He nearly laughed at the idea of offering her a drink; he wanted to blackmail her. He decided to say nothing to her; the deal would have to be struck with Cadillac Jack.

"No, thank you," she said. "I met your wife. Lisa?"

"Yeah. She's gone. For like good." He leaned down, pulled a cigarette from the pack, lighted it. "You mind if I smoke?"

"It's your apartment."

"That's not what I asked," Derry said. "I asked if you minded. If you do, I won't."

"I'm just a little bit allergic."

He stubbed out the smoke.

"You can still smoke that later, right? I don't want you … to go without." She sat on the couch, on its edge, her shorts gripping her supple thighs.

"Don't worry about it." He sat in the chair.

"Lisa told me she was leaving you. We were in the laundry room last week," she said. "It's terrible."

"You're late breaking the news," Derry said.

Gina tapped her finger against her leg. "She said it was over money."

"She wanted to live better than I could afford. I don't blame her." He hated himself as soon as he said it, because, damn it, for richer, for poorer meant just that and she'd not lived up to her side of the vow.

"I wondered if you still needed money, Derry."

"You in the door-to-door loan business?"

Gina shook her head. "I need quiet help. And I could pay you well." She nibbled on her bottom lip, knees crunched together, painted toes tipped against the carpet.

"Define quiet."

"Like you don't tell anyone."

"I don't do illegal." He thought it the safest reply.

She shrugged, tenting her cheek with her tongue.

"Why would you trust me?" Derry said. "You don't know me."

"I don't know anybody here," she said. "And you're a big, tough guy, you look like you could handle yourself." She cocked her head. "You need the money. I know you do."

"Not really."

"I'll pay you fifty thousand dollars," she said.

It was ten times what he had thought to ask for his silence. He barely kept his poker face in place. He wished he could relight the cigarette, look cool for her, stare at her through the screen of smoke. He folded his hands in his lap. "If you're so rich, why do you live in this hole?"

"Not by choice," she said. "And I won't stay here when we're done. You won't have to, either."

"Won't have to or won't be able to?" he asked.

"That's up to you."

"What am I supposed to do?"

"My boyfriend Jack has a business deal going with an old guy who's got a place out on Castaway Key." It was a sumptuous development on the edge of St. Leo Bay, a spit of island covered with grand homes and a fancy marina. "A man named Potter. Potter keeps his fingers in a lot of shady deals. Real estate in Houston, Beaumont, up and down the coast, pouring money into crappy housing developments, hiding cash for not-so-nice people. Jack helps him find the properties, get the bids for improvements that never happen, doctors the invoices. So the money they clean together looks legit."

"That's why y'all are staying here," Derry said. "Potter's pretending to pour money into this dump."

"I knew you were smart, Derry." She rubbed her thighs with her hands as though chilled. "I could drink a beer if you got one."

He had one precious Bud left and he got it for her. She sipped at it, touched the cold can to the skin above her breasts for a moment, put it back on a dried ring on the coffee table. "The people Potter works for—they are extremely not-nice. I'm thinking three-letter word, starts with M, ends with B, has O in the middle, but you never heard it from me."

He said nothing, waiting.

"They like Jack better than they like Potter. And they want Jack to get rid of Potter, take over that side of the business."

"Get rid of," Derry said.

"Don't get dense all of a sudden." Her voice was barely a whisper. "They want Jack to kill Potter."

"I can tell you I'm pretty not-interested in your business proposition."

"Hear me out. Potter's got tons of cash on hand. Usually keeps it in a safety deposit box, but Jack knows where he's got a stash, about a hundred thousand, in the house. So he's gonna get rid of Potter, make it look like an accident, a fall down the stairs. Potter broke a hip last winter; he's old, getting frail. Then Jack pockets all the cash because Potter's bosses don't know it's there."

"Potter's been skimming the till and Jack hasn't ratted on him."

"Exactly," Gina said. "Potter's not the kind of guy his mother would shed tears for. Rotten to the core. He likes girls. Young girls. Way too young girls." She shivered.

"So what do you want me to do, Gina?"

"Jack wants to make Potter's death look like an accident. So there won't be many questions. But I'm worried once he's committed murder, he's going to get very nervous about me. About what I know. I'd rather be in charge of my own future."

Her words reminded him of the trade school ads and he almost smiled. "So you want to break free from Jack and you want to take Potter's money."

She nodded.

"How free you want to be?"

"Forever free." She cleared her throat. "It would be easy to make it look like Jack and Potter killed each other."

"You want me to help you kill them."

"Not Potter. Just Jack."

He had gone, in ten minutes, from potential blackmailer to potential hitman and a trickle of fear and excitement coursed along his spine. Blackmailers were cowards, in a way, but a hitman? That would be cool. If it wasn't crazy. "You must be nuts to confide in me when you don't know me very well. How do you know I won't go to the police and spill my guts?"

"Because then you'll be the one exposing Potter and Jack, and in turn, their bosses. The people Potter works for are not the people you want to testify against in a trial." She left the silence in the air, watching him. "You don't have two cents to rub together, Derry. We do this right, you and I are both free from our sucky lives and out of here. With a lot of money."

He stared at his stubbed-out cigarette.

"What do you do, Derry?" But she asked like she already knew.

"I work shrimp boats."

"But not today, or any other day I've seen you."

Now he looked at her.

"You got fired for stealing?" Again, the rise at the end of the sentence, she knew but acting like she didn't know. "Any captains around here eager to take you on?"

Lisa and her laundry-room mouth.

"I'm not desperate enough to become your personal hitman," he said. "I won't fink you out but I don't want any part of it."

"Please. I can't do this alone."

"I'm not interested."

"You ever going to see fifty thousand in cash in your life, Derry?"

He wasn't going to see five dollars in cash anytime soon, and he knew it. Soon he'd lose the apartment, the car, the TV. He wouldn't even have the trade school ads to keep him company, to dangle a life just out of his reach. Seize your future. Embrace your potential. Be your destiny.

"You can do better than Lisa and this dump," Gina said. "It's a fresh start."

It was a sweet deal. Maybe this was his future, grabbing him by the throat, shaking him into action. It was an opportunity he'd never had before, would never get again. Money. A second chance. Maybe, as well, a new career. If he could do one hit, he could surely do another. He thought of Jack—loud, self-absorbed, a man who hit his woman—yeah. He could kill a loser like that for money. The realization was a shock to him, then the surprise faded. It might be ... cool. Like in the movies.

"Have fun living off the mold in your fridge." She got up to leave.

Derry reached out and grabbed her arm. He felt a smile break across his face for the first time in a week. "Let's do it. Seize the future, Gina. Let's take the money."

✛

POTTER'S HOUSE WAS new-money grand, fronted by two thick-trunked palms, a brick driveway, mushroom clouds of bougainvillea. The sun had set into the land behind St. Leo Bay but twilight offered no relief from the damp heat that fogged the air like devil's breath. The stars twinkled in the indigo sky. It was close to nine.

Derry wiped sweat from his forehead. Hitmen, he told himself, shouldn't sweat. The cries of cicadas and crickets blanketed the night. He sat parked two blocks away from Potter's, in front of a house owned by weekenders, empty on a Tuesday night. She said both houses on each side of Potter's were empty at the moment, owned by winter Texans, sure to avoid July swelter. She lay huddled in the back seat so that Jack would not see her as he drove past. Jack thought Gina had gone to Rockport to see a movie. She was supposed to buy two tickets to give Jack an alibi if there were any difficulties later with the police.

"Any sign of Jack?" she asked for the tenth time.

"No," he said.

Her plan was simple. They would wait for Jack to go inside Potter's house, kill the old man, and retrieve the money. Jack would then come out with a duffel bag of cash. Gina and Derry would surprise him, hurry Jack back into the house, shoot him dead, leave him tangled with Potter's body so it looked like a fight gone fatal. Take the cash, split it, run their separate ways.

Derry's resolve to kill Jack rose and fell with his heartbeat and his fear. It's not murder, he told himself, it's a job. The thought—equaling this task to cleaning shrimp or sweeping a floor or hosing down a boat deck—calmed him. The gun felt firm in his hands and he studied its architecture, the curve of the trigger, the texture of the grip, the near-perfect roundness of the eye. Not a gun; a tool to do the job. Just pull the trigger once. Just do it and be done with it and get to the airport in Corpus Christi, pay cash for a ticket anywhere in the world, just go.

"Penny for your thoughts," Gina said.

"My thoughts are about to get much more expensive."

She laughed but he could hear her nervousness in the giggle. "I went to Catholic school. Whole pleated plaid skirt gig. I was the spelling champion four years straight. The nuns would die if they saw me now."

"I'm glad your parents didn't waste the tuition."

"It's kind of a shame we need to part ways. I like you way better than Jack."

"You're a nice girl, Gina." He meant it. "I appreciate what you're doing for me."

"You meet cool people in the funniest circumstances sometimes."

He saw Jack pull up in front of Potter's house, hurry to the door, ring the bell. The door opened. "Jack just went in," he said in a low voice. He pulled his car within two houses of Potter's.

"Give him at least ten minutes," she said. "Maybe longer. He has to get Potter to tell him where the money is. And to shove him down the stairs."

They waited, Derry's throat thickening into concrete.

Fifteen minutes later the front door of the big house opened, Cadillac Jack stepped out onto the darkened porch. He carried a duffel bag, the fabric bubbled with weight.

"Let's go," Derry said. She opened her car door. The gun weighed like an anchor in his, but as they hurried across the yards and up toward Potter's porch the gun seemed to lighten with each step. He kept the gun tucked behind his back.

Cadillac Jack stared at them as they approached. He didn't reach for a gun, his gaze flicking between Derry and Gina.

"Baby, what the hell ..." he started.

"Don't move." Derry brought the gun around to aim at Jack; its weight evaporated. He nearly laughed at the *oh Jesus* look on Jack's face. He felt like a god, like he'd finally stepped into the shoes he'd always been meant to wear.

"Jack," Gina said. "We need to talk."

Jack stared at her, stared at Derry. At Derry's gun.

"Back inside," Derry said.

Jack said, "You're a moron." But he turned and he went back in the house, Gina and Derry following.

Derry shut the front door behind him. The foyer was marble, white. The old man, Potter, lay in a broken heap at the bottom of the stairs, neck twisted, eyes half-shut as though drowsing in the sun.

"Drop the bag," Derry told Jack..

Jack obeyed. Derry kicked the duffel bag toward Gina. "Make sure the money's there."

Jack said, "You bitch …"

Gina knelt by the bag and unzipped it. Derry saw a flash of green within the zipper's tracks, neatly bundled bills, wrapped in rubber bands with yellow paper notes stuck underneath the bands, numbers scrawled on the notes.

"Give me your gun," Derry said. Damn, a basic and he'd forgotten it in the charge of barking orders and getting steeled for the kill. Some hitman he was. Gina had said Jack would have a gun just in case Potter put up a fight. But he had the gun, and it was all cool.

"The gun's in the bag." Jack's eyes were wide and white. "Gina, baby, let's talk about this—"

Derry shot him, the gun booming like thunder cupped in his hands. A bright bloom of red erupted on Jack's chest, and he collapsed on the marble, two feet from Potter, a look of stunned surprise and fear vanishing as his face went slack with death.

"My God," Gina said. "My God, my God."

It was done. Ten seconds, Derry thought, ten seconds and you entirely change the person you are, he was no longer a loser, he was a hitman now. He laughed. He wasn't scared; he felt great. "I did it. Jesus. Okay. We got to fix it so that it looks like Potter shot him as they fell."

The first bullet hit him in the throat, the second and third in the chest, and as he died Derry watched Gina walk away from the duffel bag, wipe the gun, and slip the pistol into Jack's dead hand.

⊕

"I WANT TO HELP however I can," Gina said to the police investigator. He was a tall, raw-boned man named Humphrey. He looked to her like he had come from a long line of shrimpers, the sun and salt baked into his genes. "For Jack's sake."

"Did you know Derry Worrell?"

"Barely. He lived next door to us at the apartment we were staying in temporarily. He had bothered me several times, asking for dates. I told him no. His wife had left him." She shrugged. "I guess he was lonely. I told Jack; Jack wasn't too happy. But Derry was younger and tougher and I don't think Jack wanted to get into a fight. We weren't planning on staying in town long. But he followed us. Like to the Sailor's Spoon for breakfast the other day. He must have followed us to Mr. Potter's once." She shuddered.

"So take me through exactly what happened again."

Gina folded her hands on the table. "Jack and I went over to see Mr. Potter. He's an old friend of Jack's. He's mostly retired now and Jack is … Jack was worried about him. Mr. Potter wasn't in the best of health. We drove over, we found the door open. Jack carries a gun, because he keeps lots of cash on hand. Lots of his renters pay in cash. He pushed open the door, went inside, told me to stay outside. He thought maybe Mr. Potter had just forgotten to lock up. Next thing I hear shots, Jack screaming. I run down the street, find someone who's at home, and call the police." Her voice trembled; she took a long sip of water from the glass at her elbow. "Derry must've broken in to rob Mr. Potter, and Jack interrupted him … I can't believe it. I thought Derry was a harmless loser."

"Derry Worrell has a record," one of the other cops said.

"Petty theft," the detective said. "And he didn't have a job."

Gina pressed her lips together, wiped the tears from her eyes.

They questioned her for another two hours and she stuck to her story without variation. The background check on her, she knew, would reveal no criminal history. Even when Jack and Potter's mob connections came to light, it was nothing to her. The duffel bag with the hundred thousand was hidden in one of the empty vacation homes next door to Potter; she'd found a hidden house key a week ago, made a copy, replaced the key. Jack had interrupted a robbery gone wrong, committed by an out-of-work loser against a helpless old man. It was a tragedy. In case Jack and Potter's business associates appeared as the news spread and began wondering about Potter's tampered accounts, she would move the money tomorrow to a bank in Anguilla, start the slow migration of the cash to safety, where only she could find it.

And then play the grieving girlfriend. Get a job here for a few months, waitressing, so she wouldn't look like she was on the run, had a reason to hide, or was suddenly flush with cash. Then, when the time was right, disappear.

She went back to the apartment. It was lonely without Jack's big voice. The police were searching Derry's apartment; she could hear them rummaging through his few belongings, talking in low whispers. She clicked on the TV to watch the sitcom reruns. The late-night commercials fired up at the first break, the trade schools promising the brightest of prospects. Seize your future, one said, and she fought down a laugh. Derry had said the same words in his excitement over his new career. But the ads, and poor dumb Derry, were right; you had to embrace every opportunity that came your way. Derry had been the right opportunity for her.

She slid with a smile into the cool of the sheets. Seize your future. Great words to live by.

REED FARREL COLEMAN

REED was born and raised in Brooklyn, NY. His sixth novel, THE JAMES DEANS, has been nominated for the Best Paperback Original Edgar Award and he's just been elected Executive Vice President of the Mystery Writers of America. He's edited the short story anthology, HARDBOILED BROOKLYN, and his short stories and essays have appeared or will appear in DUBLIN NOIR, BROOKLYN NOIR 3, PLOTS WITH GUNS, DAMN NEAR DEAD, WALL STREET NOIR, F—K NOIR, and CRIME SPREE MAGAZINE. He writes another series under the pen name Tony Spinosa. Reed lives with his wife and children on Long Island.

On the topic of literary assassins, Reed says: "I think hitmen are the big cats of crime fiction. They're the alpha predators; hidden, powerful, aloof."

Visit Reed at www.ReedColeman.com

BAT-HEAD SPEED
Reed Farrel Coleman

WHEN I KILL for the kikes, I call meself Hank Greenberg. For the niggers, it's Hammerin' Hank. Don't love it that Hank is so popular amongst those two races, but let's face it, how many Jews were great home run hitters? Yeah ... I'm waiting, boyo. You can count the number on the thumb stuck up yer arse. Bonds stays healthy a few more years and the problem'll be solved. For the wops, it's Joe D. The spics, Roberto Clemente. When the contract is white bread, I go with Mickey Mantle. It appeals to me own sense of vanity. Like I put the Mick in Mickey. Sorry, Babe. Fook, McGwire, the cheatin' cunt. Don't kill for the Irish. No profit in it.

Me specialty or speciality, as me sainted mother would call it, is blunt force trauma. I can take it deep with a mighty blow or play "small ball", breaking every bone on me way around the bases. Either way, I always touch 'em all and never is the time I miss home plate. It's management's choice. He who pays controls the play. Nature of the business. I've rigged me iPod so to play the roar of the crowd and the explosion of fireworks in me ears when a job is complete. I'm afraid I've not yet figured out how to rig a curtain call. Some day.

When I began me career as a lad in the disco '70s, there was great affection for the long ball. Clients wanted the work done quickly, with a single swing. *And the pitch ... Oh, he got all of that one. If it ever comes down, it's a home run. Man oh man, have you ever seen a skull crack quite like that one?* The '80s saw the advent of junk bonds and morning in America. And with them, please god, came a jones for cocaine and cracked bones. Jaysus, even had the odd client wanted to watch me do me work. Discouraged it. Whenever I'd break the shins, it was vomitville. No sound like it, breaking a man's shins. Came the '90s, back we went to tapemeasure shots. 9/11 has brought back bunts and bones broken one at a time. All business is cyclical in nature. I come to the knowledge honestly.

Was the day I tried changing with the times. Mistake. Turned my back on ash as me material of choice and went aluminum. As effective? Maybe more so. Saved on equipment in the long run. But the sound! Jaysus and his blessed mother, couldn't stomach it me own self. That pinging was a horror. You kill a man, whatever the reason short of rape and child molestation, and he deserves more than a hollow *Ping!* at the end of the road. Bollocks. Embarrassing, really, killing a man that way. Give me a solid *thud, crunch, snap.* That's music for a man to die by. Lately, I've gone the way of Bonds and tried some of those maple bats from north of the border. Sweet. Lovely feel. But I'll take ash when the job's to be done right.

Yer thinking, how'd a thick-headed donkey like meself develop a taste for baseball? Fair question. First, I think it was out of necessity. Tis always the way, is it not? Came stateside when I was eleven. Da had a run-in with the Brits, the hoors. An explosive personality, me father, if ya catch the drift. Till I landed stateside, had a hurly near glued to my palms. A hurly, you say? A lethal piece of hardwood shaped roughly like a human femur. Hurling? Take a week to explain. Let it suffice to say it's bloodier than politics or ice hockey and a fair bit more entertaining. The sport the real Fighting Irish play.

Guess I saw baseball as the closest thing to it, minus the carnage, of course. I'd more than make up for that. I was quite the prodigy. Couldn't field worth shite, but I was a natural DH. Ron Bloomberg can kiss me arse. Shame me career predated the DH. Coaches tried burying me in right field. And in spite of me shortcomings, made it one game short of the Little League World Series. Didn't show the qualifying games on TV back in the day, only the final on Wide World of Sports. Would've shown those chinks a thing or three had we made it to the finals.

Pushing fifty now and still I've the bat-head speed of a thirty-year-old slugger. Tiger Woods come to me, I'd get his club head speed up a good five miles. I've got the whole setup in me house: batting cage, video tape, VR exercises on the computer to keep my hand-eye coordination sharp. Do yoga, trunk strengthening, and quick-twitch muscle exercises every day. Read every book, seen every instructional tape on hitting that's been produced. Fook Einstein. Ted Williams, now there's a feckin' genius. Charlie Lau was a cunt. Set hitting back a decade with his bat release shite.

Still, with all me own equipment, I love showing off for the colleens at the local batting cages. No matter the town I'm in or the job to be done, I manage to get a session in at the local bat-away. Particularly love the jobs in college towns or hamlets with a minor-league squad. Visiting California, Florida, or Arizona is a pleasure. Always baseball to be played. Always a blond to be had. Hustled me more money than Paul Newman and Tom Cruise put together. Though it grieves me hard to say it, I'll cede the number of blonds to them boyos.

Currently, I'm on Long Island, expensive fooking shitehole. Bad timing as well. The Ducks, the local minor-league squad, is on the road and the colleges are out of session. Needless to say, me mood's not great. I'm still waiting for me wedge and instructions. Don't like this much to be up in the air, but the money's too good to turn away from. I've waited for two days now and me patience is near as thin as me own hair. The phone, praise god. Salvation at last. Instructions of a sort.

⊕

THE BAR WAS CROWDED but dark. I was in the loose-fitting, road-gray, Detroit jersey. Very retro. No name across the back. Even if there were, Greenberg wouldn't resonate with this bunch. More likely think I was a dentist than a slugger.

"Hey Hank," she says, strolling up to me seat at the bar. Raven hair framing a green-eyed goddess' face. "Whatcha having?"

Loaded question that. Let it hang there like blue smoke. Moved on.

"Sam Adams."

"Not Guiness?"

"You'll want to watch that. Stereotypes'll get you in trouble," I warned.

"Max! Two Sams."

"Max is it? Know all the barmen on Long Island by their first names?"

"Not on the entire Island. Just Suffolk County." The sarcasm dripped off her tongue like honey. "Slainte."

Impressed me. Clinked glasses and put their contents down in a swallow.

"C'mon, Hank, let's take a ride."

Another loaded line. Curious. Said,"Where to?"

"Your motel room. I want to see your stuff."

Christ, I wondered, did she say anything that wasn't loaded?

Got in her yellow Vette. Stopped at me room. She stayed in the car. Picked up me Lousiville Slugger. Burned *The Mick* into the top of the barrel me own self.

"Now where to?"

"You'll see," she purred.

Drove through a darkened industrial park. Pulled into an empty parking lot in front of what looked to be a warehouse. The local bat-away. She had the keys. Stepped inside the darkened hall, punched numbers into a keypad, threw a light switch. Have you ever entered an empty church? Was what it felt like for me. This was me own St. Paddy's.

"Fast cage is over there." She pointed to the far right end of the facility. "What size helmet?"

"Yer joking me lady. Helmets are for pussies. No offense intended."

"None taken. It's your funeral."

Got in the cage. Stood in the right-hand batter's box. "Whenever you're ready."

Five seconds later, a yellow ball whizzed by me at the knees. I made no move. Judged the speed at ninety. Next ball, same thing. Statues have made more movement. This time I eyed where the ball was coming from. Third ball I smacked right through the square in the netting through which the pitch had come. Next ball, same result. And the next and the next and the … Jumped into the lefty batter's box. Closed my eyes. Listened. Smacked the ball just above the hole in the netting.

"Shite!"

"I'm convinced," she said. "You're the best I've seen."

The pitching machine went silent. As I stepped out of the cage, the lights dimmed. Nothing more frightening than a dark church. Got into hitting position.

"Fuck is th—"

The tail end of the question was shoved back into me mouth along with me front teeth. Something snapped. Heard it more than felt it. Coughing up teeth and blood, I was down, dazed, me arms and legs as useless as tits on a tennis racket. After a second she came back into focus. Standing over me, a hurly in her hands.

"Manny Alcazar," she hissed. "Remember him, Mr. Clemente?"

Mind racing. Yeah, shite, I recalled. A thick-bodied, squat spic, took his time dying, too. He was one of my early nineties one-bone-at-a-time jobs. Didn't know why management wanted him done or done that way. Never questioned the instructions."

"Yer father," I choked.

"You caught on about five minutes too late, asshole. Fucking shame that I snapped your vertebrae. Would have liked to have you feel the bones breaking."

"The hurly?"

"Faith and begorrah, me mother's Irish, you prick."

Last thing she said to me. She put down the hurly and picked up me own bat. Poetic justice, I suppose. I watched her shatter me legs. Well done. She'd a powerful swing. The girl had real potential and there was little doubt, with proper training, mind you, I could have added a good ten miles an hour to her bat-head speed.

LISA MANNETTI

LISA Mannetti is a former editor and adjunct English instructor who discovered she preferred full-time writing to real work when she volunteered to be the family member who cared for her ailing mother. Her work has appeared in SMALL BITES (an anthology to benefit Charles Grant), SPOOKS! published by Twilight Tales; and HELL HATH NO FURY. Her short story, "Hungry for the Flesh" will be in *Space and Time* #102. Two of her novels, as well as two other book projects illustrated by Glenn Chadbourne, are in the ninth circle of limbo on publishers' desks.

When asked about the topic of this anthology, Lisa replied: "Hitman stories appeal to the outlaw in all of us. Who wouldn't occasionally love to get rid of troublesome acquaintances (or relatives) without actually having to clean up messy forensic evidence?"

Visit her at www.TheChanceryHouse .com.

EVERYBODY WINS
Lisa Mannetti

ANXIOUS? DEPRESSED?

THINKING OF SUICIDE?
Now, there's help.
Our 24-hour line connects you
ONE ON ONE
With a New York State Certified Suicide Counselor

That was as far as Sally Grimshaw read. She punched in the phone number.

"We're here for you," a young woman on the other end said. Sally began explaining, talking faster and faster. Her black moods, her low self-esteem (and what good did it do to *know* it was low self esteem? As if knowing could make you feel less like shit).

"I want to die," Sally finished.

"Mr. Vinny can see you in twenty minutes—"

"See me?"

"Certainly." The woman rattled out an address in the West Eighties. "Can you get here?"

"Yes. Thank you. God bless you, yes—"

"Don't worry about your hair, your clothes—don't worry about a thing. Just get in a cab and come right now."

Sally hung up and rushed into her old trench coat, throwing it on over a flannel nightgown. She snagged an oversized worn black leather pocketbook from the hook inside the closet door.

Five minutes later she walked into a cold gray day and wishy-washy December flurries. But she had hope, she told herself. Now there was hope.

⊕

"**I'M FORTY-SEVEN** and I've never even had a date." Sally snuffled into a white Kleenex tissue. "I hate my job. I think they're going to fire me because I call in sick a lot. I can't help it." She twisted the soft paper to shreds, as if it might prevent her from breaking into hysterical sobs. "Four years ago at my high school reunion, not one person remembered me ..."

Mr. Vinny ("No last names here, please") held up a pudgy hand. "It's a tough old world, that's God's truth, Sal." Gold pinky ring gleaming, he was paging through the three or four sheets of paper that were Sally's file.

Mr. Vinny's office was painted dark salmon. A huge aquarium built into the wall behind his antique desk added turquoise sparkle. He closed the folder and walked toward her.

"So, Sally, how were ya gonna do it? Huh?" Mr. Vinny sat on the edge of his desk, one loafer dangling. "Pills, a gun, a dive out the window, what?"

"Pills, I guess—"

"Shit, you take pills, maybe you'll get the job done. More likely you'll wake up one morning in Bellevue, and you'll be lucky if you don't end up a vegetable in a wheelchair." He got up and paced a step or two, hands clasped behind his back. "Nope, it's not efficient." He stared at her. "I don't like inefficiency."

Sally wasn't sure what he meant.

"Ya know, nobody can tell you when it's time to check out— I mean look at you." He suddenly whirled around and snatched her file, flapping it in her face. "Overweight, nobody in your life—not even a cat. Your life is a shitpile, and nobody knows it better than you. So whaddya say? Have you had enough, or what?"

"I thought—" she stopped. Confusion mounted inside her. She touched her thin brown hair and knew she looked bad. "I hate all of it," she whispered.

"Right. That's my point. But ya know, it's not easy to kill yourself. I could show you a dozen files about how tough it is."

"Yes," she said. She had botched everything else—killing herself would be no different. She felt the hot flash of embarrassment and knew her face had turned the ugly purple-scarlet of a wine birth mark.

"Guy holds a gun to his head," he mimed, "but who knows; maybe he chickens out at the last second. Anyway, whammo-slammo. 'Cept he don't die, he just ends up with a dent in his right temple and pissing his pajama bottoms because his fuckin' catheter fell out, only he don't know it, cause there's no feeling from his neck down. Hoo-boy, and he thought he was depressed *before*." Mr. Vinny smiled, his face broadening to a double chin.

This wasn't a place that coddled or pampered; they were going to make her realize what a terrible decision suicide was. "I guess it's a bad idea."

"No it's a great idea! But amateurs … unless you got like Jack Kevorkian on the spot, there's no guarantees. You get amateurs involved, it's not efficient It's bad business."

"Oh," she said. Confused, she clutched her purse a little tighter.

"So what do you say, Sal? Should I pencil you in on my dance card or are you gonna stay miserable?"

"In? You mean like a program?"

He was rustling papers. "I got a guy here needs to be taken out, Sally, and you could—"

"Taken out? I—I … What?"

"The bastard's been beatin' the shit out of his wife, the kids. He's lappin up the booze. He's got millions, and he's still as stingy as a whore's alarm clock. But his wife—she's a woman who understands good business, so she came to us for help.

And what I want to know is, are you willing to kill him at the same time you kill yourself?"

"But—"

"We guarantee you go—no messy half-assed attempts. The lady gets her hit. Everybody wins." He paused. "Sal?"

"You're the Mafia, aren't you?" she said.

He leaned forward, his bulky arms supporting his weight, hands resting on the arms of her club chair, his heavy chin an inch from hers.

"There *is* no more Mafia."

He backed away and she breathed easier.

"Between the last three or four asswipe mayors, what we *used* to call a hitman wouldn't touch a contract. Too much risk. There's no loyalty these days. But there are still people who need services. See? This woman needs a service—and you need a service. She paid for it, but, for you it's free. And when it's done there'll be one less creep friggin' up the world."

He paused. "Uh, I was referring to the shit-sucking gentleman. Not you, of course. You're goin' to your heavenly reward."

"I don't know. I mean…" She squirmed in her seat, the thick nightgown wadding into a lump between her fleshy thighs. "How would I …?"

"You drive?"

She nodded.

"Smacko." He brought his hands together in a thunder-clap. "Head-on collision. We pump you through-and-through with your drug of choice. Guaranteed lights out and you won't feel a thing after the first ten seconds.

"No, I couldn't!" In her mind she saw glass spewing in a slow arc like water droplets from a fountain. She heard the ripping clang of metal, felt the thud of the impact hewing her instantly, saw blood.

"You disappoint me. I thought sure you'd go for the car." He sighed. "You could shoot him. Him and the assholes he hangs with. Have you had target practice? Cause we can arrange lessons at the local shooting range—"

"No guns," Sally said.

"Tough shit. Gun it is."

"I think I should go now."

"I don't think so," he said. "Not unless you want to have a messy accident … because I got ten lonely guys and five world-weary pre-menopausal ladies like yourself that's gonna call me before the close of business today." His smile was too wide, his teeth too prominent.

She understood at once. One of his other cases, a would-be suicide, would do her in. A small scritchy noise—the sound of a cornered ferret—pushed its way past Sally's lips. But so what? Death was what she wanted anyway.

"Wouldn't it be better to have time to make your preparations, write your note, call your mother? Get some closure on the mess of your life?"

"No!" She started to get up, but the menacing look on his face told her to sit. She was in a trap, caught under the bell jar of her own neurosis. She was making herself sick and depressed. Was her life so terrible that she couldn't snap herself out of it?

"Cause you can walk right out the door, if you want—but you won't know when the knife's gonna go through your cheek in some cold alley, and there'll be no time to get your shit together. And no guarantees you'd die. Nope, no guarantees. Except the guarantee that you'll suffer."

"Mr. Vinny—" Sally said.

"Just Vinny, now." He smiled. From his desk drawer he removed a plain manila folder and opened it. "Sign here."

A single sheet of white paper with black print like flea dirt came at her. At the bottom was a line marked with a huge blue X.

Sally signed.

✛

A HALF-HOUR LATER, she left with photos of "John Doe," his thinning gray hair offset by a neatly trimmed, silvery mustache. He was wearing a tuxedo in all the pictures.

She hailed a cab back to her apartment.

The contract was totally illegal, she thought,. But she had no doubt Vinny would see she kept her end of the bargain.

The last words he'd said to her were *Happy New Year*.

"Happy New Year," Sally said, sliding the key into the scratched brass of her door lock and letting herself in. "Happy fucking New Year."

Inside the apartment she opened her black purse and took the greasy towel wrapping off the .22 Ruger. Its serial numbers had been filed off.

Tomorrow she was scheduled for practice at the shooting range at eight AM. Sharp.

Vinny told her if she didn't show, he'd begin to have doubts about her intention to honor the contract. And that would be too bad.

Sally picked up the gun and aimed at an age-browned lampshade in her tiny living room. She pretended it was Vinny's double-chinned face.

"Pow," she said, and then she let the hand holding the gun fall to her side. How could she think there was any help for someone like her, or that anyone cared? How stupid could a person be?

✛

"I CAN'T." SALLY wept into the phone in her galley kitchen. "This man's never done a thing to me!"

"So what? He's hurt plenty of people. And that's all you need to know. You'll be doing the world a big favor."

"I went to the shooting range." Her tears were coming harder now. "I just know, Vinny, I just know, I mean the minute I take the gun out in the restaurant, someone will see me, I won't be able to shoot, I'll wind up in jail!"

"No you won't, Sally." His voice was ice. "You'll never see the inside of a jail."

"All right," she sighed.

"Good girl. The Moon Over the Tiber Ristorante. Nine PM. Sharp. Saturday night the 23rd and no later. We don't want to ruin his kids' Christmas Eve. It's a big night with Italians."

The phone came down with a *thunk* in her ear.

It was two days until the end of the world.

⊕

SHE STOOD OUTSIDE the restaurant. The crosswinds veered madly around the corners, and she shivered. Garlands of colored Christmas lights sparkled through the fogged glass of the Moon Over the Tiber's red door.

She pushed on the door, and a gust of steamy air scented with garlic assailed her. It was so warm it was almost tropical. Sally shivered again.

A phone call from Vinny this morning had included her final instructions.

She was to take Doe out first, and any baggy gentlemen dining with him were fair game. But no grandmas would get shot because *we're not fuckin' barbarians, capisce?*

Doe, then the linguine-slurpers. And she was told not to worry. Since she refused to use the gun on herself, all she had to do was clamp down on the little yellow capsule she'd been told to keep between her back teeth. A little blood might leak out of her mouth, but, hey, that was it. She'd seen the photos of all those crazy cultists from Guyana, right? Cyanide was a sure bet.

It lay like a dollop of dentist's gel in the gutter between her cheek and her teeth. She'd been afraid she'd inadvertently clamp down on it too soon.

If that happened, the Lifespan Treatment Center was going to bring her mother in for bereavement counseling.

Sally stood in the cramped foyer, hesitating. The gun in her purse felt like an anvil.

Have dinner, Vinny told her. *We want to keep our clients happy. But don't pay for it—you don't want anybody seeing the gun before you yank it out. Stand up like you're gonna use the can, then let 'er rip.*

She'd left no note. Nothing in the dog-eared diary she called a journal about being angry or feeling crazy or having a gun. There would be no clues.

A waiter wearing a long dark blue apron over his suit showed her to a table. Twenty feet or so away, John Doe was sucking clams from the shells. There was a white napkin tied bib-style around his neck.

"Wine, Signora?"

"Yes. A bottle of Pinot Grigio."

"Bene." He scribbled onto a small pad.

She ordered fried calamari, a caesar salad, stuffed cannelloni, and tiramisu for dessert.

Sally fingered the empty wine glass on the table in front of her. The wine would taste damn good, she thought. Then she suddenly realized the capsule was in her mouth. How could she eat or drink anything with the capsule in her mouth?

She waggled it out and placed it gently in the under the rim of her bread plate. She would shovel it back in right after the tiramisu, just before the check, just before … Yes, she sighed, that would work out fine.

The waiter brought the wine and uncorked it. "How festive," Sally said, taking a sip and nodding assent.

"Si," the waiter said, fussing over the glasses, rearranging the tableware, the glowing votive lamp.

The waiter hurried off again.

The condemned woman ate heartily. At least it was a great restaurant. The calamari had been delicious.

Sally was into her second forkful of caesar salad when she realized the waiter had taken away the bread plate.

The capsule was nowhere on the table.

Panic seized her, and she shifted the short white vase with the single red carnation, the silverware, skimming her finger around the underside of her salad plate. She even lifted the tablecloth and peered at the floor.

It was gone.

It must have disappeared when the waiter cleared the appetizer and dipping oil. Oh hell, did it matter? The capsule was probably already in a big industrial garbage bag, invisible in a soggy mess of half-eaten cream tortes, tossed lemon slices, and limp parsley.

It wasn't like she could ask for it back. *Oh waiter, I'll take the check and my cyanide capsule; I'm afraid of guns you know.*

Sally stifled a snort, drank some more wine, and ate dripping romaine lettuce, mopping the dressing with the half-eaten slice of crusty bread she'd left perched on the salad dish.

She glanced at John Doe. He was with three other men. They were eating provolone and fruit.

Everybody wins. It was so much like her own dreary, wrecked life.

Everybody else wins, she thought, *but not me.*

And she was tired of it all, tired of being the loser, watching everyone else get what they want. Was she tired enough to do anything about it?

She ate the tiramisu but her appetite was gone, and the food was no more than dust and the steely taste of gunmetal in her mouth.

And Mr. Doe became everything she hated about herself. If he was as disgusting as Vinny claimed—disgusting enough for Doe's wife to want to have him killed—then who was Sally to argue?

She pulled the gun out of her purse as she stood, and aimed it at Mr. Doe's face.

His startled expression disappeared a moment after she pulled the trigger. His dinner companions never had a chance to react as she easily dispatched them one after the other.

She was a natural at this.

The handful of restaurant patrons had fled, leaving Sally alone with her four victims. Killing them had been shockingly liberating, and she realized she finally had a talent for something in her wretched life. She smiled as she wondered whether or not she could get away with this.

She planned to try. It was incredibly fortunate the cyanide pill had been lost. Perhaps more than fortune. Perhaps fate.

She turned to leave, to begin a new life.

From out of the shadows her waiter approached, his gun drawn.

She could tell he'd been crying.

"I'm sorry, miss," he said. "I have to. I signed a contract."

He pulled the trigger.

LAWRENCE BLOCK

LAWRENCE Block is a Grand Master of Mystery Writers of America, and a past president of both MWA and the Private Eye Writers of America. He has won the Edgar and Shamus awards four times each and the Japanese Maltese Falcon award twice, as well as the Nero Wolfe and Philip Marlowe awards, a Lifetime Achievement Award from the Private Eye Writers of America, and, most recently, the Cartier Diamond Dagger for Life Achievement from the Crime Writers Association (UK).

About his character Keller, the hitman protagonist of this and many other short stories, Larry says: "The professional killer is an appealing character for writers and readers alike. His is an irresistible fantasy occupation; he does, after all, get paid handsomely for what you and I would cheerfully do for free."

Visit him at www.LawrenceBlock.com.

KELLER'S DESIGNATED HITTER
Lawrence Block

KELLER, A BEER IN ONE hand and a hot dog in the other, walked up a flight and a half of concrete steps and found his way to his seat. In front of him, two men were discussing the ramifications of a recent trade the Tarpons had made, sending two minor-league prospects to the Florida Marlins in return for a left-handed reliever and a player to be named later. Keller figured he hadn't missed anything, as they'd been talking about the same subject when he left. He figured the player in question would have been long since named by the time these two were done speculating about him.

Keller took a bite of his hot dog, drew a sip of his beer. The fellow on his left said, "You didn't bring me one."

Huh? He'd told the guy he'd be back in a minute, might have mentioned he was going to the refreshment stand, but had he missed something the man had said in return?

"What didn't I bring you? A hot dog or a beer?"

"Either one," the man said.

"Was I supposed to?"

"Nope," the man said. "Hey, don't mind me. I'm just jerking your chain a little."

"Oh," Keller said.

The fellow started to say something else, but broke it off after a word or two as he and everybody else in the stadium turned their attention to home plate, where the Tarpons' clean-up hitter had just dropped to the dirt to avoid getting hit by a high inside fastball. The Yankee pitcher, a burly Japanese with a herky-jerky windup, seemed unfazed by the boos, and Keller wondered if he even knew they were for him. He caught the return throw from the catcher, set himself, and went into his pitching motion.

"Taguchi likes to pitch inside," said the man who'd been jerking Keller's chain, "and Vollmer likes to crowd the plate. So every once in a while Vollmer has to hit the dirt or take one for the team."

Keller took another bite of his hot dog, wondering if he ought to offer a bite to his new friend. That he even considered it seemed to indicate that his chain had been jerked successfully. He was glad he didn't have to share the hot dog, because he wanted every bite of it for himself. And, when it was gone, he had a feeling he might go back for another.

Which was strange, because he never ate hot dogs. A few years back he'd read a political essay on the back page of a news magazine that likened legislation to sausage. You were better off not knowing how it was made, the writer observed, and Keller, who had heretofore never cared how laws were passed or sausages produced, found himself more conscious of the whole business. The legislative aspect didn't change his life, but, without making any conscious decision on the matter, he found he'd lost his taste for sausage.

Being at a ballpark somehow made it different. He had a hunch the hot dogs they sold here at Tarpon Stadium were if anything more dubious in their composition than your average supermarket frankfurter, but that seemed to be beside the point. A ballpark hot dog was just part of the baseball experience, along with listening to some flannel-mouthed fan shouting instructions to a ballplayer dozens of yards away who couldn't possibly hear him, or booing a pitcher who couldn't care less, or having one's chain jerked by a total stranger. All part of the Great American Pastime.

He took a bite, chewed, sipped his beer. Taguchi went to three-and-two on Vollmer, who fouled off four pitches before he got one he liked. He drove it to the 396-foot mark in left center field, where Bernie Williams hauled it in. There had been runners on first and second, and they trotted back to their respective bases when the ball was caught.

"One out," said Keller's new friend, the chain jerker.

Keller ate his hot dog, sipped his beer. The next batter swung furiously and topped a roller that dribbled out toward the mound. Taguchi pounced on it, but his only play was to first, and the runners advanced. Men on second and third, two out.

The Tarpon third baseman was next, and the crowd booed lustily when the Yankees elected to walk him intentionally. "They always do that," Keller said.

"Always," the man said. "It's strategy, and nobody minds when their own team does it. But when your guy's up and the other side won't pitch to him, you tend to see it as a sign of cowardice."

"Seems like a smart move, though."

"Unless Turnbull shows 'em up with a grand slam, and God knows he's hit a few of 'em in the past."

"I saw one of them," Keller recalled. "In Wrigley Field, before they had the lights. He was with the Cubs. I forget who they were playing."

"That would have had to be before the lights came in, if he was with the Cubs. Been all around, hasn't he? But he's been slumping lately, and you got to go with the percentages. Walk him and you put on a .320 hitter to get at a .280 hitter, plus you got a force play at any base."

"It's a game of percentages," Keller said.

"A game of inches, a game of percentages, a game of woulda-coulda-shoulda," the man said, and Keller was suddenly more than ordinarily grateful that he was an American. He'd never been to a soccer match, but somehow he doubted they ever supplied you with a conversation like this one.

"Batting seventh for the Tarpons," the stadium announcer intoned. "Number 17, the designated hitter, Floyd Turnbull."

✪

"HE'S A DESIGNATED HITTER," Dot had said, on the porch of the big old house on Taunton Place. "Whatever that means."

"It means he's in the lineup on offense only," Keller told her. "He bats for the pitcher."

"Why can't the pitcher bat for himself? Is it some kind of union regulation?"

"That's close enough," said Keller, who didn't want to get into it. He had once tried to explain the infield fly rule to a stewardess, and he was never going to make that sort of mistake again. He wasn't a sexist about it, he knew plenty of women who understood this stuff, but the ones who didn't were going to have to learn it from somebody else.

"I saw him play a few times," he told her, stirring his glass of iced tea. "Floyd Turnbull."

"On television?"

"Dozens of times on TV," he said. "I was thinking of seeing him in person. Once at Wrigley Field, when he was with the Cubs and I happened to be in Chicago."

"You just happened to be there?"

"Well," Keller said. "I don't ever just happen to be anyplace. It was business. Anyway, I had a free afternoon and I went to a game."

"Nowadays you'd go to a stamp dealer."

"Games are mostly at night nowadays," he said, "but I still go every once in a while. I saw Turnbull a couple of times in New York, too. Out at Shea, when he was with the Cubs and they were in town for a series with the Mets. Or maybe he was already with the Astros when I saw him. It's hard to remember."

"And not exactly crucial that you get it right."

"I think I saw him at Yankee Stadium, too. But you're right, it's not important."

"In fact," Dot said, "it would be fine with me if you'd never seen him at all, up close or on TV. Does this complicate things, Keller? Because I can always call the guy back and tell him we pass."

"You don't have to do that."

"Well, I hate to, since they already paid half. I can turn down jobs every day and twice on Sundays, but there's something about giving back money once I've got it in my hands that makes me sick to my stomach. I wonder why that is?"

"A bird in the hand," Keller suggested.

"When I've got a bird in my hand," she said, "I hate like hell to let go of it. But you saw this guy play. That's not gonna make it tough for you to take him out?"

Keller thought about it, shook his head. "I don't see why it should," he said. "It's what I do."

"Right," Dot said. "Same as Turnbull, when you think about it. You're a designated hitter yourself, aren't you, Keller?"

⊕

"**DESIGNATED HITTER**," **KELLER** said, as Floyd Turnbull took a called second strike. "Whoever thought that one up?"

"Some marketing genius," his new friend said. "Some dipstick who came up with research to prove that fans wanted to see more hits and home runs. So they lowered the pitching mound and told the umpire to quit calling the high strike, and then they juiced up the baseball and brought in the fences in the new ballparks, and the ballplayers started lifting weights and swinging lighter bats, and now you've got baseball games with scores like football games. Last week the Tigers beat the A's fourteen to thirteen. First thing I thought, Jeez, who missed the extra point?"

"At least the National League still lets pitchers hit."

"And at least nobody in the pros uses those aluminum bats. They show college baseball on ESPN and I can't watch it. I can't stand the sound the ball makes when you hit it. Not to mention it travels too goddam far."

The next pitch was in the dirt. Posada couldn't find it, but the third base coach, suspicious, held the runner. The fans booed, though it was hard to tell who they were booing, or why. The two in front of Keller joined in the booing, and Keller and the man next to him exchanged knowing glances.

"Fans," the man said, and rolled his eyes.

The next pitch was belt-high, and Turnbull connected solidly with it. The stadium held its collective breath and the ball sailed toward the left field corner, hooking foul at the last moment. The crowd heaved a sigh and the runners trotted back to their bases. Turnbull, looking not at all happy, dug in again at the plate.

He swung at the next pitch, which looked like ball four to Keller, and popped to right. O'Neill floated under it and gathered it in and the inning was over.

"Top of the order for the Yanks," said Keller's friend. "About time they broke this thing wide open, wouldn't you say?"

⊕

WITH TWO OUT in the Tarpons' half of the eighth inning, with the Yankees ahead by five runs, Floyd Turnbull got all of a Mike Stanton fastball and hit it into the upper deck. Keller watched as he jogged around the bases, getting a good hand from what remained of the crowd.

"Career home run number 393 for the old warhorse," said the man on Keller's left. "And all those people missed it because they had to beat the traffic."

"Number 393?"

"Leaves him seven shy of four hundred. And, in the hits department, you just saw number 2988."

"You've got those stats at your fingertips?"

"My fingers won't quite reach," the fellow said, and pointed to the scoreboard, where the information he'd cited was posted. "Just twelve hits to go before he joins the magic circle, the Three Thousand Hits club. That's the only thing to be said for the DH rule—it lets a guy like Floyd Turnbull stick around a couple of extra years, long enough to post the kind of numbers that get you into Cooperstown. And he can still do a team some good. He can't run the bases, he can't chase after fly balls, but the sonofabitch hasn't forgotten how to hit a baseball."

The Yankees got the run back in the top of the ninth on a walk to Jeter and a home run by Bernie Williams, and the Tarpons went in order in the bottom of the ninth, with Rivera striking out the first two batters and getting the third to pop to short.

"Too bad there was nobody on when Turnbull got his homer," said Keller's friend, "but that's usually the way it is. He's still good with a stick, but he hits 'em with nobody on, and usually when the team's too far behind or out in front for it to make any difference."

The two men walked down a succession of ramps and out of the stadium. "I'd like to see old Floyd get the numbers he needs," the man said, "but I wish he'd get 'em on some other team. What they need for a shot at the flag's a decent lefthanded starter and some help in the bullpen, not an old man with bad knees who hits it out when you don't need it."

"You think they should trade him?"

"They'd love to, but who'd trade for him? He can help a team, but not enough to justify paying him the big bucks. He's got three years left on his contract, three years at six-point-five million a year. There are teams that could use him, but nobody can use him six-point-five worth. And the Tarps can't release him and go out and *buy* the pitching they need, not while they've got Turnbull's salary to pay."

"Tricky business," Keller said.

"And a business is what it is. Well, I'm parked over on Pentland Avenue, so this is where I get off. Nice talking with you."

And off the fellow went, while Keller turned and walked off in the opposite direction. He didn't know the name of the man he had talked to, and would probably never see him again, and that was fine. In fact it was one of the real pleasures of going to a game, the intense conversations you had with strangers whom you then allowed to remain strangers. The man had been good company, and at the end he'd provided some useful information.

Because now Keller had an idea why he'd been hired.

✛

"THE TARPONS ARE stuck with Turnbull," he told Dot. "He draws this huge salary, and they have to pay it whether they play him or not. And I guess that's where I come in."

"I don't know," she said. "Are you sure about this, Keller? That's a pretty extreme form of corporate downsizing. All that just to keep from paying a man his salary? How much could it amount to?"

He told her.

"That much," she said, impressed. "That's a lot to pay a man to hit a ball with a stick, especially when he doesn't have to go out and stand around in the hot sun. He just sits on the bench until it's his turn to bat, right?"

"Right."

"Well, I think you might be on to something," she said. "I don't know who hired us or why, but your guess makes more sense than anything I could come up with off the top of my head. But I feel myself getting a little nervous, Keller."

"Why?"

"Because this is just the kind of thing that could set your milk to curdling, isn't it?"

"What milk? What are you talking about?"

"I've known you a long time, Keller. And I can just see you deciding that this is a hell of a way to treat a faithful employee after long years of service, and how can you allow this to happen, di dah di dah di dah. Am I coming through loud and clear?"

"The di dah part makes more sense than the rest of it," he said. "Dot, as far as who hired us and why, all I am is curious. Curiosity's a long way from righteous indignation."

"Didn't do much for the cat, as I remember."

"Well," he said, "I'm not *that* curious."

"So I've got nothing to worry about?"

"Not a thing," he said. "The guy's a dead man hitting."

✥

THE TARPONS CLOSED out the series with the Yankees—and a twelve-game home stand—the following afternoon. They got a good outing from their ace right-hander, who scattered six hits and held the New Yorkers to one run, a bases-empty homer by Brosius. The Tarps won, 3–1, with no help from their designated hitter, who struck out twice, flied to center, and hit a hard liner right at the first baseman.

Keller watched from a good seat on the third-base side, then checked out of his hotel and drove to the airport. He turned in his rental car and flew to Milwaukee, where the Brewers would host the Tarps for a three-game series. He picked up a fresh rental and checked in at a motel half a mile from the Marriott where the Tarpons always stayed.

The Brewers won the first game, 5–2. Floyd Turnbull had a good night at bat, going three for five with two singles and a double, but he didn't do anything to affect the outcome; there was nobody on base when he got his hits, and nobody behind him in the order could drive him in.

The next night the Tarps got to the Brewers' rookie southpaw early and blew the game open, scoring six runs in the first inning and winding up with a 13–4 victory. Turnbull's homer was part of the big first inning, and he collected another hit in the seventh when he doubled into the gap and was thrown out trying to stretch it into a triple.

"Why'd he do that?" the bald guy next to Keller wondered. "Two out and he tries for third? Don't make the third out at third base, isn't that what they say?"

"When you're up by nine runs," Keller said, "I don't suppose it matters much one way or the other."

"Still," the man said, "it's what's wrong with that prick. Always for himself his whole career. He wanted one more triple in the record book, that's what he wanted. And forget about the team."

After the game Keller went to a German restaurant south of the city on the lake. The place dripped atmosphere, with beer steins hanging from the hand-hewn oak beams, an oompah band in lederhosen, and fifteen different beers on tap. Keller couldn't tell the waitresses apart, they all looked like grown-up versions of Heidi, and evidently Floyd Turnbull had the same problem; he called them all Gretchen and ran his hand up under their skirts whenever they came within reach.

Keller was there because he'd learned the Tarpons favored the place, but the sauerbraten was reason enough to make the trip. He made his beer last until he'd cleaned his plate, then turned down the waitress's suggestion of a refill and asked for a cup of coffee instead. By the time she brought it, several more fans had crossed the room to beg autographs from the Tarpons.

"They all want their menus signed," Keller told the waitress. "You people are going to run out of menus."

"It happens all the time," she said. "Not that we run out of menus, because we never do, but players coming here and our other customers asking for autographs. All the athletes like to come here."

"Well, the food's great," he said.

"And it's free. For the players, I mean. It brings in other customers, so it's worth it to the owner, plus he just likes having his restaurant full of jocks. About it being free for them, I'm not supposed to tell you that."

"It'll be our little secret."

"You can tell the whole world, for all I care. Tonight's my last night. I mean, what do I need with jerks like Floyd Turnbull? I want a pelvic exam, I'll go to my gynecologist, if it's all the same to you."

"I noticed he was a little free with his hands."

"And close with everything else. They eat and drink free, but most of them at least leave tips. Not good tips, ballplayers are cheap bastards, but they leave something. Turnbull always leaves exactly twenty percent."

"Twenty percent's not that bad, is it?"

"It is when it's twenty percent of nothing."

"Oh."

"He said he got a home run tonight, too."

"Number 394 of his career," Keller said.

"Well, he's not getting to first base with me," she said. "The big jerk."

✛

"**NIGHT BEFORE LAST,**" Keller said, "I was in a German restaurant in Milwaukee."

"Milwaukee, Keller?"

"Well, not exactly in Milwaukee. It was south of the city a few miles, on Lake Michigan."

"That's close enough," Dot said. "It's still a long way from Memphis, isn't it? Although if it's south of the city, I guess it's closer to Memphis than if it was actually inside of Milwaukee."

"Dot …"

"Before we get too deep into the geography of it," she said, "aren't you supposed to be in Memphis? Taking care of business?"

"As a matter of fact …"

"And don't tell me you already took care of business, because I would have heard. CNN would have had it, and they wouldn't even make me wait until Headline Sports at twenty minutes past the hour. You notice how they never say which hour?"

"That's because of different time zones."

"That's right, Keller, and what time zone are you in? Or don't you know?"

"I'm in Seattle," he said.

"That's Pacific time, isn't it? Three hours behind New York."

"Right."

"But ahead of us," she said, "in coffee. I'll bet you can explain, can't you?"

"They're on a road trip," he said. "They play half their games at home in Memphis, and half the time they're in other cities."

"And you've been tagging along after them."

"That's right. I want to take my time, pick my spot. If I have to spend a few dollars on airline tickets, I figure that's my business. Because nobody said anything about being in a hurry on this one."

"No," she admitted. "If time is of the essence, nobody told me about it. I just thought you were gallivanting around, going to stamp dealers and all. Taking your eye off the ball, so to speak."

"So to speak," Keller said.

"So how can they play ball in Seattle, Keller? Doesn't it rain all the time? Or is it one of those stadiums with a lid on it?"

"A dome," he said.

"I stand corrected. And here's another question. What's Memphis got to do with fish?"

"Huh?"

"Tarpons," she said. "Fish. And there's Memphis, in the middle of the desert."

"Actually, it's on the Mississippi River."

"Spot any tarpons in the Mississippi River, Keller?"

"No."

"And you won't," she said, "unless that's where you stick Turnbull when you finally close the deal. It's a deep-sea fish, the tarpon, so why pick that name for the Memphis team? Why not call them the Gracelanders?"

"They moved," he explained.

"To Milwaukee," she said, "and then to Seattle, and God knows where they'll go next."

"No," he said. "The franchise moved. They started out as an expansion team, the Sarasota Tarpons, but they couldn't sell enough tickets, so a new owner took over and moved them to Memphis. Look at basketball, the Utah Jazz and the L.A. Lakers. What's Salt Lake City got to do with jazz, and when did Southern California get to be the Land of Ten Thousand Lakes?"

"The reason I don't follow sports," she said, "is it's too damn confusing. Isn't there a team called the Miami Heat? I hope they stay put. Imagine if they move to Buffalo."

Why had he called in the first place? Oh, right. "Dot," he said, "I was in the Tarpons' hotel earlier today, and I saw a guy."

"So?"

"A little guy," he said, "with a big nose, and one of those heads that look as though somebody put it in a vise."

"I heard about a guy once who used to do that to people."

"Well, I doubt that's what happened to this fellow, but that's the kind of face he had. He was sitting in the lobby reading a newspaper."

"Suspicious behavior like that, it's no wonder you noticed him."

"No, that's the thing," he said. "He's distinctive looking, and he looked wrong. And I saw him just a couple of nights before in Milwaukee at this German restaurant."

"The famous German restaurant."

"I gather it is pretty famous, but that's not the point. He was in both places, and he was alone both times. I noticed him in Milwaukee because I was eating by myself, and feeling a little conspicuous about it, and I saw I wasn't the only lone diner, because there he was."

"You could have asked him to join you."

"He looked wrong there, too. He looked like a Broadway sharpie, out of an old movie. Looked like a weasel, wore a fedora. He could have been in *Guys and Dolls*, saying he's got the horse right here."

"I think I see where this is going."

"And what I think," he said, "is I'm not the only DH in the lineup ... Hello? Dot?"

"I'm here," she said. "Just taking it all in. I don't know who the client is, the contract came through a broker, but what I do know is nobody seems to be getting antsy. So why would they hire somebody else? You're sure this guy's a hitter? Maybe he's a big fan, hates to miss a game, follows 'em all over the country."

"He looks wrong for the part, Dot."

"Could he be a private eye? Ballplayers cheat on their wives, don't they?"

"Everybody does, Dot."

"So some wife hired him, he's gathering divorce evidence."

"He looks too shady to be a private eye."

"I didn't know that was possible."

"He doesn't have that crooked-cop look private eyes have. He looks more like the kind of guy they used to arrest, and he'd bribe them to cut him loose. I think he's a hired gun, and not one from the A-list, either."

"Or he wouldn't look like that."

"Part of the job description," he said, "is you have to be able to pass in a crowd. And he's a real sore thumb."

"Maybe there's more than one person who wants our guy dead."

"Occurred to me."

"And maybe a second client hired a second hitman. You know, maybe taking your time's a good idea."

"Just what I was thinking."

"Because you could do something and find yourself in a mess because of the heat this ferret-faced joker stirs up. And if he's there with a job to do, and you stay in the background and let him do it, where's the harm? We collect no matter who pulls the trigger."

"So I'll bide my time."

"Why not? Drink some of that famous coffee, Keller. Get rained on by some of that famous rain. They have any stamp dealers in Seattle, Keller?"

"There must be. I know there's one in Tacoma."

"So go see him," she said. "Buy some stamps. Enjoy yourself."

✛

"**I** COLLECT WORLDWIDE, 1840 to 1949, and up to 1952 for British Commonwealth."

"In other words, the classics," said the dealer, a square-faced man who was wearing a striped tie with a plaid shirt. "The good stuff."

"But I've been thinking of adding a topic. Baseball."

"Good topic," the man said. "Most topics, you get bogged down in all these phony Olympics issues every little stamp-crazy country prints up to sell to collectors. Soccer's even worse, with the World Cup and all. There's less of that crap with baseball, on account of it's not an Olympic sport. I mean, what do they know about baseball in Guinea-Bissau?"

"I was at the game last night," Keller said.

"Mariners win for a change?"

"Beat the Tarpons."

"About time."

"Turnbull went two for four."

"Turnbull. He on the Mariners?"

"He's the Tarpons' DH."

"They brought in the DH," the man said, "I lost interest in the game. He went two for four, huh? Am I missing something here? Is that significant?"

"Well, I don't know that it's significant," Keller said, "but that puts him just five hits shy of four thousand, and he needs three home runs to reach the four hundred mark."

"You never know," the dealer said. "One of these days, St. Vincent-Grenadines may put his picture on a stamp. Well, what do you say? Do you want to see some baseball topicals?"

Keller shook his head. "I'll have to give it some more thought," he said, "before I start a whole new collection. How about Turkey? There's page after page of early issues where I've got nothing but spaces."

"You sit down," the dealer said, "and we'll see if we can't fill some of them for you."

⊕

FROM SEATTLE THE TARPONS flew to Cleveland for three games at Jacobs Field, then down to Baltimore for four games in three days with the division-leading Orioles. Keller missed the last game against the Mariners and flew to Cleveland ahead of them, getting settled in and buying tickets for all three games. Jacobs Field was one of the new parks and an evident source of pride to the local fans, and the previous year they'd filled the stands more often than not, but this year the Indians weren't doing as well and Keller had no trouble getting good seats.

Floyd Turnbull managed only one hit against the Indians, a scratch single in the first game. He went 0-for-3 with a walk in game two, and rode the bench in the third game, the only one the Tarpons won. His replacement, a skinny kid just up from the minors, had two hits and drove in three runs.

"New kid beat us," said Keller's conversational partner du jour. He was a Cleveland fan, and assumed Keller was, too. Keller, who'd bought an Indians cap for the series, had encouraged him in this belief. "Wish they'd stick with old Turnbull," the man went on.

"Close to three thousand hits," Keller said.

"Lots of hits and homers, but he never seems to beat you like this kid just did. Hits for the record book, not for the game—that's Floyd for you."

"Excuse me," Keller said. "I see somebody I better go say hello to."

It was the Broadway sharpie, wearing a Panama fedora with a bright red hatband. That made him easy to spot, but even without it he was hard to miss. Keller had picked him out of the crowd back in the third inning, checked now and then to make sure he was still in the same seat. But now the guy was in conversation with a woman, their heads close together, and she didn't look right for the part. The instant camaraderie of the baseball notwithstanding, a woman who looked like her didn't figure to be discussing the subtleties of the double steal with a guy who looked like him.

She was tall and slender, and she bore herself regally. She was wearing a suit, and at first glance you thought she'd come from the office, and then you decided she probably owned the company. If she belonged at a ballpark at all, it was in the sky boxes, not the general-admission seats.

What were they discussing with such urgency? Whatever it was, they were done talking about it before Keller could get close enough to listen in. They separated and headed off in different directions, and Keller tossed a mental coin and set out after the woman. He already knew where the man was staying, and what name he was using.

He tagged the woman to the Ritz-Carlton, which sort of figured. He'd gotten rid of his Indians cap en route, but he still wasn't dressed for the lobby of a five-star hotel, not in the kha-kis and polo shirt that were just fine for Jacobs Field.

Couldn't be helped. He went in, hoping to spot her in the lobby, but she wasn't there. Well, he could have a drink at the bar. Unless they had a dress code, he could nurse a beer and maybe keep an eye on the lobby without looking out of place. If she was settled in for the night he was out of luck, but maybe she'd just gone to her room to change, maybe she hadn't had dinner yet.

Better than that, as it turned out. He walked into the bar and there she was, all by herself at a corner table, smoking a cigarette in a holder—you didn't see that much anymore—and drinking what looked like a rust-colored cocktail in a stemmed glass. A Manhattan or a Rob Roy, he figured. Something like that. Classy, like the woman herself, and slightly out of date.

Keller stopped at the bar for a bottle of Tuborg, carried it to the woman's table. Her eyes widened briefly at his approach, but otherwise nothing much showed on her face. Keller drew a chair for himself and sat down as if there was no question that he was welcome.

"I'm with the guy," he said.

"I don't know what you're talking about."

"No names, all right? Straw hat with a red band on it. You were talking to him, what, twenty minutes ago? You want to pretend I'm talking Greek, or do you want to come with me?"

"Where?"

"He needs to see you."

"But he just saw me!"

"Look, there's a lot I don't understand here," Keller said, not untruthfully. "I'm just an errand boy. He coulda come himself, but is that what you want? To be seen in public in your own hotel with Slansky?"

"Slansky?"

"I made a mistake there," Keller said, "using that name, which you wouldn't know him by. Forget I said that, will you?"

"But …"

"Far as that goes, *we* shouldn't spend too much time together. I'm going to walk out, and you finish your drink and sign the tab and then follow me. I'll be waiting out front in a blue Honda Accord."

"But ..."

"Five minutes," he told her, and left.

It took her more than five minutes, but under ten, and she got into the front seat of Honda without any hesitation. He pulled out of the hotel lot and hit the button to lock her door.

While they drove around, ostensibly heading for a meeting with the man in the Panama hat (whose name wasn't Slansky, but so what?) Keller learned that Floyd Turnbull, who'd had an affair with this woman, had sweet-talked her into investing in a real estate venture of his. The way it was set up, she couldn't get her money out without a lengthy and expensive lawsuit— unless Turnbull died, in which case the partnership was automatically dissolved. Keller didn't try to follow the legal part. He got the gist of it, and that was enough. The way she spoke about Turnbull, he got the feeling she'd pay a lot to see him dead, even if there was nothing in it for her.

Funny how people tended not to like the guy.

And now Slansky had all the money in advance, and in return for that she had his sworn promise that Turnbull wouldn't have a pulse by the time the team got back to Memphis. She'd been after him to get it done in Cleveland, but he'd stalled until he'd gotten her to pay him the entire fee up front, and it looked as though he wouldn't do it until they were in Baltimore, but it really better happen in Baltimore, because that was the last stop before the Tarpons returned to Memphis for a long home stand, and—

Jesus, suppose the guy tried to save himself a trip to Baltimore?

"Here we go," he said, and turned in to a strip mall. All the stores were closed for the night, and the parking area was empty except for a delivery van and a Chevy that wouldn't go

anywhere until somebody changed its right rear tire. Keller
parked next to the Chevy and cut the engine.

"Around the back," he said, and opened the door for her and
helped her out. He led her so that the Chevy screened them from
the street. "It gets tricky here," he said, and took her arm.

⊕

THE MAN HE'D CALLED Slansky was staying at a
budget motel off an interchange of I-71, where he'd registered
as John Carpenter. Keller went and knocked on his door, but
that would have been too easy.

Hell.

The Tarpons were staying at a Marriott again, unless they
were already on their way to Baltimore. But they'd just finished a
night game, and they had a night game tomorrow, so maybe they'd
stay over and fly out in the morning. He drove over to the Marriott
and walked through the lobby to the bar, and on his way he spotted
the shortstop and a middle reliever. So they were staying over, unless someone in the front office had cut those two players, and that
seemed unlikely, as they didn't look depressed.

He found two more Tarpons in the bar, where he stayed
long enough to drink a beer. One of the pair, the second-string
catcher, gave Keller a nod of recognition, and that gave him a
turn. Had he been hanging around enough for the players to
think of him as a familiar face?

He finished his beer and left. As he was on his way out of
the lobby, Floyd Turnbull was on his way in, and not looking very
happy. And what did he have to be happy about? A stringbean
named Anliot had taken his job away from him for the evening,
and had won the game for the Tarpons in the process. No wonder
Turnbull looked like he wanted to kick somebody's ass, and pref-
erably Anliot's. He also looked to be headed for his room, and
Keller figured the man was ready to call it a night.

Keller went back to the budget motel. When his knock again went unanswered, he found a pay phone and called the desk. A woman told him that Mr. Carpenter had checked out.

And gone where? He couldn't have caught a flight to Baltimore, not at this hour. Maybe he was driving. Keller had seen his car, and it looked too old and beat-up to be a rental. Maybe he owned it, and he'd drive all night, from Cleveland to Baltimore.

✛

KELLER FLEW TO Baltimore and was in his seat at Camden Yards for the first pitch. Floyd Turnbull wasn't in the lineup, they'd benched him and had Graham Anliot slotted as DH. Anliot got two singles and a walk in his first three trips to the plate, and Keller didn't stick around to see how he ended the evening. He left with the Tarpons coming to bat in the top of the seventh, and leading by four runs.

✛

THE CLERK AT ACE HARDWARE rang Keller's purchases—a roll of picture-hanging wire, a packet of screw eyes, a packet of assorted picture hooks—and came to a logical conclusion. With a smile, he said, "Gonna hang a pitcher?"

"A DH," Keller said.

"Huh?"

"Sorry," he said, recovering. "I was thinking of something else. Yeah, right. Hang a picture."

✛

IN HIS MOTEL ROOM, Keller wished he'd bought a pair of wire-cutting pliers. In their absence, he measured out a three-foot length of the picture-hanging wire and bent it back on itself until the several strands frayed and broke. He fashioned a loop at each end, then put the unused portion of the wire back in its box, to be discarded down the next handy storm drain. He'd already rid himself of the screw eyes and the picture hooks.

He didn't know where Slansky was staying, hadn't seen him at the game the previous evening. But he knew the sort of motel the man favored, and figured he'd pick one near the ballpark. Would he use the same name when he signed in? Keller couldn't think of a reason why not, and evidently neither could Slansky; when he called the Sweet Dreams Motel on Key Highway, a pleasant young woman with a Gujarati accent told him that yes, they did have a guest named John Carpenter, and would he like her to ring the room?

"Don't bother," he said. "I want it to be a surprise."

And it was. When Slansky—Keller couldn't help it, he thought of the man as Slansky, even though it was a name he'd made up for the guy himself—when Slansky got in his car, there was Keller, sitting in the back seat.

The man stiffened just long enough for Keller to tell that his presence was known. Then, smoothly, he moved to fit the key in the ignition. Let him drive away? No, because Keller's own car was parked here at the Sweet Dreams, and he'd only have to walk all the way back.

And the longer Slansky was around, the more chances he had to reach for a gun or crash the car.

"Hold it right there, Slansky," he said.

"You got the wrong guy," the man said, his voice a mix of relief and desperation. "Whoever Slansky is, I ain't him."

"No time to explain," Keller said, because there wasn't, and why bother? Simpler to use the picture-hook wire as he'd used it so often in the past, simpler and easier. And if Slansky went out thinking he was being killed by mistake, well, maybe that would be a comfort to him.

Or maybe not. Keller, his hands through the loops in the wire, yanking hard, couldn't see that it made much difference.

⊕

"AWWW, HELL," SAID the fat guy a row behind Keller, as the Oriole center fielder came down from his leap with nothing in his glove but his own hand. On the mound, the Baltimore pitcher shook his head the way pitchers do at such a moment, and Floyd Turnbull rounded first base and settled into his home run trot.

"I thought we caught a break when the new kid got hurt," the fat guy said, "on account of he was hotter'n a pistol, not that he won't cool down some when the rest of the league figures out how to pitch to him. He'll be out what, a couple of weeks?"

"That's what I hear," Keller said. "He broke a toe."

"Got his foot stepped on? Is that how it happened?"

"That's what they're saying," Keller said. "He was in a crowded elevator, and nobody knows exactly what happened, whether somebody stepped on his foot or he'd injured it earlier and only noticed it when he put a foot wrong. They figure he'll be good as new inside of a month."

"Well, he's not hurting us now," the man said, "but Turnbull's picking up the slack. He really got ahold of that one."

"Number 398," Keller said."

"That a fact? Two shy of four hundred, and he's getting close to the mark for base hits, isn't he?"

"Four more and he'll have three thousand."

"Well, the best of luck to the guy," the man said, "but does he have to get 'em here?"

"I figure he'll hit the mark at home in Memphis."

"Fine with me. Which one? Hits? Homers?"

"Maybe both," Keller said.

⊕

"**YOU DIDN'T BRING** me one," the man said.

It was the same fellow he'd sat next to the first time he saw the Tarpons play, and that somehow convinced Keller he was going to see history made. At his first at-bat in the second inning, Floyd Turnbull had hit a grounder that had eyes, somehow picking out a path between the first and second basemen. It had taken a while, the Tarpons were four games into their home stand, playing the first of three with the Yankees, and Turnbull, who'd been a disappointment against Tampa Bay, was nevertheless closing in on the elusive numbers. He had 399 home runs, and that scratch single in the second inning was hit number 2,999.

"I got the last hot dog," Keller said, "and I'd offer to share it with you, but I never share."

"I don't blame you," the fellow said. "It's a selfish world."

Turnbull walked in the bottom of the fourth and struck out on three pitches two innings later, but Keller didn't care. It was a perfect night to watch a ballgame, and he enjoyed the banter with his companion as much as the drama on the field. The game was a close one, seesawing back and forth, and the Tarpons were two runs down when Turnbull came up in the bottom of the ninth with runners on first and third.

On the first pitch, the man on first broke for second. The throw was high and he slid in under the tag.

"Shit," Keller's friend said. "Puts the tying run in scoring position, so you got to do it, but it takes the bat out of Turnbull's hands, because now they have to put him on, set up the double play."

And, if the Yankees walked Turnbull, the Tarpon manager would lift him for a pinch runner.

"I was hoping we'd see history made," the man said, "but it looks like we'll have to wait a night or two … Well, what do you know? Torre's letting Rivera pitch to him."

But the Yankee closer only had to throw one pitch. The instant Turnbull swung, you knew the ball was gone. So did Bernie Williams, who just turned and watched the ball sail past him into the upper deck, and Turnbull, who watched from the batter's box, then jumped into the air, pumping both fists in triumph, before setting out on his circuit of the bases. The whole stadium knew, and the stands erupted with cheers.

Four hundred homers, three thousand hits—and the game was over, and the Tarps had won.

"Storybook finish," Keller's friend said, and Keller couldn't have put it better.

✛

"**TRY THAT TEA,**" Dot said. "See if it's all right."

Keller took a sip of iced tea and sat back in the slat-backed rocking chair. "It's fine," he said.

"I was beginning to wonder," she said, "if I was ever going to see you again. The last time I heard from you there was another hitter on the case, or at least that's what you thought. I started thinking maybe you were the one he was after, and maybe he took you out."

"It was the other way around," Keller said."

"Oh?"

"I didn't want him getting in the way," he explained, "and I figured the woman who hired him was a loose cannon. So she slipped and fell and broke her neck in a strip mall parking lot in Cleveland, and the guy she hired—"

"Got his head caught in a vise?"

"That was before I met him. He got all tangled up in some picture wire in Baltimore."

"And Floyd Turnbull died of natural causes," Dot said. "Had the biggest night of his life, and it turned out to be the last night of his life."

"Ironic," Keller said.

"That's the word Peter Jennings used. Celebrated, drank too much, went to bed, and choked to death on his own vomit. They had a medical expert on who explained how that happens more often than you'd think. You pass out, and you get nauseated and vomit without recovering consciousness, and if you're sleeping on your back, you aspirate the stuff and choke on it."

"And never know what hit you."

"Of course not," Dot said, "or you'd do something about it. But I never believe in natural causes, Keller, when you're in the picture. Except to the extent that you're a natural cause of death all by yourself."

"Well," he said.

"How'd you do it?"

"I just helped nature a little," he said. "I didn't have to get him drunk, he did that by himself. I followed him home, and he was all over the road. I was afraid he was going to have an accident."

"So?"

"Well, suppose he just gets banged around a little? And winds up in the hospital? Anyway, he made it home all right. I gave him time to go to sleep, and he didn't make it all the way to bed, just passed out on the couch." He shrugged. "I held a rag over his mouth, and I induced vomiting, and—"

"How? You made him drink warm soapy water?"

"Put a knee in his stomach. It worked, and the vomit didn't have anywhere to go, because his mouth was covered. Are you sure you want to hear all this?"

"Not as sure as I was a minute ago, but don't worry about it. He breathed it in and choked on it, end of story. And then?"

"And then I got out of there. What do you mean, 'and then?'"

"That was a few days ago."

"Oh," he said "Well, I went to see a few stamp dealers. Memphis is a good city for stamps. And I wanted to see the rest of the series with the Yankees. The Tarpons all wore black arm bands for Turnbull, but it didn't do them any good. The Yankees won the last two games."

"Hurray for our side," she said. "You want to tell me about it, Keller?"

"Tell you about it? I just told you about it."

"You were gone a month," she said, "doing what you could have done in two days, and I thought you might want to explain it to me."

"The other hitter," he began, but she was shaking her head.

"Don't give me 'the other hitter.' You could have closed the sale before the other hitter ever turned up."

"You're right," he admitted. "Dot, it was the numbers."

"The numbers?"

"Four hundred home runs," he said. "Three thousand hits. I wanted him to do it."

"Cooperstown," she said.

"I don't even know if the numbers'll get him into the Hall of Fame," he said, "and I don't really care about that part of it. I wanted him to get in the record books, four hundred homers and three thousand hits, and I wanted to be able to say I'd been there to see him do it."

"And to put him away."

"Well," he said, "I don't have to think about that part of it."

She didn't say anything for a while. Then she asked him if he wanted more iced tea, and he said he was fine, and she asked him if he'd bought some nice stamps for his collection.

"I got quite a few from Turkey," he said. "That was a weak spot in my collection, and now it's a good deal stronger."

"I guess that's important."

"I don't know," he said. "It gets harder and harder to say what's important and what isn't. Dot, I spent a month watching baseball. There are worse ways to spend your time."

"I'm sure there are, Keller," she said. "And sooner or later I'm sure you'll find them."

ROBERT W. WALKER

ROB Walker, a graduate of Northwestern University, is the author of forty novels, including the acclaimed *Instinct* series with FBI Medical Examiner Dr. Jessica Coran, and the *Edge* series featuring Texas Cherokee Detective Lucas Stonecoat and psychiatrist Meredyth Sanger. He also pens horror fiction under the name Evan Kingsbury. Rob was born in Corinth, Mississippi, and currently resides in Chicago, Illinois. His latest is SHADOWS IN THE WHITE CITY, the sequel to CITY FOR RANSOM.

On the subject of assassins in fiction, Rob comments: "We respond to the individual rugged character of a hitman as the ultimate resourceful soul who lives by his own means, wits, and personal code, eschewing the easy life of rules and regs. Just as we would all like to be Dracula or Superman, capable of superhuman feats, we admire the qualities of those who live on the deep fringes of the outer edge."

Visit Rob at www.RobertWWalker.com.

PET PROJECT
Robert W. Walker

When Tino the Ax Capino looked around in his grave and noticed his missing limbs, ears, nose, genitalia, and other extremities, he said to himself, "What the hell did I do this time?"

It slowly came back to him. Yeah … Binney Melvino, aka Binney the Butcher, had played slice and dice with him. He'd begun with Tino's ears, taking each off one at a time, holding the bloody things up to Tino's tortured eyes, chanting his name—"Ax … Ax … the Ax … ohhh … I'm so scared of the Ax!" Binney then tossed each ear off into the trees. Only justice he saw in this life and it had to be his own body parts being consumed by hungry woodland creatures, from rodents to a red fox that'd made off with one of his feet.

Being a hitman, Tino's old father used to say, had its bad days, and this was damned bad. It had even started to rain while he was being executed body piece by body piece; hard chinaberry pellets that sting the raw flesh areas.

Sure, he'd brought this down on himself. He recalled pleading with Binney—a useless act of contrition, as good as talking to the bark on the tree that Tino found himself lashed to. Saddest part of all, he was being killed in a vengeance thing that started when he showed a small human spark of pity, an inch of human kindness he'd never before shown … pity for a mark.

In all his career as a hitman, no one had ever asked Tino to take out a sniffer dog, a greyhound, a cat, a monkey, a canary, or a horse—or any other animal. But that side of the business had begun to thrive and the money was too good to turn down. These days anything goes, and you couldn't turn your nose away from the green so easy anymore given the state of the economy.

Tino started out an enforcer, doing odd jobs as a hefty teen while still in Carpenter Elementary. He'd been born with some kind of glandular problem that left him a giant among peers; he'd never fit in, and school simply was not for him. Certainly, not after a third repeat of eighth grade. So he asked his Uncle Sal Capino for full-time work.

Sal took him in, treated him like a son—albeit calling him Quasimodo all the time. Sal sent Tino to another kind of school—*The Squash Garden Restaurant*, a front for hitman training with an all-assassin faculty. At hitman school, the first thing he learned was to never ever let a single emotion enter into his thinking; he learned to be an automaton able to pull the trigger on anyone anytime anyhow if the bosses handed you a contract to fill.

Tino took to the work like a natural, his only drawback his huge frame—he stuck out in a crowd big time. But he learned to counter this by using his natural gifts, and even his size to throw off a mark. He could work in close when needed. On the surface, he looked the part of a slow, slight retard with a goofy grin no one would take for a mask. But for over fifteen years, he had racked up a record of forty clean kills and seventeen not so clean kills, sending fifty-seven men and a handful of women to their everlasting.

Tino had become highly respected in the business, and the family counted on him whenever a problem arose, until this thing with the iguana came along.

Capino had grown senile, a hitman's worst nightmare—a boss with senility making bad decisions and taking out contract hits on the basis of unreasonable slights. This time he insisted that Tino take out Carmine Russo's pet iguana.

Worse yet, he wanted the iguana to die mercilessly and messily—butcher fashion. Piece by piece and all of the bloody remains laid out on Carmine's bed as a sure warning. Tino had no problem with this, not initially.

But that all changed in one moment; in one blink of emotion. An emotion Big Tino the Ax had not felt since childhood.

Fucking childhood. No matter how far you stray from it, it is always there in the gut of your brain, stuck in your mind like a hard peach pit. It may be covered over, it may be forgotten, un-used for what seems forever, but that hard little core, convoluted and unbreakable, is there just waiting for you to reconnect, recall, remember a whiff of a childhood moment of perfection—the per-fect starry night, perfect breeze, perfect odor, perfect touch, perfect kiss. And it came that way for Tino—the odor of this iguana fill-ing his brain with memories of Loretta. And startlingly enough, strangely enough, the name on the iguana habitat read Loretta. And how fucking coincidental is that?

At first, he thought it just a cosmic joke, one of those things God did to pass the time—just fucking with us. But then he drew near, and the nearer he got to the iguana's habitat, the more Loretta overtook his mind. The thing's odor held pause the huge de-boning knife over his head, and when their eyes met, the liquid beauty of those black eyes were identical to those of the long-remembered, long-bereaved loss.

The fond eyes of Loretta. God how he had loved her; God how he would have sacrificed anything for her. God how he had suffered so much pain on losing Loretta.

Now this dilemma.

He steeled himself. Shake it off, he kept thinking in man-tra fashion. This ain't Loretta. This is a fucking iguana, man, not my lost Loretta from long ago.

"It ain't nothing personal," he said to Loretta, but the words were meant for himself; not his today self but his long-forgotten self, that self that remembered. "Can't let emotions rule. No feelings on the job. It's just another job."

He grabbed a willing Loretta, who looked pampered with her pink bow tied about her neck, and in one hand he held her curled, smiling face in the half-light up to his eyes, and their eyes again met. Melting eyes; eyes that had soul … eyes that—

He plunged the knife into the creature's gut as training took over, and those eyes that held him now bulged and pealed back, and an aching keen that sounded like "Whhhy?" escaped Loretta Iguana. Like air slowly exiting a balloon, and the curled smile turned to a crooked sickness, and the seed-lit eyes turned off.

But there was no mutilation. No dismemberment. Tino the Ax gently placed Loretta back in the tank and tucked in her insides.

In doing so he managed to piss off not only Carmine Russo but Uncle Sal Capino, pissed that his Tino, toward whom he'd put so much time and effort, had failed him. Tino hadn't done the job as told—cut up Loretta in twenty pieces over Carmine's bed, so the blood spatters would create a kind of Jackson Pollack painting over Carime Russo's white Russian-made down comforter. Now crazy Uncle Sal had put out a major contract on his nephew's head—to be filled only if Tino's carcass were cut into twenty pieces.

Meanwhile, Carmine Russo, pissed that Loretta had been stabbed by someone ballsy enough to get past his bodyguard and into his home, placed a contract out on his life as well.

Chicago, which had always been home for Tino the Ax, a place of familiarity and comfort—like as in comfort zone, as they say—disappeared that night he'd killed Russo's iguana. He no longer felt at ease in the Windy City. So he had made for parts unknown.

Two hitmen he knew well—Jack Divine, a scar-faced West Virginian who believed John Wayne a Shakespearian actor in cowboy boots and spurs—and Binney Melvino, the Butcher, who really liked knives and the cleaver. While Tino knew very little of Jack Divine except by reputation as out-of-town muscle, he'd had professional debates over methods and process with Binney. In fact, the two men had an odd, perhaps eerie mutual admiration society going. They appreciated one another's results.

Thank you, God, it had to've been the worst of the two, the Butcher, who had found Tino first.

The Butcher had trained in the same manner as the Ax, and he'd perfected a genuine heartlessness that any sociopath might admire. The Butcher was a hitman's hitman, a model, a master craftsman, as he felt nothing for anyone, nor for anything animate. He had laughed in Tino's face as he recounted the pussy thing he had done at Carmine's when Sal Capino wanted it done in butcher fashion.

"Shoulda offed the fucking Iguana the way you was told, Tino. So tell me, before I kill you, tell me why? Why'd you not slice and dice the damn Iguana like the contract called for? Why, man, why?"

"Why? Why?" Tino spat out blood, amazed he had any left. As Tino heaved up, gasp-driven blood pumped over his lips, yes, but it also pumped from in a hundred rents and tears and little stabs Binney Melvino had made all over Tino's body now: genitalia gone, ears, nose, hands gone. "Why, yeah ... why didn't I butcher Loretta?"

"The iguana, yeah ... gotta tell me, Tino ... why?"

"She reminded me of my own Loretta so damn much, down to how she smelled, man."

"Whoa ... really? Reminded you of a woman? I knew it. I told Sal there had to be a woman involved someplace in all this. How else you make sense of it?"

"Whoa up, what woman? My Loretta was accidentally killed when she got out of her aquarium ... crawled up under the rug and my dad stepped on her."

"Wait up ... she was an animal, a pet?"

"W-w-was my pet turtle. Loretta."

"Damn ... ohhh, shit, man, I had a special turtle once myself, name of Gigi...when I was just a little tyke."

"Hey, kill me if you must ... but don't fucking mock me ... You gonna mock what's real, huh?"

"No, man, seriously. I take that shit serious, OK? Turtle love for a child is too precious."

"Really?" asked Tino between death gasps.

"When I was like four, maybe five."

"Damn ... how about that. Me too ... same thing. But hey ... fuck this, shit," said the Butcher, and he made one final slit across Tino's throat, taking pity now.

"My turtle's name was Shane," came a voice from behind Melvino the Butcher, "named for the part Alan Ladd played in the film. But you know how Shane died? I dissected him alive myself."

This was what Tino went into eternity with, along with the sure knowledge that the Butcher was at the mercy now of Cowboy Jack from western West Virginia.

And now Tino the Ax Capino awoke in an unmarked grave with a lotta pieces missing. That was his fate, to spend eternity trying to put all the missing pieces—both physical and mental—back together again.

Lying in the dirt, Tino wondered if a search for Loretta out here in the Nether Regions was possible.

He wished Binney Melvino no ill will, and that he might find peace and Gigi again, too.

As to that bastard Cowboy Jack Divine, a man who as a boy would kill his own turtle, Tino had gotten word through the purgatory grapevine that Jack was wanted dead in twenty pieces. Ol' Sal Capino again had worded the contract placed on Cowboy Jack Divine in the same manner as that put out on Loretta. You see, Sal became pissed at Jack's unproven results, because Sal had wanted to see all of Tino's parts for himself before that fool Divine buried them all in a dozen places.

The devil's in the details.

JOHN GALLIGAN

JOHN Galligan is author of THE NAIL KNOT, THE BLOOD KNOT, and (forthcoming) THE CLINCH KNOT—installments in a fly fishing murder mystery series in which an itinerant trout bum hooked on vodka-Tang, fly casting, and grief tries to take himself out but keeps getting interrupted by other, more interesting deaths.

When asked about assassin fiction, John said: "Hitman stories present both writers and readers some of the most deliciously guilty pleasures in crime fiction. First of all, there is the amorality—the squeaky clean evil—of the hitman's profession, which when done well comes across as pure refreshment to all of us who live mired in moral complexities. Then, also pleasant, there plays out in these stories a mirror-like inversion of the murder mystery, as we identify for once with the killer and track events up to exactly the point when most other stories start. Finally, here is the guiltiest pleasure of all: In a good hitman story, there comes the chance to revel in pure craft and feel the thrill of a job well done."

Visit John at www.JohnGalligan.com.

MAN HIT
John Galligan

AS HE DEPLANED at Sea-Tac, Zoichi Oro found himself tempted by many things. He was tempted, at first, to shove through the knot of sluggish Americans laboring up the jetway. This included the temptation to try out some hard-earned Berlitz—*excuse me, please*—as he elbowed first that fat breast, then that lumpy arm, and finally that wad of crap-ass shoulder luggage that had been twice too big for the overhead bins. But Zoichi Oro restrained himself. He took baby steps. He thought about sex with the sleepy, stumbling college girl who had demanded vegetarian meals. He walked so close behind he could smell her sleepiness, her whiteness—his dry lips wrapped around an unlit Kent.

Then, at last achieving a normal gait in the concourse, Zoichi Oro was tempted by beer and giant sandwiches. But he steered his legs away. At a kiosk, he purchased a green pack of gum, tempted all the while to touch the strange black skin of the hand that made his change. He nearly bought a newspaper—tempted to sit and chew his gum and savor the blocky and simple English of the headlines: *Stocks Rise ... Body Found ... House Burns, Three Dead.* Later, on the airport train, he was tempted to dial his cell phone, call Bando-san maybe, and whisper something about the preposterous size of things, the space, the reckless waste. But instead he gripped the train's oily silver pole. He loosened his knees just like on the Osaka subway. He set his slim carry-on between his shoes and moved the knuckles of his free hand to within one millimeter of a tall woman's ass. Shit, she was tall. Taller than a human woman needed to be. Legs like a giraffe. Fine red hairs on the nape of her neck. The woman turned and Zoichi Oro nipped aside the Kent, showing his teeth. He withdrew the hand to his pocket and closed his eyes. If only, he thought. So tedious, Zoichi Oro thought, all the calculations of invisibility and tact, all the disciplines of his dull, dark trade, all the masks of his servant-warrior caste. So strong, the temptation to throw away the idea of a proper and respectable death—the urge to collapse his name to Zorro, buy a nice American gun, and simply shoot the dirty fucker.

Zorro he became then, and in a Tacoma pawn shop the pistol was shockingly easy to buy. But the object seemed unreal for a time, and in the rental sedan, heading east, temptation exchanged itself for the challenge of driving on the wrong side of the car, the wrong side of the road. Zorro settled into five hundred miles of contentment. Delighted with this new kind of danger—trucks as big as Japanese trains, speed limits in the strange and hurtling quantity of miles—Zorro smiled and lit one cigarette with another. He liked any new challenge. He admitted to himself that this property in himself, this rigor, might be lacking in the idea of a pistol blazing at point-blank, a neat bore hole, and instant death. Yes ... after all, Wakabayashi, his target, would get the clean and artful death he deserved. Annoying as the task might be, Wakabayashi would get his lovely little death poem.

Yet the pistol, as it rode heavily on the seat beside him through Washington, struck Zorro as a beautiful tool. He touched it often. He lifted it—by the handle, then by its long silencer—and then he dropped it back on the seat, enjoying the bounce. Wakabayashi was so simple, he mused, so foolish. Wakabayashi was underclass, the grandson of a comfort woman. He had been a veteran runner, steady and safe. He had carried cash payments from the Osaka road construction contractors to the LDP offices in Tokyo, where the cash had lubricated dam projects and bridge projects and all other manner of costly government make-work. But after twenty years in the business, Wakabayashi had "lost" an envelope. He had claimed he was robbed while waiting for his commuter train. Not long after, though, his ailing mother had replaced her hip and moved into a new, barrier-free mansion in the Saitama countryside, and Wakabayashi had disappeared. Or so the poor fool had thought. Like there was no bounce, mused Zorro, in the working out of things.

Eastern Washington arrived at a pack-of-Kents-and-a-half, and Zorro marveled at the landscape—the almost comic dryland rippling and wrinkling, the purple waves of grain lapping up against the majestic thrust of the Rockies. Finally, he stopped for gas and gum in Idaho and was suddenly, indescribably excited. Never before—never!—had he pumped his own gas. The rush of petroleum thronged through his fist as he stood at the edge of a vast, mountain-rimmed darkness, feeling the weight of the pistol in his jacket pocket, enjoying the smells of gasoline and meatloaf. Once more, keen-eyed Zorro appreciated the headlines of the American newspapers in the boxes across the asphalt. The headlines were short and blunt, accessible to the vocabulary of a junior high school slack like Zorro and unconfused by the hellish grammar of English text books. *Stocks Fall. Woman Saved. Mariners Drop Pair.* Maybe, Zorro thought, his fascinations were for the boldness, the bluntness, the savage vectors of America herself. He holstered the big gas gun. He started the car. He said to himself *Man Drive* and smiled.

✛

HE CARRIED A POSTCARD in his breast pocket— from the foolish Wakabayashi to his foolish sister in Gifu. *Greetings from Livingston, Montana.* The picture amazed him. He had never—never!—so much as heard of a jackalope. And yet there the strange beast was, an enormous horned rodent squatting among stones and shrubbery, just asking to be shot. When he was done gassing up, Zorro parked the car away between the restaurant and a far-off row of train-trucks that idled in soft and looping thrums. He carried the pistol into the dry and hillocky wasteland behind the truck stop. Trash blew. Small birds darted from thick, low grasses. In the chilly twilight, Zorro stalked a hidden draw and flushed a fat, long-tailed bird that flew recklessly into the gathering night. But no jackalopes. Zorro imagined a headline—*Man Shoot*—and fired six rounds into a dark hump of dirt. He drove on through the night.

In Livingston—this dry and windy place from which stupid Wakabayashi had written his stupid sister—Zorro supplied himself for the job. He bought a fly fishing rod and rubber boots, plus a many-pocketed vest and a hat that embarrassed him. When the clerk made pains to mention a license, Zorro concealed his amusement. There was no license for what he had come to do. He finished his shopping at Yellowstone Ace Hardware: a hibachi grill, charcoal, lighter fluid, petroleum jelly, and a roll of strong silver tape. That afternoon, at the Chico Hot Springs Resort, he rented a room where he could aim the pistol down three floors into the main pool. He felt tempted again. *Man Want*. He chain-smoked. He chewed gum and spat it out when the taste dimmed. He unpacked—a change of clothes, a cell phone, a carton of Kent filters, and a 1.5-liter bottle of gold-flecked *Hana Yama* sake from Wakabayashi's Saitama hometown. By the third night, relief came at last and Zorro was easing into the bath next to his mark, the pistol wrapped in an extra towel that smelled like white clouds and wind over fresh grass. Imagine that, Zorro said to Wakabayashi, two Japanese—and not even real Japanese but the shameful kind, with third-generation Korean passports, the grandchildren of kidnapped whores and slaves—all the way over here, where men could be men, finding themselves in a nice hot bath together. In minutes they were laughing and oath-making and then Wakabayashi, the jolly thief, shared his daily schedule: fish, bathe, drink. Company welcomed at any point.

Umai, said Zorro, resting a hand on the fat, hard towel. *Sweet*.

⊕

INTO THE INTERSTICES of the following morning leaked temptation again. But Zorro fought like a warrior. He wanted pancakes, meat loaf, mashed potatoes. But he bought gum and stayed slim as a fence rail. He wanted to unzip the smock of the blonde woman behind the gas station register. Instead he took a long and solitary piss on the hillside beside Highway 89, watching cars swoosh by toward Yellowstone Park like targets in a video arcade. It would be so easy. But he settled for another crack at the jackalope. Finding only brush and rocks—*Jackalope Hide*—he emptied himself with a fast pistol round into a tight little canyon where sparks kicked out and dust flew up and drifted away on the incessant wind.

At last the afternoon arrived and Zorro met Wakabayashi at a bridge on the Shields River. Wakabayashi wanted to play rock, paper, scissors to see who fished upstream and who fished down. Old pros, both men launched scissors. So they went at it again. This time, both rock. Wakabayashi giggled. But in round three, the fool went back to scissors and Zorro smashed him.

"Downstream," said Zorro.

"Swell guy, you are," said Wakabayashi.

Zorro, feeling vaguely confused as to what made him swell, or even okay—nothing, he had always heard—went downstream. He flailed the limp rod, getting cigarette smoke up his nose. He hated the way the river pushed him and topped his boots with shocking cold and made him stumble. He saw no fish. For three hours, then, he sat on the rubbled bank, smoking cigarettes from a proper posture and aiming the pistol at skull-sized rocks on opposite shore. By the time Wakabayashi returned to the cars,

Zorro waited in the shade under the bridge with the pistol in his pocket and the tall bottle of sake between his knees.

"Now, my friend, we drink?"

He watched Wakabayashi's eyes light up.

"Yes."

Zorro had to admit that Wakabayashi was a good drinker. Wakabayashi was a good talker. Wakabayashi was a good man. He hid what should be hidden. He laughed when he should laugh. He emptied his cup like a champion, this sneak-thief who had traded his life for an old woman's final comforts.

They drank. They drank more. When Zorro looked at Wakabayashi again, he saw a simple man who had simply gotten old. He saw a small-time criminal who had gotten a little tired, a little plump, a little gray—a man who wore his belt right across the middle of a surrendering belly, a man who had attempted to retire, essentially, in a business where there was no retirement. Wakabayashi had slipped the chain, so he thought, of the country that never claimed him.

They drank more still. And yet, in the country that held them, the links owed a debt to the very idea of the chain. There was, therefore, an order to things. And in that order, what Wakabayashi had done could not be tolerated. When at last Wakabayashi closed his eyes and slumped back, Zorro balled a raincoat under his head and made him comfortable among the rocks.

Then, up at the cars, Zorro went to work. He opened Wakabayashi's door and released the trunk lid. On his back, the trunk latch digging into his spine, Zorro knifed open the seams that held the rear dash panel in place. He exposed the bolts. He twisted off the nuts. When the rear dash was loose, he lifted it into the bright air inside the car. He measured the opening—thumb to pinkie, one and a half spans—and he muttered a prayer of thanks for gum, three weeks of gum—and nothing but.

From his own trunk he removed the hibachi and charcoal. He placed them on the rear floor of Wakabayashi's car. Carefully, even wistfully, like a man balancing pebbles at a shrine, he prepared the grill. And next was the strong silver tape—all seams sealed except around one back door. He laid a stick across Wakabayashi's trunk latch, so that not even a strong and sudden wind could shut the lid. And then Zorro returned below the bridge.

Wakabayashi was a good drunk. Outstanding. He trusted Zorro like his own third and fourth legs and he giggled and joked senselessly as they stumbled up through the rocks. Like a child, Wakabayashi curled up on the back seat. He took one look at Zorro—one last grin—and returned to his drunken slumber.

Zorro sat beside him. He touched the pistol in his pocket and reflected soberly that it felt like the plumping of his scrotum. He sighed then. He pulled the door shut and taped the last seam. He removed his shoes and clothes and dropped them through into the trunk. He dropped the tape next, then the lighter fluid. He lit the charcoal and tossed out the lighter. Quickly, taking shallow breaths, he greased himself with petroleum jelly and climbed up into the dash space and pushed and pushed and kinked and strained and at last squirted through with a plop and a cough onto the spare tire. He rolled, reached up and pulled the dash panel down, bolted it back.

Zorro dressed on the edge of the trunk before he closed it. He smelled no smoke. He did not look back at Wakabayashi. But suicide was a nice way to die. Honorable. Real Japanese-style. Taking responsibility for one's actions. The man's mother, the silly rest of his family, would be the right kind of sad.

But not Zorro. His sadness bloomed from a seed sowed long ago from a bush ripped and stomped and flung and left to cling and scrap in sidewalk cracks. That was how he and Wakabayashi had been cast, together, against each other. Zorro drove west, drove hard, forgetting to smoke. He felt a strange yearning, a thirst nearly, for the big American rivers that flowed through burgeoning forests, chaining and unchaining beside the highway.

And the temptations came back in force. Zorro was hungry. Zorro was desperately, ravenously hungry. The pistol rode in his fist, but every jackalope resolved into a brush heap, a rock heap, into dead vines around a crumbled fence. Every woman turned lovely and remote under his gaze, cold and safe under glass. Every man loomed big-jawed and aloof and certain of where he had come from and where he went. In the curl of a cloverleaf off the Idaho interstate, Zorro's guts bent and his head ached. He missed Wakabayashi—a man he didn't know, a man he had killed—and therefore he knew he must be insane. Therefore he knew he had nothing. No country. No longer any true name, even. Nothing.

It was the same Idaho truck stop, where big trucks idled at a distance and wind pushed fat birds at skidding angles toward the endless western flatlands. Zorro sat in the café and pointed at pictures: meatloaf, mashed potatoes, creamed corn, pie. His jacket slung to the right, heavy with the pistol. Baby, he croaked to the waitress, hey you baby. She stared at him, blank-faced, as if he had spoken Korean, or jackalope. But across the room they were smiling his way. They were laughing. Out the window, big bodies slung from big cars and pumped gas and then moved on to home.

Zorro ate. Zorro finished everything and still felt hungry. Zorro went to the restroom and pissed with one hand on his business and one on the pistol in his pocket—and then his circuits connected and the sadness in him fried up hard and hot and in an instant his troubles popped and vanished. It was only three short steps from there to the first of the toilet stalls, and the third of those steps was a high, swift kick above the door latch.

The random traveler inside was too startled to speak. The man sat red-faced and hunched, elbows on thighs, neck tucked between shoulders and a deep furrow in his brow. Zorro aimed for the furrow and hit it perfectly. The pistol coughed through its silencer. The head blew back and the bullet broke tile and the mess slid down.

Zorro closed the toilet door.

He threw the pistol into the big, chaining river.

He drove west. He smoked Camels. He ate pancakes and stayed at Super 8. He understood that he was not going home, that he was in this place now—a newborn man in a new, wide place—and the next morning, under a sky as blue and bright and sharp as ceremony, Zorro's new papers arrived, framed in a coin-slotted Seattle Times box, amidst the fumes of gasoline and pancakes.

Man Hit.

WILLIAM KENT KRUEGER

WILLIAM Kent Krueger writes the Cork O'Connor mystery series set in Minnesota's great northwoods. His work has received a number of awards, including the Anthony and Barry Awards for Best First Novel, the Loft-McKnight Fiction Award, and the Minnesota Book Award. Series books include *Iron Lake*, *Boundary Waters*, *Purgatory Ridge*, and *Blood Hollow*, which received the Anthony Award for Best Novel of 2004.

On why he enjoys hitman stories, Kent remarked: "Because the people who do the killing do it so cool and so clean. Me, I only want to kill when I'm in a blinding rage, and if I did, I'd do it badly."

Visit Kent at www.WilliamKentKrueger.com.

ABSOLUTION
William Kent Krueger

GRIFFIN FOUND THE NUN kneeling alone in the convent chapel. He slipped into the pew directly behind her, and, in the quiet candlelit sanctuary, put the gun to the back of her head.

"Don't turn around, Sister. Keep your head bowed. This isn't a crucifix I'm holding. One sudden move, or if you call out, I'll pull the trigger. Your head will explode like a melon. Do you understand?"

At the feel of the barrel against her skull, the nun stiffened. She gave a careful nod. The cloth of her habit slid with an audible, starched scraping over the metal of Griffin's Ruger.

"What do you want?" She spoke in a low, hoarse whisper. Whether out of reverence or out of fear, Griffin couldn't say.

"It's very simple. I'm looking for a man. Monk."

"There are no brothers here, only nuns."

"Monk isn't his vocation. It's his name. Frederic Monk."

"There's no one here by that name."

Griffin leaned nearer, his breath softly invading her ear. "Let me spell it out for you. Monk used to work for the people I work for, but he wanted out. In my line, nobody gets out unless we say so, and we didn't. So he ran, just disappeared. We've been looking for him. A few months ago we intercepted a letter meant for a cousin, postmarked Able, Minnesota. Three times we sent men to deal with Frederic Monk. They disappeared, too. We never heard a word from any of them. So here I am. Why me? Because I'm the best. I check out this

Able, Minnesota, a pathetic excuse for a town, if you ask me. Two-hundred sixty residents without enough brains between them to fill a shot glass. No place for Monk to hide. But on the hill overlooking the town sits this convent, and when I look up here, one word comes to my mind. *Sanctuary.*

"So I reconnoiter a little, slip in, have a discussion with the first nun I come across—"

"You didn't hurt anyone," the nun whispered quickly.

"Relax, Sister. She's sleeping right now. She'll wake up with a headache, that's all. Before I put her out, she told me that I should talk to you and that you'd probably be here. You like to pray late, she said. She also said you could tell me about Monk."

"She was mistaken. I don't know anything. I tend the gardens, that's all."

"Then why would she send me to you?" He nudged the barrel more firmly against her habit and the bone beneath it, driving home his point.

"The other nuns sometimes tell me things they won't tell someone else."

"Because you're what? Their confessor?"

"They find me understanding."

"Then understand this. Unless you tell me where Monk is, I'm going to kill you."

The nun was quiet for a while. Griffin wondered if he'd scared her so much she'd lost her voice.

"Would you really shoot me?"

"Maybe not. Maybe I'd beat you like a stepchild then strangle you with your own rosary. Do you want to die?"

"Does anyone? But if you're asking am I afraid, the answer is no."

"You'd die to protect someone like Frederic Monk?"

"To prevent the death of another, I'm compelled to silence."

Griffin lifted the Ruger, preparing to give her a good crack across her thick, nonsense-filled head. Then he had a better idea.

"I'll tell you what I'm going to do. First, I'll kill you. Then I'll kill the next nun and the next until someone tells me what I want to know. I'll waste this whole fucking convent if I have to."

"You're in the house of our Lord. Please don't swear."

"I have the gun, Sister. I'll say any fucking thing I fucking well please."

"What kind of man are you?" It didn't seem to be a question asked in outrage, but from a sincere desire to understand. "Don't you care about your immortal soul?"

"The only thing important to me is the here and now, what I have and what I still want."

"What is it that you still want?"

Was she stalling, or was she actually interested? It didn't matter; in the end, she would give him what he was after.

"To know that I'm the best," he replied. "The absolute best."

"At killing?"

"At this art, which is more than just killing. I'm a hunter, Sister, just like Frederic Monk. Man is the game."

"So this Monk is what? A trophy?"

"*The* trophy, Sister. I bag him, and there's no doubt I'm the best."

Her head shook in a faint negation. "A human life is a sacred thing."

"The soul is the sacred thing," he countered. "The flesh, that's simply the vessel. We all abandon it eventually. I'm here to send Monk's soul packing a bit sooner than he'd prefer."

"You believe in the soul? You're Catholic?"

Baptized and confirmed, he could have told her, although he'd had trouble with his faith from the beginning. His father was a brutal man, a drunk, who'd laid into his son every time he hit the bottle. As a kid, Griffin had often prayed for the beatings to stop. As far as he could tell, God didn't care. His old man's brutality finally ended when Griffin was sixteen and the cops found his father lying in a parking lot outside Willette's

Tavern, his head bashed in with a baseball bat, his brains spilled out all over the pavement

Griffin still had the bat.

"Have you lost your faith then?" she went on.

"Indeed I have, Sister. But that's not what I'm here to find."

"We don't always see the Lord's hand as it guides us, but guide us it does. You believe you're here seeking this Frederic Monk, but, in truth, it may be that you're here for something else entirely. Absolution, perhaps."

He liked the nun's voice, the low throaty whisper. It reminded him of a woman he'd once been fond of—Vera, a kickboxer with an IQ through the roof. Smart, quick, and with a voice like roughed up velvet. She'd been the target of a contract, though she hadn't known it. He'd taken great pleasure in her company, in her body, and eventually in the slow way she died. Maybe, he thought with an unsuppressed smile, he'd do this nun the same way.

"Anything can be forgiven," she said.

"I don't need forgiveness. I need answers. Where's Frederic Monk?"

"I told you, this man is not here."

"And I'm telling you he is."

"Pray with me."

"I'm not here to pray. I'm here for Monk."

"I think you're here for something you don't yet realize. I think it's something I can offer. Let me ask you a question. When you lie down at night and close your eyes what do you see?"

She had him there. He couldn't remember ever sleeping well. His brain, when he tried to drift off, was a battleground, and his dreams were the realm of monsters.

"Close your eyes now," she urged gently. "What do you see?"

"Close my eyes? You think I'm an idiot?"

"Are you afraid of me? Or is it something greater?"

He gave no response, no physical indication, but he did, in fact, close his eyes.

He smelled the place then, the distant fragrance of roses, the oil that was used to polish the wood of the pews, and faintly the smoky ghost of frankincense. The quiet of the chapel felt comforting. Like an image emerging from a thick fog, he glimpsed the truth of her words, the possibility of peace.

Then a small squeal broke the moment and he opened his eyes. A door to the right of the altar had been pushed ajar. An old nun shuffled into the chapel holding a lit candle in her hand.

"Who's that?" he said.

"Sister Agnes. She's deaf. She can't hear us."

"She's got eyes."

"It's not unusual for visitors to pray in our chapel. Just bow your head."

"How about I just pop her instead? In fact, I think it's time I take care of you both."

"He's here," she whispered suddenly.

"Monk?"

"Yes. Let Sister Agnes go quietly, and I'll tell you what you want to know."

"If you're lying—"

"I'm not."

"If you are, I'll work you over till you're a bloody lump on the floor, then I'll go back to that sweet little nun I met first thing and do the same to her. Maybe I'll have myself some fun while I'm at. I never fucked a nun before. You're all virgins, right? Or dykes?"

Sister Agnes smiled in their direction, turned, and left the way she'd come.

"I'm waiting," he said to the nun in front of him.

"It's not too late. If only you'd let yourself open up to the blessing offered here."

Griffin chambered a round. "I'm finished waiting."

She sighed heavily. "They're here. They're all here. Monk, the others. All transformed, all for the better."

"Take me to them."

With a note of sadness, she said, "It was working on you. I felt it. Maybe if you stayed just a little longer."

"Now, or I start shooting." He shoved the barrel of the Ruger into the back of her head, making her nod as if she finally saw the light.

"I understand. You've been closed too long and too firmly." She stood up. "Follow me."

"Take it very slow."

The nun stepped into the aisle. She genuflected and turned, keeping her head bowed respectfully in the dim light. She crossed her arms, slipped her hands into the loose cuffs of her habit, and led the way out the back of the chapel, Griffin close behind her. They stepped into the night air, which was redolent with the scent of roses. A dim light came from a bulb over the chapel doorway, illuminating the flowerbeds and a tool shed just beyond.

"My garden," the nun said with a note of pride that Griffin, remembering his early religious instruction, thought out of place in a religious order. "Flowers are such simple things. They ask so little and give so much. We should all be as graceful in our lives."

"Where is he?"

"Frederic Monk is no more."

"What do you mean? You said he's here."

"And so he is. He's different, however. He understood the grace of this place, its special gift to those who choose to embrace it. The others who came after him, they're here, too, changed in their own ways by the choices they made."

"What the fuck are you talking about?"

"It would take too long to explain. There's really only one thing you ought to know." The nun no longer spoke in a whisper, and her voice seemed to have dropped an octave. "In a place such as this, a suppressor is an absolute necessity."

The nun turned, and the shots came from the cuff of her habit with a muted *phht-phtt*. Griffin stood a moment, stunned, then crumpled to the grass in the dark heart of the garden.

Although he heard and saw clearly, everything after that came to him from a distance, from a place he stood outside of and could not feel, as if he were on a boat sailing into a gray sea and looking back longingly at the shore.

From the stone walkway beyond the flowerbeds came the sound of steps, a measured gait, slow and deliberate. The nun stepped between Griffin's body and the light. The shadow of her long habit engulfed him.

"Mother Superior, good evening," the nun said.

Griffin heard an old woman's voice, immeasurably gentle, reply: "You're up late."

"I couldn't sleep. I thought I'd work in the garden. Perhaps put in another rose bed. I was just about to get the spade from the shed."

"Another? But you've already planted three new lovely rose beds in the short time you've been here."

"You can never have enough roses, Mother Superior."

"They are beautiful to the senses. They so delight the eye and the nose. I believe God must be partial to roses. Perhaps that's why he sent you to us. I knew you were different from the beginning. Very special. We all did."

"Thank you, Mother Superior."

"Well, carry on then. And God bless you, Sister Frederica."

Griffin heard the tap of soles receding on a stone path. Then he heard the rustle of the nun's habit and the squeak of hinges as the shed door opened.

By then he was too far gone to be able to see anything of the world he was leaving behind. But he could still hear clearly the final sound from his old life: the cold *chunk* of thin metal as the spade bit into dirt.

PAUL A. TOTH

PAUL returned to his home state of Michigan after spending eight years in Los Angeles, Washington, DC, and Denver. His first novel, FIZZ, and its successor, FISHNET, are available from Bleak House. His short fiction has been nominated for the Pushcart Prize and Best American Mystery Stories.

When asked what is the appeal of hitman stories, Paul answered: "The hitman tale is the first story and probably the last: the race between stalker and prey. We share the fear of the hunted, or take guilty pleasure in the stalker's shoes, or steal a double thrill by sharing both viewpoints."

Visit him at www.netpt.tv

NICE KIDS CARRY GUNS
Paul A. Toth

I DON'T SPEAK MAFIOSO. I've never stalked New York, much less Little Italy. I've fired but never owned a gun. I possess no silencer and speak freely, as if drunk all the time. I do not lurk; one could step into shadows and never hear a "psst" from me. Children run not from but to me. I've clipped a few hundred flies, spiders and mosquitoes, like any human being, but otherwise my record's cleaner than a whistle, for whistles require saliva. I'm a hitman, yes, but a different kind: rap records made in Vermont, believe it or not, where if a man isn't careful, somebody might bust a snowball in his ass. Even here, rivalries emerge. Soon, magazines will trumpet the Northeast-Northwest battle, Montana vs. Vermont and Maine vs. Washington. But that wasn't my problem. My problem was Harley. Harley had a job for me, one for another kind of hitman.

Harley—what the hell kind of name is Harley?—said to me, "Uranus. He's on the take, Chet, and I can't take him out thanks to my probation. You'll have to do it, fruitfly. You're taking Uranus out." He laughed. He thought I was gay. Lots of people do. "It's a speesh impediment," I always explained, but they demanded decorating tips.

I said, "MC Uranus? He seems like the nicest kid."

"He's not. He had the keys and he stole a bunch of tapes, now bootlegged, everybody making money but us."

He tossed a gun in my lap. It might have been a truly-automatic or semi-manual pistol.

"This is Vermont," I said, "land of the spiritual, for Ansel Adams, not Billy the Kid."

"I don't know what kind of gay shit you're talking, but we're taking him out. We need the PR. We need a worse reputation."

"Can't we beat him up?"

"Look, I know you like Uranus."

"That's enough."

"It's got to be done."

"I'm not killing anyone."

"I've already considered that, Chet. Fact is, I told Uranus you've been talking shit about him. 'Small package,' et cetera. He's coming to your house tonight. It's you or him."

"Coming with a gun?"

"What do you think?"

"He seems like the nicest kid."

"Nice kids carry guns."

He ordered me to the gun range. To get there, I had to drive around the Ansel Adams mountains with my defroster providing the slowest wipe and fade in history. An hour before, I was the not-really-gay-but-get-your-jokes-in-while-you-can guy, and now I was a hitman. A sitting hitman. A hitman for a hitman, in two ways, double-crossed, and I wished for a slick cliff to spare me what security experts everywhere warned: "Don't pull a gun unless you're sure you'll use it." I didn't want to use it. I didn't want to be home that night, but I knew Uranus would follow me, as if in orbit. That day, the next, or twenty years in the future, our planets would align. I was not Mars but Pluto, the disappearing Roman god. Subtracting the "d" from "god" leaves go. Go to the gun range, Chet.

I shot at targets for an hour. I hit everything but targets. I heard laughing beside, behind and all around me. Guffaws, giggles: A man like me learns to know they're coming his direction. He also knows that men without speesh impediments feel that the Chets of the world deserve this snubbing, that to speak of sports or any other manly subject in their presence is just not done. I often thought it might be easier to simply turn gay, but I found women who appreciated all things Chet. Lately it was Carol. Carol and Chet. "One day," Harley had said, "you'll both wear matching clothes to Walmart. Then you'll have kids and the whole damn family will match. You'll keep that house spic and span. She'll have questions but won't ask. After all, her husband does the housework. What more could a wife want?"

Driving to Carol's house, I turned on the stereo. I was greeted by MC Uranus:

> *I'll fuck you up*
> *And jack your shit.*
> *Motherfuckers think they cool?*
> *I bring it old school,*
> *With fists of fury.*
> *Don't call no jury,*
> *'Cause I'll smudge the judge,*
> *Claw the law,*
> *Scale the jail,*
> *Steal my time,*
> *Give myself life.*
> *MC Uranus,*
> *God of the sky,*
> *You fuck with me,*
> *You bleed and cry.*

That was it. I had to do it. I grabbed my cell phone and called him, hoping I could cut and run. Mea culpa, Uranus.

"What the fuck?" he said as someone moaned beside him.

"Yo," I said, and anything else would have sounded equally lame. "I ain't been talking shit."

"Quit talking like a brother, motherfucker. I heard. I know. Me and you got business, bitch."

"That's right: It's just business, U."

"Bullshit."

He hung up. I pulled into Carol's driveway. Above, clouds I could almost touch. The sky had descended. Soon, astronomers could drop their telescopes.

"You could lay a hand on Uranus," Harley would have said.

"Oh, Chet," Carol said.

What the fuck? With a pair of Adidas visible just outside the bedroom, I heard Uranus say, "He's here? Get the fuck out of my house, Chet."

I ran. I could have shot him right there, but I ran.

I sped home, for Uranus drove a souped up Saturn; he hadn't quite made it yet. I steered with an alcoholic's coordination, as somewhere deep inside, tiny needles injected adrenaline in my toes, ears, tongue, nose. Everything tingled and twinkled. My body radiated. But there was something else. Carol was nothing but a pseudo fag-hag and now had switched to the old school rap game. No loss. Did I say I loved her? I didn't. Now I almost wanted to send her a thank you card, a bouquet of roses for a reason to kill Uranus. Double jeopardy and here's the final answer: "A gun does what to fake gangsta rappers?"

I called Harley. "You were right," I said, breathless from my fight and flight reaction. "That son of a bitch is at my girl's house, in her bed."

Harley laughed and laughed. He finally said, "Fuck, that's funny."

"We'll see."

"'We'll see' what?"

"What we see."

Leave 'em hanging, they say, but I hadn't yet knotted the noose.

At home, it was nearly dusk. I had a small home in a town that couldn't be called a town, but there was nothing else to call it and so we called it a town. We were free of police, except the county fellas, two, I think, and the state cops, plentiful but usually on the freeways. In many ways, this was a world of slow-motion anarchy, where anything could go unseen and unheard yet rarely deserved notice. Once in a while, we made the nearest paper's blotter: "Driver runs over mailbox, Route 3. Headlight found at scene." A more perfect place for what would commence could not be devised, not even Antarctica, which was losing snow as Vermont gained it. Meanwhile, the stars and soon the planets appeared.

I waited so many hours. I knew why: Uranus was well-known for lengthy sessions, and not the recording variety. He might have moved up to a Benz had he spent more time in the studio. I listened to his records and tried to absorb his bravado.

"You stick to avocado dip," Harley would have said. Everything rhymed in our world, but there was little reason.

Poor Uranus. Orphaned in Brooklyn, somehow ending up here in Vermont with foster parents, white, of course, and so, as he explained in every interview, "It's like I got white hair, but I'm dyeing my roots, know what I'm sayin'?" He came to us with a demo tape. It wasn't bad, nor was it particularly good, but somewhere close enough to good that we thought we might groom him. Harley encouraged U to commit petty crimes. He said, "Go to New York, show up at a club, flash a gun, and let the cops kick your ass." Uranus was happy to oblige but had so far lost three cases against the cops; we couldn't afford lawyers. Harley didn't care. "Art requires sacrifice," he'd say.

We sent Uranus on "tours" of local bars. Sometimes the kids came, and sometimes the adults, and a few times I sat in the audiences and studied the misplaced jaws of mystified homo sapiens.

We had an old school bus for these tours. We painted it black and gold and put a minifridge inside. Harley learned how to crack hotel fridges, and we'd restock the bus so that the artists thought they traveled first class. Harley drove. I gave directions from Yahoo maps. Sometimes we ended up in New Hampshire and had to cross back to Vermont. The artists never cared. We had a Playstation rigged in the back. We drove to the sound of gunfire and John Madden. In the mornings, after-noons, and nights, the bus filled with pot smoke. Sometimes

Harley took a hit or two, and then the jokes started. I memorized those jokes, every single one.

In a way, it was my job to raise these kids. Harley called me "mom," and soon the artists did, too. "Maybe you want to try a love song, like LL Cool J," I'd tell Uranus, just like a mom.

"Fuck that shit."

"What about politics?"

"Bullets and pussy," Harley would interrupt. "Listen to dad, not mom."

"What do you need me for, then?"

"To read the maps. Girls are better with directions. Guys know it. That's why we get so mad."

I wanted to say, "Ohhhhhhh, you make me so angry," but Harley would have replied, "You sound like a fruitbat, fruitfly."

A door rattled. House settling? No, that only happened on the Brady Bunch, the one where the kids haunt the house. My house had settled forty years before and wasn't moving anywhere. Therefore, I knew the planets had met the earth's surface.

"Uranus is here," U said as his Adidas shoe chopped the door in half.

He reached into the pockets of his big down coat. "Yeah," I wanted to say, "I know you got a gun, Uranus." He paused and looked at the ceiling, trying to remember something, and then he rattled:

> *I see your derriere*
> *in Montpelier,*
> *I swear to God,*
> *I'm gonna make you odd.*
> *See, you was even before,*
> *Two balls, same story,*
> *Now you got one.*
> *No guts, no glory.*

"That's what I was thinking," I said, aiming the gun at his zipper.

"You best not even think it."

"Take the gun out," I said. "You know this dialogue, right? You watch a lot of action movies. Take the gun out very slowly, where I can see it."

He did.

"Aim it at your foot."

"I lift this gun, you dead."

"You lift it once inch, you lose however many inches you got."

He sighted the gun on his left shoe. "Not my Adidas, man."

"Your shoe or your balls."

"Goddamn," he said, making the face of a little boy about to be spanked.

"This is going to hurt nobody but you."

"Man, yo, Chet, you practically my mom."

"And is that any way to treat your mother, by popping her girlfriend? Show some respect."

"We can work it out. Lemme talk."

"No more rhymes, U. I can't take it."

"Fuck that, man. You wanna know the score? This is the deal. Harley dealt those tapes, the ones from that guy you signed. He said it wasn't shit, anyway. He told me to go to Carol's house. He told me to get you worked up, scare the shit out of you, so you was ready."

"Ready for what?"

"Ready for killing, man. You the target. You was the target all along. Harley said, 'Get him out of my life. I can't stand him no more in the front seat next to me. I can't stand him no more in the studio.'"

"Yeah, but what about you? Maybe he wants you gone, too? Because the thing is, U, your records ain't selling shit. Maybe he wants us both dead."

"Fuck, man," Uranus said. "I never thought of that. But he couldn't know that would happen."

"Either way, one of us dies, right? And if he's lucky, you pull your gun, I pull mine: bam."

"Bam. Shit."

"That's right, it's shit, Uranus. So what are we gonna do about it?"

"Kill the motherfucker," he said, right on cue.

"That's right, U: Kill the motherfucker."

As I drove to the studio, U mumbled rhyming nonsense and Malice in Wonderland gibberish. It was too dark for Ansel Adams, as no flashcube could have lit our surroundings. In the canyon was another canyon that might send us for a ride, an invisible detour. After all, Harley could have been waiting for us. But I remembered then that Harley always drove the bus for another reason: He read maps worse than I did.

"You gonna be ready?" I said.

"*You* gonna be ready?"

"I'm ready," I said, patting my pocket. "Say, U, how many tracks we lay down for you so far?"

"Got to be fifty. Maybe more. Why? You ain't released ninety percent of 'em."

"I bet there might be more."

"Hell, yeah, there is. I'm just talking about the studio. At home, I got probably two hundred tracks. I even got those love songs you're always crabbing about. But I can't stand 'em. Worse than—excuse me—but worse than sleeping with Carol when I didn't want to do it, know what I mean? Somebody else's idea."

"True, but sometimes somebody else's idea works out way better than they predicted, though maybe not for them."

I knew Harley would still be at the studio. It was an alibi, just in case the police came calling. "Me?" he'd say. "I was right here all night, in this chair. It's a tragedy, is what it is. Who died, again?"

I parked next to the bus. We were no Partridge Family, that's for sure. Behind the bus was Harley's car. He drove—I swear—a Mercury. Somewhere, at least six other planets were involved in a plot I didn't care to know about.

We didn't sneak. We didn't prowl. We didn't pick locks. The overconfident asshole had left the door ajar because the heat always ran too high. He was in the soundproof booth and we came in behind him. He spun to see us.

"You worked it out, then?" Harley said. "I'm proud of you both."

Uranus slammed Harley's head into the mixing board, leaving the imprint of an equalizer on top of the wrinkles. But Harley wasn't out. He shook it off, and then he reached, of course, for a gun. I grabbed his arms.

"Wait 'til I move and then shoot," I said.

"What? You shoot him."

"I left my gun at home," I said.

"I should kill you both."

"You listen to me, U: I'm gonna let go of his arms and step aside, and then you blast him. I know what I'm doing. You've got to trust me."

He looked at me. Did he see what I hoped he saw? I tried to encourage that vision: "I'm your mom, after all."

I took my chances and let go of Harley's arms. There was a delay that I would soon apply in a most artistic fashion, and then Uranus fired.

We waited. The universe was quiet. One might think planets would make a lot of noise, but not us, not until I explained, and then Uranus got it, every word.

As president of the company, I waited three years. For once, I hired an attorney. It's a wonder what notoriety can do, and an even bigger wonder that the police bought the story that I'd never known about the gun in U's pocket. By the time he was released, Uranus had ten hit records, including two love songs sustained by a delay effect, which made U's voice sound as big and open as the universe that had closed upon us.

JEFF STRAND

JEFF Strand is best known as the creator of Andrew Mayhem, hero of the novels GRAVEROBBERS WANTED (NO EXPERIENCE NECESSARY), SINGLE WHITE PSYCHOPATH SEEKS SAME, and CASKET FOR SALE (ONLY USED ONCE). His most recent novel is the thriller PRESSURE.

Jeff says, "When I write about killers, they tend to be of the 'raging lunatic' variety. They're scary people, but in some ways a hitman is even scarier. When a serial killer is slicing you up with a knife stained with the blood of the rest of your family, at least you know he's probably getting some insane pleasure out of the process. To a hitman, you're nothing more than a paycheck. That's cold."

Visit Jeff at www.JeffStrand.com.

POOR CAREER CHOICE
Jeff Strand

IF YOU'RE LIKE ME, you spend a lot of time trying to joke your way out of socially awkward and/or potentially fatal situations. A good example of this took place one summer evening when I was relaxing in my recliner with the novel *Whose Blood Is In My Popcorn?*, which I'd been reading off and on for the past four years. I'm not an ambitious reader.

I looked across the living room into the kitchen and saw an extremely large man holding an extremely large knife. He had long greasy hair, was wearing a black leather jacket that had metal spikes around the wrists, and I sort of got the impression that he had broken into my home to kill me.

By "broken into," of course, I mean that he'd probably just casually walked in through the door in the kitchen that my wife Helen was always reminding me not to leave unlocked. She'd never specifically used a man with a knife as an example, but I'm pretty sure this is the kind of thing she was referring to.

"Are you here about the leaky faucet?" I asked.

Not my all-time funniest comment, I'll admit. Still, when you consider that I said it to a huge guy with a knife and a homicidal glimmer in his eye, it was a more than passable effort.

He shook his head. "No. I'm not."

"Oh."

I considered my options. The only weapons I had readily available were the dog-eared paperback and a grape juice box. I'd already drank most of the juice, so the box probably wouldn't even carry all the way across the living room if I threw it. However, the straw provided a defensive possibility.

I considered making a run for it. But when I say that the man was "extremely large," I don't mean that he was an obese gentleman who would chase after me in a labored waddle. Though it was hard to tell under the jacket, he looked to be all muscle. And as he walked toward me, he moved with a grace and efficiency of motion that gave the impression that he could have me tackled to the ground and nicely decapitated before I even made it to the stairway.

But maybe not. After all, I'm rather nimble myself. I decided to let this one play out and wait for the precise moment to act.

"Are you Andrew Mayhem?" he asked.

"Yes," I said, a split-second before I realized that the more intelligent answer would be "No."

He stood in front of me and held up the knife. "I've been hired to kill you, Mr. Mayhem."

I lowered the recliner's footrest. "By whom?"

"I can't say."

"You can say if you're going to kill me, right? I promise not to scrawl the name in my own blood on the carpet."

He shook his head. "No, I'd get in trouble."

"If you're going to kill me, you've at least got to let me know who wants me dead. Give my ghost something to avenge."

"I don't know …"

"It's the least you could do."

"Hey, I waited two weeks for you to be alone in the house. I could've done this while your wife and kids were home. Would you want your wife and kids to see you die? Would you?"

"Helen would kick your ass."

The hitman smiled. "She sure puts you in your place. Damn, but you're whipped."

"Not whipped. Henpecked."

"Whatever."

"Y'know, you may be here to kill me, but you're still a guest in my home. Let's be respectful, okay?"

"Fine with me. I'm not here to talk. I'm here to cut myself a slice of bitch."

I stared at him for a long moment.

"Did you just say you're here to cut yourself a slice of bitch?"

He nodded.

"Was that, like, a planned comment? Did you actually come in here with the intention of speaking those exact words?"

"What's wrong with them?"

"What does that even mean?"

"It means that you're a bitch, and I'm here to cut a slice of you."

"No, no, no, no, no, that doesn't work at all. Trust me on this. Have you really said that to other human beings? What was their reaction?"

"I haven't said it to anybody else."

"Good. Don't. What do you usually say in this situation?"

The assassin looked a bit sheepish. "Actually, you're my first hit."

"Seriously?"

"Yeah."

"Oh, well, that explains it. I know that you were trying to sound all cold-blooded and stuff, but the only reaction you're going to get is 'Oh, crap, I'm gonna be murdered by a doofus.' What's your name?"

"Victor."

"Hi, Victor." I extended my hand politely. He didn't shake it. I figured I probably should have seen that bit of rudeness coming and placed my hand back on my lap. "Listen, you need a catchphrase that doesn't make you sound like a street punk. Something sinister but classy. Because I'll be honest with you, right now I should be so scared that I can barely keep my urine on the inside, and I'm just not feeling it."

"I bet you'd feel it if I stuck this knife in you."

"I'm sure I would. But if you're an assassin, you need to be memorable. You need to be stylish. I mean, any common hooligan can run somebody over with a car, but you, you're the kind of guy who gets up close and personal with a knife. It's all about the presentation. You need to leave a lasting impression."

Victor nodded almost imperceptibly, as if he were considering my advice. Then he scowled as if suddenly realizing that he'd become the kind of assassin who listened to helpful hints from people he was supposed to kill. "No, I don't. You'll be dead!"

"Yeah, but this isn't about me. It's about you. I might be dead either way, but how would you feel if I died thinking that your hitman persona was sub-par?"

Victor shrugged. "I get paid either way."

"Is it just about the money, though?"

"Sure."

"Do you really believe that?"

"I kill for money. That's what an assassin does. When I slit your throat, I won't feel a thing."

I wasn't happy that the conversation had turned to slit throats, and I shifted uncomfortably in my seat. "How many people have you killed?"

"I told you, you're my first."

"You haven't killed *anybody*? Not even for recreation?"

He shook his head.

"What about animals?"

"No animals."

"Have you ever flushed a goldfish?"

"Look, I don't need to have dozens of corpses stacked in my closet to deal with somebody like you. I can kill you. It's not a problem."

"I'm not trying to be a pain here," I insisted. "I'm just wondering how you got the gig of terminating me without any previous murder credits."

"I sorta fell into the job. You know how it goes."

"You padded your resume, didn't you?"

"That's none of your concern."

"You did! You lied about your experience! What are you going to do if your boss finds out?"

"I didn't lie about anything."

I shook my head and made a tsk-tsk sound. "Lying by omission is still a lie."

"You know what? I've had way more than enough of you." Victor pointed the knife at my throat. "Got anything else to say before I gut you?"

"That's not where the knife should be pointed if you're planning to gut me."

"Don't tell me how to do my job."

"I'm just saying. Not many guts in my neck."

"Sure there are."

"Do you even know what a gut is?"

"That's it. You're dead, Mayhem."

"My name's not Mayhem."

He blinked. "What?"

"Are you looking for Andrew Mayhem? He lives next door. Shorter guy, glasses ..."

"You said you were Andrew Mayhem."

"Your knife made me nervous. I wasn't thinking."

He looked at me for about three seconds as if trying to decide if I was lying, and then clearly decided that I was, in fact, lying. "You know what? I'd kill you for free," he said.

"How much are you getting paid?"

"None of your business."

"Of course it's my business! I have a right to know my market value. How much?"

"I don't discuss salary with anybody. And it's time for you to die."

"You keep saying that, and yet my guts are still sealed up in my neck."

Victor looked so angry and frustrated that I thought he might scream. I used the opportunity to strike.

"Did you just throw a fucking juice box at me?" he asked, rubbing his forehead.

"I did."

"You … you … there's something wrong with you, man! How is it possible that nobody else has murdered you yet?"

"See, Victor, you're not listening. This isn't about me. It's about—"

He began to pace around my living room, wildly swinging the knife. "You know what, I didn't even *want* this crappy job! I was happy at the Wal-Mart! I'm just trying to earn enough money to go back to school! I didn't ask to get hit in the head by a goddamn juice box!"

I noticed to my horror that the juice box, which lay on its side, had leaked some grape juice onto the carpet. Helen was going to go ballistic when she got home. The juice boxes were never, ever to be consumed in the living room. Granted, the rule was intended for my children, Theresa and Kyle, but I'd get in just as much trouble. Damn.

Victor continued pacing back and forth across my floor, alternating between shouting in frustration and muttering silently. I kind of felt sorry for him. I still held the straw, and tried to figure out how good my chances were of plunging it into his eye when he wasn't looking.

Suddenly he turned to me, eyes wide with fury, raised the knife over his head, and brought it down toward my face— stopping a few inches from my nose.

It occurred to me that a substantial portion of my plan had revolved around the idea that I would break out my lightning-fast reflexes to escape from danger at the exact moment when Victor finally snapped. But if Victor hadn't stopped the knife's downward trajectory by his own choice, I would probably have a blade sticking deep into my face. 'Twas not a pleasant thought.

"I'm sorry," I said.

Victor lowered the knife. "This job sucks," he said.

"Most jobs do."

I realized that my palms were sweating profusely now that I'd come so close to being stabbed in the nostrils, and my stomach kind of hurt. What had happened to my lightning fast reflexes? The knife could have gone all the way through my nose and up into my brain! I'd be *dead*! And then Victor would collect his paycheck even though he was a below-average assassin!

I wiped my palms off on my jeans, hoping he wouldn't notice.

"Did I scare you?" he asked.

"No."

"I bet I did."

"Okay, yeah, you did, but that knife looks sharp, all right? You can't expect me not to be a little uncomfortable when you're trying to stab me with it."

"I bet you almost wet your pants."

"Would it make you feel better if I had?"

He shook his head. "That would probably be awkward."

"Yeah, for me too."

He sighed. I sighed back.

"Why didn't you finish stabbing me?" I asked.

"Dunno."

"Are you having second thoughts?"

"Maybe. I just … do you ever feel like you're playing a part that isn't really *you*? I mean, I feel ridiculous in this spiked jacket. What do you think?"

"Honestly, I thought the jacket was pretty cool."

"It's too hot. And it doesn't fit right in the back. And these spiky things keep scraping on furniture and stuff. I wonder if I should just give up the whole idea of killing people for a living. I don't think I'm cut out for it. I like being the lovable guy. I like being cuddly."

"Cuddly is good. So how much trouble will you get in if you don't kill me?"

"I'm not sure. Not too much. He was only paying me fifty bucks."

"Fifty bucks? *Fifty*?"

"Yeah."

"My life is only worth fifty dollars? Are you kidding me?"

"Is that low?"

"Of course it's low! Holy crap, I was thinking you were making at least five figures, probably six!"

"I made seven dollars an hour at Wal-Mart."

"I can't believe you would kill me for fifty bucks. That's just insulting. Who hired you?"

"Todd McBride."

"Don't know him. But people try to kill me every once in a while. It's just part of being me. But … fifty bucks? You'd pay an exterminator more than that to kill some bugs! Perhaps you should leave."

"Yeah."

"Sorry this didn't work out."

"Me too. I'll resign in the morning. I didn't really want to see sliced flesh anyway." He turned around, took a step toward the kitchen, then hesitated and returned his attention to me. "You know, I'm out fifty bucks."

"Yeah, and … ?"

"Maybe you could pitch in a little. It doesn't have to be the whole fifty, but something for my time would be nice."

"I'll be honest with you. Paying somebody not to kill me would feel sort of like paying for sex."

"You're just saying that because your wife monitors the finances, aren't you?"

"No, I'm saying it because it would make me feel icky."

Victor frowned. "Oh."

"Sorry."

He stood there for a moment, silent.

"Well, do you have any of those juice boxes left?"

"I think there's one in the fridge."

"Thanks."

"Don't take the cherry one."

"Okay."

Victor wandered into the kitchen and rummaged through the refrigerator. I heard him leave and sat on the recliner for a while, more than a little annoyed. I couldn't even get back into my book.

Still, at least I was alive. And I'd helped Victor realize that the life of a killer-for-hire wasn't for just anybody with access to a bladed weapon. So the evening wasn't a total loss. In fact, since I now knew that my lightning fast reflexes needed to be honed, I had fodder for self-improvement.

If you really thought about it, it was a very worthwhile experience.

I returned to the novel, feeling good.

Then Helen came home and I got in trouble because I forgot to clean up the grape juice on the carpet. So the rest of the night sucked.

KEN BRUEN

KEN Bruen won the Shamus Award for the Best Novel of 2003 for THE GUARDS, the book that introduced Jack Taylor. He's also written eighteen other novels, including the latest Taylor book, PRIEST. Ken has a doctorate in metaphysics (to confuse them, he says.) He lives in Galway, Ireland, but insists all of his influences are American.

When asked about literary hitmen, he responded, "I see them as the last of the samurai."

Visit Ken at www.KenBruen.com.

PUNK
Ken Bruen

Don't give me shit about ghosts

Things that go bump in the night

The fuck are you kidding?

I've seen enough monsters walking round to give any tough guy nightmares and the sooner they got put in the ground, the better

When I hit sixty, I got out … my line of work, you kill people for a living, it takes its toll and you know what, it was getting stale, kind of lame, no buzz there no more. Sure, it was a regular gig, I'm not bitching, let's get that clear from the off, I want to whine, you'll know.

But I had the bucks stashed, nice little investment plan and figured, enjoy.

My roots are Irish, I'm not saying it helps to be a Mick in the killing business, we don't have the edge in it, ask the Italians, but I like to think I brought certain poetry to my work, an artist if you will

Truth to tell, and I always tell the truth, I can't abide a liar, give me any scumbag, don't care what he's done, he fronts up, I can cut him some slack but a liar, whoa, don't get me started, the thing is, I was getting slow, the old reflexes were zoning out.

And I just didn't have the taste for it, you got to love what you do, am I right.

Don't read me wrong here, you listening, I didn't love killing ... I'm not some psycho. I relished the details, the planning, and the clean efficiency of dispatch.

My Mom was Irish, came over on the boat, got a job as a cleaning lady and then met my old man, all he ever cleaned was his plate. She was from Galway, reared me to stories of the Claddagh, the swans, the old streets of what used to be a Spanish town, and the music, ah, the wild mix of bodhrans, uileann pipes, spoons, fiddle, and the keening voice.

Jeez, she'd a grand voice, hear her sing ... Carrickfergus, fuck, that was like a prayer in action. She was real hot on religion, mass every Sunday, confession, the whole nine

Get this, my old man was an atheist, believed in nothing, especially not work, he wasn't violent, just feckless, found a woman who'd pay the freight and let go. When I was 17, big and okay, a little mean, I slung his ass on out, him whining

"Where am I going to go?"

I said

"Try the track, you spend most of your life there anyway."

My Mom would have taken him back, Irish women, that demented loyalty, but I was running the show then and she was real proud of the money I was producing. I heard he got him some other woman in Canarsie, like I give a fuck

Good riddance

I'd done my first job for Mr. Dunne, he'd told me

"Kid, I got a guy giving me lots of grief, you got any ideas on that?"

I did

The guy is in the East River

Mr. Dunne never asked for details, just handed me a wedge of serious change, said

"You're my boy."

I was

He used me sparingly, a full year before he had another problem and I took care of that too.

Automobile accident.

Grimaldi's was the place back then and he took me out for dinner there, said, handing me an envelope

"Get a good suit, we're putting on the Ritz."

He talked kind of odd but I respected him

The staff there, falling all over him and he said

"See kid, this is juice and you ... you're my main supply."

I was mid bite on the biggest steak I'd ever seen and swallowed it sweet, asked

"Really?"

He was drinking wine, lots of it, I never cared for it, give me a cold one, I'm good, and a nice shot of Jameson to round out the evening, what more do you need? He said

"See, I don't have to do a whole lot now, I hint ... you want the kid on your sorry ass and presto, the problem's gone."

He ate a half mountain of mashed potato, awash in gravy, then said

"You've a dark future ahead of you kid but you need to be real careful."

I pledged I would.

And I was

My Mom got sick last year, the cancer, and on her last night, she took off her wedding band, the gold Claddagh, put it on my finger, croaked

"Go to Ireland for me gasun (son)"

I tried to give her back the ring, me heart was torn in a hundred ways and she near screamed

"I worked for that piece of gold, you think I'm letting it sit in a box in the cold ground."

It's on my right hand, the heart pointing out, means I'm on the lookout

I'm not

Women talk

I don't do talk

My last job, I don't really like to dwell on it, it was before Mr. Dunne got his, a two bit loan shark gutted him, left him spilling his mashed potatoes all over East 33rd and Second.

Mr. Dunne had summoned me, looked bothered, said

"Frank, I have a real delicate situation."

I was no longer the kid, had moved too far along for that. He lit a cigar, his face serious, continued

"There's a teenager, seventeen years of age, name of Gerry Kane, he's knocked up my niece and is fond of hitting her, I want him brought to his senses, nothing major, you understand but he has to understand how to behave, you reading me?"

I had thought I was

It went south, badly

I'd given him a few slaps, the way you do and the punk, he pulled a knife

Can you fucking believe it?

A knife …

On me?

Didn't he know anything

And it got away from me, first time ever, I lost it, big time, they say I scalped him and other stuff

I'm not making excuses, trying to justify me own self or nothing but I'd been doing a lot of speed, you think you can just kill people and get by on the odd brew with a Jameson chaser

Grow up

He had the most amazing blond mop of hair, like Brian Jones before the swimming pool and wait till you hear this, he was seventeen, right? And on his right arm, was the tattoo, Semper Fi … the little bastard, I had my buddy buy the farm in Desert Storm and this piece of shit, this thrash, this nothing, was wearing it … for fashion?

That section of skin, I threw in a dumpster on Flatbush

The shit hit the fan, naturally and maybe it was just as well that Mr. Dunne got diced by the loan shark.

I was finished in the biz.

So, I made my move, liquidized my assets, sold my Mom's house, and flew to the West of Ireland

Rented a little cottage in Oranmore, a beautiful village on the outskirts of the city.

There's a little river runs right by my window and get this, you can fish it, got me some nice trout and cooked the suckers me own self.

My cottage looks just like the one in The Quiet Man and the locals, they're real friendly, the one place in the world where they love Yanks. They're not too nosy, I go to the local on a Saturday night, buy for the house and they like me a lot, well, they like my dollars

Same difference.

They even try some matchmaking, a widow named Theresa, she comes round after the pub on Sat and I give her a workout, she thinks I'm very quiet but her, she could talk for Ireland, and does

I like to read … you're going laugh to your socks off but I read poetry, that guy Yeats, the fucker had it … sings to me, there's a small bookstore, mainly secondhand stuff and they keep any poetry for me.

I'm getting me an education

I was reading … A terrible Beauty …

Jeez, like some awful omen that

I had that marked with my Mum's memorial card when … when … how do I describe the beginning.

I had a log fire going, the book on in me lap, a wee drop of Jameson by my arm when there was scratching on the door … I figured some stray dog.

I opened the door and no one there, then noticed a small envelope on the step, took it inside, reckoning it was another invite to some local event. Tore the flap and inside was a single sheet of paper with the words … Semper Fi

Okay, so it knocked a stir out of me

I'm not going to argue the toss

But I'd been down this road

When I arrived in Ireland, before I got this cottage, I had to stay in Galway, in a hotel, no hardship there, but the city, it was like mini America … Gap, Banana Republic, McDonalds, all the teenagers talking like hybrid rejects from The O.C.

And in the pubs, on tap, freaking Millers, Bud, Pabst … the fuck was going on?

And then I saw him, the blond kid, working the stick in a pub on Quay St … the spit of Gerry and he smirked at me … like he knew … said

"You're a Yank … been there … Dunne that …"

Unnerved me, fuck, gave me a shot of the tremors but I was lucky, a local skel, a bottom of the pond dealer, hooked me up to my beloved speed and once I got that in place, I knew what to do

Scalped him

Yeah, see who Dunne that?

I have his blond hair in my trunk

And figured that was that

Now this

Who was fucking with me and why

The next Sat night, I'm in the pub and Dolan, the owner, a smarmy schmuck, asks

"You met Gearoid?"

What?

I couldn't even pronounce it, one of those dumb Irish names that you need to be German with a bad lisp to say, so I went

"Who?"

He smiles, indicates a group of young people drinking, yeah, bottles of Bud, tequila chasers, and I see the Brian Jones look alike, Dolan says

"That's him, he's got his own band … named Punk … he's hoping to get to America, you might give him a few pointers."

I got the fuck out of there, leaving a full pint of Guinness on the counter.

I was back home, draining a double Jameson when Theresa came round, all concern, Dolan had told her I took a turn and she was fussing, like a freaking hen, the speed was hitting max in my blood and the Jameson was whispering to it, not whispering anything good. I asked

"That nephew of his, Garage … is it?"

She laughed, the dumbass Yank, mutilating the accent, and I tell you, I don't take mocking real good, she said

"Use the English form."

My teeth were grinding, I could hear them and I near spat

"Gee, I would if you'd share it, is it like a secret or something?"

She shot me a look

Me …

Shoot me a look?

Was she fucking kidding, you don't give me looks, unless you're packing something more lethal than bad attitude, but then, she changed course, like women do, said

"Gerry, it's Gerry."

I dropped my glass, Jameson leaking into the rug and she's fussing, searching for a cloth, I roared

"Leave the fucking thing, is that his name, are you jerking my chain?"

She put her hands on her hips, barked

"Don't swear at me mister, my late husband, God rest his soul, he never swore at me and I'm not going to let some …"

I cut her off, demanded

"Why he's here?"

She was thrown, asked

"What … he's on holiday, he has a band he …"

"I know about the fucking band, I asked you why he's here."

She gathered up her coat and the groceries she'd brought
for our meal, said

"Well, I know when I'm not wanted, I'll return when you
soften your cough mister."

After she was gone, I poured some Jameson, chanced another hit of speed, needed to think …

The kid in Galway, when I'd done him I'd been confused,
because when I lifted his sleeve, there was no tattoo, none.

I went to my trunk, unlocked the heavy Yale on it and
pushing aside the blond hair, I took out my knife, the blade
honed to wafer thin perfection, shouted out loud

"Let em come, I'm so fucking ready."

Later, I chilled, thinking, I'd overreacted, new country
and all, those spuds and the Guinness, that shit knocked you
on yer ass.

So I calmed a bit, was even able to read some Yeats, se-
lected a poem at random … The Stolen Child

Fuck, isn't that what the Irish love … that irony they go
on about … .I laughed out loud, laughed till the tears ran down
my face, the knife sitting snugly in my lap.

Next few days were without incident, but I kept the knife
in my jacket, I was easing down a notch but I was getting antsy,
I was ready, they could send all the Brain Jones they liked, I'd
take em all, see if I wouldn't

Changed pubs though

On the other end of the village, was a more modern place,
I preferred the traditional one but what the hell, killers can't be
choosers.

Sitting there over my pint, Bushmills as back, the Jameson
was obviously not agreeing with me, a tiny hint of speed in me
blood, reading the Irish Independent, lots of reports on Iraq, I
skipped them.

Then a feature on a new movie about the life of Brian
Jones, speculating that he'd been murdered.

A shadow fell across me, I looked up to see Dolan's nephew, sweeping the blond locks out of his eyes.

He was wearing faded flared jeans and a black sweat shirt with the logo

HARVARD HURTS

Like he'd fucking know?

He asked

"May I join you for a moment?"

His accent had that quasi-American uplift, as if everything terminated in a question, if he asked me about the Mets, I'd pop him in the goddamned mouth. I said

"Why not."

He slid onto the stool opposite, never taking his eyes off me, asked

"Get you a jar?"

Least he hadn't called it a brewski … yet. His sleeves were rolled down and I couldn't see his arms, his left wrist had all those multicolored bands they collect, the barman brought him over a bottle of Bud, packet of chips, or crisps as they call them here. No glass, he drank from the bottle, cool as the hippie choker round his neck. He raised the bottle, said

"Slainte."

I raised my pint, said

"That too."

His mouth had that half smirk going, as if the joke was known to everyone but me, I asked

"Help you with something?"

He drank noisily, I hate that, all gurgle and no finesse, he belched then

"Me and me band, we're going Stateside and I was wondering if you could hook us up with the names of some hotels in the Village, Like Greenwich Village, we're going to try for a gig at the Fillmore."

Good luck

I said

"The internet, your best bet."

Something dark flitted briefly across his face and he tossed his hair, said

"I thought you might know someone who, like, you know, would open some doors for us?"

He wanted to mind fuck, I'd gone rounds with the best of em and left em in the dumpster, … so I could play … said

"Kid, my age, most people I know, they're dead."

Didn't faze him, he signaled for another brew, said

"Ah, tis a pity but shure, never mind, 'twas worth a shot."

The speed hit a wave and I before I knew it, I asked

"Show me your right arm"

"What?"

I kept my voice steady, said

"You're not deaf, you heard me."

He stood up, gave me his tough guy eye, said

"Jaysus, you're not all in it, you need to get a grip buddy."

He was waving away the barman and the ordered drink, I said

"I'm not your buddy."

He moved to the counter and joined some gaggle of girls, I could see them glancing over, laughing out loud

Man, jeering, that's all they've got, like that rates on my radar.

I finished my drink, made my way out and grabbed his arm, whispered to him

"Hair today, gone tomorrow."

I stopped sleeping, I wanted to be ready lest someone leave something at my door, I slugged the Jameson, did some of the speed, read Yeats a lot but he'd stopped talking to me, the music was gone

Must have been a week after, I saw a poster for the band … Punk, last concert before the American tour

In the local hall.

The way I have it figured , I'll wait in the alley behind the venue, get him on his way out, … No, better, follow him home and do the business

Then I'll get to examine his arm at leisure

The tattoo's going to be on there, isn't it?

I don't doubt that other blond punks will show up but I'm real easy

The trunk has lots of room

Maybe I'll try another poet, you think?

MONICA J. O'ROURKE

MONICA J. O'Rourke has published two novels, SUFFER
THE FLESH, and POISONING EROS (with Wrath James White). Her
short fiction has appeared in more than sixty magazines and anthologies, including *Gothic.Net*, *Nasty Piece of Work*, *Fangoria*,
Flesh & Blood, *Brutarian*, *Nemonymous*, and *Red Scream*. She
lives in New York City and is working on a new novel.

When asked about hitmen, Monica replied: "Hitmen appeal
to the darker side in all of us. Someone who can so easily and
often callously take a human life is terrifying yet somehow appealing. It makes you wonder, as a reader and perhaps more so as
a writer, what kind of person is capable of killing for money."

Visit her at www.DeadlyMojo.com.

BLOODSHED FRED
Monica J. O'Rourke

IN THE ENVELOPE his client had forwarded to him, along with his usual 20K fee, was an address followed by a single line of instruction:

> *150 Beachwood Avenue*
> *Burnt Hills, New York*
> *THURSDAY NIGHT, 9:00 PM*

No further instructions, which Fred knew meant a single target. Easy job, ordinarily. Except …
Fred grew up in that house.
Was this some kind of joke?
He needed to know who ordered the hit, who the target was.

⊕

I'M WALKING INTO A TRAP, he thought as he fixed a cup of instant the following morning. He'd pick up a better cup at Starbucks on his way out of town. For now, taste didn't matter, just caffeine.

But he didn't really believe it was a trap. Besides, who'd set it? His parents? He hadn't seen them in two decades, and he couldn't imagine they'd have any reason to set him up. No matter how they might feel about him. He smirked when he thought about his overly indulgent mother and self-righteous prig of a father. Them, set him up? He imagined the world's most dysfunctional intervention.

He actually hoped his father did have something to do with this. Fred loved the thought of seeing the old man one last time. Because he imagined his fingers around the old asshole's wind-pipe ... Actually, high-tension wire was much more effective and pretty much untraceable, unlike the telltale signs of prints on someone's crushed neck. Not that it mattered, since the feds had no clue how to find Fred and didn't know who he was.

The rental car, an unassuming Ford something-or-other, rented using fake ID and a fake credit card, brought him to Burnt Hills in a matter of hours. Once there he drove slowly up and down Beachwood Avenue, looking for... what? Signs of trouble?

Signs of anything, actually.

He was surprised the house hadn't been condemned by now. It had been a mess when he was a kid and his folks never had the money to fix it. Now, it was more than twenty years since he'd last set foot in this tiny excuse for a town.

He glanced at the note. Today was Tuesday. It was after dark. He'd run out of reasons to procrastinate. He had an obligation and needed to keep to the timeframe.

He grabbed the bag containing his small arsenal and headed for his car. He wondered again if he was stepping into a trap but decided he had to take the risk. His parents were assholes, but they weren't more clever than him. He could handle this.

⊕

WITH HIS GUN DRAWN—a Glock 19 fitted with the silencer he'd made using a Pepsi can, flex coupling, PVC bushing, and a couple of band clamps—he approached the house from the front, entering through the gate long in need of a paint job. There was no need to sneak around the side—no one was on the street. And the closest neighbor lived too far to see the front of the house. He was about to pass the mailbox when he noticed an oversized red envelope sticking out. The name FRED was clearly written across the front. He snatched the envelope and tore it open.

It contained further handwritten instructions:

DOOR IS UNLOCKED.
TARGET IS IN LIVING ROOM.
WELCOME HOME.

He could still recognize his father's pathetic scribble.

Something Fred had never experienced crept into his stomach: dread. But he couldn't leave now. He'd never failed to complete a hit, and he had a reputation to uphold. If he bailed now, he'd never get work again.

At this point, his approach to the house wasn't even close to stealthy. He sauntered up the path as if he'd just returned home from a date. Not that he'd had many dates. Girls thought he was rather strange and, as one called him, icky.

The front door was unlocked, as the note had said it would be. He stepped inside the foyer and the door snicked shut behind him. By now he was past pretenses or real concern; this had become too bizarre and he wanted answers.

"Welcome home, son," his father called from the living room.

Fred smirked and shook his head, amazed at the casualness of this situation. He stepped into the living room, the Glock hanging at his side. He expected to see the old man brandishing a shotgun or rifle. Instead, his father sat empty-handed on the sofa.

"How good to see you," he said, and Fred recognized immediately where he'd learned his own particular smirk. He'd forgotten how much he emulated his father. And how alike they looked, though he'd imagined that after twenty years things would somehow be different. But not only were their mannerisms similar, so was their receding hairline. Their bodies shared the same lanky lines, same stooped posture. Fred wondered if his father had grown a backbone somewhere along the way but highly doubted it. His passive—and pacifist—father had always disappointed him.

Fred asked, "Care to tell me what the hell's going on?"

"Not much. Same old, same old."

"Answer my fucking question!" He raised the gun and aimed it at his father. "Or I swear to god I'll blow your fucking head off right now."

Then he regretted his impatience. This could be a setup, and he'd just threatened the old man's life. He waited a few seconds, expecting to see cops explode from their hiding places to arrest him.

No exploding cops.

"So it's true. You've come to kill me."

Fred lowered the gun. "So it seems. Those are my instructions. But why you? Why did *you* hire me?"

His father sat forward on the edge of the sofa. "Been a long time, Freddie. Miss me?"

Fred smirked. "I never miss."

His father licked his lips and sighed. Held out his hand as if hoping his son would take it but quickly lowered it again to his lap. "It's been so long. I've missed you so much. Please, have a seat."

Fred grinned despite the rodent gnawing on his intestines. "A seat. Well sure, what the heck, why don't I have a seat? And maybe you could get me a beer. And hey, while you're at it, maybe you can tell me why I've been brought here to kill you." He sat on the chair near the door.

"You never were patient. Want coffee or something?"

The Glock resting against Fred's knee brought him little comfort. "Are you planning to keep making small talk? Or maybe you can give me some answers."

"Is that a no?"

"Well," Fred said, standing. He sniffed once and wiped his palm on his pants. "Anyway, this has been... surreal. But I have a job to do. You understand."

His father bowed his head. "So it's true."

"What's true? That I'm here to kill you? You hired me, remember?"

His father ignored the question. "I was hoping somehow I'd been wrong. And it took years. You know?"

"No, I don't know. What the hell are you talking about?"

"I hired a private detective to find you. Your mother and I were worried sick and wanted to find out what happened to you. And finally … we learned. Rather, I did."

"Good for you."

"Your mother died of a heart attack before learning the truth. But I learned what you do …" He cleared his throat. "For a living."

"So that's what this is about?" Fred shook his head and snorted. "Do you understand your stupidity? You *hired* me to kill you. That's one fucked up way to get an answer."

"I know," the old man whispered. "But that's not what this is about. Though I *am* sorry. Somehow I failed you. Somewhere along the way something went bad. But I had to know."

"Yeah, well now you know. And you must know I have to kill you."

"I beg you not to. Not for me but for yourself. Don't do this, Fred. You still have a chance—"

"Shut up!" He raised the gun and aimed it between his father's eyes. "Don't beg for your life, old man. It won't work."

"I'm not begging for my life, I'm begging for yours! There's still a chance for you. You can change things. Please, Fred, listen to m—"

Fred shoved the gun against his father's temple and shot him in the head. The old man flew back and hit the sofa, the shocked expression on his face now nothing more than a rictus of cracked bone and shattered dentures.

Blood splattered Fred's face and clothing—the reason he rarely fired at such close range. But he wasn't concerned with appearances, and the silencer—though mostly a misnomer—

was still quiet enough to not alert the neighbors. Hopefully. But he was prepared for such an event, should someone come along to investigate. The duffel bag he brought and dropped near the front door was his own Magic Bag of Tricks.

"Jesus Christ," he muttered, wiping bits of brain matter off his cheek. "You stupid old fuck." He spat on the corpse. "This was too good for you."

He turned to leave but then stopped. There were still too many unanswered questions. If only he could control his impetuous nature better, he thought. That way he could have tortured his father into giving him answers. Fred would have enjoyed that.

A search of the house might reveal something.

He started in the parlor. Searched drawers and shelves, knocking knickknacks and useless framed memories off the bookcase, overturning chairs and cushions. Nothing but dust behind the TV or under the stereo, nothing inside the fake Ming vases his mother had collected.

He glanced at his father's corpse, reluctant to go near it, never mind touch it. Not that Fred was squeamish; he just hated the thought of touching him.

His father was in an almost upright position, and Fred reached inside his robe, separated the lapels. Nothing. He checked the pajamas—also nothing. The body tipped on its side and slumped over, almost falling to the floor.

Taped to his back was a large manila envelope.

On the outside was written, simply: FRED.

He snatched it from his dead father's body.

The unsealed envelope bulged with papers. Fred separated the seams and looked inside.

The first set were medical reports indicating his father was terminal, had been given six months to live before the cancer would claim his life. They were dated three months ago.

Fred shook his head. Dying?

The next set of papers was his father's will. A quick skim showed the beneficiary was the hospital where his father had been receiving his cancer treatments. They would get the house, the car, any money his father had in savings. Nothing for Fred. He rolled his eyes. How fucking typical.

And the next page showed a nice retirement fund, though it also showed a sizeable amount had been withdrawn just a few weeks ago. The twenty thousand he had paid to hire Fred for the hit.

This kept getting better.

But what was Fred's part in this? His father could have swallowed a bottle of pills or stuffed up the car muffler in the garage. Why involve Fred?

At the bottom of the stack of papers were two envelopes. On one was written OPEN FIRST. He read it:

> *Dear Fred,*
> *I'm sorry I failed you. Your mother and I raised you the best we could. I guess sometimes that don't matter. Sometimes the wiring just gets messed up. We blamed ourselves through the years and wondered what we could have done different.*
> *And then a year ago I found out what you do. How you kill innocent men, women and kids. Kill them for money. My whole world ended.*
> *But son, everything you do has a price.*
> *I brought you home because I wanted to save you. But since you're reading this, then that means I'm dead, and I failed you again. I'm sorry. I tried. I wanted to save you. Your mother and I loved you very much.*

That was it. Nothing else. Fred read the letter several times, looking for clues, looking for anything to explain why his father had done all of this. If he was trying to save Fred, why would he hire him for the hit? It didn't make sense.

The second envelope had nothing written on it. Fred tore it open.

> *Dear Special Agent Hobbes,*
> *As we discussed on the phone earlier this evening, I believe my son is the killer known as Bloodshed Fred. If I'm right,*

*then I am now dead, because I hired him to kill me. It breaks
my heart to do this, but I can't allow him to kill any more
innocent people. If you arrive at my house tonight, you'll
know whether or not I was right. This will be the proof you
will need to show you I was right.*

And a handwritten note at the bottom of the letter:

*I spoke to the agent a little earlier, Fred. I don't know how
quickly they'll get here, but I believe you don't have much
time. I also mailed everything to him, including your bank
account information. There's nowhere to go now. It's over.
Please make peace with that.*

How long ago had his father written the letters? Or called
the feds?

Though the thick silence Fred could hear his own heartbeat pounding in his ears.

He turned to run, to escape the madhouse of his childhood
and figure out his next plan. So what if his father had managed to confiscate his US account? He had more than one, most
overseas and untraceable. He could flee the country, hide out in
Canada or South America, he could—

And then the squeal of brakes outside, the slam of car
doors, the heavy and persistent footfalls on the driveway and
through the thick weeds and bushes surrounding the house.

This couldn't be happening. Fred bolted up the stairs two
and three at a time and reached the top landing.

His bag of weapons was near the front door where he'd
dropped it.

Eyes wild, Fred ran down the hallway, tripping over the
scatter rug, catching himself against the windowsill. He glanced
down at the dozens of agents swarming the house.

As the front door burst open and the shouting began, Fred
hoped he had enough bullets.

MITCHELL GRAHAM

MITCHELL Graham began writing science fiction novels several years ago and recently switched to legal thrillers. His first, MURDER ON THE MAJESTIC, is due out in November 2006 and has been optioned for an upcoming movie by Cherokee Productions. He holds dual degrees in law and neuropsychology.

On the topic of this anthology, Mitch comments: "The psychology of what makes a hitman tick holds a macabre fascination for a lot of people. The reader is alternatively pulled toward the victim, hoping they will escape their fate, and toward the dark side of the hitman trapped or molded by events into theirs."

Visit him at www.MitchellGraham.net

THE LOUVRE CAFÉ
Mitchell Graham

"**IT'S A FUNDAMENTAL** truth. Do you know what that is?" she asked.

The man leaned back in his chair and squinted at the courtyard across from them before answering. It was late in October and unusually warm for this time of the year. Heat waves rose from the ancient cobblestones and shimmered just above the ground's surface. A half-full glass of *Campari* sat in front of him.

"I suppose you mean that it's somehow truer than other truths, but I ask again, what will it prove?"

"It will draw attention to our cause … our suffering."

The man nodded once.

"I would like to understand this suffering you speak of."

When the young woman didn't respond he prompted, "If I'm going to die the least you can do is explain it to me. That's not asking very much."

The young woman glanced at him and then stared over his shoulder at the glass pyramid in the middle of the court-yard. Her eyes became unfocused. Against the backdrop of the elegant buildings that surrounded it, the pyramid appeared anomalous and out of place. A series of statues lined the roof-tops, looking down on people who waited patiently in line for guards to inspect their packages. Among these were a group of school children in blue blazers and clean white shirts. The man thought they were not much younger than the woman sitting across from him. She was perhaps nineteen at most.

"You can't know what it's like not to have a homeland," she said. The words seemed spoken more to herself than to him.

"No, I can't. But how will this solve your problem?"

"The world will take notice. They will put pressure on the Israelis to give us what is ours."

"Haven't they already given your people land on the Gaza Strip?"

She laughed to herself and shook her head.

"Not enough," she replied. "Not nearly enough."

"I see."

Her eyes came into focus again and fixed upon him. Her right index finger was poised above the green button of her cell phone.

"You are like all the others," she said. "The Americans think they know everything."

The man raised his hands in a placating gesture to calm her. "I am a Frenchman."

"It doesn't matter. You are all the same. You only wish to exploit us."

"Have you ever met an American?"

The woman started to say something then appeared to change her mind. She looked at the group of children who were now nearing the guard station. "No."

"Then how can you know what they are like?"

"Because our leaders and the mullahs teach us. They are holy men and I will enter the kingdom of heaven. My family will be forever blessed."

"So you are doing this for your family?"

"For my family and my people, yes."

"You must be very brave."

The woman swallowed and let out a long breath. Her hand was shaking slightly.

"No, I'm not," she said. "I'm very scared, but this is something I must do. God wants me to."

The man's eyebrows lifted in surprise.

"God? God wants you to die? I cannot fathom such a thing. In my religion God loves his people. Is yours so very different?"

"Of course not," she replied. Our God loves us as well."

"Then how do you know he wants you to die?"

"My mullah has spoken to me," she repeated.

"Ah," he said. "May I ask you another question?"

"Go ahead."

A waiter started to approach them but the man signaled him away with his hand.

"In your religion, are mullahs permitted to marry? I know your leaders are. I've seen photographs."

The woman thought for a moment. "Yes."

"And do they have children—the mullahs, I mean?'

"Of course. You said one question. That was two."

"Forgive me," the man replied. "I am scared as well. I did not think to die when I sat down here with you."

The woman nodded absently and glanced at the large clock over the entrance, its face meticulously etched with gold scrollwork. The time read eight minutes before the hour.

The café had been crowded and his choosing this particular table was strictly by chance. How ironic, he thought. Normally, we French do not begin conversations with total strangers, but the dark-haired woman seemed troubled and her cappuccino had not been touched. It wasn't until he took his chair and her coat gapped open slightly that he noticed she was wearing a vest. Then he saw the thin wires coming from it and he immediately knew why the pockets were bulging. She had sufficient plastic explosives to destroy not only the museum, but the entire block.

"You said your mullah is a holy man. By this, do you mean that he is also good?"

"Certainly he is good. Who would follow someone evil?"

"Indeed. It is just that …"

"Yes?"

"There are times evil can disguise itself, or so I'm told."

"You would not say such stupid things if you knew my people. I assure you my mullah is a good man. God's work is everything to him."

"Is the same true of other mullahs?"

The woman made an annoyed gesture with her hand.

"I don't know any other mullahs. I suppose so. Why do you not leave? I will wait."

But the man did not leave. This surprised him as much as it did the woman. He had never been brave in his own eyes.

"I am curious," he said, after a moment. "These mullahs and leaders, who you tell me are good, do they send their own children to blow themselves up?"

The young woman turned to look at him.

"What?"

"I asked if they ever send their own—"

"I heard you. I don't know. Can't you understand? I must do this. If we strike down the infidels, the unbelievers—"

"And you can tell the infidels just by looking?" the man asked.

The young woman glanced at the clock again. Her breathing was quicker now. It read three minutes before the hour.

"You should go," she said, without turning around.

"You haven't answered my question. Because if you can tell the content of someone's heart and what they believe in simply by looking at them, this truly is an amazing talent."

The young woman reached out a shaky hand, picked up his glass of *Campari*, and finished the remainder in a single swallow. "You are just trying to confuse me. You are like all the others."

"Not really," he replied quietly. "I am a Muslim."

The young woman's eyes widened and her mouth opened slightly. "You lie."

He shook his head slowly.

"Do you see that little girl over there?" he asked. "The one with the balloon, holding her mother's hand?"

"Yes."

"Do you know what their religion is?"

"No," she whispered.

"Neither do I."

A minute ticked by and then another and neither spoke. In the background, the sounds of different conversations blended together with people laughing. It was a very warm day and the sky was a crisp blue. The young woman's eyes grew bright and a single teardrop slid down her cheek. The man saw this and reached out, gently placing his hand on top of hers.

⊕

AT A QUARTER past the hour, four blocks from the museum, two bearded men in turbans sat by the window of their hotel room waiting for a different sound—that of an explosion. When nothing happened their eyes burned with outrage.

"The girl has failed us," the first one said.

His companion nodded. "She and her family will be severely punished. We will teach them a lesson that will not be soon forgotten—an example for the others."

The first man said, "If we cannot have obedience, then we must—"

The balance of his words were interrupted by a light tap at the door. His companion rose, crossed the room, and cracked it open slightly. When he saw who was there his face grew even darker and he opened it fully.

The man at the window folded his arms across his chest as the young woman entered and sat down on one of the chairs. Without speaking he reached for the curtain rod and unhooked it. It was perhaps two feet in length and slightly thicker than the quarter inch the Koran prescribed for disciplining a woman, but Allah would understand. One needed to be flexible in times of adversity.

The woman did not flinch when his companion pulled her to her feet and yanked off her coat. Nor did she flinch when the first man came toward her with his arm raised.

The blow, however, never arrived.

The man's arm froze in midair when he finally noticed her finger was resting on the cell phone's green button.

BENJAMIN M. LEROY

BENJAMIN M. LeRoy was born and raised in Madison, WI. His short stories have appeared in two collections-The Best Underground Fiction (ed. Scott Miles) and North Florida Noir (ed. Michael Lister). When he isn't worried about words, he often wishes he could have played baseball through the Great Depression.

When asked about hitmen, Benjamin says, "I want to say something cool, frame it in some Quentin Tarantino way that we can all get a good laugh out of seeing somebody killed. But the truth is, right now I think the whole thing is too tragic. Not just from the victim's standpoint, but from the hitman's perspective. How the hell did somebody end up in a place where he/she can kill another human being for a handful of cash? There is a greater struggle present that goes beyond predator and prey-the killing is only the cork popping and it's a throw away part of the story. Who? Why? How? There are real questions to be explored both in literature and on the street."

Visit Benjamin at www.benjaminleroy.com

LETTERS FROM HOME
Benjamin M. LeRoy

I TOLD MYSELF it would never come to this. Sooner or later the fall would stop. I would hit bottom. But it's three o'clock in the morning in Cleveland and I'm waiting on some two-bit diner waitress to step through her front door so I can put her brains on the kitchen tile.

I keep falling.

⊕

APRIL 1, 2004

Hi from home! I miss you so much and I can't wait for you to come back. It seems like forever since you left, I just hope the time keeps moving fast. I know that when you come home we will be together forever. I often think about what our family will be like and I've even started picking out houses. I don't know if we'll be able to afford them, but I don't care, not now. I'm only passing time until you get back and we can go window shopping together.

Where are my pictures, mister? I want to see you in your uniform holding a machine gun. Or maybe riding in a tank. I can't believe that you're really over there and I won't believe it until I see pictures.

If you're a good boy, I'll send you some pictures, too.

You'll never guess who I ran into the other day—Caleb Washburn. Can you believe it? Nobody knew where he went after high school, but it turns out he was in Kansas working on his grandparents' farm. Anyway, he said to say, 'hey.'

Love,

Baby Girl

⊕

I SET THE GUN down on the coffee table, put my head in my hands. Count to three and tell myself this isn't happening. Hasn't happened. I can still get up off the couch, disappear back into the shadows.

Fuck $500.

⊕

HEY BABY!

It's been hard without you, but I've been trying to keep myself busy. School's gonna start back up in less than a month. I'm working doubles to save up money so I don't have to work as much this fall. We've got some new people at work. We'll all go out once we close. It's a blast. I've never been sooooo drunk. There's a cool new club we'll have to go to once you get back. We'll dance all night.

Your mom came over to dinner last night. We traded pictures of you. She really is proud of you, you can see it in her eyes. How come you didn't send me a copy of the one from your bunk? You look so handsome.

Every time I go to sleep I put my head on your pillow and pray that you'll be there when I wake up in the morning. Sometimes I get sad when you're not there.

I love you.

Baby Girl

✛

I WISH I WASN'T HERE. Should have gotten into the van with Poole and gone off to wherever he was going just to get the hell out of town.

"Listen man," he said, "I know what it's like. They pump you full of everything, teach you how to be a soldier, then they leave you on the side of the road when you're done. When they're done with you. Shit, I wasn't home more than six months when I started getting sick, but when I showed up at their hospital, they acted like they didn't know who I was."

"I understand," I say. But Poole is already gone, a hundred miles an hour out of town. Destination unknown. Looking for hope at every exit.

✛

HOWDY!

I'm sorry I missed your phone call last night. I didn't think I was going to stay out so late, and when my

*cell phone is in my purse, I can't hear it ring. I wish
I could have called you right back.*

*School sucks. I'm thinking about taking the semes-
ter off and working full-time. We've got a good crew
of people, and I miss them when I'm at school. I feel
like such a loser, since most people hate their jobs,
but, I don't know, it just feels right. Caleb says he's
glad that he moved back home and that this is the
happiest he's been in a long time.*

I miss you so much. It's really hard.

Baby Girl

⊕

I CAN HEAR THE thunder in the distance. Everything
in the living room is blending into the dark. The tv becomes
the entertainment center becomes the wall. Only a few lines to
distinguish the shapes.

A car pulls to a stop in front of the house. Engine idles.
The low rumble of bass coming from a rattling trunk.

I slide the gun off the table, squeeze it tight, the snakeskin
of metal leaving the pattern on my palm.

Revisit the plan. The door will open. The door will close.
She turns on the light. I am there.

There's still time to disappear.

⊕

CHARLIE—

*Baby, I'm so sorry what happened to your mom. I
talked with your brother and the doctor. She's going*

to be ok, but she doesn't have any insurance. I feel so bad. I'm sure it'll be ok.

Love you,

Baby Girl

⊕

THE ENGINE REVS, drops into gear, the bass fades into the night. She is not home yet. I take a deep breath and get off the couch. I've memorized the layout of the tables and the furniture. Drawn the map in my head. Thumb tacks to hold everything in place.

I move to the kitchen, pick a half-smoked Marlboro from an ashtray on the counter, and light up. I hear voices in my head. Muffled voices. Strange voices coming from parts of me I wish I would have left behind in the desert.

"How'd I find out she'd been doin' another guy? She told me she was home alone, but I heard other people talking. My towels were missing. My cologne wasn't where I put it. It's circumstantial, Charlie, but I've got a feeling in my gut."

Yeah. I understand. I've got a feeling in my gut, too.

⊕

DEAR CHARLIE—
I'm very sorry about last night. I never wanted to hurt you like that. You have to believe me when I tell you that I didn't mean for this to happen this way. I love you very much and I always will.

I just can't live my life like this. I never know what's going on with you. When you don't call, I think you must have died. It's torture. I have to keep myself distracted or I start to think all sorts of terrible things about what's going on. It hurts so much to feel the way I do.

I am still here for you and I always will be. If you need help around the house because of what hap-pened to your mother and what happened to your arm, I will be glad to help out with things.

I hope you can forgive me. I hope you believe me when I tell you that I love you so much and that I always wanted to be with you. I'm so sorry, I thought I could wait.

Love,

Deena

✛

I'M WAITING FOR SOME big hand to come down. Grab me. Hit me. Stop me. Stop me from killing. Stop me from falling. Pick me up and take me back with the whole bunch of other buzz cut fuck-ups from south of the Mason-Dixon line.

I'm waiting for Poole to show up in the van, wired on trucker speed and anger. "This is what happens, soldier." Voice like gravel. I'm waiting for Poole to figure out the answer and make it all disappear.

I'm waiting. Frozen. Cigarette nearly burnt down to the filter. Cigarette burning down on my lip.

✛

CHARLIE,

*Dfsilkdsoifsdldfsiofsdkljgaskjiogvbjklwiosdiopasdklas djfdijasdjdfaskjdfiopasdfopidfp'dfsoisdldfs;ljsdfl;kas dlkasdjasdkjdas;ikdfj;laksdj;laksdl;krtdf;ldf;ljsdf*THIS COULD HAVE BEEN BEAUTIFUL*jdfsjkldaso;dsjfdid*NOT SURE WHAT I*'Madlkjfldakjsdlfjl;ajsdfl;ja;* THINKING*alj adflja;lsdjf;lajd;lfj;aldjf;lajd;lfkjsf;odsf;ljefwoidfsjdf;o ijdfs;ijdfs;oijdfs*I LOVED YOU.*lasdlkdsiodflds;lijsdjdsflk jdf;ljdsfljkdfrfdl;ljdfjjf*WHAT NOW, SOLDIER?*ladlkfd;ods ;ijasdjidc;oijds;kjd;ofiusda;lkajd;fouad;lkjdf;oiaud;lk asdj;oaifj;lksdfj;ojsdfds;lijasdij*

✛

I AM AWARE OF HER coming through the door. I hear her keys drop on the table. I feel the light as it hits my eye. There is part of me that has already disappeared, has turned to smoke.

But this time distance is no problem. Is not an issue. Not for me. Not for this two-bit girl, wide eyed with the knowledge of what has come and gone. We have an understanding in the second before the squeeze. In the second after the thunder.

MARCUS SAKEY

WITH ten years of advertising experience, Marcus Sakey has the perfect background to write about killers and criminals. His first novel, entitled THE BLADE ITSELF, will be published in January 2007 by St. Martin's Minotaur. He's at work on his second, also to be published by Minotaur.

Marcus on assassins: "Rule breakers are automatically interesting, and the hitman breaks our biggest rules; he literally defies the central principles of civilization. But to me, what makes a hitman an interesting character is not the things he does that are horrific, but rather the ones that are distinctly human—like managing to love, or trust, or even just meet his own eyes in the shaving mirror. When well handled, the tension between those opposing aspects of personality make for a character that's as much fun to write as he is to read."

Visit him at www.MarcusSakey.com

AS BREATHING
Marcus Sakey

WITH FORTY STORIES of empty air swimming beneath your feet, the constellations are close and cold.

I had a steady grip and the wet sound of Sammy's exhales in my ear. I had a ladybug crawling on my fingers and the taste of copper in my mouth.

A mile south, a radio tower rose from the Atlanta skyline. Its red beacon, dying and reborn in slow pulses, reminded me of Sherry, the easy rhythm of her breathing, breasts rising and falling in a beam of dusty sunlight. She'd slept against me as though the world was without fear, each inhale carrying the certainty of the next, and I'd stared with my neck craned sideways and never wanted to turn away.

The ladybug moved off my fingers onto the railing, and I looked at it, and at the balcony that only my heels touched.

"Go," Sammy said, his voice through the earpiece thin and sharp as broken glass, and I stepped off the ledge into the stars.

$\oplus$

WE'D BEEN SHOOTING pool in a midtown dive on the second floor of a strip mall, afternoon heat warping the world outside the windows, Cuervo warping the one within. With his head for angles, Sammy should have been a good player, but wasn't. I'd been in that automatic zone where I let my body do the work, nerves and reflexes functioning unencumbered, cue sliding smooth and sure, dropping ball after ball. Forty bucks a game and I was up two hundred, but Sammy never did know when to quit.

"I don't like it," I said, and kissed the two into the corner.

He held his tequila to the sunlight like he was checking purity.

"An apartment that swank, the guards will have experience. Could be ex-cops." I lined up on the six. "Cameras. Keycards."

Sammy shrugged in that way he does, and poured the drink back. "Why not meet with her anyway, see what she's got to say?"

The trick was not to think. The cue moves, the ball drops. Natural as breathing.

"Guy like Vincennes, he'll have security of his own. Bodyguards inside, bodyguards in the hallway."

"Nothing you can't handle." Sammy set his glass on the table upside-down.

"I don't do that anymore." I popped in the eight, and straightened.

"Right," Sammy said. "I forgot."

"Rack 'em," I said.

✛

THE ROPE WAS DARK blue with green flecks. My gloves were black. Four hundred feet below, the highway was a river of light, the rush of steel a distant murmur.

My legs wrapped around the cord, but it was my arms that drove the descent. Slide, lower, slide. Slow and easy. The first apartments were dark, only my reflection staring back, a vague ghost.

On the thirty-seventh floor the ice-blue glow of a TV revealed a living room. Framed posters on primer-white walls. On the couch, a couple sat together. The man said something that made the woman laugh and fit herself more tightly under his arm.

I tried to remember the last time I'd laughed, but all I could think of was sticky sheets tangled around our calves and the hum of the air conditioner in the window.

✠

IF YOU WERE LOOKING for specialized help and knew who to ask, they might tell you to talk to us. Sammy the planner, good with electronics, surveillance, computers. Dexter the point man, the finisher. Though word was old Dex had slipped lately. Gone soft, now making rent as a thief, cue the violins.

Sherry had known who to ask.

We'd arranged to meet her in the revolving bar on top of the Westin, anonymous amidst fat men auditioning trophy wives and tourists snapping pictures. The sunset skyline blazed like a funeral pyre.

I'd heard of Vincennes. Everyone had. Arms trader, drug dealer, middleman. Not the top dog, but certainly well up in the pack, and his teeth were supposed to be sharp. So his wife I'd imagined as a diamond: sparkle without softness, perfect and unreachable.

Instead I saw a frightened girl whose makeup didn't quite cover thumb-width bruises on her neck.

"Cash," she'd said. "A lot of it. It's supposed to go out the next day."

"Where?"

"I don't know. El Salvador. Afghanistan." She twisted her napkin. "I just pick up what I can. He doesn't tell me anything."

"Why?" I asked.

She looked surprised. "He doesn't really see me."

"No," I said, "why do you want us to rip off your husband?"

She looked at her plate, brushed a lock of hair behind one perfect ear.

"Sherry?" I leaned forward on my elbows. "Why not just leave?"

"Where?" She barely whispered. She looked up, reached out to touch my forearm. "I never meant to be here. I just want …" She paused. "I want to start again." Her gaze held mine, and in her eyes I saw myself reflected.

⊕

THE THIEF THING was new, a way to buttress dwindling finances. We used to offer a much more specialized service.

Then I stopped killing.

In the movies, when the assassin quits, it's always because of some dramatic fuckup. A child in the line of fire. A contract who turns out to be a friend.

The truth is simpler.

Sammy and I were the most sought-after hit team working the South. We'd done Big Oil V.P.s in Dallas and Cuban drug runners in Miami. While Sammy scrambled security cameras, I'd once scraped a straightened clothes hanger through the ear of a Nashville singer planning to move to a rival record label.

We made prestige kills, big scores, and lived like it. Flash pads, beautiful cars, fast women. Nothing meant anything. Put your thumbs through the eyes of an aspiring city councilman in the Ritz bathroom, snap the blood off your hands, go finish your eggs Benedict and wait for the screaming to start. Sammy once bet a homeless guy twenty grand that he couldn't sprint across the highway and back with his eyes closed. Then shot him when he made it. Sammy never did know when to quit.

It all became routine.

Then one morning, a bright blue day like any other, I woke from a dream where I was holding a man's head in a bathtub, crimson water splashing as he struggled to break the surface. My fingers dug into his pressure points, controlling his body, and all I could think about was how huge the score was going to be, how this was the one I'd been waiting for, the one I'd always wanted. Eventually he went limp, and I shouldered the body up and over to float in the tub, which was when I realized it was me staring back at me, and smiling.

"What," Sammy had drawled when I told him, "God came by, said you were on the naughty list?"

"Sort of," I said. "I think I'm done."

Only it hadn't been religion I'd found. It had been her.

Even before I met her, I'd known she was coming

✜

GEORGIA HEAT DROVE a bead of sweat through the long slow run down my side. A squeal of brakes and a car horn rose from far below. I wove the rope back and forth between my legs and shook out my arms. Paused, closed my eyes. Then I bent at the waist, the rope bowing back, gripped just below my feet, and unrolled like a Cirque du Soleil acrobat, ending up hanging head-down three hundred feet over a glimmering highway.

And just above Vincennes's balcony.

"One in the living room." The earpiece stripped the bass from his voice. We'd rented a penthouse with good sight lines two blocks away, and I pictured Sammy peering through the fifty-mag telescope, thin fingers rolling a silver dollar back and forth.

"Strapped. A second piece on the table." He described the layout of the room, like I hadn't spent a dozen hours staring at it through the same scope. "Give me a second," he said, and I heard the tones of him dialing. "Okay. You're a go."

I loosened my thighs, tendons banging like steel cables, and eased down the rope, friction and aching leg muscles all that kept me from tumbling into darkness. My arms stretched, fingertips filling with blood. One foot. Two. Three.

At five, I touched the railing, identical to our own ten floors above. Through the patio door, I could hear the phone ringing, Sammy making the call.

I slid over the railing and onto the balcony. Rolled my neck, allowed myself a memory of Sherry drinking two-hundred-dollar wine out of a plastic cup and smiling, smiling at me, and then I eased the glass door open and slipped inside.

⊕

THERE WERE STORIES about Vincennes. None of them good. One popular fave was about a lieutenant the FBI had twisted. This was a guy who'd been with Vincennes for years, been at his wedding. Two of the lieutenant's own soldiers scooped him up, dumped the wire he wore, and ran a switch on the Marta trains to lose the feds.

Then they took the poor bastard to meet Vincennes in a warehouse on the west side. Rumor had it they kept him alive for almost three days, though I wouldn't call it much of a life.

"You know he'll come after us." Sammy put his arms behind his head, his feet up on the edge of the roof. He'd bought the building cheap, a former meat packing plant southwest of downtown, and had been trying to find a buyer to turn it into lofts for yuppies. Always playing angles. "The cash we're taking, it won't be enough to cripple him."

"I know." I started to speak, stopped, words caught in my throat like fishhooks. Tried again, choked them out. "I'll take care of him."

"You mean we're back in biz?" Sammy's voice quick and eager.

"No," I said. A million reflected city lights burned in the sweat on my beer bottle.

"Huh?"

I took a last swallow. "I'm done killing."

Behind the building, a train blew a lonely whistle, the rattling of wheels on tracks a pulse to the night.

"But you'll do him?"

"Just Vincennes." I threw the bottle overhand, the dark glass whirring away. A faint clank rose from the scrub near the tracks. "Not the guards, not anybody else. Then I'm done for good."

He pursed his lips. "Tell me something, partner." He looked over, eyes bland. "Why him?"

Because she'd asked. Laying in my arms, my skin still sticky with her. She'd asked me to kill him and then never kill again, and it had been like it was me speaking.

"He doesn't deserve to live."

Sammy shrugged. "Who does?"

"Vincennes is the last," I said.

⊕

AFTER THE DARKNESS outside, the living room was garish. Schoolroom bright. No shadows, no cover.

Ten feet away a bodyguard stood with his back to me and a nine-millimeter SIG-Sauer P226 strapped in a quick-release shoulder holster.

"Who called you?" he said into the phone, the cord stretched out from the wall.

I lifted my right foot, set it down slow. Then my left. Didn't concentrate on the motion, didn't concentrate on the man. Didn't concentrate at all, actually. Just let nerves and reflexes take over. Like playing pool.

"Yeah, well, you got the wrong place." The man paused. "Yes, I'm fucking sure. There's nothing wrong with our plumbing."

When I was two steps away, the floor creaked.

He whirled, reaching for his piece. The phone was still in his hand as I speared his neck, rigid fingers slamming into his carotid artery where it branched, and then he was falling.

The phone hit the carpet with a muffled thump. The bodyguard I caught. Pressure point knockouts don't last, but a chokehold will.

I ran the list in my head. Two guards in the lobby downstairs. Two in the exterior hallway, but if they'd've heard anything, I'd already be dead. And this one outside the bedroom, now flat on the carpet.

If they followed pattern, there was just Vincennes to go. One final murder, one final chunk of me disappearing.

And then I could watch her sleep for the rest of my life, and never dream again.

⊕

IT TOOK TWO WEEKS and most of our remaining capital to prepare.

Sammy gathered intel. He worked all his angles, from the kid at the planning office who ran photocopies for a C-note to hacking the apartment's wireless network from a coffeeshop across the street.

The strategy was his idea. Instead of circumventing building security, we co-opted it. Rented an apartment ten stories above our target, using a passport I bought in the back room of a Ponce de Leon pawnshop. The building piped the lobby video cameras in with the cable TV, and I spent days logging everyone who passed.

One time I saw Vincennes half-dragging Sherry through the foyer, his fingers leaving marks on her pale arms, and put my fist through the drywall.

⊕

DARKNESS POURED IN the windows when I killed the living room overheads. If Vincennes was paying attention, he might notice the glow under the door go out, but it was better than stepping in with bright light at my back.

I put a gloved hand on the knob. Took a breath. Sammy was quiet in my ear, a good sign. If things looked off, he'd be squawking.

I opened the door. Nothing moved. I flowed inside, a shadow in dim light.

As I eased the door closed, it occurred to me that this was his sometimes-bedroom. Which meant it was her sometimes-bedroom too.

My hate rose like stinking black sewage.

Beyond the floor-to-ceiling windows, the skyline blazed. The red beacon on the radio tower died and was reborn. City light spilled in to trace silhouettes. A desk big enough to suggest Vincennes was compensating for something. Two doors on the far wall, both closed. According to the floor plans Sammy had scored, the far one was a closet, the near a bath.

The sleigh bed was beside the window, and I could barely make out the shape of Vincennes asleep in it.

I moved on the balls of my feet, alert to every motion. He didn't so much as twitch. When I made the edge of the mattress, I lifted one of the pillows, a heavy down thing soft as falling snow. Reviewed the moves in my head: straddle Vincennes with a knee on either shoulder, use the pillow to silence his shouts and a knife-hand blow to crush his trachea. Count two hundred after the struggling stopped, get the cash, and we were clear.

I was leaning forward when the lights flickered on.

✣

THE MOTEL CURTAINS were faded plaid, the carpet dotted by cigarette burns, but the dusty sunlight through the window was holy. Outside, the breeze tossed the trees, leaves rustling, and she sighed as I slipped inside her, sighed and wrapped her arms around my neck and whispered my name, William, not Dex or Dexter or even Billy, William, two soft syllables that melted in the heat of her breath in my ear.

⊕

BEHIND ME, SOMEONE spoke, but I didn't hear a word.

It wasn't Vincennes in the bed.

It was Sherry.

Her face was blue. Her body was bruised. Her amber eyes were empty.

The voice behind me spoke again, and I turned.

Larry Vincennes stood in the bathroom doorway. He wore a paisley dressing robe and a contemptuous smile, held a 0.50-caliber Magnum Desert Eagle in his right hand. The pistol looked enormous in his delicate fingers.

We stared at each other for a long moment.

"Why is she naked?" My voice like rusted metal.

Vincennes smiled. "Gave her to the boys." Then he raised the gun, the dark barrel wide enough to crawl into and fall asleep forever.

I hurled the pillow as I lunged, and the roar of the Desert Eagle was a cloud of goose-down filling the room and glass from the window falling in sparkling sheets. My eyes caught every detail, the tangents of a thousand drifting feathers, the way Vincennes's robe flapped open to expose a gold necklace laying against his skinny chest, the play of his muscles as he struggled to recover from the recoil, realizing only now that his cannon was way too much weapon to fire one-handed, and I drank the panic in his eyes as he understood he wouldn't make it, and then I snapped his neck as automatic as breathing.

When the guards raced in from the hallway, I held the Desert Eagle in both hands. Squeezed once. Squeezed twice.

✛

I WASN'T SURPRISED to find Sammy gone when I made it back to the penthouse.

Sammy. Always playing angles. If I was determined to quit the game over some woman, why shouldn't he make a buck on it? And if that got her raped and beaten to death, well, can't make an omelet, right?

His abandoned cigarette still smoldered in the ashtray, and I stubbed it out and stepped onto the balcony. The red light on the radio tower flared and died, flared and died, and I stood holding the gun and thinking of a patch of dusty sunlight and the hum of air conditioning.

He's gone, but Sammy never did know when to quit. I'll find him. Because he forgot one thing.

I only stopped for her.

It's like shooting pool. The cue moves, the ball drops.

Natural as breathing.

DAVID ELLIS

DAVID Ellis is an author and trial attorney in Chicago. His first thriller, LINE OF VISION, won the Edgar Award for Best First Novel. David followed up with the critically-acclaimed novels LIFE SENTENCE and JURY OF ONE. His latest novel is IN THE COMPANY OF LIARS.

"Why do I (and so many others) like movies and books about assassins? They are daring and adventurous. They are risk takers. They are mysterious. They are highly skilled. But most of all, they are fascinating from a psychological perspective. Taking another person's life for nothing but money? I like the quirky ones, the ones who are painfully shy (William H. Macy in *Panic*), emotionally conflicted (John Rain in Barry Eisler's series), scrawny (Steve Buscemi in *Things To Do in Denver When You're Dead*), or even a little goofy (Travolta in *Pulp Fiction*). But I'll take them any way I can find them!"

Visit Dave at www.DavidEllis.com.

THE SHINING KNIGHT
David Ellis

AN ACTION. A LITTLE SCARE. New for me. I usually scare people, but that's because I'm killing them. So this is a first. How hard can it be?

Probably not that hard, but I'm off to a bad start, spending thirty minutes standing on this isolated corner downtown. A couple of cabs drive by but they're occupied and drive past. This isn't the best street to look for cabs, because I'm standing near a stop for the elevated train; most people at this intersection are taking mass transit, and the cabbies know it.

The action will take place twenty-six blocks north of where I'm now standing. That's three and a quarter miles. Timing is, shall we say, rather critical here. I check my watch, shake my head, pick up my briefcase, and walk over to the stairs to the elevated train platform. Doesn't hurt that there's a woman arriving at the staircase just before me, a few stairs above. Doesn't hurt that she has long, athletic legs, either. I'd climb a lot more than a dozen grimy, stained, cracked concrete steps to follow her.

I slide my pass through the automatic register and head up the next flight of stairs, the princess still ahead of me.

I check my watch again. Quarter past nine. On the train platform, the humidity in the July air has mixed the odors of urine and garbage and refined them into a wretched smell.

The woman sits on the yellow bench in the glass canopy, looking meek and innocent, her leather workbag between her feet, a small purse over her shoulder. Dressed professionally in a jacket and skirt and low heels. Blond hair pulled back off her face. Delicate features. Looks to be early thirties. No wedding band. Above her is a billboard for the latest sitcom with dreadfully thin women and average-looking guys, having lots of zany fun. All of their features have been altered with magic marker, none of the changes flattering and one obscene.

Besides the beauty queen and me, the only person up here is a tough-looking kid in a muscle tee, pacing around as he talks on a cell phone. I lean against a pole and wait for the train, my eyes naturally moving in the direction of the woman. That's how it works with men, the eye always latching onto the most attractive female form. She's the only one in this case, but she'd do in most circumstances.

You look without looking. If you keep your head still as you stare, she'll eventually notice—that sixth sense, combined with peripheral vision, that tells you someone's watching. The key is to keep yourself moving—check your watch, clear your throat, adjust your position, whatever—while you ogle.

I keep my eye on the young kid, too, but not because he's black. White people are unrealistically fearful of African Americans. He says something into the phone and closes it. He looks at me just as my eyes move off him.

Over five minutes of nothing passes. My stare carries beyond the platform to the elevated tracks. Death all around us. I could throw either one of these people onto the third rail. I could push them onto the tracks, third rail aside, and leave them for a train. I could snap either of their necks. It's an honors system, really, the whole thing. But it's right there, if you're looking for the invisible.

The headlight of the elevated train appears on the horizon of the track. The lady on the bench looks up, which means she looks in my direction, but I've already moved my eyes off her, pulling down my tie and opening the collar of my dress shirt. She makes me for a professional working late, like she is. In a way, she's right.

The train stops with a heavy sigh and the doors on the cabins part in sync. There are a few people in each of the cars. The woman pauses a moment, then gets in the closest one. I notice her glance over at the black kid on the platform, wondering if he's going to move in her direction, but he doesn't. Must be taking a different train, she's figuring. I get in the same car as the woman.

Musical chairs now. The seats in the train car face in different directions. Some face north or south, others east or west. Cinderella takes one of the seats against the wall, facing east, and I sit across from her. There are two women, a couple of older Hispanic ladies, down the way. Funny how we do that. We give each other as much space as possible. We spend hours together sometimes, on airplanes or buses or trains, without saying a single word to each other. We do our very best to avoid interaction.

Wait. Another guy in the corner. Homeless guy, wearing at least three shirts, though none of them covers his belly as he lies across two seats in the corner. He is coming to, smacking his lips and moaning softly. The beauty queen hears him and watches him struggle out of his coma. Then her eyes hit mine. I give her that universal, non-threatening smile, tucking in my lips, which is closer to a grimace than a grin, especially on me. She seems disarmed by the brief contact and casts her eyes downward. I get that a lot.

The doors close, the train exhales as it starts up again.

I look at the woman without looking, because she is even more attractive in better lighting, and it's either her or the obnoxious advertisements for drug-addiction hotlines and AIDS awareness that run along a top shelf of the train. She has blond hair and soft green eyes that move across the page of the *Cosmopolitan* magazine she's fetched from her bag. She doesn't wear much makeup but her skin is tanned and healthy. She wouldn't be confused with a supermodel but she has my attention, though she doesn't indicate, in any way, that she wants it. She blinks once and looks in my direction, probably aware, as people are, that she is being ogled. Soon she returns to her magazine as I pretend not to stare. But stare I do. I make her for an athlete, for a timid woman who doesn't seem overly occupied with her looks. The type I would normally go for. Pretty but unaware of it.

I need a girlfriend, I decide. But I have no illusions about this woman.

The rear door of the car pops open. Two young black men walk through, coming over from the adjoining car, holding onto seats as the train rocks and buckles. You hear about this sometimes, gangbangers patrolling the cars, looking for prey. They are laughing about something I can't make out.

"Ho, now," one of them says, his tone less spirited.

I work the car clockwise. The homeless guy seems entirely unaware. The two Latina women, hearing the punks at the other end, look at the floor, take each other's hands. The lady across from me freezes, but her eyes come off the magazine with intensity. She's pretty sure the kid's reference was to her.

We rock as the train turns a corner, crossing the river and moving to the near-north side of the city. Now the sound of hands clapping.

"My, my, my." He's a skinny African American with a healthy stalk of hair, slapping his large hands together in exaggerated fashion. "Look-at-the-pretty-lady." He says it like a song.

That confirms it—he isn't admiring me.

His friend is shorter, stockier, actually a little meaner. Younger, too, looks like. Not the leader. You always identify the leader.

I peek at the woman, suddenly focusing on the zipper of her leather bag at her feet. She has just crossed her legs but now she adjusts, placing them together, her knees hugging each other, a defensive position.

"Ho!" the kid calls out. "Wha's yo' name, girlfrien'?"

I turn and look at the guy, make a point of holding my stare until he notices. The woman does, too—I see her look up at me from my peripheral vision. Looking without looking.

"Aw, c'mon, I's just askin' yo' name, pretty girl."

The woman's eyes dart across mine. She is, essentially, holding her breath now. Waiting it out. Hoping she can hold these bozos off until her stop.

I look over at the homeless guy, who is stirring, but he doesn't seem like he'll be much help. Then I glance back over at the kid, who is standing up again, holding one of the vertical poles as the train rocks forward again, the overhead speaker calling out the next stop.

"Tell me yo' name, pretty woman." The kid cups his mouth with a hand, like he's calling across a canyon to her, when in fact he's only about ten feet away.

"Ya got yo-self a player, lady?" Punk Number Two, the younger, stockier one, calls out. He's wearing a wife-beater tee and baggy jeans. "Ya want yo-self a *boy*-friend?"

The two of them enjoy that for a moment, menacing laughs, pushing each other. The young woman can hardly pretend not to notice now. Her eyes are intense, boring holes in the floor, darting about as her knuckles turn white gripping her magazine. She is calculating, no doubt. A non-response could be as escalating as the wrong response. But if her mind is racing, it doesn't seem to be leading anywhere, the paralysis of fear.

The train stops. No one gets off, no one gets on. I half expected her to exit here, even though it's not her stop, just to be rid of these idiots. But they might follow her, and she wouldn't even be near her house. She's probably made the safe move, in her mind.

"Now come *on*." Number One advances, followed by Number Two, gripping a pole close to her as the train starts up again. He could almost reach out and touch her now. The woman's chest heaves, her eyes blinking rapidly. She continues to look away from the morons, until her eyes catch mine.

I clear my throat. The punks are aware of me but don't show it.

"What's *your* name?" I ask Number One.

The kid, facing the young lady, turns his head so I can see his profile, moving his head slowly like I'm being a nuisance. "What-choo sayin', guy?"

"I want to know *your* name." I get to my feet, holding a pole lest I fall over as the train rocks along the track. I doubt I threaten too many people but I'm over six feet, wide-shouldered, and credible enough.

The kid chuckles, like he's impressed with my *cojones* but I'm nothing but a pest.

"I ain't *talkin'* to you, man," he sings in a threatening melody, like he's already lost patience with me. He swings around on the pole to box me out from the young woman.

"Why don't you and I talk," I say. I suppose if I were looking for something snappy, I missed, but I have a deep voice and I say it like I mean it.

Generally speaking, people looking to make trouble want easy marks. Low resistance. There's nothing personal to it whatsoever. The problem is, this isn't a purse-snatching. This is the very definition of personal.

"Don't *make* me turn around," Number One says. Punk Number Two hasn't spoken for a while, studying me.

Number One says, "Am I botherin' you, pretty lady? Huh? Now I'm *talkin'* to you." He snatches the magazine out of her hand.

Contact. An escalation. Now is the time.

"You're bothering her, pal," I say. "And you're bothering me."

"*Pal?*" Number One switches hands on the pole, shifts his feet and opens himself up so he's facing me.

The play here is to throw water on the fire, not gasoline. Chesting up to this kid might make him want to leave, but he wouldn't want to lose face. He'd probably want to mess up mine first. That's how anyone would look at it, anyway.

"Go back to your seat," I say. "Keep the magazine."

"Maybe my seat's right here." He nods in the direction of the young lady while his expression grows cold. The second kid moves to his left, like he's getting a better angle on me.

"I don't remember it that way," I say.

"No?"

Our conversation is reaching new lows.

"Listen, kid. I've got somewhere I gotta be, and I really don't need your blood all over my suit. So do me a favor—run along." I gesture with my head.

The kid pauses, blinks away our eye contact. The woman, still seated, is watching our conversation with interest, sizing me up to see if I'd be able to handle myself. To look at me, you might not think so. To know me, that's another story.

The kid makes a point of seeming unaffected, rolling his tongue against his cheek as he chuckles. Looking to save face. There's two ways he can do that. One of them is take me on.

"You might mess me up," I allow. "Wanna find out?"

The other is to gain some small victory, a minor concession from me.

He takes the latter option, predictably. "Damn right I could mess you up." He leans forward until his forehead almost touches against mine, then he's on his way back to his seat, Number Two close behind, after giving me a steely glare.

I look again at the woman, who is deflating with relief. I take my briefcase and sit next to her, her personal bodyguard.

"Thank you so much," she whispers.

I lean into her. "I'm not really a tough guy," I said. "But I play one on subways."

The kid strolls to the end of the car, by the door connecting to the next car over, and kicks an empty soda can hard, the woman next to me flinching at the echo of the aluminum colliding against the rear door.

"He's harmless," I say quietly, but evenly, to this woman. "I'm Jason," I add.

She looks at me briefly, a sweet smile. Kings have sent armies into battle, I imagine, for smiles not as endearing as this one. She shakes my hand without offering her own name, which is smart of her.

The kid is on the cell phone now, talking to one of his buddies in his own private lingo, but I've spent enough time around gangbangers to catch a few choice words, most of which describe parts of the female anatomy.

The lights inside the train make it hard to see out, leaving me with a collage of my own reflection in the window and the passing shapes outside, the sides of brick buildings and the tops of trees and billboards advertising for home equity loans and cellular phones, as the train moves on in clunky fashion. We hit another stop, the doors open and close with no one getting on or off, including the punks sulking in the corner.

"The next stop is mine." I say it like it's an apology—her Knight in Shining Armor is getting off the train.

"Mine, too," she says. I can see she's still tense, still trying to keep an eye on the punks through her peripheral vision. She has not, apparently, found them to be so harmless.

I check my watch and sigh. "Would you like me to walk you home?" I ask, quietly, looking over at the kid who is watching us with a hard stare.

"Oh." The woman looks at me again. "I don't want to be a bother."

I raise a hand. "No bother."

The overhead speaker blares out the name of her stop, and I stand with indifference, grab my briefcase and offer the young lady a hand. Quite the gallant nobleman, am I. She takes my hand and smiles. She sees what I'm doing, not looking nervous, and tries to follow suit. We walk over by the door and wait for the stop. The kid watches us, and I make a point of watching him. I whisper a joke to my female companion, again to look not the least bit unraveled.

The car doors open and we step out. "I'll be right with you," I say to the woman, and I turn back to the door I've just passed through, looking dead-on at the kid, Punk Number One. He gets up quickly, like he might move toward the door. He shouts something at me, then the doors close between us and he slams his hand hard on the window, pressing his face against the glass.

My back to the woman, I blow the kid a kiss. He winks at me, then forms his hand into a pistol and shoots it at me.

That's Charlie Watts for you. Always taking a risk. At least he got on the train in time—after getting the call from his colleague, the black kid who was waiting on the train platform for the blonde beauty and me. I assume the woman—whose name is Emily Taylor—wasn't looking his way when he gestured toward me just now. Charlie always likes to have a little fun, but he's never blown a job.

⊕

WAY I HEARD it, Emily Taylor was a prostitute with a nice, clean-cut suburban white girl's name. Only Emily wasn't suburban and wasn't so clean-cut. She worked as a secretary at a law firm during the day but spent a few evenings a week as a high-class escort, her only client being Victor Cappeletti. You gotta know Victor. He talks. He brags. Especially with the ladies. Point being, he told her things she's not supposed to know. Things about what he does for a living. Details, too.

They told him—hell, I told him—there are plenty of girls who'd fuck a mobster, stay away from the escorts, the girls who get paid. They're easier to flip. Emily Taylor was no exception. That's what the Boss told me, anyway, three weeks ago.

"Feebies got her," he'd told me. "Probably raided the escort service."

"How sure are you?" My question had surprised the Boss. That kind of thing usually didn't matter to me. But they didn't usually ask me to kill a woman.

When he didn't convince me, I'd told him, "No, thanks," and got up and left.

He'd stared at me then, incredulous, maybe offended, too. "*No thanks*?"

He had someone call me again, two weeks later. "It wasn't the feds, after all," the Boss told me, in person, same booth, same restaurant. "It's the Patanos."

That changed things. A rival crime family. That meant the woman hadn't been flipped, hadn't been forced to work for the government. She'd probably gone to the Patanos, not the other way around, looking to play both sides into a nice payday.

"I don't want her dead," the Boss told me. "Just a little action. Put a scare in her."

That made sense. If she had been working for the G, she could testify at some point and would need to be adiosed. If the Patanos were using her, that wasn't an issue. An action would be enough.

"You don't want her dead," I said. "But you want me?"

"Nobody knows you." He sat back in the booth. He looked unhappy, having to explain himself. He was the Boss, what he said was the word. But he wasn't *my* boss. I flew solo. And that, I realized, was his reasoning. If the Patano family figured out who came down on Emily Taylor, they might come looking for that person. But nobody knew me. Nobody would find me.

"I'll tell our friend Emily that we know," I told the Boss, feeling a wave of relief. I wasn't sure if his decision to scare her, not kill her, was because of my earlier reluctance. I thought that was possible. But I wasn't sure.

Either way, I was glad.

The Shining Knight felt like the right call. Emily Taylor lived in one of the gigantic apartment buildings on the near-north side, so forcing my way into her place wasn't an option.

And with the Knight, we would let her know how well we knew her routine, how easily we could invade her world.

But the thing I liked most, it kept my options open.

I told the Boss I'd use Charlie Watts. I trusted him, and he knew how to play it.

⊕

THE WOMAN AND I walk side by side from the train. She keeps looking behind her, for Charlie and his friend. I keep telling her, the punks aren't following.

"I really can't thank you enough." The woman sighs with relief. "It's just—something like this happened to me before. I really thought it was going to happen again."

I don't follow that up, because I assume that if she wants to elaborate on her history, she will.

"I'll say this," she adds. "That's the last time I take the train."

She may be right about that. I haven't decided yet.

"Look, I'll walk you home, no problem. The guy spooked you. It happens. No need to explain."

"You have to let me pay you back," she insists. "I have to give you something."

We take the steps down off the platform. I say, "You could give me your name."

The woman eases up a bit, smiles at me tentatively. "Emily," she says. "Emily Taylor."

So we're getting closer on the trust thing.

Diamond Street is all high-rises and taverns, one big agonizing traffic jam of a neighborhood when it's busy. It's a Tuesday night so the nightlife is a little slower than usual, but there is still plenty of animation tickling out of the places we pass. Bars are advertising drink specials on stand-up chalkboards or enormous signs across their windows. Some live music blares out of one place, some heavy guitar and a white kid trying to rap. What the hell is a white kid going to rap about? Some bitch at the shopping mall who didn't put enough sprinkles on his frozen yogurt?

"What do you do?" I ask.

"Oh, I work at a law firm."

"Oh, so *that* explains why you're working so late," I say. "You're a lawyer."

She doesn't answer. A natural reaction, from her perspective. She just got spooked by a couple of strangers, and now here's another stranger—albeit her Knight In Shining Armor—asking personal questions.

The shoe-shine patrol is out in force, black kids who throw some polish on your wingtips before you even know it, then charge you five bucks to spread it evenly over your shoes. I sweep my foot away at the last second, avoiding him, and the kid decides I'm not a pushover.

"I'm a lawyer, too," I say, looking the part in my suit and briefcase. "Walker, Price. You know it?"

Law firms have their own phone directory, to which virtually every law firm subscribes. I did a check and found no law firm named Walker, Price in this city, or anywhere in the state. I stopped counting the number of law firms in this city at five hundred, most of them small, so she shouldn't be surprised she hasn't heard of the name.

"We're small," I say. "Just ten of us."

"I'm sorry." She looks over at me. "I haven't heard of it."

"Where do you work?" I ask, knowing that the answer is Addison, Bell, and Myers. A firm of thirty-five lawyers practicing commercial litigation, occupying the nineteenth floor of Bentley Tower.

"Addison, Bell, and Myers," she tells me. "Actually, I'm only a secretary. My boss is starting a trial next week."

"Who's your boss?" I ask, because it seems like the natural thing to ask.

"David Rosencrantz?"

So my research was right. David Rosencrantz was listed as a partner at the firm, and his secretary is Emily Taylor.

"Don't know him," I say. "I don't do much trial work, but I hear you about the late hours." The only trial work I've done is when I was a defendant, and that was twenty-one years ago. One witness had an unfortunate accident, the other a change of memory.

I think about my conversation with the Boss. *Just a little action*, he'd said. *Put a scare in her.*

I'd agreed with him then, as he knew I would. He could probably see the relief on my face. I don't live by too many rules in my profession, and I've never set any for my clients. But if I don't want to do something, I just don't do it. I've never killed a woman and I don't want to start now. But if what the Boss tells me is true, then this one is bad news. She must have gone to the Patanos, looking for a nice lump of cash in exchange for critical information of some sort. Play in mud, you get muddy.

On the other hand, nothing is black and white. The whole fucking world is gray. I knew a guy with ice in his blood, over a hundred hits to his name, who cried like a baby when his dog had a leg amputated. Tell me that guy was all bad. This one, Emily Taylor, seems nice enough. She had a hand, she played it. It's not like she was two-timing the Pope. Vic Cappeletti is a mouth-breathing, blood-sucking swine.

But I still haven't decided what I'm going to do here.

"Oh wait—Addison, Bell, and Myers," I say, like something just registered. "Jody Franzen works over there. I never met her, but we traded some nasty letters over an employment contract. Boy, she sure was a piece of work. She was tough as nails. How is she to work with?"

Now she should have no doubt about me being a lawyer. Anyone could say that he's a lawyer. Anyone could make up a phony law-firm name. But who would know a lawyer who works in her law firm?

If she'd asked—which she hasn't—I'd tell her my name is Jason Conrad. I've worked at Walker, Price for the last eleven years. The case I had with Jody Franzen was a potential dispute where I represented a company—I'd rather not say which, thank you—that fired a woman who was friends with Jody Franzen. Jody helped her out as a favor. We avoided litigation by agreeing to a buy-out with a confidentiality clause.

I was feeling pretty good about my story. I'd given it some thought. If I said Jody represented the company, Emily might have asked which one? Companies usually have the same lawyers for years. Emily would expect to recognize the name. So I said *I* represented the company, and Jody Franzen represented the individual, a friend. The confidentiality clause, too—kept me from sharing details and showing my ignorance.

Hell, I even went so far as to call Jody Franzen, whose phone number was listed in the directory, just to make sure—hanging up, of course, as soon as the lawyer answered the phone.

The wind lifts the hair off my forehead, carries the smell of a barbeque grill. We are getting close to Dillard Street now. Emily Taylor lives at 2459 North Dillard, Apartment 8B. Usually this is when my heart goes cold, because it has to, but this time it escalates, kicking against my shirt.

Emily Taylor has one half of one city block to convince me she should live.

"I don't know Jody very well," Emily says to me. "She seems okay, I guess. I live up here."

"Sure." My pulse is at full throttle as we turn up Dillard, the frivolous sounds from the bars growing fainter now, the relative darkness of the residential block shrouding us. I work the corner so that when we turn, she's to my left. While I'm at it, I remove the nine-millimeter, with a silencer, from the back of my belt with my right hand and keep it to my side.

"What would you have done?" she asks me. "If they hadn't backed down back there?"

"I would have had to defend your honor," I answer. "I know *jujitsu*, *karate*, and a lot of other Asian words."

She should laugh, but she doesn't. Maybe she's still spooked. Maybe I'm not much of a comedian. Wouldn't be the first time someone told me so.

"I'm over here," she says, pointing to the brick high-rise near the northeast corner, about twenty floors of condos with a four-stair walk-up and green awning. God, they pack a lot of people into the north side.

We've been walking north. Emily Taylor stops at the gate to her building, facing me, as I clasp my hands behind my back. "I'm wondering," she says. "Maybe you could call me some time."

I almost laugh. To my right, two guys wearing baseball caps, each holding an open beer can, appear in the doorway of Emily's apartment building, laughing as they push the door open.

"Great," I say to Emily, turning a quarter to my right, so the guys coming out don't know what I have behind my back. I switch the gun to my left hand, tucking my finger behind the trigger.

"Let me give you my card." Emily reaches into her purse but it spills out of her hands, toppling over on its way to the ground. She squats down as the two guys come out of the building. One guy's telling the other a joke as they bounce down the steps.

I start with them. I raise the nine-millimeter, with the silencer, and put one between the first guy's eyes. I kick Emily, who is hunched down, in her shoulder, sending her to the sidewalk. The second guy pulls the same gun as mine out of his jacket but I drop him, too, before he can raise it.

And I'm not even left-handed.

"Stand up," I tell *Emily*, the name she's using. She's hardly had the chance to react and realizes that any time she had is gone. "And don't make me nervous with those hands."

She complies, showing me her palms as she rises. She's not the shooter, anyway. That's why she was ducking.

I move close to her face. "Tell me your name, and don't lie."

"Bridget," she says quickly.

"I'm going to let you live, Bridget. You understand? But I want you to tell the Boss a few things. Ready?"

She nods, and says, tentatively, "Ready."

"One: I turn down any job I *want* to turn down."

She says, "You turn down any job you *want* to turn down," using the same emphasis, with a little more strength in her voice now. She seems to understand that the messenger gets to breathe.

"Two: Even when I'm putting a scare in someone, I still bring my gun."

She nods again, repeating it back to me.

"Three," I say. "Now I'm mad."

"I can tell."

I stare at her, then laugh. "Good, Bridget."

She appraises me, the caution gone from her eyes. "So you're the man," she says.

My reputation has preceded me. I imagine she was getting a decent nickel for this job, even as the set-up.

"I'm *a* man," I answer. "And so is Jody Franzen."

I leave her, heading north, wasting no further time. But I swear I see the trace of a smile cross her face before I start running.

BIBLIOGRAPHY

Jeff Abbott
[Whit Mosley novels]
A Kiss Gone Bad
Black Jack Point
Cut and Run

[Jordan Poteet mysteries]
Do Unto Others
The Only Good Yankee
Promises of Home
Distant Blood

Panic
Fear

Raymond Benson
[James Bond novels]
Zero Minus Ten
The Facts of Death
High Time to Kill
Doubleshot
Never Dream of Dying
The Man with the Red Tattoo

[James Bond film novelizations]
Tomorrow Never Dies
The World is Not Enough
Die Another Day

*[Tom Clancy's Splinter Cell novels,
    writing as David Michaels]*
Tom Clancy's Splinter Cell
Tom Clancy Operation Barracuda

[non-fiction]
The James Bond Bedside Com-
    panion

Faceblind
Evil Hours
Sweetie's Diamonds

Michael A. Black
A Killing Frost
Windy City Knights
The Heist
Freeze Me Tender

Lawrence Block
[Evan Tanner Mysteries]
The Thief Who Couldn't Sleep
The Cancelled Czech
Tanner's Twelve Swingers
Two for Tanner
Tanner's Tiger
Here Comes A Hero
Me Tanner, You Jane
Tanner on Ice

[Chip Harrison Mysteries]
No Score
Chip Harrison Scores Again
Make Out with Murder
The Topless Tulip Caper
Introducing Chip Harrison

Lawrence Block (cont.)

[Bernie Rhodenbarr Mysteries]
Burglar's Can't Be Choosers
The Burglar in the Closet
The Burglar Who Like to Quote
    Kipling
The Burglar Who Studied Spinoza
The Burglar Who Painted Like
    Mondrian
The Burglar Who Traded Ted
    Williams
The Burglar Who Thought He
    Was Bogart
The Burglar in the Library
The Burglar in the Rye
The Burglar Who Dropped in on Elvis
The Burglar On The Prowl

[Matthew Scudder Mysteries]
The Sins of the Fathers
Time to Murder and Create
In the Midst of Death
A Stab in the Dark
Eight Million Ways to Die
When the Sacred Ginmill Closes
Out on the Cutting Edge
A Ticket to the Boneyard
A Dance at the Slaughterhouse
A Walk Among the Tombstones
The Devil Knows You're Dead
A Long Line of Dead Men
Even the Wicked
Everybody Dies
Hope To Die
All the Flowers are Dying

[John Keller Mysteries]
Hit Man
Hit List
Hit Parade

[non-fiction]
Writing the Novel: From Plot to
    Print
Telling Lies for Fun and Profit

Spider, Spin Me A Web
Cinderella Sims
Death Pulls A Doublecross
Mona
The Girl with the Long Green Heart
Deadly Honeymoon
The Specialists
Such Men Are Dangerous
After the First Death
Ronald Rabbit is A Dirty Old Man
The Triumph of Evil
Not Comin' Home to You
Ariel
Code of Arms
Sometimes They Bite
Like A Lamb to Slaughter
Random Walk
Into the Night
Some Days You Get the Bear
Enough Rope
Small Town

Jay Bonansinga

Black Mariah
Sick
The Killer's Game
Headcase
Bloodhound
Sleep Police
Oblivion
Frozen
Twisted
[non-fiction]
The Sinking Of The Eastland:
    America's Forgotten Tragedy

Ken Bruen

[Jack Taylor novels]
The Guards
The Killing of the Tinkers
The Magdalen Martyrs
The Dramatist
Priest

[Brant novels]
The White Trilogy
Blitz
Vixen

Rilke on Black
The Hackman Blues
London Boulevard
Her Last Call to Louis Macneice
Dispatching Baudelaire

Reed Farrel Coleman

[Mo Prager Mysteries]
Walking the Perfect Square
Redemption Street
The James Deans

[Dylan Klein novels]
Life Goes Sleeping
Little Easter
They Don't Play Stickball in
    Milwaukee

Max Allan Collins

[Frank Nolan series]
Bait Money
Blood Money
Fly Paper
Hush Money
Hard Cash
Scratch Fever
Spree
Mourn the Living

[Quarry series]
The Broker / Quarry
The Dealer / Quarry's Deal
The Broker's Wife / Quarry's List
The Slasher / Quarry's Cut
Primary Target
Quarry's Greatest Hits
The Last Quarry

[Mallory series]
No Cure for Death
The Baby Blue Rip-Off
Kill Your Darlings
A Shroud for Aquarius
Nice Weekend for a Murder

[Nathan Heller series]
True Detective
True Crime
The Million-Dollar Wound
Neon Mirage
Dying in the Post-War World
Stolen Away
Carnal Hours
Blood and Thunder
Damned in Paradise
Flying Blind
Majic Man
Angel in Black
Kisses of Death
Chicago Confidential

[Eliot Ness series]
The Dark City
Butcher's Dozen
Bullet Proof
Murder by the Numbers

Max Allan Collins (cont.)

[Dick Tracy series]
Dick Tracy and the Nightmare
    Machine
Dick Tracy Goes to War
Dick Tracy Meets his Match

[NYPD Blue series]
NYPD Blue: Blue Beginning
NYPD Blue: Blue Blood

[Road to Perdition series]
Road to Perdition
Road to Purgatory
Road to Paradise

[Disaster series]
The Titanic Murders
The Hindenburg Murders
The Pearl Harbor Murders
The Lusitania Murders
The London Blitz Murders

[Dark Angel series]
Before the Dawn
Skin Game
After the Dark

[On the Road to Perdition series]
Oasis
Sanctuary
Detour

*[CSI: Crime Scene Investigation
    series]*
Double Dealer
Sin City
Cold Burn
Serial
Body of Evidence

Neon Oasis
Bad Rap
Demon House
Grave Matters
Binding Tides
Killing Game
Snake Eyes

[CSI: Miami series]
Florida Getaway
Heat Wave

Jim Thompson: The Killers Inside
    Him
One Lonely Knight: Mickey
    Spillaine's Mike Hammer
    (with James L. Traylor)
Midnight Haul
The Best of Crime and
    Detective TV
In the Line of Fire
Maverick
I Love Trouble
Waterworld
Mommy
Daylight
Air Force
Tough Tender
U.S. Marshals
Mommy's Day
The Mummy
Saving Private Ryan
Elvgren: His Life and Art
Regeneration (with Barbara Collins)
U-571
Murder: His and Hers (with Bar-
    bara Collins)

Max Allan Collins (cont.)

The Mummy Returns
Blue Christmas and other Holiday
    Homicides
History of Mystery
Windtalkers
The Scorpion King
I-Spy
For the Boys: The Racy Pin-Ups
    of World War II
Johnny Dynamite
Batman: Child of Dreams
Bombshell (with Barbara Collins)
War of the Worlds Murder

Sean Doolittle

Dirt
Burn
Rain Dogs
The Cleanup

David Ellis

Line of Vision
Life Sentence
Jury of One
In the Company of Liars

John Galligan

[Fly Fishing Mysteries]
The Nail Knot
The Blood Knot
The Clinch Knot

Red Sky, Red Dragonfly

Victor Gischler

Gun Monkeys
The Pistol Poets
Suicide Squeeze
Shotgun Opera

Ed Gorman

[Sam McCain novels]
The Day The Music Died
Wake Up Little Suzie
Will You Still Love Me Tomorrow
Save the Last Dance for Me
Everybody's Somebody's Fool
Breaking Up is Hard to Do

[Robert Payne novels]
Blood Moon
Hawk Moon
Harlot's Moon
Voodoo Moon

New, Improved, Murder
Murder Straight Up
Murder in The Wings
The Autumn Dead
A Cry of Shadows
Murder on The Aisle
Several Deaths Later
Night Kills
The Night Remembers
The Marilyn Tapes
The First Lady
Moonchasers
Runner in The Dark
Senatorial Privilege
Black River Falls
Prisoners
Cages
Dark Whispers
Famous Blue Raincoat
The Long Ride Back
Such a Good Girl
Different Kinds of Dead

Mitchell Graham

The Fifth Ring
The Emerald Cavern
Legacy of the Ancients
Murder on the Majestic
Dead Docket

Jeremiah Healy

[John Francis Cuddy Mysteries]
Blunt Darts
The Staked Goat
So Like Sleep
Swan Dive
Yesterday's News
Right to Die
Shallow Graves
Foursome
Act of God
Rescue
Invasion of Privacy
The Only Good Lawyer
Spiral
The Concise Cuddy (short stories)
Cuddy Plus One (short stories)

[Mairead O'Clare novels, writing as Terry Devane]
Uncommon Justice
Juror Number Eleven
A Stain Upon the Robe

The Stalking of Sheilah Quinn
Turnabout
Off-Season and Other Stories

Libby Fischer Hellmann

[Ellie Foreman Mysteries]
An Eye for Murder
A Picture of Guilt
An Image of Death

A Shot to Die For

Julie A. Hyzy

[Alex St. James Mysteries]
Deadly Blessings
Deadly Interest

Artistic License

Rob Kantner

[Ben Perkins Mysteries]
The Back Door Man
The Harder They Hit
Dirty Work
Hell's Only Half Full
Made in Detroit
The Thousand Yard Stare
The Quick and the Dead
The Red, White and Blues
Concrete Hero
Trouble is What I Do (short stories)

J.A. Konrath

[Jack Daniels Mysteries]
Whiskey Sour
Bloody Mary
Rusty Nail

William Kent Krueger

[Cork O'Connor Mysteries]
Iron Lake
Boundary Waters
Purgatory Ridge
Blood Hollow
Mercy Falls
Copper River

The Devil's Bed

David Morrell

First Blood
Testament
Last Reveille
The Totem
Blood Oath
The Hundred-Year Christmas
The Brotherhood of the Rose
The Fraternity of the Stone
Rambo (First Blood Part II)
The League of Night and Fog
Rambo III
The Fifth Profession
The Covenant of the Flame
Assumed Identity
Desperate Measures
Extreme Denial
Double Image
Black Evening
Burnt Sienna
Long Lost
The Protector
Nightscape
Creepers

[non-fiction]
John Barth: An Introduction
Fireflies
American Fiction, American
    Myth
Lessons from a Lifetime of Writ-
    ing

Monica J. O'Rourke

Suffer the Flesh
Poisoning Eros (with Wrath
    James White)

P.J. Parrish

[Louis Kincaid Mysteries]
Dark of the Moon
Dead of Winter
Paint it Black
Thicker Than Water
Island of Bones
A Killing Rain
An Unquiet Grave

M.J. Rose

[Butterfield Institute novels]
The Halo Effect
The Delilah Complex
The Venus Fix

Lip Service
In Fidelity
Flesh Tones
Sheet Music

Marcus Sakey

The Blade Itself

Jeff Strand

[Andrew Mayhem series]
Graverobbers Wanted
    (No Experience Necessary)
Single White Psychopath Seeks Same
Casket for Sale (Only Used Once)
Mandibles

How to Rescue a Dead Princess
Out of Whack
Elrod McBugle on the Loose
Pressure
The Sinister Mr. Corpse

Paul A. Toth
Fizz
Fishnet

Robert W. Walker
[Jessica Coran series]
Killer Instinct
Fatal Instinct
Primal Instinct
Darkest Instinct
Pure Instinct
Extreme Instinct
Blind Instinct
Bitter Instinct
Unnatural Instinct
Grave Instinct
Absolute Instinct

[Lucas Stonecoat & Meredyth Sanger series]
Cutting Edge
Double Edge
Cold Edge
Final Edge

[Inspector Alastair Ransom and Dr. Jane Francis Tewes series]
City for Ransom
Shadows in the White City

Sub-Zero
Daniel Webster and the Wrong-way Railway
Brain Watch
Salem's Child
Aftershock
Disembodied
Dead Man's Float
Razor's Edge

Burning Obsession
Dying Breath
Gideon Tell and the Siege of Vicksburg

[writing as Geoffrey Caine]
Curse of the Vampire
Wake of the Werewolf
Legion of the Dead

[writing as Glen Hale]
Dr. O

[writing as Evan Kingsbury]
Fire & Flesh

[writing as Stephen Robertson]
Decoy
Decoy #2-Blood Ties
Decoy #3-Blood Tells
The Handyman

Brian Wiprud
[Garth Carson Mysteries]
Pipsqueak
Stuffed

Sleep with the Fishes
Crooked